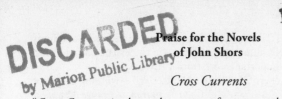

Praise for the Novels
of John Shors

Cross Currents

"*Cross Currents* is about the power of nature and the power of love—romantic, brotherly, and parental. You are held in suspense, watching the love between the characters grow, knowing that this love is going to be tested severely when the tsunami hits. And when it does, you are carried away by the clash of both forces in a maelstrom of riveting action. I loved this book."

—Karl Marlantes, *New York Times* bestselling author of *Matterhorn*

"John Shors has a great feeling for Thailand. The beauty of its geography and the pliant strength of its people are in every word of his novel *Cross Currents*, which is set in the days just before the tsunami. The suspense around what will happen to his characters (each with a vivid history and set of troubles) makes for a supremely readable tale."

—Joan Silber, author of *The Size of the World*

The Wishing Trees

"An affecting and sensitively rendered study of grief and loss, the healing power of artistic expression, and the life-altering rewards of travel to distant lands. I was deeply moved by this poignant and life-affirming novel."

—Wally Lamb, bestselling author of *She's Come Undone*

"Shors's fourth novel is a moving, emotional story about coping and coming to terms with loss. Anyone who has lost a loved one will relate to this poignant novel." —*Booklist*

"John Shors has made himself a reputation for re-creating exotic landscapes that surround heartwarming stories with captivating details. *The Wishing Trees* is no exception, as he replaces what might be a standard tale of recovery from loss with an alluring travelogue filled with colorful details of these chromatic countries." —*BookPage*

"Poignant. . . . Country by country, their odyssey transforms into a journey of worldly healing and renewal, nurtured by the wisdom and compassion they discover in the cultures they pass through, and by the realization of the commonalities—hope, death, love—that bind all fathers, mothers, and children." —*National Geographic Traveler*

Dragon House

"A touching story about, among other things, the linger...... of the last generation's war on the contemporary land........ ....nam. In a large cast of appealing charac.......... ....rt of this book; their talents, friendsh.............. ....es."

—Karen ....nd

"A wonderful novel. . . . Shors transcends politics and headlines and finds the timeless and deeply human stories that are the essence of enduring fiction. This is strong, important work from a gifted writer."
—Robert Olen Butler, Pulitzer Prize–winning author of
A Good Scent from a Strange Mountain

"Amid the wreckage of what's known in Vietnam as the 'American War,' Shors has set his sprawling, vibrant novel. All of his characters—hustlers, humanitarians, street children—carry wounds, visible or otherwise. And in the cacophony of their voices, he asks that most essential question: 'How can we be better?'"
—David Oliver Relin, bestselling coauthor of *Three Cups of Tea*

"There is a tenderness in this moving, deeply descriptive novel that brings all those frequently hidden qualities of compassion, purity of mind, and, yes, love—the things we used to call the human spirit—into the foreground of our feeling as readers. This is a beautiful heart speaking to us of the beautiful world we could and should find, even in the darkness that so often floods the world with fear."
—Gregory David Roberts, bestselling author of *Shantaram*

Beside a Burning Sea

"A master storyteller. . . . *Beside a Burning Sea* confirms again that Shors is an immense talent. . . . This novel has the aura of the mythic, the magical, and that which is grounded in history. Shors weaves psychological intrigue by looking at his characters' competing desires: love, revenge, and meaning. Both lyrical and deeply imaginative."
—Amy Tan, bestselling author of *The Joy Luck Club*

"Features achingly lyrical prose, even in depicting the horrors of war. . . . Shors pays satisfying attention to class and race dynamics, as well as the tension between wartime enemies. The survivors' dignity, quiet strength, and fellowship make this a magical read." —*Publishers Weekly*

"An astounding work. Poetic and cinematic as it illuminates the dark corners of human behavior, it is destined to be this decade's *The English Patient*." —*Booklist*

"Shors has re-created a tragic place in time, when love for another was a person's sole companion. He uses lyrical prose throughout the novel, especially in his series of haiku poems that plays an integral role in the love story, and develops accessible, sympathetic characters. . . . A book that spans two and a half weeks, set on a deserted island, easily could become dull and redundant. But Shors avoids those turns by delving into the effects of war on each character, causing readers to attach themselves to the individuals yearning for home and the ones they love."
—*Rocky Mountain News*

"[A] spirited debut novel. . . . With infectious enthusiasm and just enough careful attention to detail, Shors gives a real sense of the times, bringing the world of imperial Hindustan and its royal inhabitants to vivid life."

—*Publishers Weekly*

"Jahanara is a beguiling heroine whom readers will come to love; none of today's chick-lit heroines can match her dignity, fortitude, and cunning. . . . Elegant, often lyrical writing distinguishes this literary fiction from the genre known as historical romance. It is truly a work of art, rare in a debut novel."
—*The Des Moines Register*

"An exceptional work of fiction . . . a gripping account." —*India Post*

"Highly recommended . . . a thrilling tale [that] will appeal to a wide audience."
—*Library Journal*

"Evocative of the fantastical stories and sensual descriptions of *One Thousand and One Nights*, *Beneath a Marble Sky* is the story of Jahanara, the daughter of the seventeenth-century Mughal emperor who built India's Taj Mahal. What sets this novel apart is its description of Muslim-Hindu politics, which continue to plague the subcontinent today."
—*National Geographic Traveler*

"[A] story of romance and passion . . . a wonderful book if you want to escape to a foreign land while relaxing in your porch swing."
—*St. Petersburg Times*

"It is difficult to effectively bring the twenty-first-century reader into a seventeenth-century world. Shors accomplishes this nicely, taking the armchair traveler into some of the intricacies involved in creating a monument that remains one of the architectural and artistic wonders of the world." —*The Denver Post*

"[Shors] writes compellingly [and] does a lovely job of bringing an era to life. . . . an author to anticipate." —*Omaha World-Herald*

"A sumptuous feast of emotional imagery awaits the reader of *Beneath a Marble Sky*, an unabashedly romantic novel set in seventeenth-century Hindustan, inside the warm sandstone of its Mughal palaces." —*India West*

"Shors . . . creates a vivid and striking world that feels as close as a plane ride. Most important, he manages to convey universal feelings in a tangible and intimate way. Shah Jahan's grief isn't just that of a man who lived centuries ago; it's a well of emotion felt long before Mumatz Mahal ever lived, and is still felt today. Shors's ability to tap into that well, and make it so alive, renders the novel as luminous a jewel as any that adorn the Taj Mahal's walls." —*ForeWord Magazine*

Also by John Shors

Beneath a Marble Sky

Beside a Burning Sea

Dragon House

The Wishing Trees

JOHN SHORS

cross currents

 NEW AMERICAN LIBRARY

NEW AMERICAN LIBRARY
Published by New American Library, a division of
Penguin Group (USA) Inc., 375 Hudson Street,
New York, New York 10014, USA
Penguin Group (Canada), 90 Eglinton Avenue East, Suite 700, Toronto,
Ontario M4P 2Y3, Canada (a division of Pearson Penguin Canada Inc.)
Penguin Books Ltd., 80 Strand, London WC2R 0RL, England
Penguin Ireland, 25 St. Stephen's Green, Dublin 2,
Ireland (a division of Penguin Books Ltd.)
Penguin Group (Australia), 250 Camberwell Road, Camberwell, Victoria 3124,
Australia (a division of Pearson Australia Group Pty. Ltd.)
Penguin Books India Pvt. Ltd., 11 Community Centre, Panchsheel Park,
New Delhi - 110 017, India
Penguin Group (NZ), 67 Apollo Drive, Rosedale, Auckland 0632,
New Zealand (a division of Pearson New Zealand Ltd.)
Penguin Books (South Africa) (Pty.) Ltd., 24 Sturdee Avenue,
Rosebank, Johannesburg 2196, South Africa

Penguin Books Ltd., Registered Offices:
80 Strand, London WC2R 0RL, England

First published by New American Library,
a division of Penguin Group (USA) Inc.

First Printing, September 2011
10 9 8 7 6 5 4 3 2 1

 REGISTERED TRADEMARK—MARCA REGISTRADA

LIBRARY OF CONGRESS CATALOGING-IN-PUBLICATION DATA:

Shors, John, 1969–
Cross currents/John Shors.
p. cm.
ISBN 978-0-451-23460-5
1. Americans—Thailand—Fiction. 2. Brothers—Fiction. 3. Triangles (Interpersonal relations)—Fiction.
4. Thailand—Fiction. I. Title.
PS3619.H668C76 2011
813'.6—dc22   2011009681

Set in Adobe Garamond
Designed by Ginger Legato

Printed in the United States of America

PUBLISHER'S NOTE
This is a work of fiction. Names, characters, places, and incidents either are the product of the author's imagination or are used fictitiously, and any resemblance to actual persons, living or dead, business establishments, events, or locales is entirely coincidental.
    The publisher does not have any control over and does not assume any responsibility for author or third-party Web sites or their content.

For Allison, Sophie, and Jack

author's note

IN LATE DECEMBER 2004, ONE of the largest earthquakes in human history occurred off the coast of Indonesia, creating a series of massive tsunamis that struck countries bordering the Indian Ocean. Waves varied in height, some reaching almost one hundred feet. It is estimated that 230,000 people, representing forty nationalities, died in the catastrophe.

Ko Phi Phi is a beautiful, butterfly-shaped island off the coast of Thailand—an island that has long been a prized destination for tourists. The center of Ko Phi Phi, where people live and work, is about six feet above sea level.

Two waves struck Ko Phi Phi—one from each side of the island. One wave was ten feet high, the other eighteen. The waves met in the middle of the island, pulling restaurants, hotels, schools, and people out to sea. Approximately one-third of Ko Phi Phi's ten thousand residents and visitors died.

Yet, miraculously, thousands of Thais and tourists lived.

Cross Currents is inspired by my multiple trips to Ko Phi Phi, before and after the tsunami. It's a fictionalized account of this calamity—of what happened and of the tragedies and triumphs of that day.

A leaf before the eye hides the mountains.

—Thai saying

cross currents

SATURDAY, DECEMBER 18

consequences

Lek opened his eyes, though his body remained as still as the gecko on the ceiling. He watched it, as he often did, admiring its patience, aware of its seemingly perpetual hunger. The creature was the length of his forefinger, and the color of mahogany. Lek enjoyed gazing at the gecko, though he was jealous of its speed. If a moth landed nearby, the gecko moved as if lightning filled its veins. Yet in the absence of insects, the gecko was without motion, a silent sentinel that protected Lek's home from airborne invaders.

As he did every morning, Lek studied the mosquito net that covered him, his wife, and their baby daughter. The old net had been patched in several places, but today no such work was needed. The net remained intact and impenetrable—a necessary barrier between their skin and the denizens of the hot, humid air.

Lek looked at his wife, Sarai, who slept facing him, their daughter between them. Sarai's small frame seemed as still as the gecko. Like most Thai women of her generation, she slept in her bra and panties, which were visible beneath thin cotton pajamas. As usual, she had pulled back her shoulder-length black hair and bound it behind her head. Reminding Lek of the moon, Sarai's face was full and round and somewhat flat. Her skin was the color of wet sand. Laugh lines bordered either side of her mouth—a sight that pleased him as much as any.

Resisting an impulse to kiss their daughter, Lek remained still. Only seven months old, Achara slept in a cloth diaper and nothing else. During the day she was almost always naked, but at night the diaper helped keep their thin mattress dry. Like her parents, Achara was slight and small boned. Lek was proud of her thick black hair, of how she smiled when he whispered and tickled her belly. Though he lived in a beautiful place, and saw splendor each day, nothing was lovelier than his little girl, or her older brother and sister, who slept together in their nearby room.

"Why are you smiling?" Sarai asked quietly in Thai, stirring enough so that the mosquito net rippled.

"She's getting bigger."

"Of course she is. She suckles like those Germans eat—as much food as I can give her."

His fingers edged forward, touching Sarai's shoulder, stroking her soft skin. "I wish I could help."

"Oh, what would you know about it? Women have suffered for thousands of years while you men have dreamed away."

"Come outside. We need to talk. Remember?"

"I remember everything. Best that you remember that."

He shook his head, smiling, easing out from beneath the net, changing into red shorts and a frayed gray T-shirt. Sarai put on a purple sarong and a light green collared blouse. After stepping out of their small room and into another, Lek looked at their other children, who also slept beneath a net. Their son's arm lay across their daughter's belly, and Lek was pleased by the proximity of their bodies. Most of the narrow mattress was vacant. A few feet from their children, under a different net, slept Sarai's mother, who was facing the nearby wall.

Outside their three-room home, dawn was beginning to unfurl. The mountain behind them blocked the sun's tendrils of orange and amber, and the sky was a juxtaposition of blue and black hues. The nearby bay was smooth, more like the surface of a giant cup of coffee than an opening to the sea.

Rainbow Resort, which Lek and Sarai owned and operated, was a collection of eleven bungalows and a restaurant situated at the far northern end of a long beach. The bungalows were mainly thatch and bamboo, featuring ceiling fans, showers, double beds, and hand-flushing toilets, but little else. The open-sided restaurant was part cinder block and cement, with a thatched roof and a wooden railing. Bamboo tables and chairs occupied much of the restaurant, which included a bar, a fish tank, and several ceiling fans. For the most part, travelers used the restaurant only during heavy rains. Otherwise, Sarai encouraged people to eat outside, on the beach, where she had positioned eight low tables atop colorful tapestries.

Lek and Sarai's home was on the northern side of the restaurant, opposite the bungalows. Their sleeping quarters were only a few feet from the black, jagged boulders that marked the end of the beach. After following a path that climbed above the boulders, Lek sat down on an old teak bench, moving slowly, the bones of his right hip seeming, as usual, to grind against each other. When Sarai sat beside him, he pointed to the roof of one of their bungalows.

"See how Patch fixed it?" he asked, speaking softly, which was his custom. "He climbed up there with new thatch and mended it just right."

Sarai sighed, her breath leaving her mouth as if she were trying to extinguish a candle. "I have the eyes of a kingfisher, you know. The kingfisher sees a shiny minnow. I see a fixed roof."

"He asked me if he could fix it. I didn't even—"

"He's been here for five months. Five. That makes him illegal. What or who is he hiding from?"

"I don't know."

She started to reply but rubbed her brow instead, sand already on her fingers. "We're standing on top of a cliff. Do you know that? The wrong step, and down we go."

"But we won't make that step. We—"

"Down, down, down. We've got no money. And our bungalows are falling apart and mostly empty. What would happen if the police found him hiding here, working for us? You'd go to jail, and the children, my mother, and I would . . . We would have to leave for Bangkok. We'd be destitute. Is that what you want?"

Lek closed his eyes at the thought of such a fate. "No. But . . . but my hip. I can't work like I used to. I can't fix roofs or walls or foundations. He's helping me. All he wants is a room and some food. And he's nice to the children."

"He's wonderful with the children."

"It's good for them to see a foreigner here, working hard, not just lying on the beach and sleeping. And their English. It's so amazing. They're learning for free, and that will help them do whatever they want in life."

Laughter emerged from a distant bungalow, and Sarai wondered which of their few residents were up, and what they were doing. "You're going to turn my hair gray—you know that?"

"I—"

"Is that what you want? To age me ten years?"

"His brother is coming tomorrow. All the way from America. Coming to help him."

Sarai shifted on the bench, listening for their baby and their children. "I like Patch. He's as sweet as sugarcane to all of us. But just because he's sweet doesn't mean that bad things can't happen. If one of our neighbors talks, if the police come, they'll take you away. Do you understand that? They'll take you and Patch away together. And then it won't matter if Suchin and Niran can speak English so well. It won't matter because their father will be gone."

"Shhh. Don't get upset. You're more than I can handle when you're upset."

She scowled. "I'm always more than you can handle."

"True."

"But you're smart to bring this up now, while I'm still sleepy and open-minded. In a few hours you wouldn't have a chance. You'd have better luck fishing for elephants."

"No one's going to talk. Everyone likes him. And nobody trusts the police."

Somewhere above, a tree frog beeped, its cry a high-pitched sound resembling the horn of a distant motorbike. "You really need him?" Sarai asked, then remembered that she had to buy fresh bananas for her pancakes. She had better get going. While she was at the market, she'd also purchase stalks of lemongrass, tomatoes, onions, eggs, cucumbers, and condensed milk. Everything else she needed to feed her customers and loved ones, she already had.

As Lek thought about his reply, Sarai studied his face, which was more angular than hers. His features were almost boyish—full lips that seemed to linger in a perpetual smile, a narrow forehead free of worry lines, hair and eyebrows as dark as oil, and shiny cheeks that rarely needed a razor.

"I need him," Lek finally replied, "at least until we catch up on all the repairs. Then he can go somewhere else."

"How long will that take?"

"A few more weeks. No more; I promise."

Her fingers tightened around his. "I don't want us to leave here. I'm so afraid of leaving. What would we do?"

"We'll—"

"The children. They'd be broken."

"We'll find a way. We always have. Once the rooms are fixed, we can raise our rates. Raise them by . . . maybe fifty baht a night."

"That's too much. Thirty, maybe."

"But everyone's charging more these days. Ko Phi Phi is no longer a secret."

She looked at a group of distant hotels, which were sprawling and several stories high. "Everyone charging more has air-conditioning and satellite television and a swimming pool. Is Patch going to build us a pool?"

"We have the beach," he replied, his thumb moving against her forefinger. "Those big places, not many are on the beach."

"They're a hundred feet from it."

"A hundred feet too many."

"For you and me, yes. But for someone who lives in Tokyo or Munich? I don't think so. They walk farther than that just to go to the bathroom."

"It's better to be closer."

Sarai pushed his sandaled foot with hers, knowing that he would always see their bungalows in the best possible light. While his sentimentality moved her, she wished that he would sometimes observe what she did—that the world was overtaking them.

As his foot pushed back against hers, she wondered how she could bring in more money. Lek would try, and he might succeed, but she needed to earn more, whether through the bungalows or her restaurant or something else. Otherwise they would have to leave the island, where almost all of their ancestors were buried, where they went to school and fell in love. They would leave for Bangkok, and the colors of her life would fade.

"We have to work harder," she said. "Somehow we have to work harder."

"I know."

"The children don't want to move either. We have to work harder for them."

"And we will."

"And you think Patch can make that much of a difference? He's helping you that much?"

"He is making a difference."

A voice emerged from below, the voice of their older daughter. "Then he can stay," Sarai said, standing up. "For a few more weeks. Until you've finished the repairs. But then he has to go. Whatever he's running from, he'll have to run somewhere else."

"Three weeks. Give us three weeks."

She put her hand on his shoulder. "Don't let the children see your worry. I see it. My mother sees it."

"I'll do better."

"Your face . . . I love it more than my own, but it's still the face of a child, so easy to read. And Suchin and Niran, they need to hear us laugh and see us smile. That's what we must always do for them."

Lek grinned, rising slowly, painfully. "So you still see me as a child? After all these years?"

"I'll always see you as a child," she replied, the corners of her mouth rising, deepening the laugh lines that he so loved. "Why else do you think I married you? For your looks? No. For your money? Definitely not. It's a good thing for you that I've always seen you as a child. Because if I hadn't, I wouldn't be here right now. I wouldn't be thinking about what breakfast you'd like most or about how I'm going to let Patch stay, against my better judgment, because he'll make your life easier. So thank Buddha for giving you that boyish face. Because without it, your problems would be yours alone. I certainly wouldn't be sharing them with you."

"Thank you, Buddha."

"Thank him again. A hundred times. If I were you, I'd thank him every day. That way, he won't decide to change his mind."

DEEP WITHIN THE MIDST OF *his dream, Patch's instincts told him that the newcomer wasn't to be trusted. He acted too confident while walking up the stairs that led to the second level. In the backpack slung over his shoulder was supposedly half a kilogram of marijuana—which Patch had already partly paid for, having handed a thick wad of Thai baht to the man's partner the previous afternoon. This was the local whom Patch trusted. Patch had bought much smaller packs of dope from him on two other occasions, and he'd always been fair, and had restless eyes that seemed to search for police in every nook and cranny.*

The Thai with whom Patch had dealt, as well as the newcomer, wore trousers, tank tops, and sandals. They weren't big men, but Patch had seen Thai kickboxers at work against one another and knew size didn't matter. An elbow or a knee thrown by a trained fighter was much more dangerous than a punch swung by some brute who lifted weights from dawn to dusk.

Patch was between the Thais, and when he reached the landing, he turned to the right, toward his room. He tried to slow his pounding heart with the thought of how much money he'd make reselling the dope. The guesthouse was full of foreigners who liked to roll joints but were afraid to buy from the locals. Patch wasn't. He'd been in Thailand for six weeks and understood who could and couldn't be trusted. He'd also tried hard to learn a bit of the language, which seemed to put him in everyone's good graces.

The hallway, illuminated by sporadic, naked lightbulbs, stretched far into the distance. The cement floor was blue, the walls pitted and stained. Music, laughter, and the sounds of bodies merging and moving seeped through the wooden doors Patch passed. Reaching into his pocket, he removed a key, thanked the men for meeting him, and approached the brass padlock that secured his room.

Inside, the room's lone window was open, revealing Bangkok's Khao San Road. One story below, Patch glimpsed the usual assortment of backpackers, vendors, taxis, and chaos before he pulled the curtains shut. Turning around, he saw that the Thai he trusted was locking the door behind him.

"Do you want a Coke?" Patch asked, moving toward a battered minirefrigerator that hummed and groaned like a car dying on the roadside. "I've also got some beer. The least I can do is buy you a—"

"You get money?" the Thai asked in broken English, sweat glistening on his forehead.

Patch nodded, wishing that the man didn't seem so tense. After walking into the bathroom, Patch lifted the porcelain lid of the water tank behind the toilet and pulled out a Ziploc bag containing two thousand baht, roughly sixty dollars. "Do you have the weed?" he replied. He felt cornered in the bathroom, and stepped to the side of his sagging bed.

The unfamiliar face smiled, revealing a silver tooth. Suddenly Patch wished the door weren't locked. He started to repeat his question when his supplier pulled a shiny badge from his pocket. "You make big mistake," the Thai said as his accomplice removed a small gun from inside his pants, near his crotch. The gun darted toward Patch the way a cobra might strike. Instinctively, he batted it aside, and a bullet thudded into the ceiling. The man shouted in Thai, twisting in Patch's direction, the gun once again rising and aiming. With Patch's free hand, he punched the Thai hard in the face, his fist striking the other man's upper lip and nose. Blood sprayed on the Thai's tank top and he fell away, dropping the gun. Patch kicked it as the man's partner rushed forward, his hands open, slamming like small axes into Patch's shoulders, aiming for his neck. Stumbling backward, Patch could do little to defend himself other than avoid a crippling blow. "You die tonight!" the Thai shouted, his fury more frightening to Patch than the gun. "You die now!"

Patch partially warded off a few more blows, felt the window behind him, and leaned back. Suddenly he was falling, spinning, hitting a canopy and tumbling to the ground, landing on his hands and knees. The sidewalk bustled with backpackers, who turned in his direction. The cop put his head out the window and started yelling and pointing. Hands reached for Patch, seeming to claw at him. He beat them aside, fueled by his panic and a strength he'd never known.

Within seconds he was running, pushing people away, bursting through their outstretched arms. He saw an alley to his right and turned, bounding forward like some sort of animal on the savanna. To his horror, the men who pursued him suddenly metamorphosed into lions. They neared him, their fangs agape, their claws ripping his skin. He heard their snarls, heard the tearing of his flesh.

"No!" Patch shouted, leaping out of bed, becoming entangled in his mosquito net as he fell to the floor. The lions and alley disappeared, replaced by the familiar thatch walls of his bungalow. Dripping sweat, Patch lay on the floor, his fists balled, his eyes tearing. He trembled, recalling the dream, a replay of what had actually happened to him five months earlier. He remembered running down the alley, the two thousand baht still in his hand, twisting through a labyrinth of buildings and warehouses until the cries of his pursuers were overcome by the beating of his heart.

Patch glanced at the ceiling, worried that he'd pulled the mosquito net from its moorings. Fortunately, he hadn't. Rising to his knees and then to his feet, he stepped out from under the net and put on a T-shirt and some shorts, feeling a need to get outside. The light of dawn had come and gone, replaced by an amber blanket that seemed to have been draped over Ko Phi Phi. Trying to take deep and measured breaths, Patch moved toward the beach, eyeing his surroundings, grateful that such beauty would help pull him from his misery.

Looking to his right, Patch studied the limestone cliff that rose five hundred feet straight above the turquoise bay. The side of the cliff was partly covered in green foliage but was otherwise a slate gray. On the other side of the curving, half-moon beach, about a mile away, a similar cliff soared above the white sand and emerald waters. Between the two wonders of stone, palm trees swayed in a low stretch of connecting land. The sound of miniature waves lapping at the shore was all he heard.

Stepping into the warm water, Patch continued to breathe deeply, thinking about his prospects. He'd spent most of his two thousand baht fleeing to Ko Phi Phi. The rest of his money, as well as his passport, credit cards, and clothes, had been left behind with the police. Without his passport, he had no legal way of leaving the country without alerting the authorities. And so he had only two choices—he could turn himself in and be charged with assaulting a police officer and likely spend a year in a Thai prison, or he could try to sneak out of the country.

For five months, Patch had been hiding in Ko Phi Phi, trying to formulate a plan. He didn't want to turn himself in, but escaping Thailand presented a series of problems so severe that thinking about them often sent him hurrying off for a swim. In the water, his problems seemed to flee, at least to an arm's length away, to a place where they were manageable.

During the first few weeks of his time on the island, he'd borrowed money from fellow travelers and kept a low profile. Then he'd been lucky enough to start doing odd jobs for the Thai family who owned a group of dilapidated bungalows at the far end of the beach. In return, they fed him, let him stay in their smallest bungalow, and didn't ask questions.

As long as he kept Lek and Sarai happy, Patch had reasoned, he could stay and develop a plan. He could avoid the police. So he'd worked hard, helping whenever possible, and taking the initiative to fix whatever needed fixing.

Mulling over how a coconut had fallen the previous day and damaged a roof, Patch looked up, studying the trees above the bungalows. One tree had a cluster of green coconuts and leaned over the path that ran between all the bungalows and the restaurant. Though made of sand, the path was lined with piles of brown bricks that Lek had asked Patch to use to pave it. Patch wanted to begin work on the path right away, but he worried about the coconuts, which often fell during storms. Afraid that someone would get hurt, he walked toward the tree and was pleased to see that it didn't rise straight up, but was curved like a giant longbow.

Patch had watched local children climb such trees and knew, in theory, how to get from the ground to where the coconuts hung. He put his bare feet on either side of the trunk, reached around the tree as if he were hugging it, and pulled up with his hands while pushing down with his feet. The bark scraped against his thighs and forearms, but he smiled as he lurched higher. His progress reminded him of the inchworms he'd watched as a child. He climbed about as fast, lifting his hands, then feet, hugging the tree. Though his exposed skin continued to get scraped, he climbed until he reached the long, knifelike fronds and the nest of coconuts, about thirty feet off the ground. Holding on to one of the fronds, Patch hoisted himself on top of the tree, resting on the other fronds and the coconuts.

"What are you doing up there, you crazy man?"

Patch looked down through the fronds and spied Suchin. The daughter of Lek and Sarai, Suchin was eight years old, with a round, pleasing face like her mother's and long hair that she wore in a braided ponytail. Her hair was pulled far enough back to reveal her pierced ears, which held her first pair of earrings— matching yellow seahorses. She was almost always smiling, seemingly proud of her adult front teeth. Though Patch was used to seeing Suchin in her school uniform, since it was Saturday she wore a faded blue Hello Kitty T-shirt and black shorts.

"Be careful, Patch," she added, moving directly beneath him, her English nearly flawless. "You'll fall on your head. And you don't want to do that any more than you already have."

"You be careful. I'm going to drop these coconuts."

"Good. Then Mother can sell their milk."

"Could you please step back?"

Suchin did as he asked, watching as he twisted off one of the highest coconuts. Her brother, Niran, appeared, eating a handful of sticky rice. A year younger than Suchin, he had straight black hair and was small for his age. As usual, at least when he wasn't in school, Niran went shirtless and carried a bamboo pole with a net on one end. "What's Patch doing?" he asked in Thai, plucking the last few grains of rice from his fingers.

"Getting us coconuts."

"For what?"

"To sell, silly."

"Oh."

Patch listened to the children talk, made sure that they were a safe distance from the tree, and dropped the first coconut. It landed with a thud, rolled a few feet, and was snatched up by Suchin. "Here comes another one," Patch said, wrestling with a bigger coconut, surprised by the strength of its bond to the tree.

The coconut finally lost the battle and rolled across the sand. Niran hurried forward, then set it next to his sister's. "Don't fall, Patch," he called.

Continuing to wrench coconuts free and drop them to the children, Patch worked until only fronds remained below him. Though bleeding in several places, he smiled as Suchin and Niran picked up their prizes and hurried toward the restaurant. He knew that Sarai would set the coconuts in an ice-filled cooler and later chop off their tops, stick a straw in, and sell them for twenty baht each. To Sarai and Lek, coconuts meant that money did grow on trees, and Patch knew they'd be pleased.

Wiping his brow, Patch gazed across the bay toward the open sea. To the north sprawled the coast of Myanmar, hardly a country to escape to. More than a thousand miles to the west lay India. Patch was fairly certain that if he reached India, he could find an American embassy, get a new passport, and go home. But traveling to India was another story altogether. He might be able to stow away on a freighter, but that meant going back to Bangkok or maybe the nearby island of Phuket.

As he did every day, Patch lamented his stupidity. To make a few hundred dollars, he'd risked everything and turned his dream vacation into the worst nightmare. He was now a fugitive. He'd hurt a police officer. If he were caught he'd be shackled and thrown in prison. Even now, within the haze of relative safety he'd found on Ko Phi Phi, it was hard to forget that his future had been jeopardized by recklessness and naïveté. And tomorrow his brother would arrive and remind him of his foolishness. Ryan would be hard on him, Patch was certain. Ryan would urge him to turn himself in. They would fight and fight and fight, and Ryan would never understand. He wouldn't understand because he wasn't a coward, wasn't afraid to be held accountable. Patch had always thought that Ryan was almost incapable of fear. And Patch doubted that his big brother had ever looked into a mirror and wondered whom he saw. Patch, on the other hand, studied his reflection from time to time, musing over why he sometimes appeared as a stranger to himself.

Though the two brothers looked like twins, and were only a year apart, Patch had always walked in the shadow of Ryan's deeds, sheltered within that shadow but also weary of its influence. This weariness was one of the reasons that when Ryan had returned to business school to finish his master's degree in management, Patch had traveled in the opposite direction, flying to Bangkok with no plan, with nothing but a backpack full of T-shirts and a yearning for adventure. He was twenty-three years old and brimming with restlessness and optimism.

Patch loved his brother as much as anyone else. But he was afraid of what Ryan would say, of the looks that Ryan would give him. Nothing ever seemed to sting as much as Ryan's disapproval. And Patch had felt it on too many occasions.

Wishing that Ryan weren't drawing so close, Patch stared down the tree trunk, wondering how he would get to the ground. Climbing up had been fairly easy, but going down looked problematic. He might have to jump.

As he sat and debated how to approach his descent, Suchin and Niran reappeared. Suchin carried a drink of some sort, saying that it was for him. Niran held an old soccer ball, and asked if Patch would play with him on the beach. Suchin continued to talk as Niran tried to keep the ball in the air with his feet and knees. He wasn't successful.

"You're stuck like a cat," Suchin said, giggling. "Though I've never seen such a big cat, and I don't see your tail."

Patch poked his head down through the fronds. "Meow."

The children laughed, Niran dropping the ball.

"Come down, sweet little kitten," Suchin replied. "Mother has a nice bowl of milk for you."

"Meow. Meow."

"Come on. You can do it."

Patch put his feet on the trunk and began to lower himself. He managed to slide about halfway down the trunk before his skin was scraped raw and he jumped away from the pain, and out into empty space, falling toward the children below.

Hundreds of miles to the north, Ryan and his girlfriend, Brooke, sat on the balcony of their hotel room, seven stories up and facing the heart of Bangkok. Ryan rested his laptop on his knees. His fingers tapped its keys with relentless speed as he scrolled through emails, replying to professors, potential employers, and friends. Brooke watched him as he typed, thinking that the Thai sun might do him some good. Though she had been attracted to him since the moment she met him in business school, his pale skin seemed out of place here in the tropical heat. The rest of him looked as it often did—his short blond hair spiked upward with gel, his blue eyes covered by narrow sunglasses. As always, he was clean shaven, revealing a strong jaw and prominent cheekbones. His Hawaiian-style shirt was unbuttoned, and the defined muscles of his abdomen appeared as firm as the cement floor of the balcony.

Aware that Ryan was engrossed in his work, Brooke shifted her gaze to the city. A dozen towering office buildings reflected the midmorning light. Bangkok's SkyTrain rumbled above a congested four-lane road. The blue-and-white train followed the wide curve of the elevated platform, heading toward downtown. The train moved much faster than the thousands of cars, trucks, and motorcycles beneath it. Brake lights made the road seem to glow. Horns were incessant, chirping like the cries of exotic birds migrating en masse. The air smelled of diesel fumes, but also of spices from the restaurant below—scents of saffron and lemongrass and fish sauce.

Eyeing the zigzagging paths of scores of traditional three-wheeled taxis known as tuk-tuks, Brooke felt an urge to explore the city. She'd never been outside America and wanted to hop on a tuk-tuk and ask the driver to take them somewhere interesting.

"Can't you finish that later?" she asked, running a hand through her hair, which was light brown with blond highlights and fell well below her shoulders.

Ryan glanced up at her, then back at his laptop. "I'm going over Patch's directions on how to get to Ko . . . Phi Phi, though I can hardly make sense of what he says. Must have been in a hurry."

"It probably costs money for him to get online. And he doesn't have any."

"So, once again, his problem becomes my problem. Sound familiar?"

"We've got plenty of time."

"What a freaking mess."

Brooke rolled her green eyes, heard a screech of tires, and watched a SkyTrain approach. "Life is messy, you know. It's not some perfect business plan that'll always give you a great return on investment."

"With him it's messy."

"And what about with me? Waking you up last night?"

"That's different. It's not your fault."

"But that doesn't make it any cleaner, Ry."

He sighed, partly closing his laptop. "I need to sweat. They actually have a decent gym downstairs. Would you mind hanging out for an hour?"

"We could walk downtown instead of taking a taxi."

"Walking isn't going to do it. I have to run to work off that nasty airline food. Don't you?"

"No. And I think we'd sweat enough just walking downtown."

Ryan nodded, noticing how her skin glistened. She wore a blue Mickey Mouse T-shirt, white shorts, and flip-flops. Her legs were mostly exposed, and his eyes followed the contours of her calves. She was more curves than muscles, more soft than not. Her breasts seemed to push at her T-shirt, and he had a sudden desire to lift Mickey above her head, to kiss her flesh. Her eyes found his and he smiled. "Caught me, didn't you?" he asked.

"I always catch you."

"Usually. Usually, but not always."

"You're not as sly as you think. Unrelenting, yes. But sly, no."

"Can you blame me for trying?"

Brooke nodded, though sometimes she wished he didn't try. He forgot that men could try too hard with her, that men had tried too hard with her. "Go on," she said. "Go work off that nasty food. I'll be here for an hour. After that, you'll have to go looking for me."

He set aside his laptop, putting his hand on her knee. "I'll explore downtown with you. I promise. I'll do a few reps, hit the treadmill, and head straight back."

"You could run in the city."

"In all that pollution? No way."

She glanced at the endless cars. "Maybe you should talk to them about sustainability. Put some of your thoughts to the test."

"Maybe I should." He stood up, moving with purpose, as always. "We'll explore, see some sights, have lunch, do whatever you want. And then maybe we can come back and I can get a look at what's hiding behind Mickey."

"Really, you should study this place. It might teach you something."

He pulled off his shirt, grabbed his iPod, and then walked into their room. She watched him change into his workout clothes, wondering why the sight of his nakedness didn't stir her as it once had. He could have modeled for a famous sculptor, she thought, recalling images of white marble statues that she'd seen in some history book.

After saying good-bye, she returned to the view of the city. She should have taken the time to use his laptop to catch up on her studies as well. Though her specialization in business school was marketing, while he studied management, they were in two of the same classes, and he was wise to use the holiday break to get ahead of everyone else. But she didn't want to read about IPOs or exit strategies or venture capital. She wanted to watch Bangkok—a chaotic, mesmerizing city that seemed to inspire something within her, something that had been robbed of wings but still longed to take flight.

As usual, midday on Ko Phi Phi brought heat, humidity, and sun. The island lay near the equator and at times felt like the inside of a greenhouse. The scent of damp soil mingled with that of tropical flowers and salt-laden air. The water near Rainbow Resort was placid, as it was in all but the strongest of storms. Most of the bay was protected by the limestone cliffs, which curved inward from the north and south, forming a shield the shape of a half-moon. The water was such a bright blue that it almost appeared to be illuminated from below.

Though Rainbow Resort wasn't popular among tourists, its beach was a desirable destination, and held a few dozen wooden lounge chairs, half as many faded Heineken umbrellas, and travelers from around the world. Swedes, Danes, Germans, Brits, Israelis, Japanese, and Australians lounged in the chairs, kicked soccer balls on the beach, or waded in the shallows. Most of the tourists were in their early twenties, some sunburned, others tanned. A trio of Swedish women sat in the bay, fifty feet from shore, the water almost reaching their exposed breasts. Farther out, several Westerners used snorkels and masks to explore beneath the tranquil surface.

As they often did during the weekend, Suchin and Niran walked along the curving row of chairs and umbrellas, asking foreigners if they needed cold drinks or ice-cream cones. If anyone did, one of the children would ask for thirty or forty baht, walk to the restaurant, and give their mother the money in exchange for the treat. Sometimes Suchin carried her little sister, Achara, on her back, but when the weather was hot, Achara was usually looked after by her grandmother in the restaurant.

Today Suchin and Niran were alone. They didn't enjoy some chores, such as cleaning up the beach in the morning or at dusk, but chatting with foreigners had never bothered them. Suchin, in particular, liked selling refreshments, liked the smile on her mother's face when a sale was completed. Since the sky was cloudless, business was brisk, and the siblings walked from one end of the chairs to the other several times before deciding that everyone was content.

Niran knew that the afternoon ferry would soon dock on the opposite side of the island and that his father would want him to help lure customers to their resort. Worried that he wouldn't have time to play, he took Suchin's hand and led her toward the water. "Let's catch some crabs," he said, wondering where he'd left his net and digging spoon.

"You and your crabs. And your fish. There's no room left in your tank. The fish practically sleep on each other."

"Fish don't sleep."

"Well, your fish are going to sleep forever if you put any more in that tank."

"Maybe we can . . ." Niran paused as his father appeared in the distance, wearing a frayed canvas hat that a tourist had given him years earlier. "See, we should have worked faster," Niran said. "Now I have to go to the pier."

"I'll go to the pier. You stay with Achara."

"No, no, no."

"Wait. Let me tell you a new joke before you go."

He watched a fish break the surface of the nearby water. "Tell me."

"Why did the farmer call his pig Ink?"

"Why?"

"Because he kept running out of the pen."

Niran giggled, pushing her. "Tell me another one."

"What's skinny, has black hair, and says 'ouch'?"

"I don't know."

She reached forward, pinching his arm.

"Ouch!"

"It's you," she said, giggling. "You're the answer." Before he could get revenge, she kicked some sand at his feet, and then ran toward their restaurant, waving to her father but not pausing. Niran started to run after her but stopped, since she was much quicker. He saw that his father was carrying their sign—a piece of wood that had been painted white, with RAINBOW RESORT written in bright colors.

"You sold six Fantas, four Sprites, and three beers?" his father asked, leading him to a footpath behind the beach, limping as he walked.

"And one of Patch's coconuts."

Lek smiled, though he wished they had sold more. "You're a fine salesman. Are you sure you want to be a scientist?"

"Of course I'm sure. Then I can catch all the fish I want. Just like the French scientists who were tagging all those tuna."

"That was neat."

"It was amazing. And they get to do it every day."

"How about we tag some tourists today? We've got seven empty bungalows. And that's seven too many."

"Let's try."

Father and son followed the path, which turned to the east, toward the interior of the butterfly-shaped island. The body of the butterfly was a rise about a mile long and a half mile across. On either side lay a beach, and at the end of each beach rose the massive limestone cliffs. The main village was located between the beaches.

As they neared the village, they began to pass a row of simple one-story shops that sold T-shirts, swimsuits, balls, sunscreen, refreshments, souvenirs, jewelry, and just about anything else that a tourist might want. The farther they walked, the more elaborate the stores became—soon small, A-framed structures that mimicked traditional Thai architecture. These one- or two-room stores contained masseuses, dive centers, Internet cafés, crepe and pastry shops, minimarts, and travel agencies.

The walkway was now paved with bricks, and thinking about how Patch had started to work on their path, Lek smiled. He looked up, gazing at the main trunk of a massive banyan tree that dwarfed everything beneath it. The base of the tree was encircled with strips of red, blue, white, and yellow fabric. A little red shrine had been inset within the weblike mesh of the tree's roots. Several incense sticks burned near the shrine. A variety of soft drinks had been set nearby—opened, but not emptied. Straws were aimed skyward, offering ancestors easy access to the drinks.

The center of the village bustled with vendors, children, and tourists. The foreigners wandered around carrying large backpacks, sat in cafés, haggled with shopkeepers, or studied maps and guidebooks. As Lek and Niran approached the opposite beach, a slew of restaurants materialized. Each restaurant had some sort of wooden boat outside, which was filled with ice and fresh seafood. There were rows of squid, giant prawns, lobsters, crabs, clams, snapper, shark, barracuda, and sea bass. Patrons could order any item and have it cooked to their specifications. Lek studied the offerings, wondering what he and Niran would spear for dinner. He didn't see much tuna and decided to hunt for such a fish. More tourists might come to their restaurant if fresh tuna was available.

The pier was about three hundred feet long and filled with people, carts, and baggage. Secured to the pier near the shallower waters were almost a dozen colorful dive boats, full of glistening scuba tanks and grinning tourists. Next came several rust-stained barges that had brought goods from Phuket. Toward the end of the pier, battered two-story passenger ferries had been lashed together, so that they pointed toward shore and stretched out, parallel to the pier. The boats were empty, but in the distance a white-and-blue ferry approached.

Dozens of Thais congregated near the end of the pier, holding signs and brochures featuring their guesthouses and resorts. Lek greeted many of the men and women he saw, taking his place in line. None of them jostled for a better position or sought to create a competitive advantage. Everyone was friendly, excited by the prospect of a full boat, of travelers with money to spend.

Lek leaned against a steel railing, his hip aching. "What did you learn in school yesterday?" he asked his son.

"What?"

"Tell me, my little daydreamer, what you learned in school yesterday."

Niran shook his head. "Nothing."

"Nothing? That can't be true. Think of one thing. One thing to make your father smarter."

"Well, a whale is not a fish. It breathes air. Like us. I asked Miss Wattana about whales. And she told me all about them."

"Really?"

"A whale has a . . . a hole in the top of its head. And it goes to the surface and breathes air."

"Hmm. I didn't know that. Thanks for making me smarter. Your mother would be proud."

Niran scratched at a mosquito bite. "Some whales can hold their breath for more than an hour."

"Really?"

"They dive down so deep, and look for squid to eat. And they sing to each other while they hunt."

"How wonderful. What kind of songs do they sing?"

"Long, moaning songs," Niran answered, still scratching. "I want to hear one someday."

"Keep studying, so that when you hear one, you'll know just what it means."

"I will."

Lek pointed to the approaching ferry. "It's about ready to dock. And we need to fill up those seven bungalows. What do you think, should we drop our price?"

"To four hundred baht a night?"

"Let's try three seventy-five."

"All right."

"Will you give it your best, my son? Let's really try to reel them in."

Niran nodded, watching the ferry pull alongside an almost identical vessel at the end of the row. A few minutes passed before tourists started crossing from boat to boat, drawing nearer to the pier. Most of the newcomers spoke excitedly and eyed their surroundings. All carried large backpacks. As the foreigners approached, the Thais began to hold up their signs and, in broken English, encourage people to come to their guesthouses. Since Niran's English was much better than his father's, when he wasn't in school he often visited the pier and tried to entice people to come to Rainbow Resort. Sometimes Suchin joined them as well.

Lek realized that the boat was less full than he had hoped—which was unfortunate, because the nicer resorts would continue to have vacancies. He listened to his competitors, aware that many were also dropping their prices. After whispering to Niran to offer three hundred and fifty baht for a room, he gripped his fists tight as his son exchanged words with a group of blond-haired women. He thought that they were going to agree to Niran's offer, but in the end, one of the women thanked him, patted him on the head, and turned away. Lek closed his eyes, angry that the woman had touched Niran's head, that she didn't know Thais considered heads to be sacred and therefore practically untouchable.

Niran knew that his father was watching him, that his family depended on him. And so he smiled wide and used his best English. He told tourists about the beauty of Rainbow Resort, about how his mother was the number one cook on the island, and about how their bungalows were on the prettiest part of the beach. But many tourists already had reservations at nicer places, and Niran didn't have brochures like some of the other people offering places to stay. All he had was his voice, which he used as a poet uses words. He made people slow with his voice; he made them stop and smile. But even when he dropped the price to three hundred baht, people kept shaking their heads. And soon only a smattering of Thais remained on the pier.

Having failed his father, Niran turned and walked toward shore, watching his bare feet rise and fall. "I'm sorry," he whispered, switching to Thai.

Lek paused and, despite the pain in his hip, bent down to look into his son's eyes. "Don't be sorry. You tried your best. And you spoke so well. I've never heard you speak so well."

"Why didn't anyone come?"

"Because there are too many of us and too few of them."

"I wasn't good enough. Suchin would have been better."

Lek smiled. "You were perfect. Just perfect. Now let's go get the spear gun and catch a tuna. So many of these foreigners like sushi. Let's hit a tuna and fill their bellies with it."

"Tuna are hard to hit. They can swim up to almost a hundred kilometers an hour. Faster than cars."

"So that's why we usually miss them? Because they're faster than cars?"

"That's right. That's why it's so hard to bring one home."

Pursing his lips, Lek pretended to ponder Niran's words.

"Well . . . don't you think it's hard for air to find the hole in the head of a giant whale?"

"That would be hard."

"But the air finds the hole. Every day. And so maybe today we'll find a tuna. Such a big tuna that we can eat some after the foreigners are full."

Niran scratched at his bare, bony shoulder. "Let's go."

After slowly straightening, Lek turned to look at the ferry, wishing that it had been full. Sarai would be disappointed once again. "Let's surprise your mother with the biggest tuna she's ever seen," Lek said, increasing his pace, grimacing at a sudden bout of pain.

"Does your hip hurt?"

"No. Not today. So let's hurry, my little scientist. Let's hurry and make her happy."

SEVERAL HOURS LATER, ON THE sandy area behind Rainbow Resort, a group of about fifteen Thai children played soccer. Only two girls competed, each on opposite teams, wearing shorts and T-shirts, while the boys wore only shorts. The field, about forty feet wide and seventy feet long, had been cleared of palm trees by Lek a decade earlier, before he hurt his hip. He'd wanted his future children to be able to run, as he had fond memories of doing so as a boy. And though he'd been tempted to build bungalows on the field, he'd been able to resist this notion, convincing himself that foreigners wouldn't want to be so far from the beach. His neighbors had encouraged him as well, glad that their children had a place dedicated to the game they loved. So much of the island was devoted to tourists. Foreigners stayed on the nicest stretches of sand, scuba dived above untouched reefs, and enjoyed the best of everything. Most of the locals lived far from the beaches and worked all hours of the day.

Lek might have been able to earn a bit more money by destroying the soccer field, but he chose not to. And his wife, who was practical in many ways, and who deftly managed what little money they possessed, wanted the field to remain as it was. Sarai liked hearing the children laugh after school as she diced vegetables with her mother and prepared to feed ten or twenty people.

Now, as Lek leaned against the back of the restaurant and watched his daughter and son with pride, he wondered what would happen to the field if they were forced to leave for Bangkok. Surely it would be developed—guesthouses or a hotel put in its place. Suchin's and Niran's friends would have to find another place to play. And while several such fields existed in the middle of the island, they were closer to piles of discarded water bottles and old engines than to any beach.

Suchin had always been much better at soccer than Niran. She could defend, pass, and dribble as if she'd learned such skills in the womb. Niran often looked as if he'd just started to play. To his friends' surprise, he didn't seem to mind being one of the worst players. Though no one else knew why, the reason was simple—Niran saw his father hobble every day and he felt no need to be the fastest or strongest. His being so fast might make his father sad.

From inside the restaurant, Lek heard Sarai announce that dinner was ready. He started to call out to his children but saw that Niran had the ball and was dribbling toward the goal. "Hurry," Lek whispered, clenching his fists, releasing the tension when another boy kicked the ball away from Niran as other defenders cheered.

"Mother's waiting," Lek interjected, stepping toward the game. Suchin passed the ball to one of her teammates, waved good-bye, and turned toward her father. Niran started to do the same but saw that a small hermit crab had wandered onto the field. He bent down, picked it up, and hurried toward the restaurant, placing the crab near the corner of the structure.

Lek complimented his children on the game, smiling as he followed them toward the kitchen. Set in the back of the restaurant, the kitchen was a cinder-block room about five paces long and three paces wide. Much of the room was dominated by full-length, stainless-steel countertops. Piles of diced onions, tomatoes, garlic cloves, lemongrass, mushrooms, and baby corn occupied one area, as did a mound of fresh shrimp, and a large barracuda that Lek and Niran had killed with their spear gun. In the back of the room, a four-burner gas stove held a wok and a large pot.

Sitting in the corner of the room was the children's grandmother, whom they called Yai. Achara, naked and wide-eyed, lay between Yai's thighs. Yai seemed as large as Achara appeared small. Dressed in a loose-fitting purple sarong and a white cotton blouse, Yai leaned back in her chair and smiled at the sight of Suchin and Niran. "Did you brush yourselves off?" she asked. "Your mother can't have two specks of sand in her kitchen. One might be fine, but definitely not two."

Suchin glanced at her grandmother's wide and full face, surprised that her gray hair was peeking from beneath the red cloth that she liked to wrap around the top of her head. "I shook myself clean; I promise."

"Like a dog after a bath?"

"I did."

"And you, Niran?"

"What?"

"Did you do some good shaking?"

Niran had been thinking of a shark he'd seen when they were trying to find a tuna and, without answering his grandmother, stepped back outside and brushed the sand from his feet, knees, and elbows. He reentered the kitchen and saw that his mother was adding noodles, vegetables, and slices of pineapple to a long-handled wok, which sizzled above a strong fire. As he often did when in the kitchen with the women, Niran leaned against the far wall, watching. He would have been happy to slice up the barracuda or to help in some way, but no one cooked except his mother, which was how she liked it.

Bending over, Suchin picked up her baby sister, holding her casually, burping her without thought. Suchin's hands pressed against Achara's naked bottom and back, keeping Achara firmly positioned against her own belly and chest. She wished her father and brother had caught a tuna or a lobster, knowing that her mother would flavor their meal with pieces of the bony and bland barracuda.

"How was your day?" her mother asked, holding the handle of the sizzling wok, flipping the ingredients with a toss of her wrist.

"We sold fourteen drinks," Suchin answered, continuing to pat her sister's back.

"I know. A very impressive number."

Yai rose slowly from her chair, moving to a cutting board. "You've done well, Suchin. But I'll tell you what's even more impressive."

"What?"

"Try watching your mother run around like a headless chicken all day. Now, that's impressive."

Turning down the heat beneath the wok, Sarai rolled her eyes. "Impressive is how that body of yours continues to get bigger. Day after day after day."

"I like being fat," Yai replied. "It's my excuse for not working."

"What was your excuse ten years ago?"

"You."

"Me?"

"That's right. Watching you move so fast made me tired. Just like it does today."

Sarai began to dish up plates of steaming food for her children. "I didn't know that someone could sit for so long. Doesn't your bottom hurt?"

"Oh, it's nothing that—"

"Or maybe that's why you like all that padding. So you can sit in comfort, no matter where you go."

"Padding is good. Nothing wrong with having a built-in cushion."

Suchin grinned as her mother and grandmother continued to tease each other, as they often did. She followed her mother out into the restaurant and sat down at a table in the corner. Niran sat across from her, the small hermit crab in his hands once again. He set the crab on the floor, aiming it toward the nearby railing and beach.

Dinner was vegetables, pineapple, and barracuda flavored with a sweet-and-sour sauce. A mound of steamed white rice also rose on the children's plates. Niran began to eat, pleased to see Patch in the opposite corner, waiting patiently for his food. Patch ate whatever the children ate—rarely shrimp or tuna, but plenty of delicious food. Niran smiled when Patch waved, then turned back to his food, wanting to finish it before the hermit crab escaped.

A few minutes passed and then a group of four Italian tourists walked to one of the low outdoor tables on the beach, dropping down on the colorful tapestry spread under the table, stretching out and talking loudly. Patch watched the young men with interest, as they had been renting two bungalows for several days now, and often were noisy and borderline obnoxious. He was amazed at how many Singha beers they could consume in a night, bottles gathering around them like spent artillery shells.

Sarai placed Patch's dinner in front of him, and he put his hands together, bowing slightly. He thanked her in Thai, adding in English that her meal looked delicious.

"I so excited for your path," she answered, grinning, her English less refined than her children's.

"Thanks. I think it will be nice."

"You are nice, Patch. Nicer than my food."

"No way. Impossible."

She laughed, stepping away from him and toward the Italians, who were calling out for more beer. Patch watched her hurry toward them, as if their order might disappear if her feet didn't move fast enough. He wondered what Niran and Suchin thought of their mother so quickly rushing to meet the needs of foreigners—probably nothing, having witnessed such scenes since birth.

Sarai took the order, then walked behind the bar and removed four oversize Singha bottles from an old-fashioned, tablelike refrigerator. Patch watched her, then picked up his spoon and began to eat. As usual, the food was fresh, light, and delicious. He'd smashed his thumb laying a brick, so using the spoon required patience. Eating slowly, he thought about what his brother might be doing in Bangkok. He had been surprised to learn that Ryan was planning to bring his girlfriend, Brooke, whom Patch didn't know. She'd met their parents only once.

Though Patch was a year younger than Ryan, he had more experience with women, was more interested in them. Sports and academics had always come first for Ryan, while women often seemed an afterthought. Patch saw the world from the opposite perspective. To him, relationships were his prize possessions, and forming them was his chief aim in life. Good grades, career success, and other such achievements were of secondary importance.

One of the Italians belched, and Patch glanced in the group's direction. The sand near their table was already littered with beer bottles. To the west, the setting sun illuminated the bay with the colors of a campfire. The bay was almost empty. Most travelers had left the beach, though a few still swam and tossed a Frisbee.

The beauty surrounding him made Patch think about the inside of a jail cell. He'd waste away in such a place. Though Ryan would certainly be able to endure a year in a Thai prison, Patch knew that he couldn't. The loneliness of such an existence would suffocate him, as would the knowledge of the humiliation that he'd brought upon his family. Better to roll the dice and gamble on a voyage to India, as outlandish as it seemed. It would be far better for his parents if he stowed away on a ship for a few weeks than if the local newspaper wrote stories about his imprisonment in Thailand.

The Italians called again to Sarai, who appeared in less than a minute. Patch saw her quickly assess the mess that her guests had created. The turquoise tapestry, which he knew she had carefully washed and ironed, was covered with sand. The flowers she'd set in a small vase had been dumped out so that the vase could accommodate cigarette butts.

Patch saw Sarai smile and nod, and he was suddenly aware of her predicament, of how she wouldn't want her children to see drunk tourists or her efforts to set a pretty table defiled. Yet she had to please her guests, regardless of her dignity.

After finishing his meal, Patch said good night to Suchin and Niran. He left the indoor part of the restaurant and walked toward the beach, kneeling on the sand when he arrived at the Italians' table. "Hi," he said, his hands on his thighs.

The smallest of the foursome, who had curly, shoulder-length black hair, nodded. "Hello."

"Do you mind if I have a smoke?"

The Italian pulled a cigarette from a pack, passing it and a lighter to Patch. "Enjoy."

Patch lit the cigarette, pretending to smoke. "Thanks a lot."

"Okay."

After starting to rise, Patch paused. "Would you do me a favor?"

"What?"

"The woman who keeps bringing you beer. Her name is Sarai. Could you thank her next time? She works really hard. And it would be nice if you thanked her."

The Italians looked at one another. Their smiles faded, and their bottles remained on the table. Patch thought that they might stand to argue with him. His heartbeat quickened. His cigarette trembled. But instead of rising, a large, bearded Italian nodded. "You are the one who was working on . . . the path?" he asked, his English slow and tentative.

"Yeah. That's me."

"You work for her?"

"Just a few odd jobs."

The stranger took a deep drag on his cigarette. "We will thank her."

Patch nodded. "Enjoy your night."

Grunting, the Italian turned away. Still pretending to smoke, Patch started to walk to the beach but remembered the children. Glancing at his cigarette, he headed back into the restaurant and approached their table. He smiled, leaning toward them. "I don't smoke," he whispered. "But I had to pretend for a bit. Okay?"

Suchin moved closer to him. "Why are you pretending?"

"I . . . I had to make some friends."

"With those boys?"

"That's right. So don't ever smoke, all right?"

Niran pushed his empty plate aside. "Can you swim with us tomorrow?"

"Sure. Maybe before my brother gets here."

"Will you introduce us to him?" Suchin asked.

"Of course."

"Good. We want to meet your big brother."

Patch smiled. "You do? Why?"

"Because he's part of your family," she replied, toying with one of her earrings. "He's part of you."

"And we like you," Niran added.

Suchin let go of her earring. "Want to hear a joke?"

"Sure."

"It's a long one."

"I like your long ones."

"A young turtle was at the bottom of a tall tree. He was tired. So tired. But he took a deep breath and started to climb. About an hour later, he reached a high branch and crawled along to the end. He turned and spread all four flippers and jumped off the branch." Suchin paused, pretending to be a leaping turtle. "After landing at the bottom in a pile of soft sand, he shook himself off, crawled back to the bottom of the tree, took another deep breath, and started to climb. Watching him from the end of another branch were a mother and father bird. The mother bird then turned to the father bird and whispered, 'Maybe it's time we told him that he's adopted.'"

Patch laughed with the children, having heard many of Suchin's jokes, and always happy to do so. He complimented her, glancing across the bay. The sun had just set, and the water was awash with color. "How about a quick swim right now? Want to ask your mother?"

Niran hurried from the table. Suchin took Patch's cigarette and stubbed it out on her plate. "Don't let my mother see you with that. Even though you're my American brother, she'd still be angry at you. And believe me, you'd rather have a hive of bees angry at you."

"I believe you."

Suchin picked apart the cigarette butt, then put the remnants on her plate and covered them with some sweet-and-sour sauce. She took Patch's hand, squeezing it tight. "Let's see what she told Niran. I hope she said yes."

"Me too, Suchin. Me too."

SUNDAY, DECEMBER 19

separate ways

Though it was only midmorning, heat and humidity seemed to rise from the bay as if it were a giant pot of simmering water. The tide was out, revealing a four- or five-city-block-size expanse of wet sand and a collection of small pools. The water in the bay was so shallow that the tide dramatically changed the look and feel of the beach. When the tide was in, the white sand met the turquoise water in a long curving line, creating an image of a crescent moon against a blue sky. When the tide was out, the beach was much less defined, stretching westward into the damp remnants of the sea's retreat.

The sky was bereft of a single cloud, and the tropical sun gave life to the colors of the island—the green of the foliage, the gray of the cliffs, the gold of the beach, and the blue of the bay. A breeze wafted from the west, causing the coconut trees to sway like cobras in front of a charmer's flute. The scent of tropical flowers and salt permeated the damp air.

Most of the beach was empty, the long line of wooden lounge chairs almost devoid of tourists. They would arrive soon, Lek knew, wondering why Sarai had called out to him to come to one of their bungalows. He looked toward the water and saw his children making their way along the shore, picking up small bits of trash. Suchin carried Achara in a sling on her back. Niran held a bucket for the trash and his beloved net, and often stepped into the water, watching the movements of sea creatures. Smiling at the sight, Lek limped along the sandy trail between the bungalows, pleased that Patch was laying bricks in the distance. A paved path would be a major improvement, as monsoon rains often left the existing trail waterlogged for days. Lek had been forced to sell one of his two longboats to pay for the bricks, but he felt sure the investment would be worthwhile. Two boats had been an extravagance anyway.

He turned right, toward one of their best bungalows, moving up three cement steps and into the room. Within seconds he could tell that something was wrong. Sarai sat motionless on the side of the bed, her feet bare, her shoulders slumped. She wore a bright red sarong and a yellow blouse, but her face seemed drained of color. He sat down beside her, resting his hand on her thigh, waiting for her to speak.

She pulled back the sheet, revealing a burned section of fabric. Somehow the sheet had been set afire, then doused with water. A fist-size hole remained, black and brown at the edges. "I should have looked closer," Sarai said softly. "Right when they left. I always do, but this morning Suchin wanted to . . . she wanted me to braid her hair. So I hurried in here, looked around, then went home."

Lek nodded, aware that the British couple who had occupied

the bungalow would by now be on the morning ferry, heading back to Phuket. He and Sarai always inspected their bungalows before their visitors left the island. That way, if there was any damage, compensation could be procured before the foreigners sailed away forever. "It's not your fault," he said softly, patting her knee again.

She shook her head, her full lips pressing together, her fists clenching. "It is my fault. Of course it is. I should have seen this right away. Do you know how much a new sheet costs?"

"I don't—"

"Three hundred baht! What a waste. Three hundred baht for a sheet we already had. A good sheet, with hardly any wear."

"We'll manage."

"How? How can you look at me and say that? Our money is almost gone. We can't afford to buy the children new clothes or for you to see the doctor. How is that managing? How do we work so hard, every day, and have nothing to show for it? What are we doing wrong?"

He reached for her hand as she started to cry. "Let me rub your feet."

"No."

"Please. Lie down. Let me rub your feet."

"Rubbing my feet isn't going to buy a new sheet."

"It might—"

"What are we going to do? The children are so happy. I don't want to take them to Bangkok. How would you even find work with your hip? No one would hire you. We'd have nothing. Do you hear me? We'd have nothing."

"We'd have each other."

She wiped her eyes, wishing that her headache would leave,

chastising herself for once again forgetting to eat and drink. "Later, when we're old, that would be fine. But not now. Not with the children. They need more."

Lek started to reply but heard someone approaching. Sarai wiped her eyes again, and reached for her old-fashioned straw broom. She started to sweep, pausing when Patch walked up the steps. In some ways, Patch resembled Lek, wearing old shorts, a tattered T-shirt, and sandals.

Patch said good morning in Thai, then switched to English. "I wanted to ask you about the path."

Concentrating, Lek forced himself to think in English, a language he had long tried and failed to master. "The path?" he repeated, wondering if his instructions might not have been clear.

"Well, I was hoping that maybe I could change the pattern in the middle. You know, try to make a rainbow with the bricks. So that people would know that they were on their way to Rainbow Resort."

Sarai nodded, repeating Patch's words in Thai, then responding in English. "Could you make a brick rainbow?"

"I think so. I could go into the village, where they're building that new hotel, and use one of their saws to cut some of our bricks. Or I could buy a few bricks that were a different color, and cut them so they fit together and made a rainbow. It would be easy."

Thinking about a rainbow in the middle of their path prompted another tear to tumble from Sarai's face. She smiled, wiping it away. "Thank you, Patch. Yes, please. Your idea is good."

Patch realized that she had been crying and dropped his gaze. For the first time he noticed the hole in the sheet. "What happened?"

"Oh, it is nothing. Just time . . . time to buy a new sheet."

"What a waste."

"Yes."

Patch started to turn away but deduced that the sight of the ruined sheet must have made her cry. "I'll take it," he said. "I have a good sheet in my room. I don't need it. You can take mine and use it in here."

"No. You keep your sheet. We will take this sheet for our bed."

He shook his head. "Achara can't sleep on this sheet. No way. That's not right for a baby."

"You are our guest," Sarai replied. "You must sleep well."

"Don't worry. I'll sleep fine."

"You sure?"

"Of course."

"I will fix it for you. With a . . ."

"With a patch. You can fix it with a patch."

She smiled. "Yes. I will fix it with a patch. A patch for Patch."

"Perfect. How could that not be perfect for me?"

"Thank you," she replied, wondering what his mother was like. "Thank you so much. You have a good heart."

"Thank you for letting me make my rainbow."

"Your brother, he will arrive later today?"

"Yeah."

"I will cook something good for him. Something delicious."

"I'm sure he'd enjoy that after his long trip."

She thanked him again and then began to speak in Thai, repeating everything to Lek, making sure he understood. Lek listened, turned to Patch, and placed his hands together, bowing slightly. He thanked Patch in Thai, wishing he could communicate better with the American, wanting to talk with him about so many things.

After Patch left, Lek turned to Sarai. "See? We'll manage. We'll always manage."

"We have to."

"Come. Lie down. Give me five minutes to rub those busy feet of yours. Please. Feet that move so fast deserve to be rubbed."

"What about your hip? Shouldn't I be rubbing it?"

"It's fine."

Sarai smiled, and Lek was relieved to see her laugh lines deepen. She closed the bungalow's door, stretched out on the bed, and his hands found her ankles, pressing against her flesh, resting at first. Then his fingers began to move—hard, calloused fingers that swept across the hard, thick skin of her heels. She closed her eyes and let him carry her away to a place free of doubt and worry, where his hip didn't hurt, where their children didn't have to sell soft drinks, where the strength of their family wasn't tested on a daily basis. Sarai let him take her to this place, and for five minutes she swam within its waters.

Then she squeezed his hand, thanked him, and reached for her broom.

THE CEMENT PIER IN PHUKET looked big enough to accommodate a warship, Ryan thought as he wheeled his suitcase toward a waiting speedboat. In the distance, scores of travelers were boarding a large blue-and-white passenger ferry. The travelers—often wearing nothing more than swimsuits—carried backpacks, beer, and guidebooks. Though distant engines purred and rumbled, it was the intonations of a dozen languages that permeated the air.

A few feet behind Ryan, Brooke hurried to catch up, amazed

that they could fly from Bangkok to such a beautiful place in just over an hour. "We should go on a boat like that," she said. She was dressed in a white tank top and denim shorts, her long hair emerging from the back of her pink Race for the Cure baseball hat. "It seems like a better fit for this sort of journey."

"Why? So we can get to Ko Phi Phi in three hours instead of forty minutes?"

Brooke saw a couple kissing toward the rear of the line. "It might be fun."

"It might be."

"Look at it. Doesn't it look fun? Why so reluctant?"

"Because it might be boring too."

"How could a ride on that possibly be boring?"

Ryan watched fishermen working on a nearby boat, which was brightly colored and featured giant booms that held hundreds of lightbulbs. The fishermen were shirtless and moved fast, uncoiling a spool of netting. Behind the fishing boat was a gray-hulled military vessel of some sort, listing slightly to one side. From atop the wheelhouse, the red, white, and blue flag of Thailand rippled in the wind. No one appeared to be on board.

"We've traveled halfway around the world to see Patch," Ryan finally replied. "And we're forty minutes from him. Forty minutes. Why would we want to make that three hours?"

Glancing at the kissing couple, Brooke followed Ryan toward the large speedboat that he'd rented through a travel agency. A Thai man, presumably the captain, approached and asked in broken English for their contract. Ryan had the papers ready, and within ten minutes he and Brooke were sitting near the middle of the boat, a pair of large outboard engines powering the craft past the idle ferry. Most of the backpackers were gathering on the roof, putting their feet over the edge, leaning forward against a white railing.

Though Brooke was envious of their slow, adventurous ride, she reminded herself that of course Ryan wanted to reach Patch as quickly as possible. Leaning back in her bucket seat, she watched the mountainous, immense island of Phuket slowly recede. Once they were clear of the harbor, the captain pushed the throttle down and the twin engines roared to life. The bow rose, casting spray out on either side. Brooke took off her baseball cap and oversize tortoiseshell sunglasses, thinking about the couple who had kissed so openly. Given her history, she wasn't sure whether she'd ever kiss a man in public. But she found herself wondering what it would be like, wondering how the couple had met and what the future held for them. A part of her was envious of their connection, and she asked herself whether she'd trade places with the woman, suspecting that she would.

In her second year of business school at Northwestern University, Brooke was about the same age as most of the other travelers. Yet she felt so much older. Restless with such thoughts, she turned toward Ryan, wondering where his mind was. "Is Patch like you?" she asked, the boat humming beneath her.

He swiveled his seat toward her. "He looks like me."

"Really?"

"Growing up, people thought we were twins." Ryan paused, his fingers tracing the contours of a crack in the leather chair. "We had fun with that. He had fun with it, especially. But I did too."

"What did you do?"

"Oh, we'd confuse our babysitters, our dentists. Stuff like that. Later, in high school, we'd switch football jerseys, and he'd get to play a down or two with the varsity. He got thumped, but he got to play."

Brooke smiled, moving to the side so that her wind-whipped hair didn't obscure her view. "Did he act like you? Like another kingpin in the making?"

Ryan thought about growing up in Kansas City, about growing up with Patch. Their father had worked long hours as an elementary school principal. Their mother was diagnosed with lupus at age thirty-one and had often been bedridden. With their father usually gone and their mother sometimes nearly incapacitated, Ryan and Patch had grown up relying on each other. They'd been inseparable and best friends. And though years had passed since they had slept under the same roof, they'd always remained close, calling each other in times of need, sharing stories and secrets.

"Patch was always more of a dreamer," Ryan finally replied. "I got the good grades. I liked school. I think the whole thing bored him. He read all the time. Day and night. Just not the books that his teachers wanted him to."

"Did he have girlfriends?"

Ryan nodded. "Patch is good at making girls smile, making them laugh. Much better than me."

"Don't sell yourself sh—"

"It's okay. I know what I can do and what I can't do."

"What did you do in high school? What did he do?"

"In high school? I was the star athlete, the perfect student. I worked really hard . . . but I wasn't really happy. On the other hand, Patch hardly worked at all but was happy. He got the girls. He was the cool brother. I'd tag along with him and his girlfriends and feel like the biggest loser on the planet."

"You couldn't be farther from a loser. And you can make women laugh. You've made me laugh."

"I'd like to make you laugh more."

She studied his face, wondering whether she could kiss him in public. "I want to ask you something."

"Go ahead."

"Why . . . why have we never said the word *love* to each other? We're here in Thailand. We've traveled so far together and we have a history together. But there's a lot we've never said. And that makes me wonder . . . about us."

He turned slightly away from her. "People use that word . . . those four letters . . . way too easily."

"Have you ever used it?"

"No. Not like that."

"But could you? Someday? Can you imagine using it with me?"

"I don't know. Really, I'd rather focus on Patch right now than talk about us."

"You sound like a politician, evading my question, acting obtuse."

Ryan turned back toward her, reaching for her hands. "I look after you. I care about you."

"I don't want to be looked after."

"Sorry. That came out wrong. That was . . . condescending. But I want to help. It's what—"

"Is it because of what happened to me?" she asked, her voice speeding up, moving like the boat. "Because I have baggage?"

His fingers tightened around hers. "Everyone has baggage."

"You don't."

"Can you just be patient? Please?"

"Patient? You're about the most impatient person I've ever met. You've got the fastest computer, the fastest feet, the fastest boat." You're even impatient in bed, she thought, though she would never say such a thing.

He sighed, removing his sunglasses. "Let's save my brother, all right? Can we do that? Let's do that and then worry about four-letter words."

Flying fish started to leap near the bow of the boat, hopping across the water like skipping stones. Brooke watched them, sitting straighter in her chair, aware that she was acting self-indulgent and chastising herself for it. "There's nothing more important than your brother," she said. "Not even overused four-letter words."

"That's right."

"But how are we going to save him? Really, if he doesn't want to turn himself in, how are you going to help him?"

Ryan put his sunglasses back on, admiring the speed of the flying fish. "He doesn't have a choice. We just have to make him realize that. The sooner he turns himself in, the sooner he can get on with his life."

"And a Thai jail should be a part of his life?"

"It'll have to be. Because there's no other choice."

"He could—"

"No, Brooke. He couldn't. He's not going to escape in some old boat to India. That's insane. For once he's going to do what he has to do."

"And you're going to convince him?"

"We're going to convince him."

She nodded, shifting her gaze toward a group of distant islands on the horizon. The green clumps seemed to rise almost vertically out of the sea, serene and secluded. Good places to hide, she thought, then wondered if she'd do what Ryan wanted.

As she did most every day, Yai sat in the shallows, washing Achara's naked body. Yai wore shorts, a T-shirt, and a cap. She had never owned a swimsuit; nor had she ever wanted one. Staring toward deeper water, she watched a pair of topless foreign women who stood facing the beach. Even though Yai had seen thousands of such women, she could never get comfortable with the sight of so much skin. The display seemed boastful, and Yai wished that her grandchildren hadn't seen so many naked breasts. Surely the experience would do them more harm than good. Breasts weren't created for men, she thought, but for babies. Men had enough toys already without breasts bouncing around in front of them.

"Don't you look over there," Yai whispered to Achara, washing her privates, turning her away from the women. "That hot sun has baked their brains. Not that they had much to start with, but they've got even less now. You'll never swim like that. Never." Yai began cleaning Achara's bottom, wiping and splashing. "Yes, it's true, some Thai girls wear swimsuits these days, but not my little Achara. You'll wear shorts and a shirt. And you won't let men see your body like it's some sort of advertisement for . . . Oh, never mind."

Achara burped, causing Yai to smile.

"You agree?" Yai asked, scrubbing Achara's feet. "I knew you would. You always agree with me. That's one of the many, many reasons I love you so much. Here, do you want to practice stand-ing? This is a good place to do it." Yai lifted Achara upright, setting her feet on the sandy bottom while continuing to support her. "See? You can do it. But I tell you, sometimes it's fun to sit too. Your shadow might not be as tall when you sit, but it's so much wider. It'll keep you cool from the sun."

Leaning forward, Achara sagged against Yai's hands. Yai bent down and blew on the back of Achara's neck, prompting a toothless smile. "Let me see that belly of yours," Yai said, lifting Achara up, blowing against her stomach, laughing at Achara's grin. "Feeling better now? Is your gas gone? Your mother's still eating too many peppers. I've tried, tried like we talked about, to get her to stop, but since when does she ever listen to me? Oh, don't follow in your mother's footsteps, Achara. She's got the strength of ten men. Not that ten men are so impressive, but these days your mother can be overwhelming. She works too hard. Of course, she needs to cook and clean, which is actually good for us, because I get to spend so much time with you. I'm a lucky woman."

Yai heard Suchin's voice and turned toward Rainbow Resort. Suchin was running along the beach, giggling, pursued by her little brother. He didn't look pleased, which made Yai smile. "Go get her, Niran," she said softly. "But don't kick sand on the tourists, or your mother won't be happy. And you'd better sell some more drinks."

Niran stopped chasing Suchin, who had darted between two bungalows. He walked to the water and sat in the shallows. Yai lifted Achara's hand and waved. Niran shook his head, apparently angry at Suchin, but finally, after hitting the water, he waved back. Yai motioned for him to join her, and he stood up and waded toward her. Watching him move through the turquoise water, with the coconut trees behind him, Yai thought of her good fortune and thanked Buddha, as she often did, for her many blessings.

"What did your sassy sister do?" she asked, as Niran approached.

"A man gave her a piece of candy and she didn't tell me about it until she'd eaten it! So I tried to get her back. But she ran and ran and ran and was laughing the whole time!"

"Here, sit by me. Keep your old grandmother company."

"She should have shared it," he replied, dropping to his knees beside her.

"Yes, she should have. But we all make mistakes. I gave birth to your mother, didn't I?"

"Suchin makes the most. Much more than me."

Yai set Achara on her lap. "Didn't she catch you that glass shrimp the other day?"

"That was three days ago."

"But isn't the shrimp in your tank today? Weren't you watching it this morning?"

Niran scratched at a mosquito bite on his elbow. "It's almost invisible, except for its stomach and eyes."

"Would you rather have the piece of candy, or the shrimp?"

"The . . . the shrimp."

"So why don't you consider the candy your return gift to her? Tell her that it was your gift. And every morning, when you see that invisible shrimp, remember how she gave it to you."

Still scratching, Niran nodded. "Yai?"

"Yes, child?"

"This morning, I heard Mother and Father whispering. They were talking about moving to Bangkok."

"They were?"

"We won't have to move to Bangkok, will we? I won't be able to catch crabs and fish if we live there. And how will I ever be a scientist?"

Yai looked toward the restaurant, certain that Sarai was cleaning up from lunch. "No, we won't ever move to Bangkok. Your parents must have had too much sun."

"But why were they talking about it?"

Yai put Achara against her chest, giving herself time to think. "Well, when you look at your tank, don't you consider which kind of rock or shell will be best for your pets? You don't just throw the first rock you see in there. And your mother and father, they're just considering all the choices. And one of those choices is Bangkok."

"It's a bad choice."

"I agree. And that's why I'm sure they won't make it. Your mother's too smart. And your father moves with too much care."

"Except when he fell."

"That's right. Except when he fell. But otherwise he hasn't missed a step. And don't forget about me. You think an old woman like me could survive a move to Bangkok? Better to just set me adrift here. Let my big belly act as a sail and push me out to sea."

Niran smiled. "Maybe we could drift together."

"You're too skinny. The wind would only tug at your nose."

"I could make a sail and put it on my chest."

Yai leaned toward him, resting her free hand on his knee. "It's a deal, then. If your parents lose what little sanity they possess and decide to move to Bangkok, we'll just swim out and set sail. You and me. And we'll bring some candy. As much candy as we can carry."

Picking up a handful of sand, Niran turned it over underwater, watching it billow outward. "I should go back. It's so hot. I bet everyone's thirsty for a Fanta."

"Good luck," she said.

"Thanks."

She watched him depart, loving the sight of his small body and the thought of his wanting to sail away with her. She thanked Buddha for her gifts again, then turned her attention to Achara, kissing her forehead and smiling at the beauty of her dark eyes.

USING AN OLD TROWEL, PATCH carefully smoothed out the layer of sand that he'd poured on the path. He worked on the area in front of him, leveling it perfectly. Satisfied, he picked up a brown brick and set it on the sand, aligning it next to a brick he had placed earlier. The bricks were thick and strong enough to support the baggage carts used by porters to transport backpacks and supplies from their pier.

Turning around, Patch eyed the ten feet or so of the path that he'd finished. The surface was level and uniform, and even when he'd jumped on the tightly packed bricks, they hadn't moved. He was certain that the path would remain useful for many years and was pleased by the notion of improving Rainbow Resort. Lek would be delighted, he was sure. As would Sarai, because until now any sort of rain meant that her guests would track mud and sand into the restaurant and bungalows. The paved path would make such messes a thing of the past.

After placing another brick on the sand, Patch looked back toward the village, wondering when Ryan would arrive. Though he knew that they would argue about his future, he was increasingly excited to see his brother. Their paths hadn't crossed in more than seven months, and only now, with Ryan so close, did Patch realize how much he had missed him. They'd been best friends for so many years—playing sports together, being bunk mates at camp, riding their bicycles around their cul-de-sac. Ryan had always been there when Patch needed him. And Ryan would be there again, only this time he wouldn't be standing up for Patch against some bully or showing him how to throw a football. He'd be telling him to turn himself over to the American embassy, to imprison himself in a Thai jail.

Several months earlier, Patch had hoped that Ryan would help him escape. But it became clear from Ryan's terse emails that he had no interest in plans that might put Patch's life in jeopardy. In Ryan's opinion, an ocean journey to India wasn't an option; nor was sneaking across the border into Malaysia or Cambodia. Any of those choices, Ryan had argued, could lead to a grim fate. And because of that possibility, Ryan wouldn't discuss escape plans, no matter how much Patch wanted him to.

Patch picked up another brick, positioning it carefully. He looked back toward the village, noticing that the setting sun seemed to paint the coconut trees and the distant cliffs with amber. Suddenly he felt alone, almost as much as he had that night in Bangkok when he'd hidden from the police in some slums. That had been the worst night of his life. And though nothing on Ko Phi Phi compared to that horror, Patch needed to see his brother.

He stood up and started walking toward the pier, brushing sand from his chafed hands. On the beach in front of the adjacent set of bungalows, a Thai man was juggling burning sticks, a group of about twenty tourists around him. The fire sticks created glowing arcs as they rose and fell, moving without pause. The smell of burning oil drifted to Patch and he turned to his left, away from the beach. Though he knew that the evening ferry wouldn't arrive for at least another hour, he wanted to be on the pier when Ryan and Brooke stepped ashore.

His pace quickened, and he passed by the wooden storefronts without a glance. Reggae music and laughter emerged from the village, and he wondered which of the many restaurants or bars had organized some sort of party. There was always a party being held on Ko Phi Phi. The only questions were where, when, and what theme.

As he walked beneath a massive banyan tree and turned a corner, Patch stopped. Ten feet away, a guidebook in his hands, stood Ryan. His older brother saw him, lowered his book, and grinned. Patch noticed an attractive woman by Ryan's side, but his gaze quickly returned to Ryan's face. They came together and embraced, squeezing each other, their grips firm and unrelenting. Patch leaned back, lifting his brother off the ground in a bear hug.

"You're so thin," Ryan said, his voice deeper than Patch remembered, almost out of place amid the reggae music and the echoes of foreign languages and accents.

"And you're a rock," Patch added, finally releasing Ryan. "It's so great to see you."

"You too."

"I can't believe you're really here."

"Brooke, this is my little brother, Patrick," Ryan said, stepping back. "But we all call him Patch."

Brooke smiled, extending her hand. "Hi, Patch."

"Hi. Here, let me take your bag."

"Thanks," she replied, noticing the remarkable similarities between the brothers. They possessed the same blue eyes, prominent cheekbones, and angular noses. Ryan's blond hair had been cut short, while Patch's was below his ears and his eyebrows. A sun-bleached, tangled mess, it looked to have not seen a comb in weeks. The tropics had also left a mark on Patch's skin, which was quite tan. A white line encircled his wrist where a bracelet had been recently.

As Brooke assessed him, Patch lifted her suitcase, surprised by her tank top and flip-flops. He'd expected Ryan's girlfriend to be more serious-looking. Ryan had told him only about how the two of them had met in business school, how she was smart and strong and interested in the world. He'd never said that she would look right at home in a place like Ko Phi Phi.

Leading them toward Rainbow Resort, Patch asked about their trip and pointed out some of the island's highlights. Ryan inquired with careful, guarded questions about Patch's situation, while Brooke gazed about in apparent wonder. Patch followed her eyes, seeing what she saw, glad that the island seemed to enchant her.

He guided them to the best bungalow that Lek and Sarai had to offer. After they had settled in and changed clothes, they met him at the restaurant, where he introduced them to his Thai hosts. Sarai had prepared a feast of sorts—seafood soup in a lemongrass broth, fried rice, garlic shrimp, and vegetable curry. Just a few other patrons were seated, and after their plates had been cleared, only Patch, Ryan, and Brooke still ate. Suchin and Niran sat at a nearby table, laughing at the sight of Patch's big brother, joking in English that their mother must have given Ryan all their food. Suchin asked that the brothers roll up their sleeves, and couldn't stop giggling as she compared Patch's thin arm to Ryan's muscles. Niran brought the trio three beers and explained how Patch was building a brick path, how they were friends.

After more than an hour of eating, Ryan thanked Sarai and paid their bill, leaving her a substantial tip. Brooke had changed into a bikini that she wore under her shorts and tank top. She wanted to swim, and the brothers followed her to the shoreline. The sky glowed, alight with the energy of countless stars. Several fires burned along the beach. Music seemed to echo off the sea and the mountainous, shadowlike cliffs. Several idle longboats had been beached, miniature waves breaking against their hulls.

Brooke removed her top and shorts, and stepped into the water, which was warmer than she would have imagined. "It's like a bath," she said, gesturing for the brothers to join her.

"It is a bath," Patch replied. He took off his T-shirt and sandals, moving deeper into the water, avoiding the sight of her body. "All we need are a few toys."

"Some squirt guns would be good," Ryan said.

"Or some plastic dinosaurs. I'll be the T. rex."

"No way. He's mine."

Smiling at the beauty around her, Brooke walked farther into the bay, the water rising to her knees, waist, and finally chest. She dropped below the surface, ran her hands through her hair, and tasted the sea. Though she heard Ryan and Patch talking above and behind her, she didn't resurface until her lungs tightened with want.

Brooke swam underwater again, felt the sand with her fingertips, tried to do a handstand, and then rose to the surface and realized that Ryan and Patch's conversation had shifted to more serious matters. She stood up.

"I called the American embassy again," Ryan said quietly.

"Just before we left Bangkok. They'll help you with the police. They say you'll do a year of time at most. More likely nine or ten months. That's not so bad."

Patch closed his eyes, the water up to his chin. "A year in hell isn't so bad?"

"It won't be hell."

"I hit a cop. His blood was on my hands. How do you think they're going to treat me in jail?"

"You're an American. That'll help. And we'll be checking in on you."

"Why would being an American—"

"Jesus, Patch. The guy at the embassy said it would help. I think he knows a lot more about it than you do."

Patch reached out toward his brother, finding his elbow. "Relax, Ry. Just for a minute."

"I don't want to relax. I want to get you out of this freaking mess."

"Just look at the sky. You've come halfway around the world to a really beautiful place. Will you just look at it for a minute?"

Sighing, Ryan turned slowly in a circle, aware of the beauty, but thinking that for Patch, the beauty was an illusion, an escape from reality. His little brother had always sought out such escapes, and he was irritated that Patch wouldn't just face his fate. "Listen to me. Even a year in hell is better than getting caught trying to run. Then it'll be two years. Or something worse could happen. You think you're going to be safe as a stowaway on some ship? Don't be naive."

"I'm not being—"

"I promised Mom and Dad that I'd talk some sense into you. They were going to come, you know, but I wanted to talk to you first."

"I like it here."

"Of course you like it here. It's paradise. But that doesn't change things. Really, it doesn't."

Patch gazed at the stars again. "One mistake."

"What?"

"One mistake is going to cost me so much." He rubbed his brow, glancing at Brooke, who was watching them intently. "Should one idiotic mistake cost me so much?"

"No," Ryan answered.

"Then why should I go to jail? I'll be in danger there. I'll humiliate Mom and Dad."

"Because you don't have a choice. Because that's how you'll get your life back."

"This is my life."

"This is fantasyland. Or Fantasy Island. It's not your life."

"I'm helping these people. And they're helping me. They took me in. They treat me like a son, and I want to repay them."

Ryan shook his head. "These people? What about Mom and Dad? What about your family?"

"Mom and Dad will forgive me."

Laughter drifted to them from a distant party on the beach. People were dancing around a fire juggler, shouting out encouragement. "A week ago," Ryan said, digging into the sand with his feet, "I was in my marketing class. I had my laptop out, but instead of taking notes, I was thinking about you, worrying about you. Do you ever think about me?"

"All the time."

Brooke looked from brother to brother, intrigued by the similarity of their faces, and the differences of their thoughts. "May I say something?"

Ryan turned toward her. "Sure."

"Let's . . . let's take a hiatus from this conversation. Just for tonight."

"Why?"

"Because you're tired from our trip, and we've got plenty of time to talk."

"Being tired has never stopped me from doing anything. And I'm sure as hell not too tired to talk about this. And we're going to talk about it, Patch. We're going to talk about it until you do the right thing."

Brooke watched the fire juggler, wondering if he ever burned his hands, if he lived with pain on a daily basis. She turned to Patch. "I don't blame you . . . for thinking about escape. And I don't blame you for what happened. Neither does Ryan."

"Thanks."

She was going to ask Patch about what there was to do on the island, but then Ryan ignored her request, as he sometimes did, and started to once again pressure Patch to turn himself in. Putting her head down, she swam out into deeper water. She surfaced and studied the stars, thinking that each star had a history, and that somehow each history now included her.

The starlight comforted her, soothing her pains, her memories. She began to tread water, looking for constellations, for ancient gods and goddesses who were shown to her when she was a little girl, when life had been simple and she could be carried away by the sight of bright figures on a dark page.

MONDAY, DECEMBER 20

the beauty of others

Lek followed Suchin and Niran to the soccer field he had built long ago, in what seemed another life. In that life he was young, he hadn't hurt his hip, and his children didn't exist yet. In some ways, this earlier life was easier—certainly less painful, and full of exuberance. But now he was aware of a deeper meaning each morning when he awoke and watched his sleeping children. Their dreams had become his dreams. He shared their joys and sorrows. He realized with greater and greater conviction that his children were his footprints, his legacy. And though he still thought about himself and his pain, more often than not he focused on Suchin and Niran. His children and Sarai were, by far, the most important pieces of his life. And as long as his children had better lives, had more opportunities than he did, he would be content when he eventually faced death.

Tossing their old, frayed soccer ball toward the field, Lek watched Suchin and Niran hurry after it. He smiled. Mornings like this, when the field was empty and the other children were getting ready for school, comprised some of his best memories. Several times a week he played soccer with Suchin and Niran, laughing, feeling the sand beneath his feet.

About to step onto the field, Lek noticed Patch carrying some bricks to the far end of the path. Lek called out quietly, motioning for Patch to join them, which he often did. He set down the bricks, waved, and jogged over.

"You sleep good?" Lek asked in halting English, watching the sweat roll down Patch's face, wondering how long he'd already been working.

"Just fine, thanks."

"Sheet okay?"

"I didn't even notice it. Really, it isn't a big deal."

Lek smiled. "Maybe some soccer? Then work?"

"Sure. That sounds great."

"That make children happy."

Patch said good morning to Suchin and Niran in Thai, then jogged toward the center of the sandy field. As usual, the teams would be Lek and Patch against the children. Since Lek couldn't run, he played goalie. Either of the children could do the same, depending on who was closest to the goal when Patch was threatening to score.

Suchin nudged Patch as Niran set the ball down. "I would be afraid to play your big brother. But not you." She giggled, pushing him again. "Why did he get all the muscles in your family?"

"Why did you get all the sassiness in yours?"

"Sassiness?"

"It means that you can be naughty . . . in a silly sort of way."

"You're the naughty boy, Patch, to say such a thing. I am a

sweet little girl. I was just thinking that maybe you need to lift some coconuts or something to get stronger. Maybe you could do some push-downs."

"Push-ups. They're called push-ups."

"You need to do a lot of push-ups, I think. Maybe a thousand."

"Thanks."

"Want to hear a joke?"

"Sure."

"Why do whales live in salt water?"

"Why?"

"Because pepper makes them sneeze."

Patch smiled, shaking his head. "That's a good one."

Niran kicked the ball toward his father. "I'm playing," he said, knowing that Suchin would tell Patch joke after joke unless the game began.

Patch pushed Suchin behind him and hurried to catch Niran, who had a good start. Though Niran wasn't skilled at dribbling, Patch didn't run his fastest, so Niran had a clear shot at the goal. The ball rose and ricocheted off Lek's belly, prompting Suchin to laugh and Niran to gather the rebound with the side of his foot, and kick again, scoring this time.

"Goal!" he shouted, as his father pretended to angrily throw the ball toward the center of the field.

Niran laughed. "Did you use your real power?" he asked his father in Thai.

"Of course I did. Those were two strong kicks. But you won't be so lucky next time."

Smiling, Niran headed toward the middle of the field.

Lek watched Patch kick the ball toward the opposite goal.

Suchin and Niran converged on him, pushing him, cheating in any way they could. As the children giggled and Patch tried to keep them at bay, Lek grinned, kneeling in front of his goal, the pain in his hip forgotten. Niran jumped onto Patch's back, and Suchin turned around, heading toward her father, the ball bouncing back and forth between her feet. As he had with Niran, Lek let her score, diving toward the ball as it crossed the imaginary goal line. She shrieked and he tossed a handful of sand in her direction.

The game continued for another ten minutes, at which point Sarai called to the children. They hurried home, where they would rinse off and put on their school uniforms. Sarai and Achara would then accompany them to school—Achara in a sling on Sarai's back, Suchin and Niran circumventing baggage carts and lost tourists.

After his children disappeared, Lek stood up, brushing sand from his knees. "Good kicking," he said to Patch.

"Will they always beat us?" Patch asked, smiling.

"Yes, I think so."

Patch put his hand on the goal's bamboo frame. "Thanks for letting me play."

"My children, they like you. I like you."

"The feeling's mutual."

"What?"

"Oh. Sorry. I feel the same way."

Lek noticed that Patch's fingers were scratched, probably from laying so many bricks. "I never have foreign friend before," he said. "It good for me."

"It's good for me too."

"When you help me, you let me help my wife. This very wonderful thing. My wife, she work so hard."

"I know. I see her working hard every day."

"Can I help you?" Lek asked, wondering, as he often did, what kind of trouble Patch faced.

"What?"

"You help me. Can I help you?"

"No, that's okay. My brother's here now. And he's going to help me."

"That good. Family always come first in Thailand. Always. Same in America?"

"Yeah. It's the same."

"Then America must be beautiful country."

"It is."

Lek picked up the ball and started to limp toward the bungalows, his hip hurting again. "Two days ago, what you say to those Italian boys?"

"I . . . I don't remember, exactly. I just . . . I asked them to thank Sarai for the beer."

Smiling, Lek slowed his already sluggish pace. "I see you talk with them. And later, I see them be nice to her. That make me happy."

"Well, they should have thanked her."

"You stay here long time, Patch. Almost five months now?"

"Almost."

"So, now you like part of my family. So if you have trouble, then that trouble, it become my trouble."

"I don't want to cause you any trouble."

"No, I no mean it like that. I mean, if you have trouble, then

I help you with trouble. You understand? You part of my family. So I help you with trouble, just like I help Suchin or Niran."

Patch stopped, turning toward Lek. "You'd really help me?"

"Family, as I say before, most important thing in Thailand. So, yes, I help you. You let me know what you need, and I help you as best as possible."

Still not moving, Patch watched Lek limp ahead, toward the restaurant. He moved so slowly, like some sort of crippled animal. Yet Lek was strong and noble, and Patch felt honored by what he had said. He'd never expected to become a part of any family beyond his own, and Lek's words echoed in his mind.

At that moment, Patch realized that he'd do anything for Lek's family. He'd protect them if they needed protecting. He'd listen to them if they needed to be heard. Forgetting his thoughts of escape or capture, he headed toward a pile of bricks, his battered fingers soon lifting and positioning, lifting and positioning.

As tourists started to head toward the beach, as music surged to life in a distant place, Patch continued to work, wanting to watch Lek walk upon the finished path, hoping it might help him walk easier.

AFTER ACCOMPANYING HER CHILDREN TO school, Sarai hurried back to Rainbow Resort and entered a small bungalow that contained her washing machine and supplies. Hanging from one wall were ropes, a fishing net, electrical cords, brooms, tools, and strands of holiday lights. Hoping there were no broken bulbs, Sarai carefully removed the holiday lights and carried them to her restaurant.

Seated at a bamboo table near the fish tank at the end of the bar, Yai held Achara and rubbed coconut oil into her skin. Achara was naked, her plump body glistening, her hair spiked upward from the oil. Yai's wide face also shone, as did her hands and forearms. She sang softly as she rubbed Achara's feet, working the oil between her toes.

"She's going to drown in that," Sarai said, setting the strands of lights on a table, stroking her daughter's cheek.

"Have you seen her sweet little bottom? It's as red as your peppers."

"I've stopped eating them."

"Her bottom needs to breathe. She'll go naked until the rash is gone."

Sarai nodded, whispering Achara's name and apologizing for the rash. "I noticed it too late. I should have let her sleep naked."

"Well, she's naked now," Yai replied, balancing Achara on her own thigh. "And what are you doing with those lights? How many headaches do they have to give your old mother before you do away with them?"

"The children like the Christmas decorations. And so do the tourists."

"And what about me? Do my headaches count for nothing? Why would I want to see a thousand blinking lights?"

Sarai squeezed Achara's fingers, then began untangling the strands. "I like them too. They make me happy."

"Are you suddenly Christian?"

"I should have gotten these up earlier," Sarai said, plugging a strand into a socket, smiling when all of the bulbs lit up. "I've never been so late. But with Lek slowing down, even with Patch's help, there's too much for me to do."

"Maybe you should wrap that strand around your head. Pretend to be one of their angels. Then you'd really be in the Christmas spirit."

Sarai began to coil the strand around a nearby post that supported the roof. "See? It's already brightening things up."

"You and your lights. And your candles. Don't we already have enough light? The sun cooks me alive every day, and now I've got a thousand little suns in here. Why, sweet Buddha, why do you allow my daughter to torment me?"

"Buddha and Jesus weren't so different, you know. Why shouldn't we celebrate both?"

Achara began to fuss, and Yai cradled her so that she could blow on her sore bottom. "They'll see us from space when you're done. Is that what you want?"

"She's tired. It's time for her nap."

"Mine too."

"You're so good at napping," Sarai replied, picking up another strand and walking toward a nearby railing. "Too bad you can't get paid for it. We'd be rich."

"And what would you do with such wealth? Buy more Christmas lights? Light up the whole island?"

"Maybe. Just to work you into a sweat."

"Sweet Buddha. My daughter has turned into a mosquito. All she wants to do is torment me. Please send a bat our way. A bat to gobble her up."

Sarai laughed, wrapping the strand around the railing, thankful that its lights also worked. "You'll see. The lights will bring us more customers. They always do."

"Just watching you work makes my back ache. How did I ever raise such a daughter? It's like you have eight arms. Do you have to always move so fast? If I wanted to watch an octopus, I'd have Niran catch one for his tank."

"Maybe if you moved at all, I wouldn't have to."

Yai frowned, still blowing on Achara's diaper rash. "Moving is for the young. Old things always stay put. Did you ever see a rock move? Or a hill?"

"The ocean moves. And it's even older than you. At least by a day or two."

"Oh, Buddha, why give me such a daughter? How did I offend you? Forgive me, please. Have mercy."

"Why don't you go nap? She's getting fussier."

"She wants to defend me," Yai said, standing up with a grunt. "She's had enough of your foul behavior. If only she could speak. She'd save me. I know she would."

Sarai stepped toward her mother, kissing Achara on the brow. "You'll love my lights," she whispered. "Just wait until tonight. You'll see them and smile."

Yai rolled her eyes. "I'm going to tie you up with them next year."

"Sleep well, Mother. Thanks for soothing her rash."

"She's a beautiful girl."

"She is."

"Are you sure she's yours? There must have been a mix-up."

Sarai tried to suppress her smile, picking up another strand, moving to a different railing. She turned, watching her mother walk away, wishing that they had more time to talk, that there weren't so many things to do. In a life comprising seemingly countless uncertainties, her mother was like a song that Sarai had sung since birth. She could hum this song when she was tired. She could sing it when her spirits were low.

Wanting to make her restaurant as beautiful as possible, Sarai continued to work, uncoiling strands of lights, wrapping them around posts and railings and beams. That night, she thought, her restaurant would shine, casting light on her customers and her loved ones, letting them all sing their own little songs and celebrate their blessings.

PATCH LED RYAN AND BROOKE toward the longboat, watching miniature crabs scurry ahead. The crabs reminded him of running, of darting through Bangkok's alleys as strangers pursued him. Sweat beaded on his back, and the pace of his breathing quickened. He saw himself in a crowded jail surrounded by hostile eyes, powerless to do anything but hope. Suddenly he felt hot and almost claustrophobic. Everything seemed too close to him, too ominous.

A ship, he thought. I have to find a ship.

As usual, Patch was dressed like a Thai in an old swimsuit, a frayed blue T-shirt, sandals, and a baseball cap. He didn't own sunglasses. Ryan had on the latest styles and brands—a checkered Billabong swimsuit and a tan Tommy Bahama shirt that identified him as a tourist. Instead of a cap, he wore aviator sunglasses. His face shone with sunscreen. His shirtsleeves were short enough that tattoos could be seen on each of his formidable biceps. The tattoos were of Chinese characters. One meant "dreams," and the other "resolve."

Patch remembered how Ryan had gotten the tattoos, seemingly in an effort to fit in with the teammates of his high school football team, most of whom had them. Though Patch had never liked Ryan's tattoos, he'd never told him as much. He didn't think Ryan cared for them either.

Holding Ryan's hand, Brooke appeared to try to slow him down. Her legs were covered by a multicolored sarong she'd purchased that morning, which was wrapped around her hips, hiding the bottom half of her violet bikini. Her pink Race for the Cure baseball cap shaded her face, though she also wore oversize tortoiseshell sunglasses.

When Patch had met Brooke and Ryan a short time earlier, he had forced himself to pretend that so much of her body wasn't revealed. That her full breasts hadn't drawn his gaze. That her bare belly and arms and shoulders went almost unnoticed. He had concentrated on her face, his eyes locked on hers whenever she spoke, but otherwise settled on his brother.

Patch knew that Ryan wanted to talk privately, so he had asked Lek if he could borrow the longboat, which Lek mainly used to take tourists on sightseeing forays to nearby islands and reefs. Lek had shown Patch how to operate the boat, and occasionally he assumed Lek's place on expeditions, navigating the azure waters, talking to tourists, and wondering if such a boat could survive an extended journey at sea.

The sand was already hot, and Patch stepped into the shallows. Lek's boat resembled most of the other vessels on the island. About thirty feet long, it was made of wood and featured an upturned bow. A curved beam jutted several feet from the front of the bow and was wrapped with leis of plastic flowers. Blue, white, and red ribbons—the colors of the Thai flag, and each as wide as a hand—had been tied around the beam and fell almost to the water. On the side of the boat, someone had written *Rainbow Resort* in white paint. Above the lettering and gunwale, a blue canopy, wrapped around a rusty steel frame, cast a large shadow. An open engine featured a long driveshaft that could be swung to and fro over the water by a steering pole. This design allowed the two-bladed propeller to be positioned on the surface of the sea or just below it, enabling the boat to be driven in shallow water.

Lek had beached the longboat with its bow facing the sand. Forcing thoughts of jail away, Patch helped Ryan and Brooke into the vessel, then untied the bow from a nearby coconut tree. He hopped into the boat, moved to its stern, and pulled on a ripcord to start the engine. Without any sort of cover, the engine was loud, but the rhythmic beat of its moving parts was strangely relaxing. Patch untied the stern rope, shifted the engine into reverse, and lowered the spinning propeller into the water.

Normally Patch wouldn't have asked Lek for anything, but over the past weekend, Suchin had told him how their anchor had snagged on the bottom during a fishing trip, and when Lek had tried to pull it up, the old rope had snapped. Lek was going to attempt to retrieve the anchor, but Suchin was worried that he might hurt himself. She'd told Patch where to look, imploring him to recover it. And so Patch had asked Lek if he might borrow the longboat, which would allow him to retrieve the anchor, but also to talk privately with Ryan.

As usual, the turquoise water of the bay was calm, nearly as flat as glass. Patch stood at the stern, holding the steering pole, making sure to stay clear of reefs. Though the water was about twenty feet deep, he could easily see the bottom, which alternated between white sand and darker mounds of coral. Having often seen where Lek and Niran fished, Patch cut the engine and drifted toward the spot. He'd earlier tied a rope to a rock and now, grunting, he lifted the makeshift anchor, dropping it toward a sandy patch of seafloor.

Though he wanted to fulfill Suchin's request immediately, he'd promised Ryan that they would talk, and he made his way toward the bow, where Ryan and Brooke sat on the first bench. "Fun, isn't it?" he asked, moving past them, until he was able to lean against the side of the boat.

Ryan wondered how anything could be fun to Patch, based on his future prospects. He started to ask the question but realized that doing so would only irritate his younger brother. "It's beautiful," he replied, shifting on the wooden plank, watching Brooke remove her sarong. "I can see why you like it here."

"I love it here."

"Do you want to come back someday?"

"Absolutely."

Ryan looked to his right, his eyes following the contours of a massive cliff. "I'd like to come back with you. I really would. But do you understand that if you escaped, you could never come back? That's if you survived the journey. You'd be a fugitive from the Thai police. And coming back wouldn't be an option."

"I've thought . . . about that."

"If you turned yourself in and settled your debt, you could come back as often as you wanted. Hell, you could live here. Open a restaurant or something."

Patch removed his baseball cap and felt the sun on his face. "If you were me, you'd turn yourself in? You'd seriously do that?"

"After I'd lined up a bunch of help, yeah, I'd do that. Then I'd get on with my life."

"In jail?"

"After jail."

A longboat full of tourists passed, headed in the opposite direction. One of the backpackers waved, and Brooke waved back. "I don't really know if I should be here for this conversation," she said, turning back to Patch. "But since I am, I'm wondering what happened in Bangkok. If I understood what happened, it would be easier to think things through."

"I was an idiot," Patch replied, his heartbeat quickening as he recalled the chain of events that had led to his escape. "I tried to take the easy road. And everything . . . blew up in my face."

"What easy road?"

Patch started to respond and then paused. For some reason, he didn't want Brooke to think less of him, and his story would have that effect. "I feel stupid," he finally said, putting his cap back on. "Really stupid."

"Don't feel that way. We've all done stupid things. Everyone inherited that gene."

"Not like I did."

"If you're reticent to talk about it, that's okay. I understand."

He kept his eyes on her face, wishing that she hadn't removed her sarong. "I smoked . . . some marijuana a few times in Bangkok. In my guesthouse. Everyone was doing it. Everyone wanted it. I thought I could get a big batch and sell off little batches to the other tourists. With the money, I figured I could add another few weeks to my trip."

"You could have just asked me," Ryan said. "I would have wired you the money."

"I know."

"Jesus."

"What happened then?" Brooke asked, glaring at Ryan.

"Well, this guy who I was buying from turned out to be a cop.

He pulled a gun on me, and I just . . . I panicked and knocked it away. And then we were fighting and the gun went off and I punched him and somehow I got out of that room and started running. I didn't mean for anyone to get hurt. That's the last thing I'd ever want. It just happened. All I wanted was to stay longer. I was making friends and having fun and I wanted to stay."

Brooke nodded, replaying the scene over in her mind. "Comfort does that."

"Does what?"

"You got too comfortable. With your situation. You got too comfortable and you made a mistake."

"I should have known better."

The water around them darkened as one of the few clouds in sight obscured the sun. Ryan reached down for a plastic bottle of water and offered it to Brooke. After she drank, he did the same. "I've talked with people at the American embassy," he said. "They told me this kind of stuff happens every day. You'll pay a fine, do some time, and that will be the end of it."

"They don't know what they're talking about."

"And you do? You know their jobs better than they do?"

"I hit him, Ry. I hit him and I escaped. Do you understand what that means? He lost face. Big-time. And that's important over here. Really important. Losing face like that doesn't happen every day, and if he'd caught me in that alley, he probably would have shot me. And if I'm in jail, he'll probably pay someone to hurt me. So, yeah, I do know what I'm talking about. I've been living with the locals for five months. And some Harvard hotshot sitting in his fancy office in Bangkok doesn't know squat about that."

"Oh, that's right. He's a hotshot because he has a degree,

because he's got a great job. That makes him an idiot? What a load of crap. Why don't you stop talking like you're seventeen and grow up?"

Patch looked away from his brother, toward shore. "I'm not going to turn myself in. No way. Anything could happen to me in jail. Anything and everything."

"Do you understand that I'm trying to help you? That I flew ten thousand miles to help you?"

"That doesn't make you right."

Ryan swore, squeezing the wooden plank beneath him, the muscles of his forearms tightening. "We pay a few bribes, we ensure your safety. That's how it's done. I'll get you through this. I'll—"

"I agree with Patch," Brooke said softly, turning toward Ryan. "I think we should get him out of here."

"Are you serious?"

"Of course."

"Tell me you just didn't say that."

"I did say it. I am saying it."

Ryan squeezed the wooden plank again. "I can't believe it."

"It's the right choice."

He stood up, rocking the longboat. "You happy now, Patch? Maybe you can get Brooke thrown in jail too. Hell, why don't the three of us just go in together?"

Patch held up his hands. "Ry, let's calm—"

"Screw you, Patrick," Ryan said, removing sunglasses. "And thanks for your support, Brooke."

"You have my support, and I didn't mean to blindside you. I just think Patch is right."

Ryan took off his shirt. "Well, he's not. And you blindsided me in the worst possible way." She started to reach for him, but he shook his head, sat down on the side of the boat, and rolled backward into the sea. He surfaced, treading water. "I can't talk about this now."

"So you're going to swim back to shore?" she asked. "You're going to leave us?"

"Why not?"

She turned to Patch. "Is it safe?"

He nodded. "But, Ry, I don't want to fight. Why don't you just—"

"I don't want to fight either. That's why I'm leaving. Because I'm about to blow my top, and I don't want to do that. No matter how much you piss me off, I don't want to do that."

"Don't leave."

Ryan shook his head, squinting from the sun's glare. "You know, you've always taken the easy way out. Always. That's why you're in Thailand. That's why you're in trouble. Don't you understand that we all have to make sacrifices? I've made them. Brooke's made them. So have Mom and Dad. What makes you so freaking special?"

"I'm not special."

"I don't want you to die. Do you understand that? I don't want you to try to escape and end up with your throat cut. I came here to save you, not bury you."

"You won't bury me."

"It's time for you to leave Fantasy Island. And it's time for me to take a swim."

"Come on, Ryan. Let's—"

"See you later."

Brooke watched him turn on his back and kick toward shore.

"Do you want me to come with you?" she asked, raising her voice. "I'll swim with you."

Ryan didn't respond. A brief gust of wind caused the surface of the water to ripple.

"I'm sorry," Patch said. "I'm really sorry."

"It's all right."

"No, it's not. This is your first time overseas, to a place like this. And I'm ruining it."

"It's not your fault."

"It is my fault."

"Trust me. It's not a big deal. We're good at fighting. We excel at it, actually. So let's leave it at that."

He shook his head, feeling as if he had betrayed her as well as his brother. She sighed and closed her eyes. Suddenly he needed to make her smile, to redeem himself once again. "Let me show you something," he said, reaching down, picking up a mask and snorkel and handing them to her.

"What?"

"Put those on. And hop in the water."

"But . . . are you sure he'll be all right? That's a long way to swim."

"Ryan? He could swim the English Channel. We're only a hundred yards offshore."

"You're positive?"

"He could tow this boat back to the mainland."

She nodded, taking the mask, putting it over her face. Though she was tempted to ask Patch to start the engine and follow Ryan, she'd seen him in such moods before and knew that he wouldn't want to talk. He needed space. And so she glanced at the water, remembering how Ryan had left the boat, and she tried to repeat

his motions, sitting on the edge of the gunwale and rolling backward, somersaulting underwater. She surfaced smiling, surprised
at herself. "What now?"

Patch hurried to the back of the boat, then opened up a plastic
sack and removed three slices of bread. He glanced at the distant
form of his brother before walking back to the bow. "Have fun,"
he said, ripping off a chunk of bread and tossing it next to Brooke.
Within seconds, dozens of small fish, many with vertical yellow
and black stripes, darted to the bread. Patch tossed another piece
closer to Brooke—prompting scores of other fish, some brown
with white spots, to rise from the reef and nibble at the offering.

Brooke was about to put her snorkel in her mouth when Patch
tossed her a slice. She caught it, positioned her snorkel, and looked
underwater. Hundreds of brilliantly colored fish surrounded her,
seeking the falling bits of bread. She lowered the slice into the
water, and the competing fish seemed to rise as one, countless
miniature mouths pulling the bread from her hand, causing her
to gasp into her snorkel. The fish churned below the surface, flashing like so many moths around a flame. Only the fish were every
color—twisting bolts of yellow and blue, green and red. Several
nibbled at her fingers and she laughed, brushing them away. Un-
deterred, they came at her again, and she kicked into deeper water, fleeing what was left of the bread. From five feet away, she
watched the cloud of fish dart and devour, amazed by their patterns of color, the genius of their design.

She heard a splash and realized that Patch had jumped from
the boat, holding a rope. He swam over to her, tossing more bread
in her direction. "No!" she said, laughing, the fish materializing
near her once again.

"They like you."

"They're incredible."

"I know," Patch replied, ducking his head below the surface, smiling as she shied away from a large parrot fish that seemed interested in her toes. "Want to help me with something?"

"Sure."

He motioned for her to follow him, and he kicked into deeper water, pointing out highlights of the reef—massive clams, a school of squid, and wondrous displays of coral. It took him only a few minutes to locate Lek's anchor, which lay in a sandy area next to the reef. The anchor was about twenty feet down, and Patch wondered whether he could retrieve it, understanding why Suchin had asked for help.

Removing his snorkel, he nodded to Brooke and handed her one end of the rope. "I'll be right back."

"Be careful."

Filling his lungs with as much air as possible, he leaned toward the anchor, then lifted his legs above the water, which propelled him downward. He kicked hard, the rope trailing behind him. Grabbing the anchor's midsection, he pulled himself lower, tightened his knees on either side of the steel, and then secured the rope.

The ascent took longer than he would have liked. His lungs ached, and his instincts urged him to inhale. He blew out air slowly, trying to appease his body, swimming with all his strength. He saw Brooke staring down at him, her silhouette seeming to block out the sunlight. She appeared almost naked, as lovely as any of the sea creatures he'd just seen.

Bursting through the surface, he gasped, filling his lungs with the sweet, humid air of the tropics. Brooke reached for his hand, holding him up, supporting him. He didn't need her help, but her hand felt reassuring against his, and he squeezed her fingers, thanking her.

"Now what?" she asked, letting go of him.

He saw that she was still clasping the other end of the rope. "Just a second," he replied. "I'll bring the boat to you." Swimming fast, he approached Lek's longboat, climbed an iron ladder hanging from its side, and pulled up his makeshift anchor. He started the engine, dipped the spinning propeller into the water, and headed in her direction.

After he shut off the engine, the longboat drifted toward her, and when she smiled, he couldn't help but wonder why Ryan had left. Brooke seemed more like a destination than a departure point. Though Patch didn't know her well, he was glad she had come to the island, that she wanted to help him escape. Somehow she appeared to understand his hopes and fears—something neither his parents nor his brother managed consistently.

Moving to the ladder, he reached down, toward the water, and helped her climb into the boat.

AFTER SCHOOL, SUCHIN AND NIRAN had gone home and changed out of their uniforms and into their beach attire. Suchin wore shorts and a tattered blue tank top, while Niran went shirtless. As they did most every school day, they played a game of soccer with their friends, cooled off in the bay, and then hurried to complete their chores before dinner.

Because the sun was nearing the distant horizon, almost all of the tourists had departed. The faded lounge chairs in front of Rainbow Resort were empty, and Suchin and Niran walked from chair to chair, picking up discarded bottles, cigarette butts, straws, and candy wrappers. Both children carried baskets, which they filled with the trash. They also stopped at each umbrella and folded it shut. While working, Suchin and Niran constantly scanned the sand for coins. Tourists often set down their change and forgot it after a beer or a long swim. Most afternoons, the children found anywhere from fifty to one hundred baht— enough money to pay for their family's dinner.

Reaching the end of Rainbow Resort's lounge chairs, Suchin and Niran put aside their trash-filled baskets but continued to walk. They weren't allowed to take anything from the vicinity of other resorts' chairs, so they moved toward the shoreline, still scanning the beach. Holding his net, Niran stepped into the shallows, searching for a new creature he could put in his tank. Suchin sang softly to herself, skipping along, moving to the beat of distant music. She was happy, since she'd found several ten-baht coins and a fifty-baht bill.

Not far ahead, several tourists threw a Frisbee back and forth. Smoke rose from an unseen fire. A kitten chased a crab. Some foreigners were learning how to scuba dive a stone's throw from shore. Suchin looked from sight to sight, then turned to her brother. "Do you ever want Frisbees and radios and sunglasses and anything to eat or drink?"

Niran dropped a crescent-shaped piece of coral. "What do you mean?"

"I mean, do you ever want everything that the foreigners have?"

"I don't know. We have a soccer ball. Sometimes we get sweets."

Suchin rolled her eyes. "Is sand in your ears? Or in your brain?

I'm asking if you want what we don't have. They're rich. We're poor. They can do anything they want."

"So can we."

"You know, I should just talk to myself. It'd be a better conversation."

"Go ahead."

She kicked sand at him and he stuck out his tongue at her, stepping away into deeper water. Chasing him, she raced into the shallows, his giggles infectious. She splashed him, and he reached down, grabbed some seaweed, and doubled back at her.

Niran ran at his sister, holding a fistful of seaweed, knowing that she hated it. She tried to avoid him but tripped, and he jumped on her, stuffing the seaweed under her shirt. For a few seconds, he succeeded in tormenting her, but she was too strong—pushing him off, then grabbing the seaweed and rubbing it against his face. They continued to laugh while struggling, rolling in the shallows, arms and legs entwined.

The pair twisted, and suddenly Niran was trapped underwater beneath her. Panicking, he grabbed her tank top and pulled himself up. The old fabric ripped, creating a hole from just below her collarbone to the middle of her belly. She yelled at him to let go, and he did, his smile and laughter gone. "It wasn't my fault," he said, lowering himself into the water. "It wasn't—it wasn't."

"You grabbed it!"

"But you were drowning me!"

Suchin looked back toward home, knowing that their mother would be upset. "She's going to kill us."

"But it was an accident."

"So?"

He finally sat up in the water. "I don't want to get in trouble."

"You think I do?"

"What should we do?"

Suchin started to yell at him, angry that she was always the one who had to find solutions, wishing as she sometimes did that she had an older sister instead of a little brother. "We need to get some money for a new shirt."

"How?"

"Sell something to the tourists."

"Like a Frisbee?"

"We don't have a Frisbee, coconut brain, so how would we sell one?"

"Oh. What about some rocks?"

She threw up her hands. "Who's going to buy rocks? You might. But you're the only one."

He nodded, scratching at a mosquito bite on his leg. "We could sell them some drinks."

"No, but we can ask them to eat at our restaurant. See those foreigners down there? The ones who are scuba diving? Let's tell them about the tuna Father speared today. It's so big, and I bet they just saw some juicy ones swimming around. They're probably hungry for tuna. Let's say they can eat all they want for two hundred baht. If five or six of them come to our restaurant, Mother won't be mad at us."

"Promise?"

"I promise that she'll be mad if we don't do anything. Is that good enough for you?"

Standing up, he looked at the setting sun. "We'd better hurry."

"Here," she replied, extending her hand. "I'll do the talking. You just smile and be friendly. You're good at that."

He nodded, taking a step toward the shore and then pausing.

"Maybe we could find some flowers and some pretty shells. For her tables."

Suchin turned to him, smiling for the first time since her tank top ripped. "The sand must have fallen out of your head. What a great idea. She's already got all her Christmas lights up. The prettier we can make her restaurant, the better. That way, when the tourists come for the tuna, they won't believe how beautiful things are. They'll be happy, and we'll make a lot of money."

"And she won't even care about your shirt."

"There's my little brother. My little scientist. Now tell me, how many gills does a shark have?"

"At least five on each side of its body."

She squeezed his hand. "I'll talk with the foreigners. You know where the pretty shells are. Find some. And remember those flowers we saw, on the trail to the lookout point?"

"They were blue."

"Grab enough for each table and I'll meet you back home. We'll give her the shells and the flowers, and we'll let her know about all the people who are coming to our restaurant. Then she'll be happy."

"And busy."

Suchin smiled again. "Did you eat some of that seaweed and it made you smarter? Because you're right—she'll be so busy that she won't even think about my ruined shirt."

Niran mused over where to find the best shells. They were usually on the other side of the island, on a small beach by the pier. Though he needed to hurry, he didn't want to leave Suchin. He was happy to have made her smile. She was better than he was at so many things—at soccer, at English, and in school. He knew more about the ocean. But that was all.

"I'll eat some more seaweed tonight," he said. "I promise."

She laughed. "Good. Eat it every day. Gobble it down like ice cream. Now go get those shells and flowers. I'll do the rest."

Feeling light on his feet, he ran through the shallows, across the beach, toward the opposite side of the island. Soon he'd found his first shell. He thought about his mother as he searched, looking for beauty next to footprints, for treasures that so many people had walked past.

AFTER THE SUN HAD DISAPPEARED, the bungalow felt like some sort of cocoon to Ryan. It was small and primitive, but also warm and comforting. A fan gyrated on the ceiling. A single naked lightbulb illuminated wooden walls and floorboards. A double bed occupied most of the available space, surrounded by a mosquito net that hung off to the side of the fan. The windblown net moved like the surface of the sea, full of restless waves.

Lying on his back, Ryan studied the net as he and Brooke made love. He also watched her face and eyes, of course, but the net sometimes appeared to mimic the rise and fall of their bodies. The tropical heat seemed to intensify the friction between them, sweat coating their skin, dripping from their brows and chests. So much sweat should have made the experience even more intimate, but Ryan felt only the physical connection between them. He moved with her, shuddered with her, but mostly looked at the net, watching it ripple, wondering what it would be like to sleep under a net every night of his life. In some ways, he envied the Thais. From what he had observed, their roles seemed so clearly defined.

The men fished and worked on their boats. The women cooked and watched the children. Ryan had never known what to do with Brooke. His father had always taken care of his mother, and Ryan had hoped to do the same with Brooke. She had wounds and he wanted to shelter her. But she'd never seemed interested in being sheltered.

She cried out, dropping onto his chest, their movements frenzied. He held her tight as desire tore away his thoughts, made him forget who he was. His body continued to rush forward, elevating him to a summit that he never wanted to descend. But descend he did, gasping, becoming aware of her weight, of the damp sheets. He kissed her, tasted salt on her lips, and she pushed her hair back and shifted to his side.

They didn't speak. The fan hummed, and creatures beeped and croaked outside. Ryan had never heard such sounds and wondered what could make them. Tropical frogs, perhaps? Some sort of strange birds? Whatever created the noises, he was comforted by the harmony of the night.

Though he wanted to step outside and listen, he decided that since he was already sweaty, he might as well do a few push-ups first. After kissing Brooke again, he put on his boxers, slipped out from under the net, dropped face-first to the floor, and began to thrust himself up and down. He felt full of strength, buoyed by lovemaking, aware that it had the opposite effect on Brooke, but wanting to rid himself of the two beers he'd consumed at dinner. He had eaten too much as well—mounds of fried rice and slices of raw tuna. The restaurant had been abuzz with feasting tourists, the liveliness somehow contagious.

"Why can't you just lie here and listen?" Brooke asked, out of his sight.

"I want to listen with you. Outside. But just let me do a few reps first."

She didn't respond, and he continued with his push-ups. He did two sets of fifty. Then, dripping sweat, he changed into his swimsuit. "Let's go," he said, lifting the net for her.

After putting on her bikini, she followed him outside, walking toward the shoreline. The sea was so warm she wondered if she'd stop sweating. Moving farther from the beach, she finally lay back in the water and, floating, studied the countless stars. They sparkled like diamonds and hinted of wealth, yet they were free for everyone to enjoy. Inland, the beat of techno music contrasted with the sounds of the jungle creatures. The smell of roasting seafood drifted over her. The water was so still that it was easy to float on her back, and she stretched her arms above her head, breathing deeply.

"I'm sorry . . . about bailing on you today," Ryan said, standing next to her, chest-deep in the water.

"It's all right."

"But, you know, you really need to support me with Patch. I didn't bring you here to stand against me."

She kicked away from him. "You didn't bring me anywhere. I brought myself."

"Wait. I didn't mean it like that."

"That's exactly how you meant it."

He reached for her hand, holding it. "That came out wrong. Really wrong. And I'm sorry. I don't want to fight with you."

"Sometimes you sound like you do," she replied, letting him hold her even though she was tempted to swim away.

"I don't."

"I don't either."

"So why . . . why do we do it?"

She saw the lights of a plane heading east, toward the mainland. "Because . . . we both want more. We're unfulfilled."

"What do you want? What can I give you that you don't have?"

The plane disappeared. "I don't know," she answered, still floating on her back. "But sometimes . . . sometimes I'm right next to you, but I feel like you're a thousand miles away. And I don't think that's normal. It's not good."

He lowered more of his body into the water. "I'm busy. I'm thinking about things. Like school. Like my future."

"See? You say 'my future.' Why don't you say 'our future'?"

"That's not—"

She stood up, facing him. "But that's it, Ryan. That's totally it. You want to look after me. I know that. But at the end of the day, really, it's all about you. It's about what you want. You want to look after me, but you don't consider my future. It's like . . . if my plans line up with yours, great. But if they don't, you'll just go ahead by yourself. Follow your own agenda."

"Just because I work hard and want to succeed doesn't mean that I'm some sort of selfish jackass."

She nodded, dropping lower into the water. "I didn't mean to insinuate that. Of course you're not. But you have your own way of doing things. Your own methodology. Just like with Patch. Have you really thought about the situation from his perspective? Have you? He's scared. He doesn't want to go to prison, and I don't blame him. Why should he have to suffer so much for one idiotic mistake?"

Ryan ran his hands through his hair, then rubbed the back of his neck. "You shouldn't have disagreed with me in public, in front of him."

"Why don't you stop living in the eighteenth century? I'm not wearing a corset, am I?"

"Brooke . . ."

"I'm going to speak my mind. Every time. That's who I am, and it's not going to change."

"And you think it's appropriate to speak your mind in front of him? In front of someone you barely know? You think that's helpful to me? When I know him a million times better than you do?"

At the far end of the beach, someone started a longboat's engine. The low sound of the rumbling contraption carried over the water, mixing with the cacophony of island noises.

"I love him, you know," Ryan continued. "I worry about him all the time. I don't want him to suffer in some crappy jail either. If I could get him safely out of here, I would. But I can't."

"Would you get me out?"

"Get you out? You wouldn't be in this mess."

"You don't know that. What if I do something stupid? What if I do something like what Patch did? Would you turn me in, or would you risk everything to help me escape?"

"I . . . I don't know."

She shook her head. "That's the problem with us. Right there. Because I'd risk everything to help you. I would."

"I—"

"And that doesn't make me better than you. Not a bit. But it makes us different. And it puts space between us."

Ryan avoided her eyes, looking past their bungalow to the restaurant, which glowed from hundreds of holiday lights. During dinner he'd seen Patch help their hostess with a faulty strand of lights, seen how the children sought to gain his attention. "You make me sound so shallow," he finally replied. "And that makes me sad."

"I don't mean it that way. I wouldn't be with you if I thought you were shallow."

"You're not with me."

"I'm here, aren't I?"

"You don't know me as well as you think you do. You don't know what I'm capable of." He bit his lower lip. "If I'd been there . . . that night . . . I would have helped you."

"That's not what I'm talking about."

"I would have. Just remember that."

She looked away, not wanting to talk about her past. "I think we want different things. Things maybe we can't give to each other."

"Maybe."

"It's no one's fault. But that's the way it is. Like it's in our DNA."

He watched her, standing still, not two feet from him but seeming to fade away. He didn't want her to go, but he didn't really want her to stay either. In some ways she was right—he needed to walk his own path, to move toward a future of his own making. Only in such a place would he be happy, which would allow him to make his loved ones happy.

Though he cared about Brooke, he knew with increasing certainty that he needed to let her go. He'd hoped that Thailand would bring them closer together, but he felt only farther removed from her. Their differences seemed to be heightened rather than diminished by the stress of Patch's situation. At a time when they should be of one mind and purpose, they were drifting away from each other.

"Do you think the stars feel far apart?" he asked.

"What do you mean?"

"I mean, they're millions of miles apart, but if you look up . . . they seem right next to each other."

She gazed above. "I think they feel close together. I think they always have."

"Me too. Lucky, aren't they?"

"Definitely."

Nodding, he continued to study the sky, wondering if someday he might look upon himself and another woman and see such a beautiful proximity.

TUESDAY, DECEMBER 21

eyes of the island

Aware that a full day lay ahead of him, Patch had awoken at dawn, hurried into the village, and sent his parents an email letting them know that everything was fine. Though his typing was rushed and peppered with mistakes, he had been as detailed as possible, telling them he'd gone swimming several times with Ryan and Brooke, and how they'd spoken about his options. He had tried to sound optimistic, though in the past few days confusion had seemed to be his most constant emotional companion.

Now, as he sat beside the path and laid bricks, he thought about what Ryan had said. He wondered, as he had on many occasions, whether he ought to just give up and turn himself in. He had committed a crime, had hurt someone, and felt that a debt needed to be paid. If only he could talk with the police officer he'd punched, tell him about his guilt and regret and longing to make amends. He felt confident he'd be able to redeem himself to this man, if given the chance. He'd spend a month helping him work on his home, or assisting one of his family members with some sort of pressing problem, or doing whatever was needed. But, much to his dismay, such an opportunity wouldn't come to him. His redemption, which would be gained through incarceration, would be a painful, dangerous, and humiliating affair.

Smoothing out the sand with his trowel, Patch tried to quell his mounting anxiety as he prepared to position more bricks. As he had hundreds of times before, he wondered what a Thai prison would be like. He'd be alone and vulnerable. And while his status as an American might help him in some ways, it might also lead to jealousy among the other inmates. Maybe he'd be attacked. Maybe the police officer he'd injured would bribe someone to exact his revenge.

Even if Patch was never hurt while in prison, he knew that he'd emerge a changed person. Living in a cage would cast a shadow within him, a shadow that would darken his spirit. Much of this darkness would stem from the embarrassment that he'd cause his parents. Their friends would whisper. The local newspaper would write a story. And his parents would wonder what they did wrong.

Patch closed his eyes, silently assailing himself for his stupidity, for putting himself in such an appalling position. He set down a brick and squeezed his fists, wishing that he could reverse time, return to Bangkok, and follow a different path.

"You sure you have enough bricks?"

Patch looked up, surprised to see Ryan standing nearby. His older brother wore a swimsuit that appeared to have been starched, as well as a Hawaiian-style shirt. Ryan's short, spiked hair was tousled and held in place with styling gel. His sunglasses were perched on top of his forehead. He held his iPod.

"I don't know," Patch finally replied. "I think I have enough. I hope so."

Ryan could tell by the length and width of what remained to be covered with bricks that Patch needed more supplies. But he nodded. "What you've finished . . . it looks good. Really good."

"Thanks."

"I thought I'd go write Mom and Dad. Let them know what we're up to."

"I just did."

"Oh. What'd you tell them?"

Patch started working again. "Just that we've been talking. That it's great to see you."

"You said that?"

"Of course. It's true."

Ryan handed Patch a brick, wondering if Brooke was still asleep, and if he should bring her a cup of coffee. She'd been up for much of the night, turning and twisting, sweating under the wobbly fan. He'd tried to talk with her, but clearly she was more interested in her own thoughts. And so he had slept.

Setting the brick down, Patch looked up. "The children who live here don't have much, but they're happy."

"I noticed that."

"I was thinking about building them a tree house, next to their soccer field. There's some sort of big old tree and it would be easy to build on."

Ryan thought about the tree house that he and Patch had built with their father. It still remained, twenty feet off the ground in an oak tree behind their childhood home. "You always liked our fort, didn't you?"

"So did you. You designed most of it. Dad and I just did what you said. You were like a little Frank Lloyd Wright, bossing us around, telling us where you wanted everything nailed up."

"Well, you needed some bossing," Ryan replied, smiling. "Otherwise, the thing would have fallen apart."

"Blah, blah, blah."

"Why do you think it's still standing?"

"Because I pounded four thousand nails into it. That's why, Frank."

Ryan pushed Patch off his path. "Sure. Build a tree house for those kids. I'll even let you design it."

"No, you design it. Walk on over, check it out, and then tell me how you think it should be. I'll follow your plans."

"All my plans?"

Patch wiped sweat from his eyes. "None that involve American embassies and Thai prisons. But a tree house? Absolutely."

Ryan pushed him again. "Such the little smart-ass. Think you've got it all figured out, don't you?"

"No. Not everything. Just you."

"I'm going to grab some grub. Want to come?"

"I need to finish more of this," Patch replied, standing. "Lek really wants it done."

"All right. See you in a bit."

As Ryan started to turn away, Patch reached out to him, touching his elbow. "Hey, will you do me a favor?"

"What?"

"Do something fun today. Something for yourself."

"Like what?"

"Well, we've got some of the best scuba diving in the world, right here. You're certified. Is Brooke? Why don't you guys go out for the day? Get a great dive in. People are seeing whale sharks out there."

Ryan gazed toward the bay. He'd scuba dived off the coast of California and in the Florida Keys, but never overseas. "She's not certified."

"So? She can take a one-day class. It's just a few hours, really. And then you could go out together."

"She wouldn't want to do that."

"Why not?"

"Because she gets claustrophobic."

Patch waved away a troublesome fly. "Why don't you go? I'll hang out with her for—"

"We fought last night."

"You did? Why?"

Ryan shook his head and then lowered his sunglasses until they shielded his eyes. "I don't want to talk about it."

"You're the one who brought it up."

"I just . . . I don't really feel like being with her right now."

"But why not?"

"Because, as usual, I don't know what she wants. I'm sure you'd figure it out in two seconds, but I have no freaking clue."

The noise of a longboat's engine sputtering to life drifted to them. Nearby coconut trees swayed in a slight breeze.

"Why don't you go, Ry?" Patch asked. "Go diving for a few hours. Everyone says it's incredible. And if you don't go you'll regret it someday."

"Can you look after her? Just for the morning?"

"Sure. I'll take her on a hike or something. Go have breakfast and then I'll take you into the village, get you set up with the right people."

Nodding, Ryan started to walk away, but then stopped. "You . . . you really love it here, don't you?"

"Why do you say that?"

"Because you said, 'We've got great diving here.' You made it sound like you were a local."

"I guess . . . after five months, I feel like a local."

"Don't you miss life back home?"

Patch listened to the longboat recede. "I'll be home soon. One way or another."

"Mom and Dad would come, you know. They'd visit you in jail."

A gecko scurried across the unfinished trail to consume an overturned green beetle. "You think I want Mom to see me in jail?" Patch finally replied. "That would crush her. She couldn't handle it. Just getting over here would be hard enough for her."

Ryan shook his head. "You think you know her better than I do? What she can or can't handle?"

"I—"

"If you know so much, why are you in this mess?"

"I didn't say that."

"But you act like it. You act like you know more than everyone else. Jesus, Patch, you sit here and build a path when you should be talking to the American embassy, trying to figure a way out of this nightmare. You want me to go scuba diving like I'm on some sort of vacation. Well, I'm not. I came here to save you. Nothing more. Nothing less."

"I didn't ask to be saved," Patch replied as he picked up another brick. "I didn't ask you to come here. I can save myself."

"How? By running again? By getting killed?"

"I can—"

"Look how great things turned out the last time you ran. You nearly got shot. And now you're screwed."

"It was an accident. It wasn't planned. It wasn't—"

"Plans? You don't know anything about plans."

"That's not true."

"It's not?"

"No."

Ryan's gaze followed the unfinished path. "You need more bricks," he said, walking toward the restaurant. "You're going to need a lot more bricks. Unless you planned on running out three-quarters of the way through."

∾

BREAKFAST AT THE RESTAURANT WAS usually a quiet affair. While their mother cooked for the tourists, Niran and Suchin sipped steaming soup, which they ate almost every morning. The soup was made from water, white rice, shrimp, celery, garlic, fish sauce, and pepper. Their mother always used leftovers from the previous night, so the meat of the soup varied from shrimp to chicken to fish. As Niran studied a foreign coin that he'd found, Suchin alternated between sipping her soup and a cup of tea rich with condensed milk and cane sugar.

Both children wore their school uniforms. Suchin's consisted of a blue skirt and a white, buttoned, short-sleeved blouse with a rounded collar. Niran wore green shorts and a similar shirt, except that his had a traditional collar. Though they always went barefoot at home, each wore worn plastic flip-flops.

As the siblings ate, Niran often gazed at his fish tank. It rested at the far end of the bar, away from the beach. He had named all the tank's creatures, which he'd caught in the island's tidal pools as well as in its deeper waters. There were miniature shrimp and crabs, brilliantly colored fish, and several kinds of snails and anemones. An old air pump hummed behind the tank, causing bubbles to rise from behind a piece of coral. The tank had never contained a filter. When it got dirty, Niran and his father emptied it, cleaned the glass, and then poured in fresh water from the bay. For as far back as he could remember, Niran recalled catching fish with his father, adding them to the tank, and watching as they grew comfortable with their surroundings. At first the fish were skittish, but after a few weeks, they recognized his face and darted toward the surface, eager to be fed.

Niran finished his soup and looked around the restaurant. In a corner table near the beach, a trio of Scandinavian women ate yogurt with fresh fruit and muesli. Patch's brother sat near them, listening to his iPod, staring at the sea. On the other side of the restaurant, two shirtless men smoked cigarettes and took turns playing some sort of electronic handheld game. The rest of the tables were unoccupied.

Gathering his empty bowl, spoon, and mug, Niran was about to head to the kitchen when his grandmother appeared carrying his little sister. Yai put Achara over her wide shoulder and patted her granddaughter's back. As Suchin started to chat with Yai, Niran cleaned up the space in front of him, carrying everything into the kitchen, where his mother was already getting ready for lunch and dinner—dicing cloves of garlic and glancing at a to-do list that she'd taped to the wall.

"Should we go?" she asked, then rinsed her hands in a stainless-steel sink next to the stove.

He shrugged. "We're always early."

"Well, that's how it's supposed to be. It would be rude to keep everyone waiting."

Nodding, Niran followed his mother out of the kitchen. He knew she didn't like to leave her restaurant when someone might be ready to order, but Yai could take any order, and his mother could fill it as soon as she returned from walking them to school. Niran said good-bye to his grandmother and baby sister, and followed his mother into the morning light.

As usual, Sarai walked hand in hand with her children, leading them along the path between the bungalows. Patch was working at the far end of the path, laying more bricks. They said hello to him, and he replied in broken Thai, asking how they were doing. Suchin giggled, leaping onto the finished part of the brown path. While his mother switched to English and told Patch that she'd make him something delicious for breakfast, Niran studied how carefully the bricks had been laid. They resembled the scales of a fish, he decided, forming a simple pattern of lines and surfaces. He complimented Patch on the work and then hurried to catch Suchin, worried that she might step on one of the small hermit crabs that sometimes scurried across the path. More often than not, Niran looked for such treasures on the way to and from school. Sometimes he found bugs that he fed his fish. Sometimes the flash of sunlight on a coin caught his eye.

Turning to her left, Sarai headed toward the village. As usual for the time of day, more Thais than tourists were about. Vendors opened their stalls—removing plywood covers, aligning rows of sunglasses, sweeping sand from tiled floors. While men swung hammers and erected or improved shops, women tidied trinkets on shelves and counted money. Uniformed schoolchildren of various ages moved toward the island's center, a few riding rusty bicycles but most on foot. Cats chased geckos at the bases of banyan trees. Tropical birds sang from within bamboo cages. Porters used carts to wheel supplies and baggage away from the distant pier.

As Sarai walked, she recalled being a child on the island, thought about how much it had changed. Thirty years earlier, Ko Phi Phi had been little more than a collection of fishermen's huts and coconut plantations. Sarai had grown up mending nets, gutting fish, and exploring the island. Few tourists ever made it from the mainland, and Sarai knew almost nothing about the rest of the world, or even Bangkok. Her reality was defined by the movement of tides, the scarcity or abundance of fish, the laughter of her mother.

Glancing at her children, Sarai worried about their futures. Ko Phi Phi had changed so much, and she wondered if a shift would occur from her childhood experiences to theirs. So far, Suchin and Niran delighted in the same things that she had—the fierce tropical rain, the feel of warm sand on their feet, the jesting of their elders. But what if their family was forced to move to Bangkok? Would Suchin still act so free? Would Niran continue to study the ocean and dream about being a scientist? And would Achara feel slighted for having no memories of waves and water?

When Suchin began to tell Niran a joke, Sarai felt an urge to gather them in her arms, to sense the press of their skin against hers, and to take comfort in that connection. She could usually sweep the burdens of her life into a small corner and smile at her many blessings. But this morning she was troubled. Lek had moved so slowly rising from bed, rubbing his hip as he left to begin his chores. She hated seeing him in pain and lamented her inability to do anything about it. Medicine and doctors cost money, and they had little—less, in fact, than before his accident, when he caught more fish and was able to keep their bungalows in excellent shape.

Sarai approached the large cinder-block school and stopped, dropping to her knees. Her children turned toward her, clearly surprised. "Tell me what you like most about living here," she said, squeezing a hand of each child.

"Why?" Suchin asked, glancing at her classmates.

"Just because."

Suchin's gaze drifted back to her mother. A mosquito landed on her mother's forearm and Suchin slapped at it—missing the pest and then slapping again. "I wouldn't get to whack you if we moved somewhere else," she said, pleased that she'd succeeded with her second strike. "And I love whacking you."

"Maybe I'll whack you. Ever think of that, you naughty little girl?"

Smiling, Suchin shrugged, pretending indifference. "You're too slow. You're too slow and Niran is always daydreaming about something. That's why you both get bitten so much. I'm the opposite. And that's why I never have to scratch."

"And how about you, Niran? What do you like most about this place?"

Niran thought about his friends, playing soccer, and catching fish. He loved all of those things, loved them as much as he did himself. "If we didn't live here, I'd miss being together," he finally replied.

His mother's brow furrowed. "But we'd be together in Bangkok too."

"No, we wouldn't. Father would work at some factory. We'd hardly see him."

She nodded, biting her lip at the thought of Lek being pulled from them. They would make do, of course. And in most ways they would be fine. But ultimately his absence would take a toll on them, the way the sun fades the colors of a beach umbrella. Such thievery went unnoticed, day to day. Yet at the end of the year the umbrella would be a pale replica of its former self.

Sarai's gaze drifted from Niran's to Suchin's face. "What would you think if I started giving massages?" she asked. "On the beach in front of our resort?"

"Massages?" Suchin repeated, shaking her head. "But why?"

"Just for some extra money. I don't have much to do in the afternoon anyway."

"Would you still walk us home from school?"

"No, probably not. But you're old enough to do that alone. You don't need me slowing you down."

Suchin looked at her feet, unaware of a group of her friends calling her name. "But this is what we do. You're cooking the rest of the day. We hardly see you."

"You see me in the kitchen. Every day you do. That won't change. We can talk and laugh and chop up tomatoes together."

Niran squeezed his mother's hand. "But if you're not with us, and I find something pretty, who can I show it to?"

"Just bring it home. Show it to me at home."

"But—"

"And if it's a rainy day, I'll come get you. No one will want to get a massage in the rain."

Niran looked to the sky, which was as blue as deep water. "Then I'll hope for rain."

Sarai hugged her children, straightened their shirts, and said good-bye. She watched them walk ahead, moving much slower than usual. The habit of meeting them at school had created a special tradition for them, one that she was loath to break. That tradition to her was what religion was to some people, lifting her, making her feel steady on her feet, and filling her mind with bliss and laughter.

Though Sarai didn't want to sit on the sand, to rub the backs of rich tourists while her own ached, she had no choice. Just two massages a day would mean four or five hundred extra baht, money that might make the difference between their staying or leaving, between a future she could control and celebrate or one that she could not.

Sarai watched her children depart. As usual, Niran followed his sister, climbing up the cement steps to the school. Upon reaching the top step, he turned toward his mother and waved. She waved back, but unlike most mornings, her wave didn't bring a smile to his face. He disappeared inside, and she felt a loss as he vanished, as if the laughter in her mind had suddenly grown quiet.

After blinking away the wetness in her eyes, Sarai hurried back home, knowing that she had to dice and clean and keep her customers happy. And then she would bring a towel to the beach, going from person to person, asking who'd like a massage for two hundred baht, degrading herself, but also ensuring that the lives of her loved ones didn't change.

Sarai knew little about the intricacies of giving a massage. But she'd seen it done so many times and was sure that she would learn. She would learn, treat the flesh of strangers with the greatest of care, and when the rains came, she'd hurry to her loved ones and the laughter would return.

PATCH WASHED HIS HANDS AND face in the sea, then walked toward Ryan's bungalow. He'd just returned from the village, where he had arranged for Ryan to go scuba diving with a dive master he trusted. To Patch's delight, Ryan had seemed eager to board the boat, put on his gear, and talk to the other divers about the prospects of seeing a whale shark. The two brothers had made amends over their disagreement, and Patch had wished Ryan luck, waving good-bye, proud of him for his journey to Ko Phi Phi.

Just before the boat had departed, Patch had again promised to look after Brooke, and now, as he stepped toward their bungalow, he wondered what she was doing. His knock went unanswered. As Achara cried somewhere nearby, Patch walked to the beach, where Brooke sat in a lounge chair beyond the reach of an umbrella's shade. She wore a bikini, sunglasses, and her Race for the Cure baseball hat, and she was reading a dog-eared book. Though Patch tried to not look at her body, he noticed that her skin glistened, seemingly brighter than the midmorning sun.

"Hi, there," he said quietly, not wanting to startle her.

She looked up, setting her book on her lap. "Hi."

"I just saw Ryan off. He won't be back for a few hours."

"Was he excited?"

"Yeah."

"Good," she replied, brushing sand off her shins and then standing up. "You don't need to be my chaperone, you know."

"I know. But I want to show you something."

"What?"

"Feel like going for a hike?"

She nodded, putting on her sandals, sarong, and a blue T-shirt. "Let's hike."

Patch led her away from the beach, following a sandy trail toward the island's northern cliffs. They soon passed run-down bungalows, a mini-mart, and several stalls that sold the usual trinkets. Three middle-aged women in pink, button-down, short-sleeved shirts sat outside a sliding glass door and asked if Patch and Brooke wanted massages. Patch knew the women well and replied in Thai, telling them that they looked lovely. The masseuses laughed.

"She your girlfriend?" one of the women asked in broken English, gesturing toward Brooke.

"My brother's."

"Then he more lucky than you. Sure, sure he is."

"You've got that right."

The masseuses continued to laugh as Patch smiled and increased his speed. The path zigzagged past worn one-story structures that served as repair shops, Laundromats, and money exchange centers. Tourists haggled with locals, toddlers chased rolling bicycle tires, and palm trees stood so still that they might have been painted into the landscape.

The ground began to rise, and soon all buildings disappeared, the jungle seeming to leap forward in the absence of steel and paint. Tropical trees stretched skyward, tendrils of vines hanging from branches. Some of the vines sprouted flowers. Other vines ran from tree to tree, creating brown webs suitable for catching monsters. Head-high ferns competed for light. Geckos rested on logs and awaited six-legged meals. Butterflies drifted about orchids, the wings and petals an assortment of vibrant colors. The trail turned from sand to dirt, exposed roots running like veins across the island's skin.

Brooke followed Patch, surprised by how quickly one world had given way to another. She'd been on beaches before, but never one near a tropical jungle. The trees were massive, some with pale or even green trunks. Monkeys played in the thick canopy above, dropping from limb to limb with more determination than grace. Frogs and insects created a cacophony of hoots, beeps, and screeches. Occasionally rays of sunlight penetrated the thick canopy and slanted toward the ground. Brooke felt as if she were in a cathedral of sorts, with trees replacing soaring arches and flowers mimicking stained-glass windows.

Her gaze went from the jungle to Patch. She noticed how he didn't hurry up the trail the way Ryan would have. Instead, Patch paused to point out sights to her—a fallen leaf the size of her torso, a purple flower that resembled exploding fireworks. He always made sure to greet the Thais they passed in their own language, using English only for encounters with fellow tourists. He was deferential to everyone, letting people take the easiest path while he skirted roots and rocks.

The incline grew steep, and Brooke started sweating. She would have liked to take off her T-shirt but didn't feel right about wearing only her bikini top. The blue fabric of her shirt darkened around her chest and back. To her surprise, she didn't feel self-conscious. The sweat, which dropped off her face like rain from a wind chime, seemed natural and somehow cleansing. Whatever was leaving her body, she thought, was being replaced by the moist, aromatic tropical air.

As they continued to climb, Patch asked about her family and her studies. He conversed the way he moved, with no sense of haste. She was used to schedules and deadlines, and found herself reveling in his indifference to time. Her answers grew longer and more detailed. She watched the rise and fall of his sandaled feet. Several times she thought about Ryan, and where he might be, but such musings didn't linger. She began to question Patch about his past, pleased at how much he revealed, at how little he seemed to care about his successes and failures.

After about an hour, they reached the peak of what Brooke considered to be a small mountain. Patch led her toward an open area dominated by immense horizontal slabs of limestone. A few tourists and Thais sat on the upper slab, and so he headed toward a lower one, climbing up it, extending his hand toward her, pulling her higher.

Brooke smiled at the scene before her. All of Ko Phi Phi was revealed, and for the first time she understood why the guidebooks inevitably compared it to a butterfly. Opposite her position was a series of lush mountains—perhaps a mile long—that ended in steep drops to the azure sea. The faces of the cliffs were gray and shadowy. She could tell that their side of the island mirrored the other. Between the two wings spanned a curving swath of land bordered on each side by an immense beach. In the middle, the land couldn't have been more than a few blocks wide and seemed hardly to rise above the water, supporting several large hotels but little else. Dozens of sailboats were moored beyond the southern beach. In the distance, beneath the almost cloudless sky, a series of islands appeared to rise from the sea like moss-covered stones set in a puddle.

The view was one of the most beautiful Brooke had ever beheld, perhaps because of the contrasting colors and geographical shapes. The sea seemed to glow in neon blue. The two beaches were nearly snow white. And the island was a striking combination of greens and grays. Though the sea was flat and serene, the giant wings of Ko Phi Phi jutted almost straight out of the water, as if they'd been below the surface, gasping for air, and somehow had been able to leap into the light.

Patch smiled, then walked to the only nearby structure, a dilapidated stall, and returned with a bottle of mineral water, which he offered to her. She drank deeply, then handed him the bottle. "Could you stay here indefinitely?" she asked, having never considered the question until now.

"I love it here."

"But could you stay forever?"

"Probably. As long as my family could visit."

She nodded, wiping sweat from her brow, enjoying the warmth. "I still don't think you should do what Ryan wants."

"Really?"

A memory unfurled within her, and she pushed it away. "Once . . . something was stolen from me. And I don't want anything to be stolen from you."

"Why not?"

"Because some things . . . you just can't replace."

"The best things?"

"That's right," Brooke replied. "The best things." She thought about how he hadn't asked what had been stolen from her. He'd sensed her need for privacy and chosen to respect it. "You're so unlike your brother," she said, gazing at the distant sailboats, wondering where they'd come from. "The two of you are connected, but different. Kind of like yin and yang."

"In some ways."

"Ryan wants action. He wants to protect me."

"But you don't want to be protected?"

"I don't know what I want. But it's not . . . some sort of knight in shining armor."

Patch smiled. "It worked for Julia Roberts."

"What?"

"In *Pretty Woman*. At the end. She asked Richard Gere to be her knight in shining armor."

Brooke remembered the scene, and turned toward Patch. "Tempting. But extravagant. I don't need all that."

"Good. Then maybe I have a chance with the ladies. Because for a while, my prospects haven't seemed great. Not without a job or any money." He leaned toward her, smiling again. "Plus, I am a fugitive," he whispered.

"Does that make me one too? Because I'm with you?"

"Probably."

"Then we've got something on Richard Gere and Julia Roberts," she replied, grinning.

Patch was glad to see her smile, and gestured for her to follow him away from the lookout point, along a little-used trail that ran into the jungle on the other side of the mountain. It took about ten minutes to reach a half-constructed home that had been framed, but never completed. The structure, which was little more than a collection of sun-bleached boards, had been built on and around limestone outcroppings and overlooked the northern beach.

"They ran out of money, I guess," Patch said. "Suchin told me it's been like this for a year. Some foreigner bought the land, started building, but never came back."

Brooke wondered what would make someone walk away from such a dream.

"I'm going to take a few of those," Patch said, pointing to a pile of unused boards. "If it's all right with you."

"Why?"

"I want to build Suchin and Niran a tree house, but I don't have any wood."

She gazed from one end of the structure to the other. "It's just going to rot up here."

"That's what I think. A bunch of trees were cut down for nothing."

"I'll help you carry them," she said, reaching down to hand him a plank.

"You sure?"

"We're fugitives, aren't we? The Bonnie and Clyde of Ko Phi Phi?"

His smile returned. "I know a back way down to Rainbow Resort. No one will see us."

"I'm not worried." She handed him another plank, then lifted one. "Thanks for bringing me here. For taking your time with me. You don't have to, you know."

"I want to."

"Why?"

"Why wouldn't I?"

Brooke followed him away from the unfinished structure, seeing how slight he looked compared to the two long boards he carried. He didn't appear to have muscles or stature, and yet he walked with a hidden strength. He'd found a new world and fit himself into that world as if he had been born into it.

For a moment Brooke was envious of him, of how he seemed able to make a new life. But the envy passed as she realized that she could easily carry two boards, and so she set her board down and hurried back to the site to grab another.

A minute or so later, she rounded a bend in the trail, a board in each hand, and saw that Patch was waiting for her. He hadn't rushed back after her or told her to hurry, but was simply waiting. She nodded, smiling, following him deeper into the jungle, into a place of dampness and discovery.

LEK FOLLOWED HIS CHILDREN TOWARD the pier, wondering why they hadn't changed out of their school uniforms, even though they'd been home for more than an hour. After all, such outfits were ill suited for soccer games or swimming. Usually Suchin and Niran shed their uniforms as if seamstresses had left needles inside the cuffs and collars.

More often than not, Lek took only one child to the pier, but he'd heard that the afternoon ferry was particularly full of tourists and had asked both Suchin and Niran to help him. He wished his English were good enough for him to approach the foreigners in a quick and precise fashion, but it wasn't. Moreover, the tourists tended to respond favorably to the overtures of a child. And though he hated exploiting his children's smiles and friendliness to lure customers to his resort, no other choice existed. Everything depended on snaring a tourist or two each day, and no one in his family was better at this task than Suchin and Niran.

The pier was more crowded than normal, and Lek was sure that his competitors also knew about the full ferry. He greeted them all politely, careful not to bump anyone with his sign. Remembering how Suchin had spelled out *Rainbow Resort* using brightly colored paints, Lek smiled. The sign had been her idea, and she'd spent a rainy afternoon working on it, following a design that her teacher had helped her draw on paper.

Lek moved to an open area of the pier. He didn't see the ferry and hoped it wouldn't arrive too late. Nearby, bungalow owners and hotel employees chatted, leaning against the long railing. These men and women wore frayed clothes, sun-bleached caps, and flip-flops. None of the Thais used sunglasses, their dark eyes accustomed to the bright, tropical sun. Lek knew everyone around him, knew that their challenges were the same as his.

Suchin and Niran started to jostle against each other, arguing about something that had happened at school. Niran pushed Suchin, then stepped away from her, staring across the empty sea. Though his children didn't often fight, they were skilled at tormenting each other when the mood struck. Usually Niran was the first to complain to Lek, but now he just kicked pebbles into the translucent water below.

"Why so quiet today?" Lek asked, seeing a scab on Niran's big toe and wondering how he'd hurt himself.

Suchin looked up. "Why do little brothers have to be so annoying? He's like some sort of mosquito buzzing around inside my net."

"You're the mosquito," Niran answered, moving closer to her, his face tight with anger.

Lek spread his hands apart. "Easy now. The ferry will be here soon, and we need to be all smiles. No one will want to stay with a couple of grouchy children."

"Bzzz," Suchin hummed.

Niran tried to kick her but missed, provoking her to make the sound again. Lek smiled at their antics, repressed his grin, and asked them to stop. "Why so grumpy today? And why didn't you change out of your uniforms?"

Neither child answered him. He wondered if they might be upset because Sarai hadn't met them after school. "Does this have to do with your mother?" he asked, the sight of her rubbing a customer's foot still fresh in his mind.

"No," Suchin replied, and glanced toward the approaching ferry, which was only a blur on the horizon.

Lek turned toward his son. "Niran?"

"It's no fun walking home alone. I found a huge hermit crab and Suchin didn't even want to look at it."

"You find a lot of hermit crabs," she replied. "If I stopped to look at all of them, that's all I'd ever do. I might as well be a rock."

"This one was special. It had a red shell."

Lek nodded, wondering whether he had the time to occasionally meet them after school. "Have you both been studying hard?" he asked as an idea struck.

"So hard," Suchin answered. "Today I learned that there are one hundred and ninety-five countries in the world. We counted them all out on a map."

"That many?"

"Sure, that many. And some of them are huge. I bet twenty Thailands could fit into China. Kind of like how Niran crams all those fish into his tank."

Lek smiled, and twisted toward his son. "And what did you learn?"

"What?"

"I asked, my little dreamer, what you learned in school."

"Nothing."

"How can that be?"

"Oh, I learned that trees need sun, air, and water."

"Really? I didn't know that."

Niran nodded, his expression finally animated and alert. "And dirt, I guess. Their roots take food from the dirt. And that helps the leaves grow green."

The ferry was now close enough for Lek to see people on its roof. "Have either of you missed a single day of school this year?"

Suchin shook her head. "Not one. My stomach hurt a few days but I still went. Mother wanted me to."

Lek dropped to his knees, leaning toward his children, longing to make them happy. "You've both worked hard, I know. And as a reward, why don't you stay home tomorrow? Just do your chores, practice your reading and numbers, and then have some fun."

"Really?" Suchin asked, taking his hand. "You're not joking, are you? That kind of joke wouldn't be funny. And I like funny jokes."

"I'm not joking. Let's get a few customers; then you run home and play."

As his children spoke excitedly, rising on their toes, bouncing up and down, Lek watched the ferry approach. To his surprise, a police boat darted from behind it, creating a turbulent wake. The police boat was made of fiberglass and featured a pair of outboard motors. Lek's heart thumped with increasing vigor as the boat neared. Though he rarely sweated, he wiped his brow, glancing around to make sure Patch was nowhere to be seen.

The boat pulled up to the pier. Three police officers were aboard. They wore brown uniforms, and batons and pistols hung from their black belts. The men secured their boat, then climbed onto the pier. One officer began chatting with bungalow owners, while another headed into the village. The third man held pieces of paper and walked to the base of the pier, approaching a wooden bulletin board that provided tourists with official announcements concerning their health and well-being. Lek watched the officer staple four sheets of paper to the board.

Though the ferry was docking, Lek continued to stare at the bulletin board until Suchin tugged on his hand. He turned, aware of approaching tourists, raising his sign. Suchin and Niran waved to the foreigners, asking in their best English if people wanted to see Rainbow Resort. Suchin promised a free mango milk shake to anyone who looked at her bungalows. Niran added that some of the best snorkeling on the island could be found in front of their resort, and that he knew where to see lionfish. Though a group of blond-haired women stopped next to Suchin and began to chat with her, Lek, for once, didn't follow his daughter's every word. He knew that the police officer had stapled photos of criminals to the board, as they did every month or two, and his stomach was churning.

Within a few minutes, Suchin was telling him that the women had agreed to see Rainbow Resort. Lek smiled at the tourists, apologizing for his bad English, and then promising that they would enjoy his resort and, better yet, his wife's cooking. He asked Suchin and Niran to lead the women back, while he stayed and introduced himself to other ferry passengers. Suchin pursed her lips at his words, since by routine he always returned with her. But he nodded again, and so she turned and gestured for the strangers to follow her. As she walked, she began to tell them about what they could do on the island, her tongue moving faster than her feet.

Lek continued to hold his sign and point tourists toward his bungalows. Soon all of the foreigners had disappeared into the village and the pier had almost emptied. To Lek's relief, the policemen returned, stepped into their boat, and headed back out to sea. He waited until they had vanished before walking toward the bulletin board, his heart threatening to burst from his chest when he recognized Patch's photo on one of the flyers. Uncertain what to do, Lek moved closer to the board, leaned against it, and pressed his shoulder against Patch's face. Lek studied his surroundings, following the actions of dozens of Thais and tourists, who were involved in the usual selling and buying of goods and services. No one appeared to be looking in his direction, and Lek reached behind his back, pretending to scratch his shoulder but actually pulling the flyer from the board. He crumpled it into a ball, still scratching. Finally he lowered his clenched hand but remained leaning against the board, sweat dripping from his forehead to his neck.

A fellow bungalow owner walked past, turned, and asked Lek if he was all right. Lek smiled, wiping his brow and stepping away from the board. He told his friend that he'd eaten some old leftovers that hadn't agreed with his stomach. He was going to head home for a nap, he added, wishing his acquaintance well.

As he walked into the village, Lek wondered whether anyone would notice the missing flyer. Perhaps he should return, late at night, and remove the others as well, even though they were of strangers. He'd also talk with Patch and let him know that the police were looking for him, that maybe he should disappear for a few days.

What else can I do? Lek asked himself, grimacing at the pain in his hip as he stepped aside for a porter and his luggage cart. I need Patch. My family needs him. And I promised I'd look out for him, that his problems would become mine. He carried wood down from the mountain and he's building Suchin and Niran a tree house. Of course, I'll ask him why he's in trouble, why he's hiding. But I don't fear him. I've seen his heart, and it's a good one. Criminals don't build tree houses. They don't take the time to thank someone for a meal, to make a child laugh, to work on a path until their fingers bleed.

Still sweating, Lek made his way to the beach. Though he rarely swam, he waded out into a stretch of empty water, sighing as it rose above his belly. He walked deeper, finally unclenching his fist, holding the flyer next to his thigh, ripping the paper into smaller and smaller pieces. A blue fish darted forward to nibble at one of the pieces, then swam away.

As more fish came, Lek twisted and tore until Patch's face had been reduced to white granules that moved with the waves, drifting forward and backward, tumbling over the sand, now a part of the sea.

BROOKE SAT ON A LOUNGE chair, watching people explore and enjoy the beach. After carrying the boards to the big tree near the soccer field, she'd showered and changed into fresh clothes. Yet perspiration still formed on her skin, dampening her white tank top. She had thought about staying at the tree with Patch and helping him build a ladder, but decided to wait for Ryan. Soon he'd return from scuba diving, a sport he was passionate about and surely would want to discuss.

As Brooke waited, her gaze drifted from sight to sight. Niran held a net and chased a fish in the shallows. Suchin had finished asking guests if they wanted anything to eat or drink, and now she drew in the sand, chatting with her grandmother, who carried an infant on her back. Brooke had met the three newcomers whom the children had led to the resort. The Danish women lay in the shallows, soaking up the remains of the weakening light. Farther down the beach, the usual activities persisted. A foursome of tourists hit a volleyball back and forth, using their hands, forearms, and feet. A Thai toddler rolled a coconut into the water and giggled as diminutive waves pushed it back toward her. Longboats came and went, ferrying people to distant islands and snorkeling destinations. The low, throaty hum of the boats' engines mingled with the ever-present music that emanated from thatched restaurants and bars. Lingering in the air were the scents of lemongrass, flowers, salt, and damp wood.

Though she couldn't see him, Brooke thought about Patch working on the tree house. He wanted to make a ladder and, as Ryan had suggested, tie it to the tree rather than pound nails into the trunk. This way the tree wouldn't be damaged. Patch also hoped to find or buy rope to bind the floor of his fort to the larger branches. He expected to use only about twenty big nails, which would ensure that the boards didn't move.

Brooke was still thinking about Patch when Ryan approached, his face and arms red from too much sun. He must have bought a mask, snorkel, and fins, because he placed a dive bag on the sand and then sat down beside her. At first he only smiled, his sunglasses speckled with sand, his hair spiked and matted from seawater.

"What are you grinning about?" she asked, sitting up and swinging her legs over the lounge chair until her feet rested on the warm sand. "Did you find a sunken galleon?"

"We saw a whale shark."

"No way."

"Yeah. We did. A juvenile, but still about fifteen feet long. He was brown with white spots. And his belly was all white."

"Were you scared?"

Ryan shook his head. "There's no reason to be scared. They eat plankton and stuff. And this guy, he just swam around without a care in the world."

Brooke wondered if the shark had been a she but didn't say anything. "Did you touch it?"

"I was tempted to. But our dive master told everyone that touching wasn't allowed. So I just shadowed him, swimming beside him, watching his giant mouth open and his eyes stare at me." Ryan paused, positioning his sunglasses atop his head. "I couldn't freaking believe it when we came across him, but on our way to the dive site we did, and they stopped the boat and within five minutes everyone was in the water. I found a buddy who had dived all over the world, so we were the first in."

"And the last out?"

"People breathe too hard and fast. That's why they burn through their oxygen. If you ever go diving, you have to breathe slowly."

"I suspect it helps to be in great shape."

"It does."

Brooke smiled. "Well, I'm glad you saw it. You wouldn't come across one of those back home."

"Maybe. Maybe not. But it was cool. Definitely cool." He picked up his dive bag. "Would an early dinner be okay with you? I'm starving."

"Sure."

Ryan stood up and hurried into their bungalow, returning in a few minutes after changing into a clean outfit. "What did you do today, anyway?" he asked as they walked toward the restaurant.

"Patch and I went for a hike."

"Where?"

"To the top of the mountain."

"Was it fun?"

"It was a good change of pace. And the view was amazing."

"I bet," he replied, stepping onto the bricks that Patch had laid. They soon saw him, nailing short planks of wood against a much longer beam, creating steps that were about a foot apart. Suchin and Niran were helping him—Niran cutting the steps from a longer board while Suchin swung the hammer with him. As soon as she saw Brooke and Ryan, Suchin paused, letting the hammer rest against the wood. "Your big brother is here," she said, and sat back on her heels. "Maybe he can hammer better than you."

Niran giggled beside her. "I hope so."

"You're the reason we're bending the nails," Patch replied, pretending to scowl. "If you nailed as well as you talked, we wouldn't have wasted so many."

Suchin looked up at Ryan. "He hit his finger twice. That's why he is being so difficult."

"That's because you moved the nail. It's hard to hit a moving nail."

"Hard for you. Not for me."

Patch nudged Suchin with his elbow and stood up. "We'll finish tomorrow. Why don't you two little troublemakers go help your mother?"

"Maybe we'll put a jellyfish in your soup," Suchin replied, bending away from Patch's feigned kick.

"Or some sea slugs," Niran added, and ran behind his sister. "I have three in my tank."

Patch smiled. "And if there aren't three in it tomorrow morning, I'll build a tree house for some other children."

As Suchin and Niran laughed and took back their threats, Patch asked Ryan about his dive and walked toward the restaurant. The sun was about to set, and frogs and insects had begun to beep and screech. Patch was glad to hear that Ryan had seen a whale shark and he asked numerous questions about the experience.

Sarai must have heard them approaching, because when they were ten steps away from the restaurant, the holidays lights went on. The building glowed as if a thousand fireflies had descended on it. Music also sprang to life—a Thai pop song that Patch had heard countless times over the past few months.

Brooke, Ryan, and Patch walked through the restaurant and stepped onto the beach, sitting down at one of Sarai's low tables. She appeared within seconds, lighting candles and handing them laminated one-page menus. "I will make you something special tonight," she said, brushing hair out of her face. "Whatever you like."

Patch thanked her in Thai and asked if she would bring them each a Singha beer. She turned, pausing in the main part of the restaurant to acknowledge the arrival of the three Danish women. Sitting with his legs crossed, Patch smiled as Niran and Suchin carried a long piece of lumber to the water and tried to use it as a boat. Soon the children were laughing and splashing each other as their craft foundered and sank.

"They're always laughing," Brooke said, then thanked Sarai for delivering the beer.

"My children?" Sarai asked. "Soon someone will get hurt; then the laughing will turn to crying."

Brooke noticed how Sarai's gaze lingered on her children, and how her face seemed to soften at the sight of them playing. "Could we buy them something sweet to eat?" she asked. "After their dinner, of course."

Sarai's smile widened. "You are as kind as you are beautiful." She put her hands together, as if she were praying, and bowed slightly. *"Kob kun ka."*

"Kob kun ka?"

"Thank you."

Repeating the phrase as Sarai turned around, Brooke raised her beer. "To whale sharks."

Bottles clinked and Brooke, Patch, and Ryan drank. Suchin and Niran continued to play with the board, laughing in the fading light. Ryan leaned back in his chair and turned toward Patch. "I've got good news," he said quietly.

"What?"

"After I dove, I checked my emails. My contact at the American embassy said that if you turn yourself in before the end of the year, the Thais will go easy on you."

"What else did he say?"

"He asked where you are. And I—"

Patch set down his beer. "You didn't tell him, did you?"

"No. But I gave him my word. I said you'd be in Bangkok by the new year."

"Your word?"

"You heard me."

"But . . . you don't speak for me. Your word isn't worth anything."

Ryan took a long swallow from his bottle. "I also got an email from Mom. You know how much pressure she's putting on me to get you to turn yourself in? Or how upset she is? She's a freaking mess. Her email looked like it was written by someone who'd never touched a computer. You think dragging this out is helping her?"

"So what, you told her that you were going to save the day?"

"I told her what she needed to hear."

"And what was that?"

"That in a week we'd be in Bangkok."

Patch shook his head, angry that Ryan couldn't have savored Brooke's toast about the whale sharks, that he'd immediately turned to more serious things. "You think I want to hurt Mom?" Patch asked. "That it doesn't kill me to know what I'm doing to her? And to Dad?"

"I don't know what you think. But it's got to end. Hiding out on Fantasy Island has got to end. Jesus, Patch, you need to get a grip."

A mosquito landed on Patch's arm, and he watched it try to sneak under his hair. When it touched his skin he killed it, then wiped his hand on his shorts. "A week is too soon. I need more time. I have to help Lek. He's got a bad hip and—"

"You've got a week. Then we're going. So you'd better get used to the idea."

"I won't—"

"You did something stupid, and you're paying for it. And I'm not going to let you make another mistake like that. You hear me? You're not going to make another mistake. Not when I can save you, not when there's still time to save you."

Patch nodded, stood up, and left the table, headed toward the water. In his absence, Brooke leaned toward Ryan. "Why are you pushing him so hard? He's not you, Ry. And he can't be bullied. Don't you see that? You're backing him into a corner."

"He needs to be backed into a corner."

"If you keep pushing him like this, what do you think will happen?"

"What?"

"We'll wake up one morning and he'll be gone. That's what. He'll try to get out on his own."

"Maybe."

"Do you know what he's doing here?"

"He's hiding."

"He's building a tree house. He's helping these people. And he's probably coming to peace, in his own way, on his own time-table, with what he did and what he has to do. So just give him some space. Give him some space and he'll come back to you."

Ryan leaned forward, looking into her eyes. "And you? Will you come back to me?"

She started to speak and then stopped. "You're brothers, Ryan. You'll always come back to each other. You and I . . . we don't have that."

He nodded, staring out at the silent sea. "Then we don't have anything, do we?"

WEDNESDAY, DECEMBER 22

believe in me

E ven at seven in the morning, the humidity made it uncomfortable for Ryan to run wearing his shirt. He'd tossed it
onto a chair, and now, slick with sweat, he jogged up and
down the crescent-shaped beach in front of Rainbow Resort.
Though Ryan typically ran with purpose and pleasure, today he
moved with less intensity than usual. His legs felt heavy. There
was an ache in his right knee. His spirit didn't rise, as it almost
always did, when his feet left the ground. Just as surprising, listening on his iPod to Otis Redding's "(Sittin' on) The Dock of the
Bay" didn't give him any solace. Still, a few other joggers were out,
and he passed them, leaving deep footprints in the sand.

He and Brooke had shared their bed the previous night but
had hardly touched. And while he knew in his core that she wasn't
right for him, he still felt a sense of loss. Somewhere within her
was a brightness, a source of light that he simply couldn't see. His
strengths seemed to be hidden from her as well. She didn't under-

stand that beneath his intensity was a simple desire to love and be loved, to nurture someone who needed nurturing. He'd watched his father look after his mother for many years and yearned to do the same. Brooke thought he was old-fashioned and sexist, but he didn't see himself that way. He saw someone who wanted to build a family, to shelter his loved ones with his vigor and ambition.

Increasing his speed, Ryan looked around, sweat pouring from him. He liked Ko Phi Phi the best in the morning, before the restaurants surged to life, before tourists frolicked in the sea. In the morning, the beauty of the island was so pronounced. Colors seemed richer, fragrances more intense. Patch had certainly found the right sort of sanctuary. The real world seemed so very distant here, as if the giant wings of the island blocked out threats and responsibilities. And behind these shields sprang hopes and contentment. Though Ryan wasn't experiencing these emotions at the moment, he could tell that others were. People looked happy. Their movements and smiles were carefree. The Thais all seemed to love to laugh, and their laughter was infectious, bringing grins to the faces of people from all corners of the world.

Reaching the chair where his shirt lay, Ryan stopped, fell to his knees, and began to do push-ups. Though his legs burned from his long jog, his arms had escaped a workout. The tattoos on his biceps seemed to stretch and surge as his body rose and fell. He counted without conscious effort, wondering what Brooke was doing, if she felt any sort of pain over the thought of losing him.

After doing fifty push-ups, Ryan walked to the water, his muscles tight and throbbing. He washed himself off, put on his shirt, and then headed into the village to buy something to drink. Thais were out and about—uniformed schoolchildren holding hands, shopkeepers cleaning their stalls, workers hammering wood and cutting tile. Ryan walked past a jewelry store and into a shop the size of his bungalow. A middle-aged woman wearing a traditional head scarf greeted him. He'd seen a small mosque somewhere nearby and wished he knew more about Islam.

Walking to the rear of the store, he approached a glass refrigerator and removed a bottle of mineral water. As he neared the counter, he saw soccer balls for sale and remembered the frayed one that Patch's young friends had been kicking around. Picking up a new ball, he felt its weight and headed toward the woman.

"You want drink and ball?" she asked, swiping at a fly that had landed on his arm.

"Please."

"Four hundred baht."

Ryan reached into his pocket and handed the woman some colorful bills. "There you go."

She thanked him in Thai, then picked up a broom.

Stepping outside, Ryan drank the entire bottle of water, dropped it into a trash bin, and started to walk back to his bungalow. The journey took about five minutes. He thought that Patch would be working on the path, but he didn't want to talk with his brother just yet, and so he proceeded along the beach, heading toward the restaurant. The owners' two older children sat at a corner table, the boy shirtless, the girl in a tank top. Ryan wondered why they weren't dressed for school but didn't ask. Instead he walked up to them, holding out the ball.

"For looking after my little brother," he said, and handed the ball to Suchin, who had risen from her chair.

"This is for us?" she asked. "Really?"

"Patch told me that you play soccer almost every day. Seems like you could use a new ball."

She tossed the ball into the air, catching it with ease and confidence. "Such a beautiful ball. Thank you, Mr. Ryan. Thank you, thank you, thank you."

"You can call me Ryan. Or just Ry. That's what Patch calls me."

Niran stood up and plucked the ball from Suchin's hands. "Thank you, Ry," he said, bowing slightly. "Thank you for our new ball."

"You're welcome."

"Do you want to go kick it with us?"

Ryan glanced toward the kitchen, where he heard women talking. "Don't you have school?"

"Not today," Suchin replied, and picked up her bowl. "We haven't missed a day all year, so we're taking today off."

"Really? Not a single day? That's awesome."

Suchin shrugged. "Well, sometimes Niran's body is at school, but his mind is somewhere else. It kind of moves around like a kitten, chasing butterflies and things. I'm the talker. He's the imaginer."

"That's true," Niran said, handing Ryan the ball, then picking up his soup bowl and hurrying into the kitchen.

Suchin followed him. "Just a minute."

The children disappeared, and Ryan started to sit down, but they almost immediately returned. "Are you a better soccer player than Patch?" Niran asked.

"I don't know. But let's find out."

Suchin surprised him by clasping his hand. "You and Patch look so much alike. If you lost your muscles, you'd be twins."

"I'd still be his big brother. Luckily."

"What did you do when you were little like us? What did you do with Patch?"

"Oh, we played a lot of sports. The two of us against two other kids. Sometimes we snuck into movies together, or we'd ride our bikes downtown."

"And was it always difficult, being the big brother?"

Ryan glanced at Niran. "I liked having a little brother. I still do."

Suchin shrugged. "Can I tell you a joke?"

"Sure."

"What kind of hair do oceans have?"

He thought for a moment as they walked toward the field. "Blue hair?"

"Wavy hair, silly. Wavy hair."

"You got me."

Niran kicked the ball onto the field.

"Let's hurry," Suchin said, still holding Ryan's hand, leading him away from his sense of loss, his regrets, and into a place that was soon filled with her laughter, a place where he remembered what it felt like to be a child, to giggle and run, to jump and be unencumbered by the burdens of maturity.

LEK CRAWLED FROM BENEATH THE foundation of a bungalow he'd been repairing and dusted the sand from his legs and back. The laughter of his children prompted a smile to spread across his youthful face. Suchin and Niran must have finished their chores and were celebrating their rare reprieve from school.

As he wondered where he might find Patch, Lek walked away from the sea, wincing at the pain in his hip. He glanced at the sky, which to his surprise was cloudless. Usually when the ache of his old injury flared up, it meant a storm was approaching. But there were no hints of rain or wind. The day was dominated by the bright sun and tranquil sea.

Hoping that movement would chase away some of his discomfort and stiffness, Lek walked toward the soccer field, soon arriving at what would become a tree house. He saw that Patch had finished building his ladder and had tied it to the trunk. The top rung was slightly higher than several large branches that spread out in different directions. At the base of the tree was an assortment of tools, ropes, and boards. Lek tugged at the ladder, nodded at its strength, and headed toward the half-finished path.

Lek thought about how he would tell Patch that the police were looking for him. He didn't want to alarm the American, or to scare him off, but felt that Patch should probably disappear for a few days. It wasn't normal for any foreigner to stay on Ko Phi Phi for five months. The typical tourist visa for Thailand was for thirty to ninety days, and if tourists fell in love with Ko Phi Phi, they might stay until their visa was about to expire, go to another country, and then return to Thailand with a new visa. What Patch was doing was so out of the ordinary that someone was bound to notice. And that someone might also come across a flyer and tell the police.

Seeing Patch at work on the path, Lek slowed his already tedious pace. Patch was using a group of precut and pale bricks to spell out *Rainbow Resort* in the middle of the path. Lek hadn't asked him to create such a sign and stopped, admiring his friend's work.

"I'll add a rainbow above the words," Patch said, and wiped sweat from his forehead. "A big rainbow that goes from one side of the path to the other."

"Where you cut these bricks?"

"I just took some to where they're building that hotel. I asked if I could use one of their saws for an hour. Nobody minded."

Lek grinned. "Did Sarai see?"

"No, not yet. I haven't been here long."

"She be so happy. What you make, it so good. Thank you, Patch."

"You're welcome."

Lek watched as Patch went back to work, picking up specialized pieces of brick and placing them beside one another as if he were building a puzzle. He moved with care, smoothing out the sand near each brick before fitting its neighbor into place. The letters were longer than Lek's hand, almost perfectly shaped, and he wondered how Patch had cut them so well.

As Lek leaned against a coconut tree and watched Patch work, he felt an unusual contentment wash over him. He and Sarai had looked after tourists for so many years, and the thought of such a person helping his loved ones made him happy. Patch saw something in Lek's family that many foreigners didn't see—beauty and joy and love and so many other wonderful things that filled Lek with pride.

Suddenly Lek didn't want Patch to leave, regardless of the danger created by his continued presence. He didn't want to talk about the police for fear that the American would disappear forever. "Patch?" he asked, moving away from the coconut tree.

"Yeah?"

"Did you see Sarai, on beach, giving massages?"

"She was there an hour ago."

"She still there. She be there most of day. And so now I go into village, buy some vegetables and fruit for dinner."

"Okay."

"The women from Denmark. They pay me to take them to Viking Cave today. Three hundred baht each. But I cannot take them if I go to buy vegetables, and do other things for Sarai. Can you take them? You been there before. You know how to drive longboat. If you take them, I can help Sarai."

Patch put down a brick. "Sure. I'd be happy to take them."

"Just do regular Viking Cave tour. Go out, stay thirty minutes, and come back."

"No problem."

"You can bring your brother. And his friend. And maybe Suchin and Niran go with you too. They stay home from school today. And I hope they have happy day, special day."

Standing up, Patch wiped his forehead again. "I'd love to take them. I'll be careful; I promise."

"I know you be careful. I trust you." Lek nodded, looking up at the much taller American. "Whatever happen to you, why you maybe in trouble, it not matter to me. What matter is you make my children, my wife, happy. That the big thing. This trouble, it the little thing."

Patch glanced away, his heartbeat quickening. "Well, to be honest with you, I am . . . in trouble." He bit his lower lip. "I should have told you about it a long time ago, but I was . . ."

"What?"

"I was afraid that you'd send me away. I'm sorry."

"What you do? Why you in trouble?"

Patch started to speak, then paused. He rubbed his sweaty brow. "I . . . bought some marijuana from a cop. He pointed a gun at me and I . . . I panicked and punched him. I ran away and I've been hiding here ever since."

Lek nodded, having guessed that something like that had happened. "Do not worry. I not angry at you."

"You're not?"

"No. Because you good to my family. That why I not angry."

"I should leave here. I should—"

"Later. Next month." Lek debated telling Patch about the flyer the police had put up, but decided not to. Fleeing to another part of Thailand wouldn't help Patch. And more important, the police came to Ko Phi Phi only once every month or two. Patch's short-term presence most likely wouldn't place Lek's family in danger.

"Why not now?" Patch asked. "I think I should leave now."

Lek shook his head. "You safe here. Next month, when so many tourists go home, you should go home too. But for now, you fine. And you my friend. You also my wife's friend, my children's friend. You . . . like a blessing for us. And I not tell a blessing to leave. Maybe I not very smart, but I not so stupid as to tell a blessing to leave."

Patch put his hands together and bowed slightly. *"Kob kun krup."*

"Kob kun krup."

"I don't know what I would have done," Patch said, "if I hadn't found your family. I wouldn't have made it. So, really, you're the blessings."

The older man smiled, revealing crooked and crowded teeth. Pride washed through him as he bent down and handed Patch a brick. "Now I must go and buy vegetable." He shook his head, knowing that Sarai and her mother would laugh later at the sight of him returning with full bags of produce. He hadn't bought such things since he was a boy and his mother sent him off to trade and haggle.

"Good luck," Patch replied, knowing that Thai women typically did all the shopping, and understanding why Lek continued to shake his head and smile. "I think you'll need it."

"You funny, Patch. Yes, I need good luck. Sure, sure I do. I need it like women need to talk. You have a good day. Thank you for helping me with Viking Cave."

"You're welcome."

Lek walked toward the village, his feet falling on the finished part of Patch's path, his hip still hurting but not as much as before. If rains were coming, they were still distant and untroubling, clouds and squalls that for now had no power to darken the sky.

The path was sound, like a single stone, seemingly as permanent as the cliffs that soared in front of Lek. He took off his sandals so that he might feel the path with his bare feet. The bricks warmed his toes and heels.

He began to whistle, stepping from brick to brick, feeling blessed and buoyant and free of the many worries that so often assailed him.

⁓つ

AN HOUR LATER, PATCH STOOD at the stern of Lek's longboat and guided the craft into deep water. Near the bow sat the three Danish women, their long hair streaming behind them. They chatted excitedly in their native language, gazing at their surroundings, taking pictures, and laughing. Niran and Suchin sat on the next plank. Holding the soccer ball that Ryan had bought, Suchin joked with her little brother, who leaned over the gunwale and let his hand rise and fall into the clear water. Closest to Patch were Ryan and Brooke. His brother wore sunglasses, his iPod, and a swimsuit, but nothing else. He held on to his seat, listening to Janis Joplin, nodding to the cadence of her voice. Whenever a swell approached and the longboat lurched up and over the wave, Ryan's muscles tightened. Brooke had wrapped a new, indigo sarong around her legs. A white bikini top covered her breasts, which moved as the boat moved, rising and falling as swells sent the boat lurching from top to bottom, from side to side.

This far out the water was rough, but Patch knew the longboat was capable of handling much stronger seas. The boat was heavy and stout, and at least thirty feet from bow to stern. As long as he headed into the swells there was almost no chance of anything going wrong.

A longboat passed going in the opposite direction, and the Thai driver waved at Patch, who returned the greeting. For a moment he worried that he had made himself too visible to the island's inhabitants, that surely hiding away in a bungalow somewhere would be a safer course of action. But he had learned that the Thais were an extremely accepting people who didn't seem to care what others did. Patch had seen several "ladyboys" on Ko Phi Phi—young men who'd undergone sex changes and now looked like beautiful women. The Thais appeared to treat ladyboys the same as they did everyone else, greeting them with smiles. And Patch often reassured himself that if the Thais didn't care what ladyboys did, they probably didn't care what he did.

The island that contained Viking Cave was a fifteen-minute ride from Ko Phi Phi, and as they approached a stark, almost vertical rise of limestone cliffs, the sea began to quiet. Patch eased back on the throttle, wondering why Ryan and Brooke hadn't exchanged a single word. The awkwardness between them was as tangible as the worn wood beneath Patch's feet. He felt responsible for their unsmiling faces and leaned down to touch Ryan's shoulder. "Want to be captain?" he asked, his voice rising above the rumblings of the engine as he gestured toward the steering pole.

Ryan pulled out his earpieces, glanced at the steering pole, and shook his head. "No, but thanks."

Shrugging, Patch turned to Brooke. "How about you? It's easy."

"Really?"

"All you have to do is push this pole from side to side. Here, I'll show you."

Holding on to the gunwale, Brooke stood up and stepped over the bench she'd been sitting on. She moved beside Patch and gripped the pole, feeling how the boat responded to her touch. If she pushed the pole to the right, the bow of the boat swung to the right.

"We need to head over there," Patch said, and pointed to the far end of the island.

"Okay."

"I'm going to let go now. Just head straight into the waves."

"Wait. I'm not—"

Patch grinned, releasing his grip on the pole. To maintain his balance, he grabbed onto one of the steel rods that supported the small canvas roof. He remained standing, watching Brooke's face express doubt and anxiety, which, after a few minutes, changed into confidence and pleasure. She didn't take her eyes off the waves, her lips widening into a smile.

A large swell approached, and Brooke thought Patch might

reach for the pole, but though his hand was near, he let her steer the boat into the wave. The bow rose and fell, casting up spray. The Danish women whooped excitedly, as did Suchin and Niran. Brooke's heart seemed to tumble as the stern was lifted and dropped by the swell. She had never driven a boat and found the act of doing so empowering. It was as if she sat in the saddle of some great stallion and was riding forward, faster and stronger than she had ever done.

As Patch reduced their speed, she wondered why he hadn't grabbed the pole when the large swell had come. With two children on board, even though they wore life jackets, he must have had faith in her. And although she'd never shown him any sort of strength, he believed in her, a conviction that even she didn't always share. She wanted to ask him what he saw in her, and to ask herself why she was happy that he was standing beside her. But she didn't give voice to either question. Instead she followed his directions and swung the boat inland, toward a gaping chasm in the cliffs that was known as Viking Cave.

A dock made from hundreds, if not thousands, of bamboo poles ran from the base of the cave out into the sea. Patch finally put his hand on the steering rod and then further reduced the throttle. Brooke thanked him, releasing her grip on the wood and staring ahead. The cave, cut into the stained gray-and-black limestone, was maybe twenty feet tall and a hundred feet wide. Long bamboo poles stretched from the rocks beneath the cave's entrance up the jagged limestone cliffs above. The ends of some poles were tied together and reached forty or fifty feet high.

Patch pointed toward the tallest poles. "The Thais use them to collect birds' eggs for soup. That's where Lek fell and hurt his hip."

Brooke looked at the children, surprised that they'd want to come to a place where their father had been seriously injured. But as she thought about Lek, she realized that he was often smiling, that even though he limped and moved slowly, his spirits seemed high. Maybe his children didn't realize he was often in pain. Maybe he kept it from them so that his wound wouldn't become theirs.

As soon as a man on the dock had secured the longboat, Suchin and Niran pulled off their life jackets and climbed onto the bamboo platform. The Danish women were next, followed by Brooke and Ryan. Patch handed the man some coins, then followed his group toward the interior of the cave, stepping from wood to rock. The cave was much bigger than it looked on the outside, and, in fact, it could have easily contained a sprawling, two-story house. Stalactites hung from the limestone ceiling. Bamboo poles reached toward crevices. And on the far wall were paintings of ancient sailing ships. These vessels had curved bows and sterns, as well as several masts and angular sails. Some ships were smaller, featuring a single mast, as well as about ten long oars that jutted from each side.

Patch had read a little about the cave and pointed to a ship that sprouted oars. "It's probably a Chinese or an Arab ship from a few hundred years ago," he said, feeling obligated to act as a tour guide for the Danish women, who had paid for the trip. "But it looks like a Viking longboat, and that's how the cave got its name."

One of the women, who had long blond hair and a soft, pleasing face, took a picture and then turned to him. "Were they traders? What did they want?"

"I . . . I'm not exactly sure, but I think—"

"He doesn't know," Suchin interrupted. She smiled, still holding the soccer ball. "He's trying to make you happy. He tries to make everyone happy. But he doesn't know."

Patch opened his mouth, started to speak, and then pretended to kick Suchin's backside. "She doesn't know what she's talking about."

"Oh, yes, I do."

The woman who had asked the question laughed. "Maybe he wants a nice tip."

"A huge tip," Patch replied, taking another swipe at Suchin.

She leaped back. "Don't give him one." She giggled as he moved toward her, and ran behind Ryan. "Your big strong brother will protect me."

"That's right," Ryan said. "So stay back. Don't make me pin you."

"You wouldn't."

"I would."

Patch scowled at Suchin, then led the Danish women to another part of the cave, pointing out a drawing of an elephant. Suchin stayed behind Ryan's back, watching a bird as it flew in small circles near the ceiling. She was about to approach the elephant when she saw Niran start to climb a bamboo pole in the corner of the cave. After yelling at him in Thai to get down, she tugged on Ryan's hand. "Why are little brothers so difficult? He wants to climb that pole for what? To find an egg? He wouldn't know what to do with an egg if it fell down and landed on his nose."

"Little brothers are like that," Ryan replied. "And they don't change. So you'd better get used to it."

"I'd rather get used to having nine toes. Why me? Why must I always watch over him?"

"Because that's what big sisters do."

"Maybe I'll crack him over the head with that pole."

"You'd better. It looks like he's about to climb another one."

Suchin mumbled to herself in Thai, then hurried off toward Niran. Ryan smiled, watched her berate him, and then caught up with the rest of the group. Patch was trying to describe the origins of the cave, which impressed Ryan with its size and artwork. As Patch talked about pirates using it as a hideout, Ryan imagined sleeping in the cave centuries ago. He would have liked living then, when all that mattered was the number of fish he caught or the strength of a shelter he built.

After spending another fifteen minutes in the cave, everyone returned to the longboat. Patch started the engine and backed the craft away from the dock. Once they were in deeper water, the attractive Danish woman moved to the back of the boat and asked Patch if she could steer. Brooke, who was sitting nearby, pretended not to watch their exchange, but saw Patch step aside so that the woman could grab the pole. The Dane smiled at him, standing closer to him than was necessary.

To her surprise, Brooke found herself wishing that the woman would tire of steering and leave Patch alone. But the Dane didn't leave, and as the swells grew larger, Brooke could only hold on to the gunwale and wish for impossibilities—that Ryan would have let her steer such a boat alone as a large wave approached, that she'd met Patch before his brother, that she didn't have to leave Thailand in a week.

The thought of her departure filled Brooke with unexpected anxiety. Once she left, she and Ryan would break up and she'd likely never see Patch again. He'd never smile at her and step aside, putting his faith in her, his trust.

Brooke wanted to drop everyone else off at the shore and take the longboat out again, just her and Patch. She wanted to hear his voice and know that it was directed only at her. But when the bow touched the beach, Patch shut off the engine, jumped into the waist-deep water, and hurried ahead to secure the craft.

ﱞ

BACK IN THE RESTAURANT, YAI laid Achara on a thick blanket, tickled her thigh, and stood up and started cutting oranges in half. As she worked, her gaze alternated between her granddaughter and the oranges. Achara was trying to roll onto her belly, and Yai encouraged her, telling her how close she was, how nice it would feel to rest her head on her hands. As Achara pushed and struggled, Yai took the sliced oranges and used a stainless-steel press to squeeze the juice out of them. Since oranges were expensive and a luxury, Yai squeezed as hard as possible, working up a sweat, extracting every drop of juice.

When she had finished, Yai poured the juice into two glasses and bent down to pick up Achara. She carried her granddaughter and the glasses toward the beach, moving slowly, shuffling her feet through the sand. "Your mother's working so hard," she whispered. "And it's time we brought her a treat." Yai turned her head, pressing her nose against Achara's neck and breathing deeply. "You still smell like a baby, my sweet. Better than flowers or perfume or anything else in the world."

Yai eased her way between two vacant lounge chairs and saw that Sarai had moved her massage operation under the scant shade provided by a coconut tree. Sarai was on her knees, positioned behind a dark-skinned woman who lay on her back and wore a one-piece bathing suit. Holding up the woman's head with one hand, Sarai used the strong fingers of her other hand to stretch and massage her customer's neck. Sarai was focused, and she didn't notice Yai approach until her shadow blotted out the sun. The foreigner sensed Yai's presence as well and opened her eyes.

"Achara and me, we make you drinks," Yai said in halting English. The woman sat up, and Yai handed her a glass, then gave Sarai the other one. "If you no drink, you dry up and blow away."

"Thank you," the foreigner replied, then tasted the juice. "It's delicious."

"It is very good," Sarai added, smiling at her mother before reaching up to tickle the undersides of Achara's feet.

Yai knelt in the sand. "You brave," she said to the foreigner. "Sweet Buddha, you brave woman. My daughter no give massages before. Be careful or maybe she break your neck, or stick you in eye."

The foreigner finished her drink. "She's good. Quite good."

"My mother is good at talking," Sarai said, resuming the massage. "She would talk, talk, talk all day if I let her. If she got money for talking, then we would all be rich. But no one will pay her for talking, and so we are poor, especially since she eats all our food."

"I eat more if you know how to cook," Yai replied, smiling, glad to be entertaining her daughter. "So sorry, sweet Buddha, that I teach her so little. She learn nothing from me, her special mother."

Sarai glanced up. "Do you like the sun?" she asked her customer.

The woman nodded. "Yes, it feels good."

"Then my mother will have to go. She blocks out the entire sun. It is like we are inside right now."

Yai mumbled to herself in Thai, shifting to her right so that sunlight fell on the woman. "You have daughter?" she asked the tourist.

"Yes. Two, actually."

"They treat you like this? So bad? Even after you carry them inside you, and you feed them milk, and your body turns into old fruit. Even then they laugh at you?"

"Sometimes."

"Your daughter better than mine. Mine laugh all time. No care for her tired mother."

Sarai grinned. "You are tired from talking. That is what you are. It is too bad for me that your tongue cannot go to sleep."

Yai stood up, grunting. "Maybe the next time I'll put sand in your juice," she said, switching to Thai. "Why does an old mother have to take care of a young daughter anyway? Bringing you juice was another of my mistakes. A big one."

"Everything about you is big. That's a perfect word for you."

"Help me, sweet Buddha," Yai said. "Remove this curse. Please remove it as soon as you can." She collected the glasses and repositioned Achara on her shoulder. After scowling at Sarai, Yai turned and made her way higher up the beach. She sat on an empty lounge chair. Achara squirmed from being away from the sound of her mother's voice, displeased with that separation. "It's all right," Yai whispered. "She'll come to you soon. She'll come to you like a butterfly finds a flower."

Achara opened her toothless mouth, arched her back, and started to cry. Worried that Sarai would be distracted by her daughter's distress, Yai stood up again and walked farther down the beach, trying to soothe Achara, who had no interest in settling down. "It's all right, my little one," Yai whispered. "She won't be long."

Some foreigners shrieked in the shallows, chasing one another. Yai glanced at them and wondered how so many were young and rich and slim. Were they aware of their blessings? Most of them didn't seem to be.

Though at one point in her life, Yai had been envious of the good fortune of strangers, those days were gone. While she might not have money or possessions, her blessings were unmatched. Nothing could replace the joy that her loved ones gave her, a realization that had come to her along with her first gray hairs.

Thanking Buddha, Yai sat down on another chair. Achara continued to squirm and fuss. "Your mother's a busy woman," Yai said, rocking Achara back and forth. "If you want to be with her, you have to learn how to walk. That's the only way you'll keep up with her." Changing her grip on Achara, Yai held her upright on the sand, supporting her. "There. You see. Standing isn't so hard. You're so good at kicking with those legs. It's time to put them to real work."

Achara stood, swaying in Yai's grasp, drool running down her chin. Yai wiped it off and looked toward the distant form of Sarai, who was now bent over the foreigner. Suddenly Yai wished that it were years earlier, and that she were holding Sarai's little body and teaching her how to walk. How many laughs they'd had. How many moments when their hearts had seemed tethered to each other's.

Watching Sarai slide toward the woman's legs and begin to rub her feet, Yai lifted up Achara, holding her close. "We're both in you, you know that?" she asked. "Your mother and I, we're in you. And we'll always be in you. So when you're older, when I'm gone, remember where you came from. Remember this place by the sea. Remember how you once slept beside your mother, how she put all of her children before herself. I'm proud of her, you know. So proud. And you be proud of her too. Be proud of her, and of yourself, and then one day, you'll embrace your grandchild; you'll see her or his beauty; you'll remember your own. And though you may feel old and tired, you'll smile at the thought of your memories. You'll hold them against your chest like I'm holding you. You'll think about all the gifts of your life. And those gifts will lift you up. They'll carry you, so that the oldness and tiredness of your bones are like grains of sand beneath your feet."

SEVERAL HOURS LATER, AFTER THE sun had just vanished and was pulling a black blanket over the island, Ryan, Brooke, and Patch sat on the frame of the unfinished house from which Patch and Brooke had taken the lumber. The western horizon looked like a line of crushed embers. The sea had darkened, as if color had been drained from it. Lights sparkled and throbbed on both beaches, as well as in the village. Several fire jugglers attracted onlookers. Music seemed to echo off the water and the cliffs.

Patch needed more wood for the tree house, and Ryan and Brooke had followed him up the mountain. To Patch's relief, no one had mentioned his situation. Instead, they'd spoken about their trip to the cave, life back in America, and their plans for the following day.

Now, as they sat on a beam that might have comprised a part of the master bedroom, Brooke reached into her pocket and removed what looked like a cigarette. She'd never smoked marijuana before and had been surprised when she'd walked past the Danish women and seen them giggling as they each tried to roll a joint. They'd offered one to Brooke, which she'd accepted out of curiosity. At first, she was tempted to throw their gift away, but the longer it remained in her pocket, and the more she held it against her nose and inhaled its sweet fragrance, the more she wanted to smoke it. In the past she'd been afraid of certain experiences, of making herself vulnerable. She'd done so in college and it had cost her dearly. But now, as she sat on the beam, she wanted to smoke the joint, to emerge from a world of doubt and fear into a better and brighter place.

"I brought something for us," she said, holding up the joint.

Patch leaned closer and smiled. Ryan's movements were similar, though no grin graced his face. "Where did you get that?" he asked, moving nearer to her on the beam.

"One of those girls gave it to me."

"The Danish girls?"

"The tall one, who was so enamored with Patch."

"And you're going to smoke it?"

Brooke nodded but made no reply. She didn't know how to smoke a joint and felt unbalanced, both from her position on the beam and from Ryan's questions.

"I don't think you should," Ryan replied. "Not that it's wrong. But because of what's going on with Patch. It seems . . . irresponsible."

She started to lower the joint, not wanting to argue, but Patch shook his head, remembering how she had supported him and feeling compelled to come to her defense, even though the thought of smoking the marijuana made him nervous. "Wait," he said. "Just wait."

"Why?" she asked.

"Look around you. See how beautiful everything is?"

"It's more than beautiful. It's idyllic."

"See how the cliffs seem to float over the water, how the sun left a line of itself on the horizon?"

"Like a remembrance."

"I think we should smoke it," Patch said. "Just this once. Let's smoke it and enjoy the island, because everything you see now . . . all of that will take on new dimensions if we smoke it. Even the breeze will feel different."

Ryan ran his hand through his hair. "Jesus, Patch."

"I'm just—"

"What the hell's wrong with you? You're about to go to prison for buying dope and now you want to smoke some? With Brooke?"

"Just once."

"I've never done it," she said, pulling out a lighter that was another gift from the woman, her heartbeat quickening. "And I want to try it. There's nothing wrong with trying it. No one's going to find us up here. Those girls were smoking it right on the beach."

"Then they're idiots," Ryan replied. "Maybe you can hang out with them in jail, Patrick."

Patch raised his hands. "Come on. I don't—"

"Can't you see what a moron you are? How stupid you sound? It's like . . . you never learn anything."

"Thanks."

"How do you think Mom and Dad would feel about you smoking dope right now? You don't want to humiliate them, but what, you think they'd be proud of this choice?"

"It wasn't his idea," Brooke interjected. "He had nothing to do with it."

"But he's all for it. The last time he touched dope in Thailand he almost got shot, and now he's ready to start all over again."

Patch shook his head. "That was different. This is safe. This island is safe."

"That's what you thought about Bangkok."

"I'm not wrong this time. Bangkok and Ko Phi Phi couldn't be more different."

Ryan jumped down from the beam, landing in knee-high weeds. He looked up at the sky and saw the first stars. "Why do I always feel like the odd man out?"

Brooke held out her hand. "You're not."

Though he had felt her hand on him, in so many intimate ways, he felt no desire to reach up, to touch her again. "I am. It couldn't be more obvious, just like it was in the old days with Patch and me and his girlfriends. I'm the odd man out, and it feels more that way every time the three of us get together."

"You're reading too much into this," she replied. "The Danish women were having fun. They said I should try it. I want to try it. I was afraid of it after . . . I was afraid of it for a long time, but now I'm not. What I'm afraid of is being afraid."

Ryan started to reply, then stopped. A part of him was angry with them both, while another part wished that he hadn't said anything. Brooke was one of the brightest students in their entire graduate program. He shouldn't tell her what she could or couldn't do, and he didn't want her to be afraid of anything. "I'm sorry," he said. "I . . . I pulled something in my back when I was lugging my scuba gear around. It hurts. And it's making me cranky."

Brooke had seen him wince when walking up the trail, and she lowered the joint. "Why don't we go find you a painkiller?"

"It's all right. I took one already. But I think I'll head into the village and check out one of the massage places."

Patch swatted at a mosquito. "Sarai could give you one. Or if she's not around, I know where a good place is in the village. I'll show you where to go."

"No, don't worry. I'll find one."

"Are you sure? You guys could do it together. We don't have to stay here."

"Yeah, I'm sure. You two stay. Enjoy . . . enjoy the night."

"Well, at least take my flashlight," Patch said, reaching toward his brother. "We can find our way back."

Ryan thanked him and started down the trail. Brooke and Patch watched him go, both wishing that he had stayed. Feeling guilty, Patch jumped down from the beam and hurried after his brother, saying that the joint could be thrown away, that they could all walk down together, grab a beer, and then find a masseuse. But Ryan was tired of being the bad guy. His back ached and he needed some silence. And so he said good night and disappeared into the jungle.

Patch returned to Brooke, climbing back up beside her. They spoke about Ryan for a few minutes, agreeing to be more inclusive of him, to try to avoid making him feel uncomfortable. Then Patch sighed, studied the sky, and explained how to smoke the joint. Brooke held it too tightly, though as he lit it, he didn't notice the press of her fingers so much as the fullness of her lips when she prepared to inhale. She took a shallow drag, pulled the smoke into her lungs as he'd taught her, and held it there for as long as possible before exhaling. Patch took the joint and repeated the process.

They smoked until only the smoldering tip of the joint

remained, which Patch rubbed against the sole of his sandal and then put in his pocket. Above, stars began to congregate as if waiting to hear a sermon. Bats chased insects, a monkey screeched, and a breeze tugged at the treetops. Though night had fallen and the wind was picking up, like any living thing, the island continued to exude warmth.

"He wants to help you," Brooke said, her thoughts slowing, the beam comfortable beneath her.

"I know."

"He just doesn't know how to do it. His mind is ideal for a lot of tasks, but this situation . . . is nuanced. And that's not his forte."

"I'm not mad at him. It's my fault."

A palm tree near them swayed, its fronds seeming to whisper as they rubbed against one another. "Are you scared about going to prison, about trying to sneak away?" Brooke asked, breathing deeply, bringing so many fragrances into her. Her senses seemed heightened, her body at ease yet acutely aware.

"Yes."

"It's all right, you know. It's all right to be scared."

He nodded but didn't answer. It seemed to her that the marijuana was making him quiet, while it made her want to talk. It was as if the muscles that kept her repressed thoughts and emotions in check were relaxing and releasing. "I know about being scared," she said, swinging her legs beneath her, wanting to share her secrets with him.

"You do?"

She followed the flight of a plane, its red lights twinkling like magical stars. After a while, the plane disappeared, and she remembered his question, which seemed to echo in her mind.

"That's why I've never smoked a joint. Because once when I was in college, after I'd had way too much to drink, a man hurt me. I'd been at a party, and I went back to my room. I was all alone. And he . . . he pushed his way into my room and stole something from me."

"Stole what?"

"I . . . I don't know."

"It's okay. You can tell me . . . if you want."

She watched a distant fire juggler on the beach, trying to forget, as she had ten thousand times before, the image of the stranger forcing his way into her room. "He hurt me. And I think he stole a part . . . of my spirit . . . of my soul."

Patch edged toward her. She felt his hand rest on her shoulder. His skin was warm and soft and somehow serene. She'd never felt such a touch, and wondered whether the tingling sensation on her shoulder was from the presence of his hand or the drug.

"No, he didn't," Patch said, her obvious pain compelling him to speak.

"Didn't what?"

"He didn't steal a part of your soul."

"What . . . what do you mean?"

"He hurt you, yes. He scared you. He made you cry. But you're still whole. Every bit of your soul is still whole."

Her eyes watered. Sniffing, she wiped away her tears. "How can you say that?"

"Because you can't steal something that you can't feel. And he . . . he didn't feel your soul. He didn't come close to feeling it."

She sniffed again, her hand on his knee, squeezing it tight. "You think?"

"It's impossible to steal something you can't touch. Impossible.

The only person . . . the only person who will ever touch your soul is the person who falls so in love with you that you're all he can think about. You're in his thoughts and dreams and his . . . his every waking moment. And this person . . . whoever he is . . . he'll treasure your soul. He'll protect it." Patch paused as a shooting star blazed across the sky. "That man . . . who hurt you . . . he didn't see your soul. He didn't touch it. And he certainly didn't steal a part of it. So don't ever worry about that again. Not for a second."

Her mouth opened, but no sound came forth. She thought about what Patch had said, wondering if he could be right. She silently repeated his words, and as she did, the wind gained strength, caressing her, answering her as if he had spoken again. Her emotions seemed heightened, perhaps from the drug, perhaps from Patch's belief. Or more likely a combination of the two. But whatever the case, she smiled at the thought of her soul being intact. For so long, she'd thought that part of it had been stolen, that she would have a hole within her for as long as she lived.

But maybe Patch was right. Maybe he had answered many of her questions with those few simple statements. Maybe he'd handed her a key with which she might unlock herself and emerge anew.

⌒

THE MOSQUITO NET RIPPLED, GIVEN life by the wobbling ceiling fan. Lek sat at the end of their mattress, rubbing Sarai's feet. She wore her thin cotton pajamas, as well as panties and a bra. Lying on her back, she watched his face and smiled faintly.

"You rubbed a lot of feet today," he said, massaging her toes. "It's only right that you get yours rubbed too."

"Does your hip hurt?"

He shook his head, though his old injury ached as usual. "It's fine. Better now that I'm with you."

"Six hundred baht. Can you believe it? I made six hundred baht rubbing feet."

"A small fortune. Though you barely got to the restaurant in time. Our guests were getting impatient."

"True. And you need to learn how to shop like a woman. I need firm tomatoes that can handle heat, not those old mushy ones you got me."

"They were cheaper."

She grinned. "Because they were half rotten, you simple man."

Lek pinched her smallest toe and she let out a muffled squeal. Asleep beside her, wearing a cloth diaper, was Achara. Lek watched their daughter stir. "Do you think she's dreaming?" he asked, his fingers growing tired but not pausing.

"She always dreams. I can see it in her face."

Someone laughed outside, and foreign voices passed by. Lek wondered where they were going. He couldn't identify anyone he knew. "I see that Patch brought more wood down for the tree house."

"I saw it too."

"Suchin and Niran can hardly wait."

Sarai noticed a hole in the mosquito net and made a mental note to mend it the following day. "Have you heard anyone talk? About Patch? He's been here so long. People are going to talk."

Lek remembered pulling down the police flyer and was tempted to tell her the truth about Patch's situation, but he didn't want to argue. He was afraid that Sarai would immediately send Patch away, which Lek believed was unnecessary. "I've heard nothing," he finally replied, pretending to focus on her toes.

"But you're not a woman. Women hear everything. And men hear nothing."

"I hear you and your mother all day. That's enough for me."

Sarai glanced at Achara. "What do you think he's hiding from?"

"Knowing Patch, it must be something small. Something not worth worrying about."

"Ask him. Stop acting like a man and ask him."

"After he finishes the path and the tree house," Lek replied. "I'll ask him then. I promise."

"You're so good at waiting. You realize that you're not fishing, right? That life isn't about holding your spear gun and waiting for a tuna to pass by?"

He stretched her toes, one by one, until they popped. "That's how you catch the biggest fish, the best fish. That's how I caught you."

Her smile was broad and pleasant. "I should have swum faster. You wouldn't catch me these days."

"Yes, I would."

She jerked her feet away from him, laughing quietly.

He grinned, crept up the mattress, and began to rub Achara's heels. "She's had a busy day too."

"She's a busy girl. And I'm going to teach her how to be busier, how to swim so fast that no spearman will catch her."

Lek studied his daughter's tiny toes and leaned down to kiss the soles of her feet. "I'm a lucky man," he said, and lay down so that Achara was between Sarai and him.

"She's lucky to have you."

"Maybe . . . maybe she'll grow up here, like her brother and sister. Six hundred baht. That's a lot of money."

"If I make that much every day, we'll have enough. We'll have enough to stay."

He watched her eyes. "But can you clean and cook and rub so many feet? Isn't that too much for you?"

"It's not too much. For some maybe, but not for me."

"Did you drink enough water today? Did you remember? You need to take care of yourself as well as you take care of everyone else."

"I did. All day long."

"Good," he replied, pausing as a gecko scurried after an insect on the ceiling. "I'll help you. I'll fix things and find guests and do the shopping. And I won't buy any more old tomatoes."

She smiled and reached over Achara so that their hands might meet and clasp. Rubbing the knuckle of his thumb with her forefinger, she thought about discovering him, about hearing his laugh as he helped fix her father's longboat. "I'm glad you were patient," she said. "That you caught me."

"I know."

"There's a sea full of fish out there, and you found me, just the right fish."

"I waited for you. I would have always waited."

She squeezed his hand but didn't release it. Their arms descended, dropping below Achara's feet. They continued to whisper as the fan hummed above and the insects screeched outside.

Sarai fell asleep first, as she usually did. And though Lek's hip ached, and he wanted to rest on his other side, he stayed still, holding her hand, grateful that he had somehow found her amid so vast a space as a sea.

～

IT HADN'T TAKEN RYAN LONG to find a massage parlor, since they were all over the island. This particular structure was located only a dozen paces away from the water, and he could hear longboats come and go as a young Thai woman clad in pink shorts and a matching T-shirt rubbed oil onto her hands and then worked that oil into his sore back. He wore only a thin pair of boxer shorts that she'd given him after he had washed sand from his feet in a stainless-steel basin. She'd pulled a curtain shut between them, and he had undressed quickly, uncomfortable with his nakedness.

The woman was beautiful. Her face was dominated by wide, dark eyes and full lips that had been drawn up into a smile ever since he arrived. Her body was small, but not lacking curves. Straight black hair fell well below her shoulders. Dao was her name, and when he'd asked her to repeat it, she had done so, and added in broken English that it meant "star." She'd smiled then, helping him lie down on a narrow futon, hands immediately at work on his shoulders.

"You so big," she said, laughing, squeezing his muscles with her slippery fingers. "You like King Kong."

"King Kong?"

"Yes, though you no have hair."

He smiled, his face pressing against a pillow. "You're the strong one."

"So, why you come to Thailand?"

"For . . . for a vacation."

"You have Thai girlfriend?"

"What?"

"You find girl here? Or maybe you a butterfly boy?"

"A butterfly boy? What's that?"

She laughed, moving until she knelt, straddling the small of his back, and could massage his neck. "Butterfly boy fly from girl to girl, enjoying them all. Thai men, they often butterfly boys. Sometimes *farang* are too."

"*Farang?*"

"Foreigners."

Ryan grunted as she pressed her thumbs along either side of his spine. "I'm not a butterfly boy."

"Sure, sure?"

"Do I have wings?"

She paused, then began working on his shoulders again. "Why you no butterfly boy? Easy for you here. Thai women must love you. You handsome man, with nice smile."

"I'm not so exciting. I like to work."

"You never have girlfriend?"

"I . . ."

"You can tell me. Massage feel better if you talk."

"I had one. But it's over."

Dao paused again and reached for more oil. She slid down so that she sat on his thighs. Her fingers pressing and rubbing, she worked on his lower back. "Why it over? She butterfly girl?"

"No."

"Then why?"

"You ask a lot of questions, don't you?"

"Why it over?"

"Because I . . . I'm too traditional for her."

"What you mean?"

He closed his eyes, enjoying the feel of her fingers against him. To his surprise, she pulled down the top of his thin shorts a few inches so that she could rub around his tailbone. Not wanting her to stop, he thought about her question. "I want to work, to have a

career, and to support my family. I don't . . . don't expect my wife
to have a job. Raising children is hard enough work. She doesn't
need to do anything else."

"That good. Maybe your girlfriend is crazy. Why she want to
have job and to have baby? That too much."

"You think?"

"Sure, sure. Now I work. I make money, give to my parents.
But when I marry, I take care of children. As you say, that hard
enough."

"You give your money to your parents? Why?"

"That Thai way. They poor. I make good money. So I give it to
them. I live with them, in middle of Ko Phi Phi. Far away from
where *farang* go."

"Why don't . . . *farang* go there?"

"Because it not nice."

Ryan nodded slightly, his face moving up and down the pillow. "Do you have a boyfriend?"

"Once, yes. But he move to Bangkok."

"And now no one?"

"No one. Poor me."

"But . . . but you're so nice. And beautiful."

Dao laughed again, slapping the side of his thigh. "You drinking tonight? Too much Thai whiskey in you?"

"No, nothing."

"Then why, King Kong, why you say such a thing?"

"Because it's true."

She started to speak and then stopped, instead helping him to
roll over. Her fingers found the muscles of his upper chest, which
she kneaded like dough. "Thai men want woman with big boobs
and blond hair, like they see in American movies. That not me."

"Their mistake."

Dao slapped his shoulder. "You think I give you free massage because you say nice thing?"

"No, definitely not. Whatever this costs, it's worth it."

"One million baht."

"That cheap?"

"Two million."

They laughed together, and she began to rub the front of his arms, working on his biceps, sometimes following the patterns of his tattoos. As she rubbed away his stress and tension, they continued to talk and smile.

Much later, after a sixty-minute massage had turned into a ninety-minute massage, she pulled the curtain shut, and he dressed in privacy, reluctant to leave.

But leave he did, turning back to wave at her, glad that she stood in the entrance of her parlor, smiling and standing on her tiptoes.

THURSDAY, DECEMBER 23

a light to bring you home

The day hinted of a storm, though so far only a light rain left dimples in the sand. The sky was gloomy, permeated with haze and shadows. The wind seemed indecisive, nonexistent one moment and stirring to life a few heartbeats later. As he worked on the brick path, Patch asked himself how raindrops formed so far above, fell thousands of feet, and landed precisely on his head. The odds against such an outcome seemed preposterously large. What were the chances that a single raindrop would be born miles above him and fall to touch his face?

His thoughts shifted to Brooke, and he wondered what exactly had happened to her. He would never ask, but if she wanted to talk about it, he would listen. It seemed as if she had cracked open a door to her inner self and hoped that he might peek inside. But he wasn't sure what to do. If anyone was to look through such an opening, Ryan should be that person.

Had Ryan not known Brooke, Patch would have tried to be

what he thought she needed. But because of his brother's presence, Patch saw himself as a raindrop that was falling toward Brooke but would inevitably be swept aside by the wind.

As Patch thought about this raindrop, he reached for a brick, only then realizing that Ryan was standing nearby, holding their old leather football. "Remember when we'd throw it in the rain?" Ryan asked, and tossed Patch the ball. "We'd stay out until our fingers were numb. Mom would call us in for dinner and we'd have to strip in the mudroom."

Gripping the football, Patch stood up. "You brought this? All the way here?"

"I've always brought it on our trips. Why change a good thing?"

Patch smiled. "Let's go to the beach. You can be Joe Montana. Just like old times."

Ryan left the path, walking between bungalows, glad for the rain, since it meant the beach was empty. He headed toward the water's edge, feeling buoyed rather than weighted down by the wetness. Patch started to move away from him, but Ryan motioned him forward. "Can I tell you something?" he asked, his voice much softer than usual, softer than the little waves tumbling on the shore.

"What?"

"You have to promise to keep quiet about it."

"Don't worry."

Ryan leaned closer to Patch. "Last night, I went into the village and got a massage."

"I know."

"Well, this Thai woman, maybe nineteen or twenty, gave it to me." He smiled, glancing toward the village. "And she made me laugh. And later, I told her she was beautiful."

"Really?"

"And I think she was glad when I told her. I don't think she wanted me to leave."

Patch wiped rain from his brow, surprised that Ryan had said so much. His older brother had always been private, seemingly not interested in talking about girls and first-time loves. "How . . . how did she make you laugh?"

"What do you think I should do?" Ryan asked, seeming not to hear Patch's question. "I don't know Thais like you do. Would it be weird if I went back for another massage? Would she expect anything from me?"

"But what about Brooke? Don't you—"

"She doesn't love me. And I feel the same."

"But I don't understand. You came all this way together."

Ryan glanced at his bungalow. "Coming here was . . . naive. Like all our problems could be solved by going on a trip together. It was wishful thinking. And I think we both knew that before we even left."

"How did things go wrong?"

"How did they ever go right? Whatever she wants, I can't give her. This trip . . . It's just reminded me of that, and how we're so different. She knows it and I know it, and there's no point in pretending that we have a future together."

Patch watched a distant longboat cut through the rain and disappear around a cliff. "And Brooke knows how you feel?"

"Jesus, Patch. Aren't you listening? She feels the same way."

"I just . . . This is a surprise. A big one."

"I've hardly seen her for the past two days and you're surprised?"

"Well—"

"What did you two talk about last night anyway?"

"Nothing, really. We just smoked a little and laughed."

Ryan's brow furrowed. "I don't know what to do about this massage girl."

"The Thais are playful. Are you sure she wasn't just doing her job? Keeping you happy?"

"I don't know. Maybe. But she did go to the door. She waved good-bye."

Patch spun the football in his hands, thinking about how his brother should proceed. Ryan almost never came to him for advice, and Patch didn't want to let him down. "Don't ever talk to her about money," he said, still spinning the football.

"Why not?"

"Because you'll never know what she really wants if she thinks you have money. You'll wonder about her motives. Right or wrong, you'll wonder. Because for some women around here, that's what it's about. Not that I judge them."

"What else? She gave me this incredible massage for almost nothing. Should I bring her something?"

"No, that's too much. Too fast. In Bangkok, that might work. But here, the women are more traditional. They move a lot slower."

Ryan cracked his knuckles, a nervous habit he'd had since childhood. "So what should I do?"

"Well, it's raining out. It's a great day for a long massage. Just go back. Spend a couple of hours with her and see if she still makes you laugh."

"And nothing else?"

"Anything else would be too much. At least for now." Patch spun the football again. "Why her? Why do you want to hurry back to her?"

Ryan remembered how Dao had looked after him, taking his clothes, folding them neatly. He'd always tried to shelter women, to watch over them, to think about their needs. But he'd never had a girlfriend take his shirt and fold it as if it were wrapping paper. He'd never felt a woman's fingers in the small of his back, kneading a knot of muscle until it loosened. He thought about telling Patch these things but guessed that his little brother would look at him the way Brooke did—as if he were too old-fashioned to live in this century.

"I just like how she made me feel," Ryan finally replied.

Patch nodded. "I understand."

"You do?"

"Just go back there, after breakfast. Be sure to wipe the sand from your feet, to make her job easier. If she's as beautiful as you say, she's probably had a hundred *farang*—I mean foreigners— tell her the same thing. So don't get stuck on that. Tell her something else."

"Like what?"

"Ask about her family, her brothers and sisters. Thais love to talk about their families. Ask how to thank her in Thai. How you should address her mother, if you met her on a path. Things like that."

Ryan smiled, reaching for the football, pulling it from Patch's hands. "You sure you want to tell me all your tricks?"

"Oh, I'll keep a few to myself. Don't worry."

"Like you did in high school?"

"I told you everything in high school. Besides, it sounds like you don't need any help with her."

"You're not going to steal her, are you? If she gets wind of you, I won't have a chance."

"Don't say that."

Thunder rumbled in the distance and the grin faded from Ryan's face. "It's complicated, isn't it?"

"What?"

"Life."

"Maybe. Maybe not."

"For you it's not? Even with all that's going on?"

Patch turned his face upward, letting the raindrops find him. "I just don't want regrets. When I'm old. I think about that. How I'll be dying in bed someday, and I don't want to look back at my life and feel regret. That'd be the worst. To know that you could have had something incredible and that you screwed it all up."

"So sneaking out of Thailand—you don't think you'd regret that?"

"If I had turned myself in, you wouldn't be here. You wouldn't be asking me about some pretty girl."

"Dao. Her name is Dao."

Patch took the football back. "Why'd you bring this all the way from home?"

"Because . . . I knew we'd fight. And I wanted to do something with you other than fight."

Stepping back, Patch lobbed the football to Ryan, who caught it with one hand. "Always the show-off," Patch said, grinning, still backpedaling. "All right, Mr. Montana. Show me what you can do."

Ryan laughed, threw the ball high, and watched Patch catch it and run backward. The distance between the brothers increased. The warm rain continued to fall, leaving dimples in the sand. The football sailed and dropped in great arcs, spinning as it flew, connecting the two boys as it always had, a relic of good, sweet days long since past. Days gone, but hardly forgotten.

~⊙

AS IT WAS STILL EARLY in the dreary morning, Sarai's restaurant was almost empty. Suchin and Niran were getting ready for school, and only Brooke was present, sipping tea, dressed in a colorful sarong, a white tank top, and her familiar baseball cap. As Sarai chopped vegetables in the kitchen and chatted with her mother, she thought about the American, wondering where her boyfriend was.

Setting down her knife, Sarai grabbed a pot of hot water and walked to her mother, who sat on a plastic chair and held Achara. Sarai pinched Achara's cheek, then went out into the restaurant. She approached Brooke and refilled her cup of tea. Brooke thanked Sarai in Thai, which pleased her.

"Where is your boyfriend?" Sarai asked in English, shrugging her shoulders. Since her restaurant had no gutters on its roof, the rain rushed down, falling from the roofline in a thick sheet of water. Sarai glanced up, looking for leaks, but saw none.

"He's on the beach," Brooke replied, and sipped her tea. "Throwing a football with Patch."

"In this rain?"

"I think it's a tradition of theirs."

Sarai smiled. "You look bored. Come. Come back to my kitchen. Any friend of Patch's, she is a friend of mine. I will show you how to cook a Thai breakfast."

Brooke lowered her mug, surprised by the invitation. She

nodded and followed Sarai into the kitchen, passing Yai and Achara and saying hello. Though the kitchen was old and worn, Brooke noticed that every item of food was fresh. Bamboo baskets held mounds of onions, garlic bulbs, peppers, tomatoes, baby corn, lemongrass, and bok choy. Glass jars lining a shelf contained spices. Thick shrimp lay on a cutting board.

"I am making Thai breakfast soup," Sarai said, moving toward the cutting board. "I work, and my mother sits and rests. It is always the same, every morning."

Yai shook her head. "She forget that I already work for many, many years. I her slave when she baby."

Grinning, Sarai handed Brooke a knife. "Will you cut up the peppers? Be careful. Do not wipe your eyes. The peppers are too spicy."

Brooke took the knife, stood next to Sarai, and began dicing the peppers. "These go in the soup?"

"Yes, please. Thais love spicy soup. Even for breakfast. Niran and Suchin, if their soup is not spicy, their stomachs will be bored."

Achara burped, prompting Yai to smile. "You see, Sarai? I told you. You feed her too fast. You always in hurry, so she drink in hurry."

"I have to move fast," Sarai replied, deveining shrimp with rapid flicks of a small knife. "If I moved like you, like a big snail, then everything would fall apart. No one would get fed. No rooms would get cleaned."

Yai clucked her tongue. "You talk with your mother like this?" she asked Brooke. "You call her big snail? You say this to woman who give you life?"

"Maybe . . . maybe not exactly like that."

"Sweet Buddha, he bless your mother. I must do something to bother him, long, long time ago. He give me Sarai for revenge."

Sarai laughed, finishing with the shrimp. She set them into a stainless-steel bowl and placed them in the small refrigerator. "Where are Suchin and Niran? School will start soon."

The peppers were so spicy that when Brooke wiped her nose, the insides of her nostrils began to burn. "They had fun yesterday at the cave."

"Good," Sarai replied. "Thank you for having your eye on them."

"You're welcome."

"Do you like Ko Phi Phi?"

"I adore it."

"Why? Why do you adore it?"

Brooke sniffed, her nose running. "It's lovely. And the people . . . they're full of life and they make me smile."

"Can you cut some green onions next?"

"Sure."

"Thai people, they like to have fun. That is why everyone calls Thailand 'the Land of Smiles.'"

Brooke thought about a group of children she'd seen the previous day. Dressed in frayed clothes, they'd been chasing a gecko, laughing without end. "I think you're lucky," she said, and started to dice the green onions.

Sarai nodded, breaking two eggs above a pot of boiling chicken stock, then glancing at a to-do list that she'd taped to the wall. "In some ways, yes, we are lucky. We have no pollution. No crime. But we are poor. We cannot always go to the doctor. We cannot buy our children everything we want."

"But they seem happy."

"Yes, they are happy. We are all happy. But our life is hard and happy. Of course, sometime it is okay to mix two things, like sweet-and-sour pork."

Brooke kept cutting, thinking that her own life was much the same. She started to ask Sarai about that combination when giggles emerged from outside the kitchen. Suchin appeared in her school uniform, putting her hands in front of her face, almost doubled over with laughter.

"What?" Sarai asked, still speaking in English. "Why do you laugh so much?"

Suchin turned around, motioning someone forward, her laughter incessant. "You know . . . you know how Niran . . . he wants to be a scientist?"

"Yes."

"Well, he . . . he changed his mind. He wants to become a Buddhist monk."

Niran entered the kitchen wrapped in an orange sheet. His hair had been completely buzzed away, and he held a wooden bowl. He pretended to chant, closing his eyes, holding the bowl in front of him.

"Niran!" Sarai dropped her knife and stepped toward him. She spoke quickly in Thai, glanced at Brooke, and then switched back to English. "What did you do?"

Suchin pulled him forward. "The German men in bungalow number seven. They have a haircutter. I borrowed it and turned Niran into a monk."

"Sweet Buddha, please be napping," Yai muttered in Thai, shaking her head. "You don't want to see this."

Niran pointed at his bowl, giggling. "I'm asking for alms. Rice and curry will do."

Sarai laughed, bringing her hands together. "What a cute monk you are," she said, returning to Thai. "You're the cutest monk I've ever seen." She wanted to rub his head, but since the head was considered to be a sacred part of another person's body, and not to be touched, she dropped to her knees and took his hands in hers. "Was this Suchin's idea?"

"Yes."

"And you let her?"

"I wanted her to."

"So you could ask for alms?"

Niran cocked his head to the side, running his tongue over his gums. "We thought it would be funny. Asking for alms on the way to school."

"And your uniform is underneath?"

"Yes. And I'm hot."

Sarai squeezed his hands. "What a clever joke, Niran. Go and show your father. Make him laugh too. But you can't ask for alms. That wouldn't be right."

"And then you'll walk us to school? Since it's raining?"

"You'll have to find me a hermit crab, my little monk."

"I'll find you one. They'll be out in the rain for sure."

"Good."

Suchin and Niran departed, laughing and holding hands. Sarai watched them go. Though the day was dark and dreary, they'd brought such a light into her tidy kitchen. Needing to finish their soup, she stirred the contents of the pot and added the shrimp.

"You really are lucky," Brooke said, and handed her the tray full of diced green onions.

Sarai smiled, liking the American woman. "Someday you will be lucky too," she replied.

"Why . . . why do you say that?"

"Because Suchin, she told me how you drove the boat yesterday, how you smiled. And so I think good things, they will happen to you. Because you are not afraid. You do not sit still and wait for good things, but you stand and walk to them. You look for them, and when you look for something, when you look hard, you will find it."

Brooke nodded, wondering what she was looking for, whether it was near or far, whether she would recognize it when it came. "Did you know when you found it?" she asked.

The knife paused in Sarai's hand. "No. But it found me again and again. And when it does that, when it keeps coming to you, that is when you stop, when you see what you need to see. That is how I discovered Lek. He was working every day on my father's boat. And one day, after so many days of seeing him smile at me, that day I knew that he would be with me. That I would be as lucky as you say."

THE ELEMENTARY SCHOOL WAS A cinder-block structure divided into several classrooms. Since Suchin and Niran were close in age, they shared the same teacher—a young woman whom Suchin adored. This teacher was responsible for close to thirty boys and girls dressed in uniforms who studied reading, writing, math, science, history, and English.

On this day, as he did toward the end of every month, Lek volunteered at the school, making repairs that didn't require strength. These moments were among his favorites, since he was able to watch his children in their element, a place where Suchin made her friends laugh and Niran asked questions about creatures large and small. The children enjoyed Lek's presence as well and often turned to smile at him as he mended a broken chair, rewired an old light, or patched up cracked floor tiles.

Lek now stood to one side of the classroom, staring at a punctured window screen, which might have been damaged by a pencil or a tool of some sort. He had a great deal of experience making such repairs, as sometimes tourists cut pieces out of the screens of his bungalows in order to make filters for marijuana pipes. Usually Sarai caught the offending guests upon their checkout and was able to assess them an appropriate fine. But Lek would have preferred that they didn't cut his screens. He didn't like waste, and few things were as wasteful as cutting a coin-size hole in a nice screen.

After taking a needle, some fine fishing line, and a square piece of screen from a small leather pouch, Lek used a pair of scissors to cut the screen to just the right size. He then held it against the damaged screen and began to sew it into place. Long ago he had realized that fishing line worked much better than cotton thread, which rotted in the humid air and didn't last longer than a year. As far as he could tell, fishing line lasted forever.

While Lek worked, he glanced at the teacher and her students. She was in the process of explaining how newspapers were written and assembled, and she held up old newspapers from Bangkok and other cities around the world. Her students were attentive, shifting in their chairs but rarely chatting with one another. After the teacher finished her explanation, she pulled large pieces of white paper from a drawer and handed one to each student. "I want you all to create your own front page," she said, passing out rulers and black pens. "Write an article about something, make your headline, and draw a picture."

The students appeared eager for the task and hurried to collect their supplies. Lek paused in his repairs, watching Suchin and Niran as they sat down at desks that wobbled despite Lek's previous efforts to stabilize them. His children didn't work at first but fiddled with their pens, apparently musing over what articles they wanted to bring to life. As Lek swatted away a mosquito and reminded himself to closely inspect all the screens, Niran turned in his direction and smiled. Lek grinned, holding back a laugh prompted by the sight of Niran's buzzed head.

His fingers making miniature movements, Lek began to sew again, determined to create a barrier through which no pest could enter. He stitched with care and patience, thinking about his children, pleased and saddened by the notion of their growing up. Sarai and he had always planned on having a large family, perhaps with as many as five or six children, but recently, because of their financial troubles, talk of a big family had been put to rest.

As Lek worked, he contemplated the beauty of Suchin, Niran, and Achara. He recognized the unique wonder of each child, and how each was a magical gift that he and Sarai had brought into the world, into their lives. And he wanted to make more such gifts, to watch more of their children step forward and smile. The concept that he had the power to create another miracle or two, but wouldn't be able to do so because he couldn't earn enough money, troubled him. A child whom he would love more than himself, who would love him, would never be born. Because of his own failings and weaknesses, such a child would never sit on his lap or wrap his or her fingers around his, would never go out and color the world with his or her beauty.

Still, as Lek stitched, he thanked Buddha for his good fortune. He had never been tested harshly by life, never been forced to endure more than he could bear, and he prayed that his fate would remain so. Several of his acquaintances had experienced hardships and woes so vast that Lek found it difficult to imagine what their days and nights must be like. Let us all live long and happy lives, he prayed. And then take me first. Please take me first.

Suchin and Niran had started to draw, and Lek wondered what articles they were working on. After moving to a second screen that needed repair, he leaned toward his children, smiling at the strokes of their pens, at their eagerness to learn.

After about thirty minutes, the teacher asked the students to present their front pages to the rest of the class. The older students went first, holding up their sheets and pointing to articles and drawings that focused on sports, movies, and weather forecasts. Most of the children were confident as they read their articles out loud or pointed at their drawings. When Suchin's turn came, Lek stopped his work and stood straight, inching closer to her, squinting when she held her work aloft.

Suchin nodded toward her teacher. "My headline is: 'Miss Wattana Becomes First Female Thai Prime Minister.'"

Her schoolmates laughed and clapped. Miss Wattana placed her hands together, beaming.

"'Today,'" Suchin continued, "'Miss Wattana, a teacher of brilliant students on Ko Phi Phi, was elected as Thailand's first female prime minister. Miss Wattana promised to end crime, increase jobs, and build new schools. She also said she would make it illegal for clouds to rain on holidays, and for more than one bee to sting a child. Also, from now on, anyone who leaves their trash on a beach will have to eat one kilogram of sand. Despite these strict new laws, Miss Wattana also promised to give all children free ice cream on really hot days. Miss Wattana will bring her students to Bangkok, so that they can work as her official assistants. The end.'"

Suchin grinned as the children clapped and Miss Wattana examined the paper, held it up, and pretended to nail it to a nearby wall. Lek smiled, finding his daughter's eyes with his own and nodding to her. She hurried back to her seat, leaned forward, and watched as the next student stepped to the front and held his paper aloft.

Niran was one of the last students to present his work. Though he didn't smile as Suchin had, and no one clapped over his words, he was obviously proud of his efforts. His article was about a boy who rescued an injured sea turtle from a fishing net, nursed the animal back to health, and released it. Niran was quite scientific in his article, talking about the turtle's weight, age, and injuries. He had drawn a picture of it trapped in a net, as well as one of it swimming free.

When Niran returned to his seat, Lek raised his hand just enough so that Niran detected the movement and looked up. Lek smiled, nodding. He and Niran had gone fishing so many times together, and he was proud that Niran's love of the sea mirrored his own. That pride grew each day as Niran spoke more openly about becoming a scientist, about how he wanted to study the ocean's creatures.

Rubbing his hip, which ached more when the rains came, Lek prayed that he wouldn't have to take Suchin and Niran from the school, from their teacher and friends. They would survive a life in Bangkok, of course. But Lek had been to the capital once and knew that his children would feel caged in the city. Most children would be fine there, but not Suchin and Niran, who had been raised on the beach, who swam and played and had never been confined by concrete and overcrowding. If his family had to move, Lek knew that they would share a small room in a squalid part of the city. A factory would be his home. He would be gone, unable to rub Sarai's feet during the day, to comfort her, to smile with her. And their children would suffer so much. Suchin's laughter would be less of a constant. Niran would never see the sea. And Achara would not remember it.

Lek glanced at his children, then moved to the final screen that needed mending. As he worked, he wondered how he might make more money. Sarai's massages would help, certainly, but they needed more guests and had to somehow attract foreigners who could afford to stay at the nicer hotels and bungalows.

Lek was a simple man. His father had been a fisherman. His mother had mended nets. He had never gone to school and wasn't sure how to lure more tourists. He'd thought of so many ways to earn more money over the years—some of which had worked, but most hadn't. Yes, he could spear a tuna. He could make Sarai smile and forget her worries. He could play soccer with Suchin and Niran, and could hold Achara against him and whisper to her that the world was a beautiful place. But could he protect that beauty? Could he ensure that his loved ones' happiness and dreams and comfort remained precious and safeguarded?

The last screen was mended. Lek nodded to Miss Wattana, waved at Suchin and Niran, and then stepped from the school and into the rain. His stride was feeble, as usual, but his mind, focused on how he could keep his family on the island, moved with the strength of the currents and tides he knew so well.

THE RAIN LESSENED, TRANSFORMING INTO a damp veil that hung around the island. Ryan walked into the village, avoiding muddy puddles, not minding his wet clothes and skin. He hadn't known that rain could be warm, that experiencing a storm in the tropics was almost like stepping into a shower. Having finally realized that his clothes made him look like someone who had just disembarked from a cruise ship, he'd bought a black T-shirt that depicted the Thai flag and left his Hawaiian-style shirts in his bungalow. He had also set aside his running shoes for flip-flops. His iPod was in place, and Jimi Hendrix's "The Wind Cries Mary" drifted in his head, seeming to lead him forward.

Ryan hadn't checked his emails or studied in more than twenty-four hours—an unheard-of lapse that surprised him. Though he continued to think about Patch's situation, and how best to deal with it, he was no longer obsessed with getting his brother to the American embassy. He'd certainly do that, but time didn't seem as pressing as it once had. Perhaps that was because on the island, time seemed strangely irrelevant. No one wore watches. Clocks didn't appear to exist. The passage of hours was measured by the voyage of the sun, the rise and fall of the tide. People didn't set alarm clocks but awoke at the sound of distant roosters announcing dawn's arrival. No one ate lunch at noon but waited until they were hungry.

As he neared the massage parlor, Ryan felt his heartbeat quicken. He cracked his knuckles, wondering whether Dao would be there, or if she'd be serving another customer. If she was busy with someone else he'd wave to her, continue his walk, and most likely not return. His pride would keep him from appearing desperate, and making repeated stops during the same day to see her would mark him as someone whose needs were too many.

The sky lightened and one end of a rainbow appeared over the mountainous cliffs. Ryan studied the arcs of color, looking from hue to hue, wondering whether Patch and Brooke saw it too. He wished that his heart still fluttered at the thought of meeting Brooke, of touching her and seeing her reaction. But it didn't. She no longer moved him and had blended into the social landscape that comprised his friends and acquaintances. And while he had a history with her, a shared experience that was both intimate and compelling, that experience was over. They were two pieces of a puzzle that didn't fit together. They had tried to force that merging, but failed.

The massage parlor appeared quiet and dark. Ryan hoped it wasn't closed. He pushed his hair back, straightened his shirt, and walked up the cement steps. "Hello?" he called out, and took off his flip-flops.

A curtain opened on the side of the room and Dao stepped forward, again wearing pink shorts and a T-shirt. She smiled, pushing her long, black-as-night hair behind her ears and tying it in a ponytail. "You all wet," she said, and moved closer, tugging on his T-shirt. "My King Kong all wet. You go for a swim in your clothes?"

"No. But the rain . . ."

"You have such big muscles, but your brain, is it big too?" She laughed, pulling again on his shirt. "You supposed to stay inside in rain. Not go for walks."

"But it's warm here. In my country . . . where I live . . . the rain is cold."

"It cold here too."

"You think?"

"It make me shiver."

He smiled. "You don't know anything about the cold."

"And you know everything? You so smart?"

"That's right."

She handed him a pair of thin shorts. "You put these on. Then I give you good massage, make you feel warm again." After stepping into the other room and pulling the curtain shut, Dao turned on some traditional Thai music.

Ryan undressed and for a few seconds was naked with her no more than ten feet away. For a reason he couldn't explain, this casual intimacy comforted him. He pulled on the shorts and then lay facedown on the nearby futon. "I'm ready," he said, and was pleased to hear the curtain slide open.

"Look at you," she replied, kneeling beside him. Her oily fingers began to work on his neck, pressing and kneading. "You body tight today. You go out last night? You find beautiful Thai girl and go boom-boom all night?"

"Boom-boom?"

"So you butterfly boy after all?" she asked, pinching his skin. "You lie to me?"

He laughed. "Ouch. I'm not a butterfly boy, and I certainly didn't go boom-boom last night."

"Maybe in your dreams. That why you all tight today."

"I was throwing the football. With my brother. That's why I'm tight."

She paused; then her fingers began to trace the contours of his spine. "Your brother here, in Ko Phi Phi?"

"Yeah. He's been here for a while."

"And you come to visit him?"

"That's right."

Her fingers pulled down the top of his shorts a few inches, and she began to work on his tailbone. "Why you come back to me today?" she asked, her hair brushing against his lower back.

Her directness surprised him. "I . . . I just wanted another massage."

"Sure, sure?"

"Sure, sure."

"Well, I glad to see my King Kong again. I so bored today. No customers for me. Too many massage girls here. They all come from Bangkok, looking for jobs. So now, we have too many massage girls and too few customers. It hard on everyone."

"Could you . . . do something else? Some other kind of work?"

Dao paused, her fingers resting on Ryan's skin. "Do what? I have to make money for parents. Cannot look for another job."

As she began to massage him again, Ryan reminded himself to leave her a large tip. He knew so little about her but wanted to help. "What happens . . . when you get married? Will you always have to take care of your parents?"

"Yes, of course. They poor. So I will always give them money." She moved so that her legs were on either side of him, and, resting on her knees, she leaned forward, using her oily palms to rub up and down his back. "You no take care of your parents?"

"No, not really. They have enough money. But I would. Just like I will for my family."

"Your old girlfriend, why you not with her, again?"

He grunted as Dao found a knot in his lower back and began to press her thumbs against it, rubbing with strength and determination. "I don't know, really. I think . . . maybe I work too hard. I'm too focused. I think she wants something else."

"Working hard is good. That how you help your family, pay for your house. Too many Thai men no work hard. Maybe they say nice thing to me, but I watch them, and if they no work hard then I no interested in them. Why I want to take care of some lazy man for my whole life?"

"So you won't care if your husband is out, working hard, and you're home alone with the children?"

"Me care? That good thing. That mean he love us very much. And that make me love him more." Dao began to rub his calves. "You so strong. How you get such big muscles? You basketball player or something? Or maybe from flapping your butterfly wings?"

He smiled into the pillow. "I don't have any butterfly wings. Never have. Never will."

"You want one-hour massage today, or two hours? I think two hours is perfect for you."

"Two."

"That good. Good for me. Better for you."

"Yes, much better for me."

As she worked on his calves, he wished that he could see her. He imagined her small hands and her full lips and smile. He wanted to untie her ponytail and watch her black hair fall upon him. Her hair would be like a blanket over him, warming him, keeping his troubles at bay.

Ryan wanted to touch her as she was touching him, to soak his hands in oil and run them over her naked body, caressing her curves and contours. He had never touched a woman in the way that he would have liked to touch her. Nor had he been touched as she was touching him.

"Thank you," he said quietly, closing his eyes.

"You are welcome."

"You know . . . just where to press."

"Of course I do. That my job."

The music stopped. "Can I tell you something?" he asked, unsure of himself, of his words.

"What?"

"I'm glad you didn't have another customer when I stopped by."

"Why?"

"Because you . . . you make me feel good."

Her smile was unseen by him, but her fingers spoke, moving in circles, treating his flesh as if it were sacred, as if soothing its aches and imbalances were like whispering an endearment, like sheltering a candle from the wind.

Dao rubbed and stroked, happy to feel his muscles relax, his tension disappear like footprints swallowed by the sea.

THOUGH THE SKY HAD CLEARED, as if it were a churned-up tidal pool that had finally settled, drops of water occasionally still fell from the leaves above Patch, keeping him cool in the heat and humidity. He sat with his legs on either side of a thick beam that he'd secured to a Y-shaped pair of branches. Wielding Lek's hammer with precision, he drove a nail into a beam that ran parallel to the one that supported him. The nail pierced the beam and entered the tree. Patch hammered until only the head of the nail remained visible. He repeated the process with a second and a third nail, then wrapped a rope around the beam and branch until both were securely fixed together.

Studying the two beams, which were separated by three feet, Patch wondered how many smaller crossbeams he'd have to put in place before nailing a thick piece of plywood on top of the structure. He thought several two-by-fours would be necessary, but decided to ask Ryan. Patch guessed that once he had finished the tree house, it would be often filled with children. And so it needed to be as safe and strong as he could make it.

Patch looked down, wondering what would happen if a child fell from the twelve-foot-high perch. The ground below was firm, and he decided to borrow a wheelbarrow and bring up sand from the beach. A six-inch layer of sand would help cushion the ground.

As he debated whether he should build some sort of giant box to keep the sand in place, Patch noticed Brooke walking in his direction. She wore cutoff jeans shorts and a purple tank top. Her hair was pulled back and partly covered with a violet bandanna.

"Hi," he said, moving on the beam so that he had a clearer view of her.

"Hey. Making some progress?"

"So far, so good."

She smiled and walked to the base of the tree. "I was just talking to Niran and Suchin. They're so excited."

"I know."

"I asked them if they'd seen Ryan. They haven't. Have you?"

"Not since around lunch."

"Where could he be?"

Patch wondered whether Ryan was getting another massage, whether it was right to keep Brooke in the dark. "I don't know," he finally replied. "But he's probably working out, running ten miles, or climbing up and down the mountain like it's his own StairMaster."

"Maybe."

"Want to come up? The sun's going to set in a bit."

She nodded and climbed the ladder, pleased that she had

helped him carry down some of the building material. The ladder was tied so tightly against the trunk that it almost felt like a part of the tree. She straddled the beam across from him and looked out over the bungalows toward the sea. Longboats prowled the tranquil waters, bringing tourists back from snorkeling or fishing tours. A few people still swam in the shallows. Somewhere a dog barked.

"Do you mind if I ask you something?" Patch said, setting down his hammer.

"What?"

"You seem . . . kind of quiet. Is everything all right?"

"Sure."

"The Thais would say, 'Sure, sure.'"

The corners of Brooke's mouth rose, a smile spreading across her face. "Everything's fine."

"But?"

"Well, actually, it's my birthday. Ryan and I . . . We were going to celebrate tonight. But I don't think that's going to happen."

"It's your birthday? Really? Why didn't you tell me this morning?"

"It's no big deal."

"Yes, it is. We should be celebrating."

"No, that's not necess—"

"Of course it's necessary. How often do you have a birthday in Thailand? Really, how often is this night going to happen?"

Her smile came again. "I don't know. You tell me."

"How old are you?"

"Twenty-four. You're twenty-three, right?"

"Yeah, but wait. Just wait here a minute."

"Patch, you don't need to—"

"Just a sec," he replied, moving toward the ladder, hurrying down, jumping as he neared the ground.

Brooke watched him jog toward the restaurant. He turned, waving, and she laughed and waved back. When he disappeared, she shifted her gaze toward the setting sun. As the sun approached the horizon, its light changed colors, as if it were penetrating stained glass at an ancient cathedral, illuminating the island and sea in scarlet and amber. The sun's descent was slow and peaceful, as were the sounds of dusk—the beeps of tree frogs mingling with the distant drone of longboat engines.

Realizing that dawn was unfolding back in her hometown of Portland, Oregon, Brooke thought about her family. Her mother would already be at the television studio where she produced the morning news. Her father would be drinking a Diet Coke and watching the broadcast, his ritual before he left for the county courthouse, where he was a judge. And her brother would probably still be asleep in his college dorm in Eugene, a guitar lying next to him. Brooke knew they'd want to wish her a happy birthday and decided to find a pay phone before she went to bed. She thought about how her parents had struggled after she'd been attacked, how she'd slept between them for almost a week. They had sheltered her when she needed it most. And though she no longer wanted such shelter, she'd be forever grateful for their love.

A few more minutes passed before Patch's voice interrupted her thoughts. "Close your eyes," he said. "No peeking."

She did as he asked, glad to no longer be alone on her birthday. "What are you doing?" she questioned, hearing him grunt as he climbed the ladder.

"Don't worry about me, birthday girl. Just keep those eyes shut."

"Don't fall."

She felt him brush past her. Near her head, leaves rustled. Resisting the urge to peek, she bit her lower lip, smiling again.

"Almost done," he said, and she heard the strike of a cigarette lighter.

"With what?"

"Wait, wait, wait. Okay. Now, open your eyes."

Patch had wedged five table candles into the branches surrounding them. He'd also set a single white-and-pink orchid on the beam in front of her. "Happy birthday," he said, facing her, holding four opened beers.

The candles flickered in the breeze. Brooke picked up the orchid, her forefinger tracing the outlines of the white petals and then the pink center. She brought the flower toward her nose and inhaled, drawing the sweet fragrance deep into her lungs. "It's gorgeous," she said. "Perfect, really."

"Well, I saw that Suchin had picked some. So I asked her. It's really her present."

"Thank you."

"You're welcome."

She looked at the flower again, then carefully placed it above her ear, moving the bandanna down so that it held the orchid's stem in place. "How does that look?"

Patch glanced from the flower to her smile, wondering which was more beautiful. "It . . . it looks great," he replied, and then handed her a beer. "To the birthday girl," he said, raising his bottle.

Their drinks touched, drawn together for a moment longer than necessary. She sipped the cold beer. "Thank you, Patch."

"I would have done more, but the sun is setting and there just isn't enough time to—"

"You don't need to do more. I wouldn't want anything different."

He smiled at the sight of her. "I wish I had a camera."

"You do?"

"Absolutely."

Somewhere toward the village, Bob Marley's voice sprang to life. "Did you arrange that too?" Brooke asked, grinning. "Or is it divine intervention?"

"Just another part of my plan."

She drank again, swinging her feet on either side of the beam. "So, tell me, why are you building this? Tell me the real reason."

He started to speak but stopped. A gecko scrambled up a nearby branch, chasing an ant. "I'm close to Suchin and Niran," he replied. "They remind me of my cousins."

"How?"

"Oh, when I was maybe twelve or thirteen, I used to babysit my little cousins a lot. They lived right down the road. Our families did so much stuff together. Picnics and pizza nights. And then one day . . . they had to move. Someone bought their house and changed everything about it. And I never walked by that house again. It felt too weird."

"And that made you sad?"

"It did."

"So . . . this tree house . . . it's something to remind Suchin and Niran of you? Something that will stay the same for a long time?"

He smiled. "Are you, like . . . clairvoyant?"

"Hardly."

"Well, you're right. Because I want to make something here that will last. Something that will remind them of me. Because we're close and I don't want them to be sad."

"So you're leaving? Soon?"

The gecko fell, landing on a branch below. Patch watched it right itself, not wanting to speak about the inevitable. "I'll go to Phuket, and from there, I'll sneak onto some freighter. As soon as I finish the path and the tree house, I'm going to leave."

"How long will that take? A few days?"

He nodded. "Please don't tell Ryan. I'll sneak away before you take off. Otherwise, he'll never let me go."

Her feet stopped swinging. She didn't want him to leave, to be separated from him. But she couldn't imagine him in jail. His spirit seemed too free. He was too good. "I'll help you," she said, and then finished her beer.

"What do you mean?"

"I'll go to the port ahead of you. I'll find whoever's in charge and I'll ask him which ships are going where. I'll get the destinations, the departure dates, the manifests. Everything."

"But he won't . . . he won't tell you."

Brooke took the flower from her hair and smelled it again. "He'll tell me."

"Why?"

"Because I'll smile and giggle and act so impressed with him. I'll ask about the big, strong boats and he'll tell me whatever I want."

"But—"

"And I'll get you some cash. In case you need to bribe someone. On the ship or when you land."

Patch lowered his drink. Ryan had never told him about this side of her. "It's too much," he finally said. "You're risking too much."

"Would you do it for me?"

"Yes."

"Then it's not too much," she replied, reaching for her second beer. "Because you might be a lot of things, but a hypocrite isn't one of them."

In the growing darkness, the light from the candles became more prominent, the flames gyrating in the slight breeze. A bird squawked from the branches above. The smell of the sea permeated the air.

Patch moved closer to her until their feet nearly touched. He took the orchid from her fingers, smelled it, and then placed it back above her ear. "Can I ask you something?"

"What?"

"It's just . . . because I'm going to leave soon. I want to ask you something, and I'll regret it if I don't, because I'll probably never get the chance again."

"I'm not a fan of regrets. They're hard to exorcise."

"I agree."

"So go ahead."

"What would have happened . . . if you and I had met first instead of you and Ryan?"

She'd asked herself the same question and remained unsure how to answer it, though she was pleased that he had asked. "I . . . I don't know."

"Guess."

"I can't guess. But I wish . . . I wish it had happened that way."

"Me too."

"Why?"

He resisted the urge to touch her, remaining still when every instinct told him to move. "Because I could sit here with you on this old beam for the rest of the night. Just talking. Just getting to know you. And I wish we'd had that chance—to really get to know each other without having to worry about anything else. I think if we'd had that chance . . . things would have been . . ."

"Don't stop."

"I wouldn't . . . I wouldn't have had to hold back. Like I do now. You'd have seen other parts of me . . . good parts . . . that you don't see now, that I can't show you now."

"Like what?"

"I . . . I wouldn't be sitting here . . . not moving. I'd be showing you how I feel, not telling you how I feel."

She closed her eyes for a moment. "What else are you thinking?"

Somewhere in the distance a child laughed. Patch recalled the many things that had occupied his mind over the past few minutes—how her promise to help made him feel safe, how her presence brought a smile to his face as quickly as one of Suchin's jokes, how he wondered whether the skin beneath her eyes was as soft as it looked.

"I'm still wishing . . . that we'd met a few years ago," he finally replied. "When things were simpler."

"My life hasn't been simple for a long time."

A candle blew out, and he lifted it from a crook in a branch and relit it on another flame. "Why would you help me with the boat?"

"Because you shouldn't have to lose so much for one mistake. I don't think life should be so . . . intolerable."

"But—"

"And I don't know you very well . . . but I believe in you."

"Ryan will be mad."

She shrugged. "We're finished, so his getting upset is just water under the bridge. At least to me. I'm sure it's different for you."

"It is," he said, then sipped his beer. "But still, thanks for sticking up for me."

"Of course."

"You know something else?"

"What?"

"You remind me . . . of me. Except that you're smarter . . . and prettier."

She smiled, shifting on the beam. "I'm neither. But how do you think we're the same?"

"You're up here, in a tree. You're an adventurer. And though you have some regrets, they don't rule you, and they never will."

"They tried."

"It's like . . . when I was ten, I broke my arm, and the doctor told me that my bone would heal, would grow back stronger than ever. I've never forgotten that. And I think you're like that. You had that break. But you're stronger than ever."

The beep of a nearby tree frog sounded. Brooke looked for the creature but saw nothing. "My break didn't mend that way. I'm not stronger than ever. I'm only what I want you to see. I'm an illusionist."

"I don't believe that."

"It's true."

"Why didn't it work with my brother? I don't understand why it didn't work."

A pair of backpackers walked down Patch's path toward the restaurant. Brooke watched them disappear into the open-air structure, which flickered with hundreds of holiday lights. "I was too hard on him," she finally replied. "Too unforgiving."

"How so?"

"He's got a lot of endearing qualities. A ton of them, actually. Buried down, deep inside him. But instead of thinking about them, I focused on his shortcomings."

"Why?"

She turned away. "I don't want to say anything negative about Ryan."

"But why did you focus on his shortcomings?"

"Because I felt like . . . I was going backward with him. And that's not where I need to go. That's not where I'll thrive."

He nodded but didn't reply, relighting a candle once again. The sky was finally bereft of color. Yet stars were being born, awakening as they had for millions of years. In the distance, the pulse of reggae music continued to thump. The scent of burning wood lingered in the air. Crickets called out to one another in the darkness, their chirps incessant and comforting.

"Happy birthday," Patch said, moving closer to her on the beam.

"Thank you."

"No, I mean it. It's your day. I want it to be special . . . because you're special." He held up his beer. "Here's to going forward."

Their bottles touched and they drank. She watched him, awash in the candlelight, his face aglow. She was aware of how he leaned toward her, of his desire. She could see it written in his expressions, voiced in the pauses between his words. If she hadn't felt the same way, perhaps she wouldn't have recognized his yearning, and she asked herself why she felt so strongly about him. She was falling toward him and longed for him to catch her, to lift her as she'd never been lifted.

Is it because he thinks of me as being whole? she wondered.

No, it's more than that. It's the way he looks at me, as if he sees me and nothing else, like I'm all that matters. Ryan never looked at me like that. No one ever has.

"Did you spike these beers with whiskey?" she asked, smiling.

"No. Why?"

"Because they've gone straight to my head."

"That's what birthday beers do."

"Really? I'll have to remember that."

"Should we . . . should we get another? I could go get another."

His uncertainty about how to proceed was as obvious to her as the gyrating candle flames. She knew he hoped to continue their talk. He wanted to cross the bridge between them, just as she did. He wanted to feel her touch, to confirm his suspicions and hopes. But he was reluctant to cross that bridge because of his brother. And she wasn't sure whether he should.

Still, she needed to touch him, to let him know that her thoughts mirrored his. So she reached out, brushing away a few grains of sand from his knee. She squeezed his knee once, thanked him for her birthday present, and then climbed down the ladder, moving away from the light of the candles, from the sound and sight of him, from the place where she longed to be.

FRIDAY, DECEMBER 24

follow me

I t was her fingernails that woke Ryan, digging into his forearms, leaving welts. He'd been dreaming about Dao, about
being shipwrecked with her on a tropical island. But as Brooke
thrashed in her sleep beside him, Dao's voice fled, replaced by the
hum of the ceiling fan and Brooke's gasps. He gathered her in his
arms and held her tight, telling her to open her eyes. Finally she
did, flinching beside him, glancing from corner to corner as if she
were a trapped animal that sought escape.

"Everything's all right," he whispered, remembering the two
other occasions when nightmares had gripped her. She struggled
against him. "Brooke, it's me. It's Ryan. You just had a dream. A
bad dream."

"No."

"Shhh. It's okay. You're safe."

She looked up at him, and her grip on his arms relaxed. Nodding, she closed her eyes and ran the back of her hand across her

sweaty brow. The dream, which was really a memory, came back to her then. She saw herself open the door, the stranger step inside, forcing her backward, a knife flashing in his hand. "Stop, stop, stop," she muttered, sitting up in bed, twisting the sheet. Tears fell to her cheeks and she wiped them away, the aches and miseries of that distant day suddenly flooding into her. "I have to get up."

"Sure. Let's get up."

"Hurry."

Ryan slipped out of bed, wearing his boxers and a T-shirt. He put on running shorts and sandals. Brooke, still in her light cotton pajamas, stepped outside. Dawn had just broken and the sky was somewhere between blue and black. Without glancing behind her, Brooke walked to the beach and sat down near the waterline. She wanted to kick and punch and scream but did nothing except stare across the flat water. An image of the stranger materialized and she forced it away, shaking her head, telling herself that he was gone forever, that Patch was right and the stranger hadn't stolen any part of her soul.

After giving her enough time to gather herself, Ryan sat down beside her. At first he didn't speak—letting her get used to his presence, unsure whether she wanted him there or not. Finally, he asked, "Are you okay?"

She nodded.

"Do you need anything?"

"No."

"You sure?"

Somewhere in the distance a rooster announced the sun's looming arrival. The sound was helpful to Brooke, pulling her from the past into the present. She wiped her eyes and turned to Ryan. "Did I . . . scratch you?"

The undersides of his wrists were still red and gouged from where her nails had dug into them. He showed her the backs of his hands that were fine. "Not a bit."

"Sorry."

"Don't be."

A miniature crab emerged from a hole near her feet. She watched it scurry toward the water, then vanish into a diminutive wave, reappearing when the wave retreated. Breathing deeply, Brooke smelled the sea and the damp sand. Her heartbeat slowed to its normal rhythm. She wondered why the dream had come. Maybe because the night before she had wanted to get her own bungalow but was afraid of being alone, and had convinced herself that a few more nights with Ryan wouldn't hurt anything. He'd apologized for forgetting her birthday and she had accepted his words. And yet they hadn't touched or spoken affectionately. Those moments, it seemed, were gone.

"I should have gotten my own place," she said, moving her feet in the sand. "Then I wouldn't have woken you up."

"I was already awake."

"You were?"

"Yeah. So don't worry."

She sighed, her feet once again resting still. "Thanks, Ry."

"You're welcome."

"I think . . . I think tonight maybe I'll get my own room. It probably makes sense at this point."

"You're sure?"

She nodded, determined to face her fears, not to let the stranger win. "There are so many empty bungalows. I might as well rent one. I'm sure it would make Patch's friends happy."

"Whatever you want."

Hoping to change the subject, she recalled their conversation before going to sleep, wondering why he had seemed so pleased. "Last night, you kept smiling," she said, her toes moving again in the sand.

"I did?"

"While you spoke, there was this little smile on your face. And I heard it in your voice too."

"You could hear my smile?"

"What made you so happy?"

He watched a distant jogger, wondering whether Brooke should know about Dao. "I met a girl," he finally replied. "A woman. She gave me a massage . . . and . . . we talked and laughed."

Brooke turned toward Ryan, her brow furrowing. "Really?"

"Yeah."

"Yesterday?"

"The other day, actually. And then again yesterday."

"And . . . and you laughed with her? About what?"

He smiled. "She calls me King Kong. Teases me. Stuff like that."

"And that's what you were thinking about last night?"

"I'm sorry about your birthday. I didn't—"

"I don't care about that. Tell me about her. How did she make you smile?"

Ryan shifted on the sand. "She's . . . spunky."

"Spunky? That's it?"

"She makes me laugh. I don't know how or why, but she does."

"Is she beautiful?"

"I don't know. The room's dark. I'm on my stomach most of the time."

"So, she's spunky and beautiful. Anything else?"

As Ryan, with some reluctance, spoke more about Dao, Brooke nodded and asked questions. To her surprise, she wasn't jealous. She was glad that the woman knew how to make him smile, glad that he was happy, and that he was being honest about the situation. And if she was honest with herself, she knew Ryan's obvious infatuation with the woman was a good thing for all of them.

Brooke could now spend more time with Patch and not feel guilty about it. She could help him with his tree house, help him leave the country. And later, if she wanted to, she could find him in America. They could sit and talk all night. They could touch.

As long as Patch escaped safely, time was on their side. If her instincts were right, if she fell for him as she thought she might, time would give them the chance to be happy together.

Still smiling, Brooke continued to ask Ryan about the woman, believing that he had fallen for her, glad that the morning had gone from a place of pain to one of promise.

SUCHIN AND NIRAN, WEARING THEIR uniforms, left earlier than usual for school. They each carried ten flyers that advertised Rainbow Resort, as well as its restaurant and massage services. At Sarai's request, Patch had made a master copy the previous day, using colored pencils to brighten a sheet of blank white paper. Patch had drawn a brick path that led to an inviting group of bungalows perched near a turquoise sea. Above his sketch, he'd written down prices and additional information. Lek had a friend who worked at the island's only health clinic and had been able to use the facility's copy machine to replicate Patch's original.

Circumventing or hopping over puddles from the recent rain, the siblings hurried toward the village, eager to hand out their flyers. Niran had asked if they could hang one in their room. He liked the way that Patch had drawn the scene, which was vibrant and warm. The bungalows looked new, and the fish that Niran had suggested seemed to speed through the sea.

"I think we should go after women," Suchin said as they started to pass vendors and shops. "The women will be sweeter."

"You think?"

"It's too early for the men. They'll be tired and cranky. The women will listen to us. And they get more massages. They like to feel good. Men just want to drink beer and play sports."

"That's not true."

Suchin studied the people ahead, knowing that she didn't have many flyers and wanting to make the most of them. "You're un-usual, Niran. You're a good thinker. Almost my equal. But most boys aren't like you. They'd rather throw a ball than read a book, or chase pretty girls than learn anything useful. I just hope you stay the way you are. We need more boys like you. If we had more boys like you, us girls wouldn't have to be so perfect."

"Perfect?" Niran repeated, leaping over a puddle. "If you're so perfect, how come you're afraid of bees? How come you don't like math?"

"Have you sat on a bee? If you'd been stung on your bony little bottom, you'd be afraid of them too."

Niran laughed, recalling how Suchin had jumped up from her chair. "That's the fastest you've ever moved."

"I don't remember."

"Yes, you do."

She scowled at him, then pointed to a foursome of foreign

women. "You see them? Let's give them a flyer. They look nice. Let's make them laugh and they'll want to come stay with us."

"How should we make them laugh?"

"Just do what I do," she replied, and headed toward the women. As Suchin walked, she started thinking in English, forcing Thai thoughts and phrases out of her mind. When she was a few feet away from the women, they looked down at her. "Good morning," she said in English, handing them a flyer. "My brother and I would like to invite you to our parents' beautiful Rainbow Resort. At Rainbow Resort, you will find soft beds, the most delicious banana pancakes in the world, and a very good massage. And all of this is so cheap that it's almost free."

One of the women thanked her but said that they already had accommodations.

Suchin smiled. "But does your bungalow have an ocean view?"

"Yes."

"Does your restaurant have food that makes your belly laugh?"

"Well . . ."

"You see? My mother is the best cook on the island. Everyone who comes to her restaurant leaves with a laughing belly. And if you've never had a laughing belly, you should definitely experience it. Look at my brother. See his silly smile? Where do you think he ate breakfast?"

The woman shrugged, grinning. "Your mother's restaurant?"

"That's right. You're as smart as you are beautiful. But your belly seems sad. Don't you want to make it happy? I tell you, if you come to my mother's restaurant, you'll understand what I'm talking about. And you'll thank me so many times."

"And your mother . . . does she give massages too?"

"Of course. Right on the beach. The best beach in all of Ko

Phi Phi. After lunch, you can lie there, with your laughing belly, and she'll rub your back until you feel like Rainbow Resort surely must be in heaven."

The foreigner studied the flyer. "It looks nice, but we leave tomorrow."

"Then please come today. Please. If you return to London or Amsterdam or wherever, and you didn't taste our mother's cooking or get one of her massages, you'll feel so empty inside. Your stomach will be sad and your back will hurt. Don't you want to leave with a happy stomach and back?"

"Is it far from here?"

"No, not at all. Just down the trail."

"Where?"

Suchin glanced from her distant school toward her home. She wanted to lead the women to her mother but didn't like to be late for school. After hesitating for a few seconds, she took the woman's hand. "Come, I'll show you. You haven't had breakfast yet, I can tell. So you should definitely try my mother's pancakes."

The woman turned to her friends, spoke in a language that Suchin didn't understand, and then nodded. "We will follow you."

Suchin switched to Thai and told Niran to go on to school. But he shook his head and said that he wanted to tell the women something. Rolling her eyes at him, aware that they would get into trouble for being late, Suchin led the women toward her home, chatting with them along the way, advising them about what they might want to do after breakfast and a massage. They didn't know about the hike to the lookout point and were pleased to hear that it was near Rainbow Resort.

When they reached the beach, Suchin turned to Niran. "My

little brother," she said, "wants to tell you something. I don't know what he'll say—probably something about his fish tank, which you'll see in our restaurant."

Niran looked up at the tall women. Their faces seemed kind, he thought. Faces to trust. He hoped to tell them so many things—to please compliment his mother, to give her a tip, if possible. But he didn't have Suchin's confidence when it came to being bold with foreigners, and so he simply smiled and introduced himself. He saw that one of the foreigners carried a camera. Wanting them to remember Rainbow Resort, he asked politely whether he could take their picture. The woman agreed, handed him the camera, and moved closer to her friends.

Proceeding carefully, Niran studied the viewfinder, lining up Rainbow Resort so that it was to the right of the four women. He counted backward from five to zero, then gently pushed the button when everything was perfect. The picture materialized in the viewfinder and he grinned. The women looked happy, and Rainbow Resort appeared just as it did in Patch's drawing—beautiful and perfect.

Niran glanced at his sister and realized that she was impatient to get moving. He wondered whether he should hurry to school without her, but decided that if she was going to get into trouble with their teacher, then so should he.

"You were good," he said in Thai, taking her hand.

"Too good, I think. We're going to be late."

"Could you tell them to compliment her, if they like her massage? She likes compliments."

Suchin shrugged. "Can't you tell them?"

"No. Not like you can."

She nodded, knowing he was right, though tired of speaking

English and eager to get to school. Still, she did as Niran asked, changing his words into hers, getting the women to laugh and smile and agree to tell her mother how wonderful she was.

Shortly thereafter, their mother appeared, stepping from the restaurant, welcoming her guests. As the women settled next to a beachside table, Sarai turned to Suchin and Niran, reaching for the remaining flyers. "I love you," she said in Thai. "Now hurry to school. And stay late. Sweep the floor and make your teacher happy."

Suchin and Niran nodded, waved good-bye to the foreigners, and ran down the beach, their footprints deep and intermingled. They ran like two parts of the same body, weaving beside each other, racing as they had a thousand times before.

Sarai watched her children. She smiled, her eyes following their movements, her ears straining to hear their laughter. Only when they turned away from the sea and headed toward the village did she again remember her customers, hurrying back to them, determined to ensure that the efforts of Suchin and Niran weren't wasted.

IT HADN'T TAKEN LONG TO get Brooke situated in her new lodgings. Ryan had carried her suitcase to the seaside bungalow and made certain that she was secure and content. To his surprise, she'd seemed eager to have her own place and had managed to forget about her nightmare. She hadn't dwelled on it as she had in the past. Instead, she had opened up the curtains and windows of her room, smiling at the caress of the breeze.

Ryan had left her alone, and, feeling as if a weight had been lifted from him, he ran up and down the beach for an hour, pushing himself, enjoying the flight of his feet and the music that thundered from his earphones. He did a hundred push-ups before cooling off in the sea. After showering, he went into the village and emailed his contact at the American embassy, proposing a meeting between himself and the policeman whom Patch had injured. Ryan knew that Patch's greatest fear was that this man would exact revenge during Patch's incarceration. If Ryan could meet him and convey Patch's remorse and willingness to turn himself in, it would be possible to gauge the man's capacity for forgiveness. And if forgiveness was offered, Ryan was certain that he could convince Patch to surrender himself.

Pleased with his plan, believing that it could be the answer to their problems, Ryan headed toward Dao's massage parlor. His spirits sank when an older woman answered his knock. He asked whether Dao was working, but the woman shook her head.

"You Mr. King Kong?" she asked, wearing a pink outfit identical to what Dao worked in.

"I'm sorry?"

"Dao, she tell me about Mr. King Kong. You him?"

"Yes . . . that's what she calls me."

The woman smiled, revealing a silver tooth. "She not working today. She home."

"Oh. Is . . . is her home near here?"

Surprise flashed across the woman's face. "You want to see her home?"

"Sure."

"Okay. I show you. For one hundred baht. If I leave work, I must pay one hundred baht every hour to owner."

Ryan reached into his pocket and handed her two hundred baht. "For your time."

"Kob kun ka," she said, rubbing the bills together for good luck. She then shut the door and walked down the steps. "Follow me."

So far, Ryan had seen only the main village and both bays of Ko Phi Phi, which were flanked with beachside resorts. He was surprised when the woman led him from the village into the jungle. They followed a well-worn trail for about five minutes before coming to a large clearing. Within this open space ran rows of dilapidated one-story wood-and-tin homes. Many of the homes shared a common wall. Others were separated but seemed as if they might fall to one side or the other. Laundry hung from old ropes strung between tree branches. Roosters and cats strutted about. Babies sat in the dirt and played with rocks while their mothers mended fishing nets or washed clothes in steel tubs. A fire smoldered in a corner of the clearing, fueled by wood, corncobs, fish remains, and split-open crab legs.

Ryan watched a naked toddler try to climb atop a battered bicycle that was much too big for her. The child's mother appeared and pulled her from the bike, prompting instantaneous cries of protest. The pair disappeared into a home made from old, sun-bleached boards.

"You follow me," the masseuse said, motioning Ryan forward.

He did as she suggested, cracking his knuckles as his gaze swept up and down the clearing. A hundred feet away, Dao sat, head down, on what appeared to be a plastic chair. She wore a sleeveless white shirt and a blue sarong. Her fingers were busy with a needle and thread, and a blanket was draped across her knees. After quietly thanking the woman, Ryan stood still, wondering whether he should leave. He felt out of place, and though children smiled and waved at him, he wasn't sure whether the adults appreciated his presence.

Dao's long hair fell on her shoulders and back as if it were a black shawl that mimicked her movements. She called out to someone Ryan couldn't see, laughing as she sewed. Then she looked up, saw him, and lowered her needle. His heart thumping with increasing vigor, he waved and walked forward, trying to appear confident. After setting her work aside, Dao stood up and stepped in his direction. The distance between them disappeared, though she did not offer her hand or make any attempt to initiate physical contact.

"Hello, Mr. Ryan," she said, a trace of a smile gracing her face.

"Hello."

"You want massage?"

"Yes . . . well, no, actually. I just wanted to say hi."

A middle-aged woman appeared in a nearby doorway. "That my mother," Dao said, grinning. "She cannot speak English. Since you come here, to our home, she must think you want to marry me."

"What?"

"We Thais very traditional in some ways. If a man visits a woman's house, sure, sure he is going to ask to marry her."

"I . . . I didn't know—"

"It okay. You *farang*. That make it okay."

"I didn't have any idea."

Dao walked toward her mother, speaking in Thai. At first her mother's face was blank and her body still, but as Dao continued to talk, the older woman nodded and then went back inside. Dao returned to Ryan's side. "Yes, I was right," she said, smiling. "She think that maybe you want to marry me."

"What'd you tell her?"

"Only that you my number one customer. That you want another massage. Come, follow me. I show you something."

They left the clearing, walking back toward the village. Watching Dao as she led him forward, Ryan realized for the first time how little she was. The top of her head might have risen to his collarbone. Yet she had the curves of a woman, and he couldn't help but watch her hips as she stepped over roots and fallen branches.

"Sure, sure, my mother will have many questions for me tonight," she said, turning to glance at him. "And my father . . . oh, King Kong, how surprised he will be!"

"I'm sorry. I didn't know."

"That okay. Do not worry your brain. It muscle too. It will get tired. But I cannot massage it. So sorry."

He listened to her laugh, wondering where she was taking him. Soon they were in the main part of the village, passing shops and pubs and clusters of tourists. Dao said hello in Thai to many of the locals she passed, sharing a few words or a smile. Ryan noticed that everyone seemed to light up when they saw her.

She proceeded past the start of the pier, followed a trail toward the nearby beach, and stopped at a vendor, speaking again in Thai. Ryan watched as an old woman dropped a spoonful of butter on what looked like a giant saucepan. As the butter heated up, the woman patted and shaped two balls of dough. After flattening the dough until it was no thicker than a few sheets of paper, she set it on the saucepan, then added half of a banana, sliced down its length, on each of what were soon two crepes. The woman sprinkled cane sugar on her creations before holding a can of chocolate syrup above each crepe, dripping chocolate strategically. Once the crepes were flipped, the vendor used her steel spatula to set them on a paper plate. She handed the plate and several napkins to Dao, who gave her some money and waved good-bye.

Dao walked to the beach and sat down on the sand near the water's edge. More than a dozen longboats were moored here, sterns tied to anchored buoys and bows secured by ropes to nearby palm trees. The longboats swayed back and forth in the breeze like horses awaiting their riders. In the distance, a passenger ferry approached—a rectangle of blue and white dwarfed by the island's massive cliffs.

"This good treat for you," Dao said, handing Ryan the plate. "Give you more muscle to chase pretty girls."

Ryan thanked her and bit into one of the crepes. The combination of butter, chocolate, and cooked bananas made him smile. "I can see why you like this. It's just about perfect."

"Of course it perfect. Like me, right?"

He laughed, handing her the plate. "That's right. Like you."

She ate the crepe in a well-practiced manner, rolling it tighter, then biting one end. Ryan watched her eat, aware of how her full lips glistened from the butter. After finishing the treat, she dabbed at her mouth with a napkin and set the plate down. "I so surprised today when you come to my house. Nothing ever give me bigger surprise. I ask myself if I am dreaming, if King Kong really come out of jungle, like in the movie."

Ryan raised his sunglasses so that they were perched atop his head. "Are you always home on your days off?"

"One day. One day off every week. And yes, on that day I home."

"What do you do?"

"Help parents. My father, he not see so well. My mother have . . . how you say . . . arthritis? So, I help them. Washing clothes, making the dinner, sweeping the floor."

"Just you? Do you have brothers or sisters who help?"

"Yes, I have three brothers and one sister. But they all younger. Still in school. So, as oldest child, I have to take care of parents."

"What about you? Do you ever do anything for yourself? Buy something nice for yourself?"

Her brow furrowed. "For me? No. Never. My money, it go to my parents. They use some for food, for clothes. They save some to use if my little brothers or sister want to go to university on mainland. My mother and father, they want one child to go to university. No one in our family ever go before."

The ferry neared, approaching the pier, which was filled with Thais. "But what about you?" Ryan asked. "It's your money. Do you want to go to a university?"

She looked away from him, her smile fading. "It not matter what I want. I cannot go. I have to make money."

"That's not fair. It's your—"

"It fair. It what we do. Then one day, if my brother go to university and later get good job, maybe he can help me, help my children. That how it work."

"Would you . . . if you could . . . would you go to a university?"

"Of course."

"How old are you?"

Her smile returned. "A smart woman never answer that question. And a polite man, he never ask."

"Tell me."

"Nineteen. But why you ask?"

Ryan shook his head, saddened by the thought that she wanted to go back to school, but never would. He knew that she was bright and eager. How must she feel giving massages to rich tourists, day after day, listening to their stories, seeing the thickness of their wallets? "You're still young," he finally replied. "You could still go to school."

"Impossible. For me, anyway. But please, do not worry your big head, King Kong. I am fine. Am happy. And if my brothers or sister go to university, then I even more happy."

A Thai man untied a nearby longboat, started the engine, and backed it out into the azure waters. The familiar and repetitive cough of the two-stroke engine filled the air.

"I . . . I came today because I wanted to thank you," Ryan said.

"Thank me? For massage? It great massage, I know. But you not need to thank me twice."

"That's not what I wanted to thank you for."

"What?"

"It's just . . . you make me laugh. And you . . . appreciate me for who I am."

"What you mean?"

Ryan scratched at a mosquito bite on his arm. "Most women . . . they don't seem to understand me. I annoy them, I think."

"Why?"

"I don't know. Maybe I . . . I worry too much about what I want to do."

She pushed her hair aside, so that it lay on the shoulder that was farthest from him. "What you want to do?"

"Study. Exercise." He smiled. "And get massages from girls on Ko Phi Phi."

"Girls!"

"I mean, from one girl on Ko Phi Phi. A beautiful girl named Dao."

"That better. Much better."

"But I'm the opposite from you. You work for everyone else. I just work for myself."

"But someday, when you have good job, you can take care of your wife, your children. So you not only work for you, but for them."

"You think so?"

She nodded. "Of course I think so. Your wife will be lucky woman. Same, same for your children."

He resisted a sudden urge to touch her bare shoulder, which glistened in the sun. "You see? That's why I wanted to thank you."

A breeze stirred her hair. She smiled. "You are welcome, my big gorilla."

Watching her grin, Ryan thought about the differences between them. Their histories were as varied as water and sand. And yet, they were also connected. She saw him for who he was, and though he had spent very little time with her, he wanted to spend more. He wanted to watch her sit on the beach, to listen to her laugh, to somehow, someday help her as she had helped him.

His eyes found the place where the water and the sand met. He watched this place, saw how little waves tugged at the sand, pulling and pushing it, bringing movement to what had once known stillness, changing patterns that had seemed so permanent.

He looked up again, smiling as she chided him for not listening, then laughing as she picked up a strand of seaweed and threw it at him.

THE DAY HAD BEEN PRODUCTIVE and somewhat celebratory for Patch. He'd finished his path a few hours after breakfast, positioning the last brick into place and then inspecting the entire project, making sure that nothing had shifted or loosened. The path was better than he could have imagined, strong and eye-catching. He knew that it was a significant upgrade from the sandy trail that people had previously used and that it might draw more customers in Lek and Sarai's direction, which pleased him.

After finishing the path, Patch had worked on the tree house, nailing a thick piece of plywood on top of the support beams. He then added railings to every side of the structure, leaving an opening by the ladder. Decorations came next, pieces of coral that he'd found on the beach soon gracing nearby branches. He also painted the top of the plywood, re-creating what Ko Phi Phi looked like from above. He'd seen such pictures in guidebooks, and it wasn't hard to paint the butterfly-shaped island surrounded by the turquoise sea.

Lek had walked to the tree house and slowly climbed up the ladder. He had sought out Patch to thank him for the path, but was equally pleased with the tree house. Both Lek and Patch had wanted to show the children right away but would have to wait until after school. So they sat and smiled, Lek swinging his feet over the edge, feeling years younger, as if the weight and burdens of time had slipped off his shoulders.

Hoping to repay Patch for the path and the tree house, Lek had asked whether he wanted to borrow the longboat for the afternoon. Patch understood the generosity behind the offer, as fuel was expensive, and frivolous excursions on the boat were rare sights. A part of him had been tempted to politely refuse, but he also understood that Lek longed to repay all the hard work. And so he had said yes, smiling at the way Lek had grinned and then tried to hurry down the ladder.

Patch had seen Brooke on the beach reading, and as Lek led him toward the longboat, he'd called out to her. She had set down her book, wrapped a sarong around her hips, and caught up to them. Patch had tried to find Ryan as well, but his brother's bungalow was empty. Once Lek ensured that the engine was working fine, he had patted Patch on the back, which he'd never done before, and helped the two Americans get under way.

Now, as Brooke stood near the stern and steered the boat toward a distant cove, Patch wondered whether Ryan was getting another massage. Brooke had told Patch that she knew about the woman, that she was happy for Ryan. And while Patch worried Ryan might object to Brooke and him spending so much time together, he was comforted by the knowledge that Ryan seemed eager to seek out the masseuse and didn't appear to have any desire to be with Brooke.

The sea was almost flat. Gentle swells caused the bow of the longboat to rise and fall. Standing next to Brooke, his hand on one of the steel poles that supported the canopy, Patch watched her steer. The serenity of her lightly tanned face seemed to match the still, smooth surface of the water. The wind blew her hair back, causing it to flutter like a flag.

As they approached the cove, Patch eased off on the throttle and the longboat slowed. Though the area was a popular destination for world-class snorkeling, it wasn't always crowded. People tended to congregate here in the late morning or early afternoon, and Patch was glad to see that they had arrived after all but two boats had gone. The cove didn't have a beach or anywhere to land, so Patch pointed to a large buoy and asked whether Brooke could steer toward it. Her aim was true and he cut the engine, hurried to the bow, and grabbed the buoy. After securing the longboat, he picked up a bag of snorkeling gear and headed back to Brooke. She had taken off her sarong and was in the midst of applying sunscreen to her legs. Patch tried to busy himself but found it hard not to glance in her direction. The sight of her bikini-clad body left nothing to his imagination and nearly overwhelmed him with desire.

"I want to introduce you to a friend of mine," he said, needing to break the silence. "Actually, a friend of Niran's and an acquaintance of mine."

"What friend?"

He handed her a snorkel and mask. "She's green and has big teeth. And as long as you don't get too close to her, you'll be good to go."

"What about sharks? Are there sharks out here?"

"Some. But most are on the other side of the island. And they're all just black-tipped reef sharks anyway. Nothing to worry about."

She tied her hair into a ponytail. "Sure, sure?"

He grinned. "Sure, sure." After taking off his shirt, he reached for his mask and snorkel. "You ready?"

"You should wear sunscreen. Your back's peeling."

"Sunscreen costs a lot. If I wore it every day, I'd be broke."

"You are broke."

Chuckling, he put on his mask and snorkel, held them against his face, and jumped out of the boat. Brooke did the same, bubbles obscuring her vision for a few seconds. The water, which seemed as transparent as the air, was about fifteen feet deep. She surfaced, cleared her snorkel, and then looked to where Patch was pointing. Putting her face underwater, she saw that closer to land sprawled a vibrant reef. Circular mounds of brain coral the size of basketballs were the first things she noticed. Soft coral, the shape of leafless trees, also swayed in the gentle current. Nestled between the brightly colored varieties of coral were anemones, urchins, sea cucumbers, and clusters of hiding fish. White clams with purple interiors grew between gaps in the reef. Most of the clams were a foot or so long, though several were much larger.

Brooke again followed Patch's pointing finger and saw a school of diamond-shaped squid swimming through the deeper water. The squid were almost translucent, their oversize eyes seeming to lock upon Brooke's. She watched the creatures glide past, thinking that they looked to have come from another planet.

Following the outer contours of the reef, Patch swam on, often lowering his head, kicking his legs out of the water, and descending quickly to the bottom. Once, ten feet down, he took off his mask and snorkel, opened his eyes, and smiled at Brooke. She waved, aware that he was showing off but pleased that he was trying to impress her.

A few coral heads were damaged from anchors and feet, but otherwise, the underwater world looked to be in near perfect condition. Brooke mimicked Patch's dives and was able to study the coral from a foot or two away, always careful not to touch it. She glanced at Patch on occasion, ensuring that she hadn't kicked away from him. Despite his lack of well-defined muscles, she felt safe with him next to her, safer than she ever had in Ryan's presence. This sense of safety, she thought, came from what she perceived as his selflessness. The people around him seemed like his first concern.

Patch motioned for her to kick to the surface, and she did, pulling out her snorkel. "The Jolly Green Giant is right over here," he said. "Let's say hi."

"That's what you named her?"

"Yup."

Brooke followed him again. After a few strong kicks he pointed to what looked like some sort of hole in the reef. At first Brooke didn't see anything other than colorful coral, but then she spied a moray eel. Its green head was almost as large as hers, and its long body was thicker than her thigh. The eel was nearly motionless—only its gaping mouth opening and closing ever so slightly. The creature, while beautiful, made Brooke feel out of place for the first time since she'd entered the water. Though Patch dived to within a few feet of the eel, Brooke had no desire to be any closer to its massive jaws and knifelike teeth.

Floating on the surface, she watched Patch circle the eel. After a minute or so, as he was near the bottom and facing her, she saw an immense manta ray approach him from behind. The animal glided like a kite on a breeze, the almost imperceptible fluttering of its wing-shaped fins propelling it forward. Brooke assumed that it would steer clear of Patch, but the manta ray came within a few feet of him, passing above his outstretched hand. He must not have seen it coming, for as soon as it entered his vision he jerked his hand away and let out a muffled cry. The ray didn't change its direction or speed, but Patch kicked quickly to the surface.

"That scared the crap out of me!" he said, pulling off his mask and then splashing Brooke. "Thanks for the warning."

She splashed him back. "Did you think it was a shark?"

"Hell, yes. I thought it was going to take off my arm."

Laughing, she kicked away from the eel, not wanting it near her dangling feet. "I thought the sharks here were safe. That they were nothing to worry about."

"That doesn't mean I want one coming up from behind me while I'm floating around like some sort of tasty treat."

"You jerked your hand away like a great white was after you." He splashed her again, smiling. "No, I didn't."

"Yes, you did."

"Well, that was a monster manta ray. Its shadow might as well have been from a great white."

"Oh, poor baby. How frightening."

He kicked after her and she tried to swim away. But she was laughing too hard to get far. He soon caught her, grabbing her by the shoulder and threatening to pull her under. She spit a mouthful of seawater into his face, so he tugged her down, dunking her. When she resurfaced he dunked her again and then kicked toward the boat.

She wasn't sure if he let her catch him, but she swam as fast as possible and managed to grab his foot as he tried to climb aboard the longboat. She pulled down, laughing as he fell back into the water. Crying out, he reached for her shoulder but missed, and his fingers swept down her arm and thigh. When he resurfaced it was her turn to dunk him, and she pressed her weight down on him, sending him under once again. A few seconds passed before his hands emerged, his fingers making peace signs. She nodded and pulled him up, helping him grab hold of the boat.

"Shark!" she yelled, and he went rigid once again. Then he was laughing. She laughed with him, everything but the sight and sound of his joy fading from her senses. She wasn't aware of the longboat approaching, of the voices drifting across the water. All she saw and heard was Patch. His happiness was infectious. His eyes were on hers, drawing them together as if eyes could communicate more freely than voices, could generate intimacy more powerfully than touch.

The connection between them was so strong that suddenly she had to kiss him, to taste him. She put her hand around his neck and drew him closer, her lips parting, her laughter gone. Pulling him tight against her, she felt his lips press on hers, a gentle sensation at first, but he must have been as hungry for her as she was for him, because his tongue found hers and the bond between them strengthened. Her hands traced the contours of his body. She heard a soft moan emerge from between his lips and then hers.

Brooke had never known that a kiss could consume her. But at that moment, she traveled somewhere, traveled within the union between them. The destination she arrived at was as beautiful as the reef, full of grace and wonder and creation. And though a small, distant part of her knew that she needed to open her eyes and draw away, she waited for him to do it. And when he finally did pull back, the scent and taste of him remained within her, keeping her journey alive, hinting of the road ahead.

She opened her eyes, and the world appeared so much richer than it had a few minutes earlier. Her senses seemed heightened, her body ready to take flight. She imagined his lips on hers, his body on hers, and, needing to quench her desire before she reached out to him, before she consumed him, she plunged underwater, letting herself sink toward the reef, heedless of whatever lurked below.

AFTER PREPARING DINNER FOR ELEVEN customers and her own family members, reading a story to Niran and Suchin, and putting them to bed, Sarai returned to her kitchen. Though she usually tried to clean as she cooked, the night had been chaotic, and dishes were stacked on counters and piled in the sink. Seeing the mess, she sighed. After emptying the sink, she began to wash the dishes by hand, scrubbing them carefully and setting them on a drying rack. A few minutes later, Lek entered, carrying Achara. She was asleep on his shoulder.

He sat on the kitchen's only chair, moving slowly. Achara stirred and he hummed, patting her back. Sarai watched their daughter settle against him and returned to the dishes. Most of what she'd made had been eaten, but several plates were nearly full, and she thought about the work she had put into each dish. Normally she would have saved the leftovers, but the food had sat for too long on the table while the women who ordered it shared a cigarette and drank Singhas.

Using a brush with force and precision, Sarai scrubbed plates and pots. When she saw that Achara was asleep once again, she asked Lek about his day. To her surprise, he didn't smile but shook his head. "They shouldn't be handing out flyers on the way to school," he said. "They must have been so late. And they already do too much."

She shut off the water but continued to scrub. "They brought us four customers. Four bellies to fill with my pancakes, and two bodies to rub. That's nine hundred baht. Nine hundred. Would you rather that we didn't have it?"

"I'd rather that they weren't always peddling."

"You think I want them peddling? That it makes me happy?"

"I—"

"Don't think like a man, like a dreamer. We don't have the luxuries of dreamers. Suchin and Niran will have to peddle as long as we live here."

He leaned back until his head touched the wall. "Hunting for coins? Chasing down tourists on the pier? And now spreading flyers around half the island? When does it end? It's shameful."

Sarai turned on the water again. She gripped a plate, her knuckles whitening. "What do you know about shame? You walk around fixing leaking roofs and toilets. You don't need to swallow your pride. I swallow mine. Every day. I peddle food, drinks, massages, and anything else I can think of. I clean up messes all day long. So I know about shame. It's with me like my shadow. But I'm not afraid to walk with it. Why should our lives be so perfect that we don't have such burdens? Are we so much more deserving than our friends?"

"No, but—"

"Stop your dreaming, Lek. Stop acting like a twelve-year-old boy. In your heart of hearts, you know that we'll always peddle. That's the price we pay for living here. And it's a small price. Our children are happy. We're happy. So don't become so prideful that you lose sight of that. I can't have a blind man in my life. I already have to take care of too many people. You hear me? Too many people."

"Easy, now," he said, standing up, moving to her side. "You'll wake Achara."

Sarai started washing the dishes again, wanting to hold her

daughter but knowing that first she needed to clean the kitchen. "Don't be prideful. Remember what Buddha said about pride: that it's like standing on the top of a tall mountain and looking down on all the other peaks, thinking that everyone is beneath you."

"I don't see things that way. I don't look down."

"Don't start."

"I just don't want Suchin and Niran to think that they're beneath others. And I see how they hang on the answers of tourists. A yes makes them smile. A no makes them sad. That's too much power in the hands of others, too much power over our children."

"But that's why we work hard. That's why we peddle. So that they can continue to go to school, so that someday they can do whatever they wish. If we fail, then they'll look up at everyone else. Then they'll always be powerless. But we won't fail. And they'll look everyone in the eye. Straight in the eye."

Lek nodded. "We put too much pressure on them to sell."

"Maybe. But they're happy. And even happiness has a cost."

Achara stirred against his shoulder. "And the cost to you?" he asked. "What's the cost to you? You look too thin. Are you remembering to eat? To drink?"

"I'm fine."

"I haven't seen your smile all evening. Where did it fly off to? I want it to return. I feel lonely without it."

"You'll never be lonely."

"And your smile?"

"It's coming back."

"Good. Do you want to hold her? She'll bring it right back. She always does."

Sarai leaned away from him. "And let you scrub my dishes? I might as well have people eating off the dirt."

"I'll try."

"And I'll try to walk on water."

"But I'll be careful. I'll get them clean. I promise."

"And I'll be careful too, when I try to walk on water. But I'll still sink like a stone."

A burst of firecrackers exploded in the distance. Someone, likely a Thai, was celebrating the approaching new year.

The corners of Lek's lips rose, and he reached for Sarai's shoulder with his free hand. "Maybe later, after your smile is back, we can—"

"Wait. Before you start romancing me, I need to tell you something else."

"What?"

"Before dinner, I went to Patch's room, and I asked him. I asked him why he was hiding."

Lek frowned, then blew a mosquito from Achara's arm. "What did he say?"

Sarai started scrubbing again and retold Patch's story. She left nothing out. When all the dishes were clean, she started to wipe the countertops. "I like Patch," she said. "I like him a lot. And I don't blame him. But he has to leave. His presence endangers our family."

"Maybe—"

"We'll help him. We'll support him. But he has to leave." Lek started to speak again, but she shook her head. "Open your mouth only if you agree with me."

"I . . . I agree. He has to leave. But I still need his help to rethatch a few roofs. Give us ten days."

"Five. You have five. Tomorrow is Christmas. And he shouldn't have to work on his holiday. But after that, you have until the first of the year. Then he has to go."

"Fine, if you insist. But I'll need to hire help for a roof or two."

She rinsed out her rag, hung it up to dry, and then began to sweep the floor. She thought about telling him how she had taken the nine hundred baht and hidden it, starting a fund that she hoped would someday allow him to visit a doctor on the mainland. But until then, he would have to endure the ache in his hip. No other choice existed. "I want to laugh," she finally said, her broom creating a pile of sand and debris. "I was born to laugh. Not to force a friend from our home. If he wasn't in trouble, he could stay forever. He could become a part of us. But I can't risk our family. Now that I know the truth, I can't risk our family."

Lek put his foot in front of her broom. "Could you still laugh tonight?"

"I don't know. I'm tired. Let me finish."

He didn't move. "Wait. Just wait and watch." With his free hand, he reached for one of Achara's bare feet and gently tickled her toes. She pulled her foot away, but he continued to tickle her, and a smile spread across her face.

Sarai bit her lower lip, setting her broom aside. Suddenly she needed to hold her child. She reached for her, soon cradling her, soon tickling the same toes. Achara smiled again, dreaming perhaps, unaware of the tears she brought to her mother's eyes. Her father caught one such tear from her cheek, rubbed it between his fingers, then picked up the broom and began to sweep.

Bending down, Sarai kissed Achara's forehead, praying for her health and happiness. She imagined her daughter running along the beach, laughing with other children, playing in the waves. The promise of such days, as well as that very moment, filled Sarai with love and wonder and joy, filled her like the sun pours light into the sky.

She's a miracle, Sarai thought. Our own little miracle.

SATURDAY, DECEMBER 25

brothers

Not long after first light, when Patch was adding the final touches to the tree house, Lek sought him out. The two walked along the beach, and Lek said that despite their bond and Patch's wonderful work, he had to leave by the first of the year. Lek told him about the police flyer, about how he'd taken it down, how Patch's presence was a threat to Lek's family. Patch apologized profusely and informed Lek of his plan to sneak aboard a freighter. Though the plan worried Lek, and he told Patch as much, there was little he could do. The two thanked each other, walked in companionable silence, and then decided to start applying fresh thatch to a vacant bungalow.

It was difficult to bind and tie the thatch. Lek was an expert at the process, though, and as Patch stood on a bamboo ladder and worked, he tried to mimic the older man's movements. He made many mistakes, for he was consumed with conflicting emotions. A part of him was dominated by joy, by the bliss of the most passionate and electric moment of his life—kissing Brooke. But that kiss came at a price—turbulent feelings of betrayal and guilt. Ryan had never betrayed him, always protecting him, always doing what Ryan thought was right. But now, after Ryan had traveled around the world to help him, Patch had put his own feelings before his brother's. He'd acted passionately, but also selfishly, disregarding how his actions might hurt Ryan.

Lek saw Patch's clumsiness and misinterpreted it, believing that Patch was upset about having to leave. He leaned closer to the American, putting his hand on a cord Patch was using to tie up some thatch. "Happy Christmas," he said. "A most happy Christmas to you."

"Thanks."

"I want you to have happy Christmas. You my friend. And my family's friend. Please . . . do not leave this place unhappy. You blessing for us."

Patch stopped working, and thanked Lek in Thai. He then added in English, "You've all been the blessing. And I won't ever forget you."

"Someday you come back?"

"I . . . I don't know. I'd love to. But it won't be easy. Maybe someday . . . you could all visit me in America."

"That impossible. We never get visa. Not enough money. Americans can come to Thailand, but we cannot go to America."

A dragonfly landed on Patch's sweaty arm and he brushed it away. "Maybe someday . . . if I have some money I could sponsor you. Maybe Suchin and Niran could study in America. I think it's a lot easier to get a student visa. And if you were serious about it, if they were serious about it, I'd really try to help."

Lek's mouth opened, but no words came forth. He'd dreamed

of such opportunities for his children but never dared to hope that they might come true. He bit his bottom lip, his eyes glistening at the thought of Suchin and Niran at an American university. Suchin might not want to leave Ko Phi Phi, of course. She was so happy here, and Lek would never do anything to disrupt that contentment. On the other hand, Lek was certain that Niran was serious about becoming a scientist. And where better to become a scientist than at an American university?

"You too kind," Lek finally replied. "You make me happy. You make a father happy. And a mother."

"I want to keep in touch. I want to help you."

"You already help. For sure. More than you know."

Patch started to reply but saw Ryan jogging down the beach. Guilt flooded back into Patch, and his smile faded. Though Lek had just called him kind, Patch didn't feel anything of the sort. He felt dirty. He wanted to step back in time and not take Brooke out in the boat. Though he had fallen for her, and though he had wanted to let her know about his feelings, the kiss had been too much. Words would have been just as effective, and infinitely less harmful.

The longer Patch watched Ryan, the worse he felt. He thanked Lek again for everything, and then asked if he could go down and speak with his brother. Lek smiled, nodding, still thinking about how someday his children might be able to study in America.

Patch hurried down the ladder and over to the beach. Ryan was at the far end of the curving stretch of sand. Walking toward his brother, Patch tried to settle his emotions. He wasn't sure what he wanted to say or do, but he had to say something. He couldn't escape the island and spend weeks hiding in a freighter without somehow honoring his relationship with his brother.

After a few minutes, Ryan and Patch approached each other in front of a small hotel that was being renovated. Ryan slowed his pace, stretching as he moved, holding his hands up and behind his head. He pulled out his earphones. His body glistened with so much sweat that he might as well have stepped out of a shower. The brothers greeted each other warmly, touching fists and exchanging wishes of a merry Christmas. Patch thought Ryan seemed in unusually good spirits and was happy for him. "Is she so great?" he asked as Ryan began to stretch his legs.

His older brother looked up, smiling. "Yesterday I went to her home."

"Seriously?"

"She laughed at me. Said that her mother thought I'd come to propose."

"Of course she did."

"Well, thanks for warning me."

Patch shrugged. "I didn't know you were going to look for her house. I wouldn't have guessed that in a million years."

"Why not?"

"Because . . . because that's something I'd do. Not you."

Ryan lifted his right knee toward his chest and held it in place. "I told Brooke all about her."

"I know."

"She told you?"

Patch hesitated, glancing away. "She's . . . she's told me a lot. You've been gone so much lately, and we've just become . . . close."

"How so?"

"Really close. I didn't plan it that way, but it just—"

"What do you mean, really close?" Ryan stopped stretching. "What do you mean, Patch?"

"I swear, I didn't—"

"What the hell are you talking about?" Ryan asked, his voice no longer friendly.

Patch took a step backward. "We . . . I made a mistake. A huge mistake. You guys had broken up. You were with Dao. And I . . . I just got caught up in the moment."

"Jesus. What happened?"

"We . . ."

"What happened?"

"We kissed. Just once. And that was it."

Ryan's hands rose up, pushing Patch toward the sea. "You kissed her?" Another shove sent Patch stumbling. "You kissed my girlfriend?"

"Ryan, I'm trying to be honest here. Just listen. We were—"

"You kissed her or she kissed you?"

"It wasn't . . ."

"Open your mouth or I'll open it for you."

"I kissed her. Just for a second. It was a mistake. We both know—"

The punch came fast and hard, striking Patch on the side of his jaw. The pain was instantaneous and almost blinding. He fell with a grunt, his palms and knees driving deep into the sand.

"That's what I get?" Ryan asked, towering over Patch. "I come halfway around the world to help you, and that's what I get?"

"I—"

"Shut up, you worthless piece of shit."

The world spun around Patch. The inside of his mouth was torn, and he spit blood. "I'm sorry."

"You're sorry? Great. That's just great. You're sorry. That makes everything fine. That makes the world perfect. You and your goddamn apologies. I bet you weren't sorry when you were kissing her, were you? Did you say sorry then? What else did you do with her? Did you sleep with her?"

"No. And you'd left her."

"So? You think that gives you the green light to kiss her? Just because I met a girl, and I was happy, you thought you could kiss Brooke?"

Blood dripped from the corner of Patch's mouth. He tried to stand but couldn't. "It . . . just happened."

"Brooke and I might be done, but that doesn't mean that I don't have feelings for her, that I don't want to be her friend. You think I want to hear about . . . about you kissing her? Why can't you ever think of me? I've always tried to be like you with women. I've sucked at it, and have always been jealous, a third fucking wheel. And now you have to move in and take Brooke from me? To show me once again how you're so much better than me?"

"That's crazy, Ryan."

"No, it's not."

"You're way better than me."

"Bullshit."

"Then why . . . why have I always looked up to you?"

An image of Patch and Brooke kissing unfolded in Ryan's mind. He remembered touching her for the first time, remembered the feel of her lips. "I'm finished here," he said, his voice flat, drained of strength. "You . . . you can rot in jail or go jump on some ship. I really don't give a crap."

Patch grabbed his brother's leg. "Wait. Just wait. Please."

Ryan stepped away, stumbling toward his bungalow. He'd seen Patch spit blood, and though he was so enraged that he wanted to scream, the sight of his little brother's blood and the memory of his fist striking Patch's face were almost as painful to him as thoughts of Patch's betrayal.

He had to leave the island. No matter how much he cared about Dao, or how happy he'd felt an hour earlier, he had to leave. Beauty and promise existed here, but so did confusion and sadness and angst. Though the island had put him at ease, had made his stresses and responsibilities seem so far away, he'd been deluding himself. He wasn't like Patch. He couldn't escape into a new world and forget where he came from. And though Dao was tempting, though he didn't want to walk away from her, he knew he had to. His feet needed to be more firmly planted. Only then would he be able to go where necessary, to create a place where he would feel at home.

He might have fallen for Dao. He might have loved her. But she was an illusion, a dream.

He had to rest somewhere else.

THE TREE HOUSE HAD BEEN full of children for most of the morning, full of children who giggled from the platform, chased geckos on branches, and pretended that they were giants. Only when a soccer game unfolded on the nearby field did the tree once again sway quietly in the wind.

Now, as Lek and Niran fished and hunted for the food that would provide the restaurant's patrons with an annual Christmas feast, Sarai, Suchin, and Yai walked toward the tree house. Sarai and Suchin carried six dried ears of corn, while Yai held Achara. Suchin had been playing off and on in the tree house since she'd arisen and was pleading with her grandmother to make the climb.

"It's so easy," she said, dropping the wooden bowl that would be used to gather kernels of corn. "All you have to do is take about ten steps up."

Yai wiped her sweating brow and wished for clouds. "Easy for you to say. You move like a monkey. Me, I'm more like an old water buffalo."

"No, you're not. You just say that."

"Have you seen my backside? You think it's better for sitting or climbing?"

Suchin pointed to the ladder. "Look, it's not far up. And no one's there right now."

"I'd bring the whole tree down. All of Patch's work, done for nothing. Your friends would chase me off the island. And with good reason."

"He made it strong, didn't he, Mother? Tell her. Tell her how you climbed up there with me after breakfast."

Sarai nodded, trying to suppress a smile. "She's right. I think the tree would hold you. Look how thick it is. It might just be strong enough."

"Oh, how my own daughter mocks me. Sweet Buddha, what did I do to deserve such a daughter? Did I curse you once? Did one of your monks get on my nerves and I sent him scurrying?"

Suchin tugged on Yai's free hand. "Just try it. Please. Don't listen to her. I know you can climb it. You were young once; you were a little monkey like me. So I know you can do it. Everyone in our family has been up there but you."

"Can't an old woman just find a spot of shade and rest?"

"No. Not today. Today you have to climb the tree for me. For my Christmas present."

"For your Christmas present?"

"I've seen drawings of Santa. And he . . . he likes his food. He's big. And they say he can climb through windows, through holes in the roof. So if he can do that, you can climb too."

Sarai reached the tree and gestured for Achara. Continuing to protest, Yai handed over her granddaughter. With one arm, Sarai spread a small blanket on the sand, kissed Achara's chubby cheek, and laid her on the blanket. Sitting so that her shadow covered Achara, Sarai began to use a knife to pry dried kernels from a corncob. The kernels fell into the bowl that Suchin had carried. Later that night, after dinner was finished, Sarai would heat the kernels in a covered pot until they popped.

"Oh, sweet Buddha, don't let me fall," Yai said as Suchin pushed her toward the ladder. "Don't let me bring your tree down on top of my loved ones. They don't deserve to die like that. Sarai, maybe. But please let Achara live."

Sarai laughed, continuing to work on the cob. "You'd protect us. You'd hit the ground first and would protect us like a giant shield."

"Why, Buddha? Where is your mercy?"

Suchin put her hands against her grandmother's bottom and pushed. "Come on, before the soccer game is over."

After testing the strength of the bottom rung with her weight, Yai looked up. "I might as well climb to the moon."

Suchin pushed harder. "Don't stop."

"Please, sweet Buddha, please protect Achara. Not the other one. But the little one. Please keep her safe." Yai moved higher on the ladder, surprised that it held her. "Don't let me squish you," she said to Suchin. "Really, you should have gone first."

"I need to push you. I can't push you if I'm not below you."

"Oh, what a sight you must see. Close your eyes, dear. Save yourself."

"Just go. Don't stop."

Yai stepped higher, aware of Sarai's laughter. She smiled, pleased that Sarai was happy today, when so much work needed to be done. Her heart thumping faster as she continued up, Yai reached the top of the ladder and moved carefully onto the platform. She was certain that it would crack and groan beneath her, but no such sounds emerged.

"See?" Suchin said, hurrying beside her, crawling on hands and feet like a spider. "I told you everything would be fine. I knew you could do it. Of course you could do it."

Yai patted Suchin's knee. "Thank you, child."

"You're welcome, adult."

The pair exchanged smiles as children shouted nearby, chasing a soccer ball, sending it flying in one direction and then another. Suchin knew everyone who played, and cheered on her closest friends, none of whom were the best players. Those children scored and danced, often doing celebratory cartwheels and headstands. Since it was Saturday, several adults participated in the game and were nearly as exuberant as the children.

Yai watched Suchin follow the game, happy that she was so confident and poised. "Did you really believe I could climb up here?" Yai asked, pulling a twig from Suchin's long hair.

"I climbed beneath you, didn't I?"

"Yes, you did."

"So I believed."

Below, Achara cried. Sarai set a corncob aside and picked up her little girl, whispering. She covered her torso with a small blanket as she began to nurse Achara.

"Don't be afraid to climb," Yai said, nodding. "Life is full of trees to climb."

"What do you mean?"

"I mean, when I was your age, girls couldn't do much. We didn't play soccer. We hardly went to school. By the time your mother was born, things had started to change. And one day, when she was older, she asked me if she should open Rainbow Resort with your father. It was their dream."

Suchin turned from the game. "What did you tell her?"

"You think my memory is so sharp?"

"No. Probably not."

Yai chuckled, her fingers tracing the contours of Suchin's face. "I told her that they should build it together. But that she would have to be the engine to make it go."

"Father does his best."

"I know, child. I know."

"Patch has helped him a lot."

The game ended and children started to head toward the tree house.

"Remember, Suchin. Don't ever be afraid to climb. One day, when I'm gone, and when a tall tree stands before you, remember how I climbed up this one. If I can climb this one, you can do anything. You can go to a university on the mainland. You can say no to a strong man. You can be who you were meant to be. Not who someone else says you should be."

Suchin reached for her grandmother's hand. "But you'll help me. I know you'll help me."

"Of course I will. And so will your mother and father. And even Niran and Achara. But someday . . . someday you'll have to look up, without fear. And when you're not afraid, so many beautiful things will happen. Just like they've happened for your parents."

Children started to call out to Suchin. She waved and told them to wait a minute. "You're a good climber," she said. "I don't care if you think your backside is like a water buffalo's. You're a good climber, and I'm glad that you came up with me."

Yai clapped. "You make me so happy."

"Let's go."

"All right. But let me go down first, just in case I'm better at falling than climbing."

"You'll be fine."

"Oh, I'd just bounce, I suppose. Bounce like that new soccer ball of yours. Just don't let me roll away too far. Your mother would think that's much too funny."

"I won't."

"Why don't you tell me a joke as I go down? To pass the time before my doom. Let me die laughing."

Suchin pursed her lips, helping Yai grasp the top rung. "What dog keeps the best time?"

Yai's foot slipped, and she let out a grunt, pulling herself back up. "Hmm . . . that must be a watchdog," she replied, stepping down once again.

"You always get them!" Suchin said, giggling. "Why do you always get my jokes?"

"Because I'm a jokester. And jokesters get all the jokes."

"I'll think of a better one."

Yai smiled. "Take your time. At the rate I'm going, there's no need to rush. Just don't tell any jokes about falling water buffalo. That would strike too close to my heart."

"Mother is laughing."

"Drop something on her, will you? Any coconuts up here?"

"No."

"I'm going to tape her mouth shut."

"You tried that once. It didn't work."

Yai paused, clinging to the ladder. "You're a beautiful girl, Suchin. Inside and out. How Sarai produced you will always be a mystery to me. A wonder of the world. Right up there with the pyramids. You're such a beautiful girl and I couldn't love you more."

It hadn't taken Ryan long to get organized. He'd thrown all his possessions into his suitcase, showered, and put on fresh clothes. After hurrying into the restaurant and paying for his lodging, he returned to his room. He had tried to avoid an encounter with Patch or Brooke, but in the end, just as he did a final check of the bungalow, she found him. She was wearing shorts and a T-shirt, and must have been running, because her body was slick with sweat.

"Don't go," she said, reaching out to him. "Patch told me what happened. Please let me explain."

He zipped his suitcase shut. "Don't pretend that you care."

"I do care. So does he."

"Right. Thanks for reminding me."

She put her hand on his shoulder. "Please don't leave. Not like this. It only happened . . . it only happened because you found someone else. You fell for someone else. And so did I."

"My brother."

"So? What's wrong with that? Wouldn't you rather have me fall for him than for a stranger?"

"He—"

"It was my fault, Ry. I initiated it. Not him."

"That's not what he said."

"He was protecting me. But I'm telling you, I started it."

Ryan began to reply but stopped, rubbing his aching hand. "I can't help him any more. He won't listen to me. So there's no reason for me to stay."

"But the woman. Don't you—"

"Dao. Her name is Dao."

"Don't you have something with her? Something worth pursuing?"

He opened and closed his hand, wishing that it hadn't formed into a fist. "I have to leave. That's what I have to pursue. Because . . . because staying here is making me crazy."

"How? Tell me how."

"You need it spelled out? Seriously?"

"I—"

"You kissed my brother. He's a fugitive. And I'm falling for a girl I hardly even know. Maybe that works for you. For Patch. But I can't stay in his little world. I'm not Peter Pan."

"I know you're not. But you were so happy the other night. Happier than I've seen you in a long time. You seemed . . . fulfilled."

Ryan shook his head. "I have to go. Right now."

"It's Christmas. Don't leave on Christmas. Please. Stay until tomorrow." She reached for his hand, holding it in hers. "I didn't mean for this to happen. It's my fault. It really is. Don't blame him. He's a wreck right now. He's—"

"I do blame him."

"He loves you so much."

"The people he loves . . . He puts them through a lot. So be careful."

"Don't say that."

Ryan bent down and picked up his suitcase. "Good-bye, Brooke."

She let go of his hand and watched him step out the door. Her legs felt weak, and she started to sit down, but an idea came to her, and she hurried outside, running now, moving away from Ryan, ignoring the looks of strangers as her feet rose and fell on the warm sand.

FIFTEEN MINUTES LATER, PATCH RAN toward the village. Though the side of his face throbbed, he was barely aware of the pain. Instead he focused on where to find Dao. Brooke had told him her name, saying that only she could stop Ryan from leaving.

Most of the massage parlors were located on the far side of the island, and based on Ryan's description of the area, Patch felt he was headed in the right direction. He wasn't used to running and soon became winded, stopping in front of a vendor's stall. Patch asked the woman if she knew of a Dao who gave massages near the beach. To his delight, she nodded and told him in broken English where he might find her.

The small parlor by the sea was open for business. Patch stepped inside, forcing himself to slow down in case she had a customer. He softly called out her name and, shortly thereafter, a curtain opened on the side of the room. A young woman with long black hair said hello and asked him how he knew her name.

"I'm Ryan's brother," he replied, breathing hard.

She looked at him curiously, noting the striking similarities of their faces, as well as the differences between their bodies. "He not here," she said. "You want massage? I give good one. Best one on Ko Phi Phi."

"I know he's not here. He's headed to the pier. He's going to leave."

Her smiled faded and she suddenly looked older. "He leave? Why?"

"Will you do something for me? Please?"

"What?"

"Will you please go to the pier and talk to him?"

She stepped back. "I think you crazy. Why I go find him? I cannot leave job."

"He told me about you. He was so excited about you."

"Excited? If he leave, then he not excited. I sure, sure of that."

Patch closed the door behind him so that another customer wouldn't appear. "I did something terrible to him. I hurt him. It doesn't have anything to do with you. But he's leaving. And I think he should stay."

"He punch you? That why your face all red and big?"

"Yeah, he punched me."

To his surprise, she laughed. "Not good to get punched by King Kong. You want a beer?"

"You're not . . . you're not following me. I need you to go to him. And tell him something."

"What? Tell him what?"

"Tell him that . . . that his brother will do what he wants. I'll turn myself in. Tell him that I'll turn myself in."

"I no understand."

Patch smiled. Now that he'd said those words, now that he'd made a decision, it felt as if a great weight had been taken from his back. "But he will. He'll understand, Dao. He'll understand if you say that I'm going to turn myself in. Because I trust him . . . and I love him."

"What your name?"

"Patch."

"Batch?"

"No, Patch. Like you . . . you sew a patch on your shirt."

"I get in trouble if I leave shop."

"I'll stay," he replied, liking her. "I'll stay and say that you'll be back soon."

She scratched her scalp. "Why you come to me?"

"Because he cares about you. He'll listen to you."

"He say . . . he care about me?"

"Yesterday. He told me that yesterday."

"My mother think he want to marry me."

Patch grinned. "I know."

"It good dream, for now," she said, nodding. "A happy dream. Okay, I go get King Kong. Be more careful next time, so he no punch you again."

"Thank you."

"Sure, sure."

He watched her depart, wishing her speed, wanting Ryan to stay for her sake as much as his.

RYAN STARED AT THE DISTANT ferry, his iPod filling him with Bill Withers's "Ain't No Sunshine." The singer's melancholy voice and words roused a feeling of nostalgia that seemed to seep into Ryan's every pore. He remembered arriving on Ko Phi Phi in the private speedboat and realized that Brooke had been right. It would have been better to land in the ferry along with everyone else. The speedboat was a luxury in a land that needed none.

He hadn't ever expected to be alone when he left the island. A profound sense of loss resided within him. Three people he cared about were being left behind, three people who were nearby, at that moment, but would most likely never occupy the same space with him again. In a few hours everything would be different. Cars would honk. People would hurry. He would go back to being himself, to rushing from one destination to the next, from one task to the next.

Worst of all, he had failed. He'd soon have to tell his parents about this failure, about how Patch insisted on trying to escape. Ryan had been so confident of convincing him otherwise, which was one of the reasons that his parents had stayed behind. His mother's health would have made the voyage hard for her, but his father would have come. Ryan had talked him out of the journey, however, saying that he could best approach Patch alone.

His hand still ached, and he wondered if he might have fractured his pinkie finger, which was red and swollen. Cursing his temper, he unzipped his suitcase and searched for a painkiller. He swallowed two pills without water, then looked at the ferry again, wishing it were only a speck on the horizon.

Ryan didn't want to leave but felt he had to. He reminded himself of this need time and time again as the ferry approached. Passengers aboard the ship waved to people on the pier. Not as many people waved back, and it was obvious that the spirits of those arriving were higher than those departing.

The ferry docked, and a few minutes later, passengers began to disembark. Ryan glimpsed the father and son from Rainbow Resort as they tried to get the attention of new arrivals. He had started to walk toward them, to thank them for their hospitality, when he felt a tap on his shoulder.

Dao stood behind him, dressed in her pink shorts and T-shirt, the breeze stirring her hair. "Why King Kong leave so soon?" she asked, scowling. "Why you no get last massage?"

He pulled out his earpieces, surprised to see her. "You . . . found me?"

"Why you go?"

"I have to."

"I have to breathe. To drink water. I not have to go anywhere. Why you have to go? What so important?"

Ryan moved closer to a railing, so that people could walk past them. "But . . . how did you know I was here?"

"Your brother . . . your crazy brother . . . he find me. He tell me where to find you."

"He did?"

Her brow furrowed. "Maybe I need to clean out your ears. You not hear so good today."

"How did he find you?"

"Why you ask me so many questions? I boss here. I ask the questions."

Her petulance made him smile. "All right, boss. Ask away."

"Why you leaving so soon?"

"My brother and I . . . we had a fight. I punched him."

She laughed. "I know. I see his face. It red like a tomato. I tell him it not a good idea to get punched by King Kong."

"You're right. Though . . . though I think I broke my finger."

She reached for his hand and inspected his swollen finger. Supporting it, she moved it back and forth. "This hurt?"

"A little."

"If it broken, I think it hurt a lot. Come, we go put ice on it. We fix it."

He didn't move. "Dao, I have to leave. I'm sorry. I don't want to . . . but I have to."

"You make no sense. You been drinking Thai whiskey?"

Ryan glanced around and saw that the pier was almost empty of waiting passengers. "I came here for my brother. To help him. But he doesn't want my help. And so I have to go."

"He tell me something. To tell you."

"What?"

"I no understand it. He acting so crazy."

"What are you supposed to tell me?"

"He say . . . he say that he turn himself in. He want you to stay. Because he going to turn himself in. I no understand what he talking about, but he ask me to tell you this. He say he trust you. And he love you."

"Are you sure?"

Dao frowned, slapping his arm. "Sure, I sure. I no forget such thing."

A smile spread across Ryan's face. The heaviness within him disappeared. Impulsively, he reached for Dao with his good hand, squeezing her forearm. "That's good news. That's really good news."

"Why? He now turn himself in instead of turning himself out? You and your brother make no sense to me. You both crazy, I think."

Ryan glanced at the ferry, no longer worried about its presence. "Thank you, Dao. Thank you for coming here."

"You are welcome. Now . . . do you stay or do you go?"

"I'll stay."

"Good. Because I must get back to shop, before I get into trouble."

She started to turn away, but he continued to hold her arm. "Where should I stay?" he asked. "I don't want . . . to be near Patch. Is there a resort on this side of the island that would be good?"

"Sure, sure."

"Will you show me? When do you get off work?"

"Six o'clock."

"Will you meet me here? And then you can show me?"

Dao started to speak but stopped, unsure whether she should see him once more outside her massage parlor. He'd been ready to leave, ready to leave without even saying good-bye. And though she liked him and hoped to see him again, she didn't want to get hurt. "You not nice to me," she said, shaking her head. "You come to see me. You confuse my mother. And then, next day, you try to leave. That make me look bad. That embarrass me. So why should I help you again? Why should I meet you?"

He saw the hurt in her eyes and released her arm. "I'm sorry. I've . . . I've thought about you. A lot. But I had to leave."

"In movie, King Kong never leave the woman. Maybe you should have a new nickname. Batman or something."

"Can I make it up to you? Tonight. Can I take you out for a special dinner?"

"Too many people will see. Then, when you leave, I look even worse."

Ryan wished the island weren't so small, that she didn't know everyone. He cracked a knuckle. "What if I brought dinner to my room? Could you . . . could you meet me there?"

Dao nodded but said nothing.

"At six?" he asked.

"My family eat dinner together. Every night around seven o'clock. But I can leave my shop earlier, if I pay a fine to my boss."

"I'll pay it. I'll gladly pay it."

She glanced around, looking for familiar faces. "You go find the Hillside Bungalows. It at far end of island. Get room there, and put dirty clothes outside your bungalow's door. I see you there at five o'clock."

He replied, but his words might have been unheard, because she turned from him and hurried back toward her shop, darting around carts and piles of luggage, a blur of pink that held his eye until she vanished into the village.

AFTER EATING LUNCH AND HELPING with the dishes, Suchin and Niran hurried to meet their father on the beach. By the time they arrived, he was already knee-deep in the water, holding Achara as he spoke to Yai. Though he wore only an old pair of shorts, Yai was dressed in loose-fitting pants, a white collared shirt, and a thatch sun hat. Niran pulled off his shirt as Suchin ran into the water, wearing everything but her sandals.

The siblings rushed toward their father, glad that he had taken a break from his work to play with them. Lek barely had time to hand Achara to Yai before his oldest children started splashing him. He fought back, moving toward the open sea, knowing that they would soon jump on him. The deeper water would allow him to lift and throw them while not putting too much pressure on his hip.

Suchin and Niran guessed his intentions and tried to drive him toward shore. Their laughter was nearly incessant as their splashes struck his face and he pretended to choke on the seawater. He stumbled, falling backward, and Suchin pounced on him. She pressed down on his chest, trying to force him underwater. After letting her briefly succeed, he stood up and threw her as far as possible.

Seeing her disappear into the water, Niran came at him. "My turn, my turn!"

Lek picked up his son, grimaced as pain shot through his hip, and then tossed Niran toward his sister. "Off with you!"

"Come here, you big sea slug," Suchin said while splashing him.

"If I'm a big sea slug, then you're a little one."

"But you're slimier. So, so much slimier."

He dived at her, swimming underwater until he was able to pull her legs out from under her. She twisted, falling on top of him, pushing him down. Suddenly both children attacked him and he had to kick away.

A distant figure emerged from amid their bungalows. Lek was glad that Sarai had finished sweeping the floor and had come to join them. They both would work for most of the afternoon, preparing a Christmas feast for their guests and anyone else who might stop by. That morning Lek and Niran had caught several varieties of fish and turned over underwater boulders so that they could spear crabs. Then, as Sarai had given a massage to an Israeli, Lek and his children had gone into the village and bought fresh vegetables and fruit at the market. Though he spent three hundred baht, Lek hoped that they would profit ten times that amount before the evening ended.

Sarai hesitated at the water's edge and Lek waved her forward. "Help!" he shouted. "I need—"

"No, you don't, you slimiest of sea slugs," Suchin interrupted, then laughed as he grabbed her wrists and tickled her.

Niran came swiftly to his sister's aid and tugged on his father's arms. The three of them went down together in a splash.

Fifty feet away, Sarai watched her loved ones play. She waded in up to her hips, holding her shirt out of the water. Though she wanted to join her family, so much work still needed to be done— fresh tapestries placed beneath the beachside tables, the sand raked free of debris, the food prepared. She would have help, of course, but still worried about getting everything finished on time. Based on previous Christmases, she knew that foreigners might show up at any moment expecting a big meal.

Sarai glanced from her restaurant to her family. Shaking her head, she plunged beneath the water, then surfaced and headed toward her mother. After taking Achara and kissing her naked body, Sarai smiled. "Isn't she beautiful?"

Yai lowered herself deeper into the water with a sigh. "Too beautiful to have come from us. There must have been a mix-up at the clinic."

"She was the only baby there. Don't you remember?"

"I remember how you didn't want to share her with me, your own mother."

Sarai grinned, then kissed Achara's ear. "That's true. I don't deny it."

"Suchin is calling for you. I think she needs your help."

"And she'll have it. In a minute." Sarai lowered Achara into the water and began to clean her bottom.

"I already did that," Yai said. "You want to make her rash worse? Please don't take care of me when I'm old. I don't want that kind of help. Just set me adrift."

"It's going to be a good year, isn't it?" Sarai asked.

"Why do you say that?"

"Because we've worked too hard for it to be anything but a good year."

"You deserve a good year."

Lek started to call for Sarai's help. Laughing at her normally quiet husband, she handed Achara back to Yai and hurried into the deeper water. The day was perfect, she reflected, full of sunlight and a gentle breeze. Tourists and Thais swam in the bay. Longboats drifted on tranquil waters. And laughter came to her from a dozen sources.

Her hands soon met with her husband's, but instead of helping him, she held him in place so that Suchin and Niran could do as they pleased. As he called her a traitor and tried to escape, she grinned, then found herself giggling much as her children were. And as they laughed together, she felt the strength of the bond among them, a strength more powerful than steel or stone.

Still smiling, Sarai whispered her thanks, then picked up her son and threw him into the air.

A FEW CLOUDS HAD DRIFTED over the island by the time Brooke and Patch sat down at one of Sarai's beachside tables. The bamboo table, placed on a green tapestry, had a glass top and a centerpiece fashioned out of coral and orchids. Half of the other tables were occupied—two with small groups of tourists and one with a pair of Thais. People snacked on plates of vegetable fried rice, spring rolls, and garlic shrimp. Sweating glasses held watermelon smoothies, Singha beers, Thai whiskey, and various sodas.

Brooke and Patch had ordered two beers and sat at the same side of the table, facing the water. She wore her swimsuit and a full-length yellow cover-up. He was barefoot and dressed in shorts and a T-shirt that he'd bought in Phuket. The shirt was white and featured a faded blue map of Thailand.

Though they sat beside each other, they didn't touch, only their words mingling, their expressions hinting of their connection. An hour earlier, Patch, desperate to hear word from his brother, had gone to an Internet café to check his email. To his delight, a message from Ryan had awaited him, saying that he'd decided to remain on the island for a few more days. He wouldn't return to Rainbow Resort but would stay somewhere else. No reference was made to Brooke other than to say that Ryan would find them the following day, at which point they could discuss when and where Patch would turn himself in.

Patch's relief at hearing from Ryan had washed over him like waves, and he and Brooke had ordered the beers, wished each other a merry Christmas, and made a toast to Dao. Without Dao, they both knew, Ryan would have left.

"What was she like?" Brooke asked, and then sipped her drink.

Patch watched a group of Thai children far down the beach chase a falling kite. "Funny. She seemed really funny. And smart. Pretty, too."

"And you think she likes him?"

"Yeah. Otherwise she never would have left her work. When she came back she kept asking me if anyone had stopped by. She was really nervous."

Brooke nodded. "I'm glad you like her."

"She could be just what he needs. And that makes me really happy."

"But I'm worried about you. I wish you hadn't agreed to turn yourself in. I think our other plan was smarter."

His gaze swung from the kite to her. "I don't want to go to the police. I don't trust them. But I'm doing it for him. Because if I don't do it, he's going to stay mad at me. And that'll mess everything up."

"Define everything."

"My relationship with him. With . . . with you."

"With me?"

"I need him to trust me again. If he trusts me, he'll let me be with you."

"You don't need his permission for anything, Patch."

"I know. But I want his support. It's important to me."

She started to talk him out of his decision but stopped herself. "I want to meet with people. With embassy people. With Thai officials. I'll go with Ryan and we'll make sure that you'll be safe."

"Thanks," Patch replied, knowing that he would never be safe in jail. "But then . . . when you get back to America, I need you to forget about me. At least for a while."

"What? What do you mean?"

He took her hand, moving his thumb back and forth against her palm. "You know I care about you, right?"

"I know."

"I wish . . . I wish we were here in other circumstances. Just the two of us. That would be so amazing. In so many ways."

"How can you say I should forget about you, and then say that? It's a complete contradiction."

"Because I'm going to be gone for a while. Six months. A year. Eighteen months. Who knows? And it will be harder for me in there; my guilt will be even worse if I know that you're waiting

around for me, that my mistakes are making you miss out on opportunities."

She shifted on the tapestry, squinting against the glare of the
sun. "Miss out on opportunities? You think I'm some weak-kneed
girl who won't be able to function without you around? And that
life is just going to pass me by?"

"I don't mean that."

"What do you mean then?"

"It's just that . . . I've already hurt enough people. I hurt my
parents, Ryan, myself. And I don't want to hurt you. I'll do worse,
in jail, if I think I'm hurting you."

She felt his thumb moving against her, which seemed to release her tension. She tried to see things from his perspective and
understood that he was just trying to protect her. Though his
words weren't right, he had her best interests at heart. Watching
his thumb, she thought about kissing him, remembered how his
fingers had briefly explored her body. "What did you feel . . . in
the water?"

"At the boat?"

"After the Jolly Green Giant."

He glanced toward the bay. Some women were lying topless
on the nearby beach, but his gaze didn't linger on them. "I need a
second for that," he replied, looking at Brooke once again. "Because it's hard to explain something . . . that I experienced for the
first time."

"Try."

Still stroking her palm with his thumb, he recalled the sensation of her lips against his, the overwhelming desire to caress every part of her. "When you kissed me," he said quietly, "it felt
more sensual, more exciting than anything I'd ever felt."

"Why?"

"Because there wasn't some sort of gradual buildup. You kissed me, and bam, we were there. Wherever we were going, we'd already arrived. And that place . . . in it . . . all I wanted was you."

A child's shrill laugh interrupted her thoughts. She squeezed his hand, wanting to kiss him again. "You know, that night when you told me that my soul wasn't hurt, that's when you first really touched me, when I first felt intimate with you. Our skin might not have come in contact, but you still touched me, just in a different way. You told me what I'd tried to tell myself. With only me saying it, I could never believe it. But when you said it, it felt true."

"It is true."

She bit her bottom lip, then smiled. "I wish you'd let me help you escape. Ryan doesn't have to get his way. He gets it enough, believe me."

"I know."

"If you escaped, we could see each other in a month or two. Instead of a year or two. Shouldn't that count for something?"

"It does count. But he stayed here because I asked him to, because he loves me, and he thinks he can help me. So I need to stay. If I run now, I'll be turning my back on him. And he's never done that to me."

"Never?"

He nodded. "And I've been thinking about something else."

"What?"

"After I get out of jail, I want to do something good. I want to help people who've made mistakes, who just need a second chance. That's what I've learned from this whole disaster—that sometimes people need a second chance."

"And sometimes people just need a chance. Period. Like Sarai and Lek."

"Actually, I'd like to help them. I told Lek that I'd try to sponsor Suchin and Niran if they wanted to go to college in America."

"That's a wonderful idea."

"I hope it works out."

A breeze brought the smell of burning coconut shells to them. Not far out in the bay, a group of Thai children were having some sort of swimming contest.

Brooke's gaze swung from one end of the beach to the other. "Can you wait another few days to turn yourself in? I just want a little more time."

"With me?"

"With us."

He kissed her palm and rose to his feet. "Come here."

"Come where?"

"I want to show you something." He helped her up and started walking to the water. He headed to the end of the beach, which was dotted with boulders and free of people. "Stand still," he said, lying down on the damp sand and rolling away from her.

"What are you doing?" she asked, laughing.

"Just wait. It's your Christmas present. I don't have any money to buy you one, so I need to make you one."

"What is it?"

He shook his head, stood up, and started walking, dragging his feet across the sand. At first she thought he was making a giant circle around her, but soon the shape became curved and then tapered.

Finally he stopped and smiled. He'd created a heart around

her, a vast heart with her at its center. "That's how I feel," he said. "Now you know exactly how I feel."

DAO WALKED UP THE PATH leading to the Hillside Bungalows, which had been built into the base of the limestone mountain on the southeast side of the island. The bamboo bungalows were perched several hundred feet above the water and provided guests with a breathtaking view of the Andaman Sea. Pleased that most of the bungalows appeared empty, Dao climbed higher, finally spying a pile of clothes outside the topmost dwelling. The sight of the clothes made her trek seem more real, more fateful, and she stopped, uncertain whether she should go up or down. In all likelihood going up would lead to fulfillment and pleasure, but ultimately disappointment. Dao had already once fallen for a tourist—a Swede who loved and left her. And clearly Ryan would leave the island. He would treat her well, smile at her jests, make love to her, and in a few days return to America. Some emails might be sent to her, some pictures perhaps, but at some point he would grow silent.

Her heartbeat quickening, Dao glanced at the clothes again. She wanted to be strong, to resist the temptation above. Certainly her parents would expect such resistance, and she wanted to please them, as well as to protect herself. But she also longed to laugh, to touch, to experience something unique and magical, and to visit a place, a height, that could not be reached alone.

After shaking her head at her indecision, Dao continued upward. She tried to stand tall as she stepped in front of the bunga-

low and knocked on the door. Inside, footsteps sounded, a lock
was unlatched, and the door swung open. Ryan, dressed in shorts
and a blue T-shirt, smiled and said hello. He asked if she'd like to
come in, and she nodded, stepping forward. Inside, the bungalow
was dominated by a double bed, a mosquito net, and the hum of
a ceiling fan.

"Thanks for coming," he said, motioning toward a table in the
corner of the room. Plates and bowls contained fried rice, cubed
watermelon, and two crepes. A pair of tall glasses held bubbling
soda. Toward the center of the table was a lacquered vase containing a single bird-of-paradise. She smiled at the sight of the flower,
then thanked him.

Ryan pulled out a chair for her. "My brother's the romantic.
He'd have the room full of candles and flowers and God knows
what else. Plus I'm sure he'd have music and incense and—"

"Stop," she said, touching his arm. "This . . . it beautiful. It
perfect for me."

"It is? Really?"

"Why I need candles when I can see? Why I need music when
I can hear birds outside? I am hungry. Food is what I want. And
food you have."

"I remembered the crepes. I went back to that same lady."

Dao smiled. "King Kong has a good memory. To find her
again."

"And I have something else. Just one more thing."

"What?"

"Just a little something." He handed her a wooden box the
width of a teacup. "A little Christmas present."

Her smile came again, lingering as she took the gift. She
opened the box, then removed a pair of earrings. Each rectangular

earring was bordered and backed with silver, and featured a jade interior highlighted by a slice of a spiral white shell. Dao bit her bottom lip, stroking an earring, thinking that she'd never owned anything as pretty. "Thank you," she said, looking up. She held the earrings against her chest, as if afraid of letting them go. "They so beautiful. So lovely. Too lovely for me, I think."

"They're perfect for you."

"I . . . I so happy that you find them for me."

"I'm glad. Merry Christmas."

"Thank you."

"You're welcome."

She pulled her old studs out and replaced them with Ryan's gift. Seeing him smile at the sight of her, she stood up, walked into the bathroom, and studied her reflection. The earrings seemed to sparkle, as did her eyes, which glistened with tears. She wiped them away and returned to the table, thanking him once again.

He motioned that she should eat. "The food's still hot. I had to run up and down those steps a few times, but I'm glad. I like it up here."

"These my favorite bungalows on whole island. I can see so far."

"It's a beautiful view. Just perfect, really."

She tasted the fried rice, then ate a cube of watermelon. Her heartbeat still hadn't slowed, and she felt silly sitting at the table, eating, when she wanted to be touching him. "You hungry?"

"A little."

"Come, I give you free massage. Then we eat."

"No, you don't need to—"

"Lie down. On back."

He pulled the mosquito net aside and moved to the bed. She followed him, helping him off with his shirt. Once he was settled on his back, she reached for the bowl of watermelon and returned to him. "Taste this," she said, picking up a cube and raising it to his lips. His mouth opened and she held the fruit so that he could bite it in half. His movements were slow and careful, and despite the swirling fan, sweat began to glisten on his forehead. She wondered if he was as nervous as she was, but then pushed the thought aside. The remainder of the watermelon went into her mouth. It was as cool as shade and as delicious as anything she'd ever tasted. The juice filled her mouth, so sweet and strong. She put her knees on either side of his flat belly, straddling him. Another piece of watermelon was held near his lips. Only this time she squeezed the fruit and let its juices drip to his chin. The world began to speed up, to move with the rise and fall of her chest, and she leaned forward, kissing the wetness on his skin. He tried to embrace her, but she held him still, squeezing the watermelon again, then tasting the drops that had fallen to his neck and shoulder. His skin was firm, smooth, and warm. His breath came and went with increasing quickness. He whispered her name, which made her long to feel more of him, to savor the movement of his skin against hers. Without thought or hesitation, she removed her shirt and let it tumble away. Her bra fell next, and his fingers traced the outlines of her breasts. Though she knew they were small compared to those she saw in American movies, she noticed that his eyes were transfixed by them. She reached for another cube of watermelon, pressing it against her chest and then moving forward on him, lowering herself so that he might taste her. His tongue swept along her collarbone to the base of her neck to her right breast, circling her nipple, coming closer and closer until she felt his mouth on it. Her body shifted against his, arching forward and backward—movement without thought or premeditation.

Her name sounded again on his lips, and he whispered of her beauty. Because she knew that beauty was fleeting and that this moment would be fleeting, his words made her slow down, despite her desire for haste. More fruit was crushed, dripped, and tasted. She covered him with such a rich, delectable sweetness that it didn't leave, no matter how many times she kissed and licked him. Her mouth made love to him, consuming his lips, the lobes of his ears, the length of his fingers. Though she had never before done such things, her movements were fluid and serene. His body had become an extension of her own, to do with as she pleased.

The watermelon lasted until the sun had lost much of its strength. Then he lifted her up, laid her on the bed, and began to move in the way that she wanted him to, as if, despite their different histories, they shared the same mind—a mind full of want and wonder, more focused on the future than on the past.

He became an explorer, delighting in discoveries, treating her body like an unknown country that he alone could search and cherish. And as he cherished her, as he empowered her through his tenderness, she rose higher and higher, moving like the sea beneath him, stirring and trembling and merging into another body that for a moment felt like her own.

SUNDAY, DECEMBER 26

ten ripples and a wave

About eight in the morning, hundreds of miles to the southwest of Ko Phi Phi, the crew of a fishing boat hauled in their net, which had been left in place overnight. Though the men had worked on the water all their lives, and could read its face like those of their children, they were unaware that miles below the sea's surface, something was happening.

A massive tectonic plate, the India Plate, shifted, as it had for millions of years. Only on this occasion, a portion of the India Plate slipped beneath the Burma Plate. The collision of the two tectonic plates created a rupture that released more than twenty thousand times the energy produced by the atomic bomb at Hiroshima. The seafloor above the focal point was suddenly thrust upward by six feet, displacing a colossal amount of water, flipping the fishing boat over like a toy, killing the crew, and creating a series of powerful waves.

As they approached nearby coastlines, the waves gathered

strength in shallow waters, rising as they rolled forth, engulfing landmasses as if islands and coastlines had been dropped, from far above, into the sea.

Though no one knew it, Ko Phi Phi lay in the path of the waves.

In less than two hours, everything would change.

FROM THE LOOKOUT POINT ATOP the island, Ko Phi Phi seemed even quieter than usual. Sailboats were moored offshore and longboats were lined up along each curving beach. The water of both bays was flat and immobile, almost as if a coat of turquoise paint had been applied to some sort of model ocean. The day was remarkably still—a few clouds seemed stuck in the southern sky, the wind asleep.

Brooke and Patch were the only people at the top of the island. Perhaps other travelers were sleeping off their holiday celebrations. Or maybe the looming heat of the day had kept people from making the arduous climb. Whatever the case, Brooke and Patch sat in solitude on a limestone outcropping that marked the highest point on Ko Phi Phi. They held hands but didn't otherwise touch.

Though Brooke was usually comfortable with silence, she had only a few more days with Patch and felt the need to hear his voice, and to tell him what she'd been thinking while he gazed into the horizon. "Last night," she said softly, "I wanted to go to your room. I actually left my bungalow . . . and walked toward yours. But then I stopped."

Patch turned toward her. "You did?"

"Around midnight."

He sighed, studying her face. "I wanted that too. But I'm glad you stopped."

"Why?"

"Because I couldn't be with you . . . like that . . . with Ryan nearby. I don't want to hurt him any more than I already have."

"I hurt him too. That's why I turned around." She rubbed an insect bite on her shin and realized that she hadn't shaved her legs for a few days. To her surprise, she didn't mind if Patch saw her stubble. "If Ryan was back in America, if a few months had passed, what would have happened last night?"

"Something beautiful."

"Tell me."

A long-billed bird with a blue chest and yellow wings landed nearby, hopping closer to them. "I would have tried to give you something . . . an experience you've never had before."

She smiled. "I'm not a virgin, you know."

His face remained serious. "There's more to making love than touching someone."

"So . . . what would you have done?"

"Really? You want to know?"

"I want to know everything."

"Well, I'd have tried to make the night special, so that we would always remember it." He studied her face, his mind replaying a scene that he had imagined over and over. His heartbeat quickened as he wondered whether telling her everything might be too much. "I would have asked Lek to borrow his longboat, and I'd have driven us around the island, to a secret cove I know about. We would have anchored there, shared a swim, another kiss by the boat, and later a bottle of wine. Then I would have lit a hundred candles and put them at the front and back of the boat.

And I would have created a little bed out of tapestries and blan-
kets, and then . . . made love to you like it was the first and last
time that I ever would. Nothing would be rushed. Just savored.
And later we would have blown out the candles and watched the
stars."

Brooke bit her bottom lip, sweat building between their hands.
"You . . . you thought about this already?"

"Last night. I couldn't sleep."

"I want that night."

"I know. Me too."

The bird hopped closer, as if eavesdropping. Brooke shut her
eyes, envisioning the scene that he had described. She longed to
ask him to reconsider his decision to turn himself in. If he was
imprisoned, anything could happen. As likely as not, the night he
had described would never occur.

But needing to honor his wishes, she stilled her desires and
reached into a nearby backpack, removing an envelope. "Yesterday, when you were with the children in the tree house, I went
shopping for you."

"For me?"

"I wanted to get you something that would help you, and that
would remind you of me. It's not really a Christmas present, but
more of a . . . token." She handed him her gift. "I'm not through
helping you, but this is a start."

Patch thanked her and carefully opened the envelope. Inside
was a small glass vial. He raised it to the light, his eyebrows coming
together as he tried to discern what was sparkling inside the glass.

"They're little diamonds," Brooke said. "Ten of them. I bought
them at that jewelry store in the village."

"Why?"

"When the time comes you can sneak them into jail, maybe by carrying them in the corner of your mouth. Then, if you need to, you can bribe a guard, another prisoner, someone who can keep you safe."

"I—"

"And whatever ones you don't give away, you can keep. And you can look at them, and remember that night we had, under those stars. That night when you told me that I was still whole."

"I don't know what to say."

"Don't say anything. You don't need to. I just want you to be safe. And I think . . . I think these little diamonds will help."

He saw tears forming in her eyes and leaned forward, kissing her. "How is it . . . that I just met you . . . but that I want you so much?" he whispered. "I didn't know it was possible . . . to feel like that."

"Neither did I."

"I think I'm falling in love with you, even though I hardly know you. Am I crazy? Am I so worried about jail that I'm just . . . reaching for something?"

She kissed his lips, his cheek, his forehead. "You tell me."

"I'm not reaching," he replied, then shook his head. "Just falling. Falling toward something beautiful."

"Whatever you're doing, don't stop. Just keep doing it."

"I will."

Hearing the emotion in his voice, and then asking herself how scared he was to go to prison, she put her hands behind his head and ran her fingers through his hair. "I'll help you," she whispered. "The diamonds are only a beginning. I'll help you get through this. And you will. You'll persevere. And then . . . we'll meet and whatever we want to do, we'll do."

"All I want is the chance to be with you."

"Good. You think about that . . . when you're in there. You think about me waiting. That'll keep you strong. And you'll need to be strong. Strong and resolute."

His lips touched hers, so gently that she wondered whether he was actually kissing her or she was just imagining it. And so she kissed him harder, needing to feel his presence, to know that he was real. He responded in kind, moving faster, with urgency, not stopping until the glass vial fell from his grip. It shattered, sending the diamonds tumbling onto the limestone.

Nearly breathless from a multitude of desires, they drew apart, cleaned up the glass, collected all of the glittering stones, and then walked, hand in hand, back toward the beach.

⁂

SARAI LOOKED FROM SUCHIN TO Niran. "Patch has to leave us," she said softly, reaching for their hands, unaware of the other people on the pier. "He loves you both, but he has to leave us."

Suchin shook her head, her mouth opening and shutting as if she were a fish out of water. "Why . . . why would he leave?"

"He doesn't want to. But he has to. His family needs him back in America."

"But we need him too."

Squeezing her daughter's hand, Sarai glanced at Lek, wondering where his thoughts had taken him. The four of them stood at the end of the pier. A ship carrying supplies had just docked, and Lek held the handle of a cart, which would soon be filled with crates of beer, bottled water, and soda. "You'll see him again," Lek said. "Someday, you might even see him in America."

"That's if you work hard," Sarai added. "If you study hard, anything is possible."

Niran released his mother's hand. "But he just finished the tree house. And now he won't even get to play in it."

Men started to carry supplies off the ship, loading nearby carts with electronic goods, building materials, medicine, foodstuffs, and mattresses. Sarai dropped to her knees so that she was eye to eye with her children. "There are some people, Niran, who will come into our lives, and who we will never see again. And there are some people who we will meet, leave, and then who will come back to us, time and time again. I think Patch is one of those people. I think you'll see him again. You'll play with him again."

Suchin saw that Niran was trying not to cry. As her mother rubbed Niran's back, Suchin turned to her father. "But Patch helps you. He does so much. And if he goes, who will lift the heavy things? Who will climb up and fix the leaky roofs?"

"You will," Sarai answered. "You and Niran will help your father, just as I will. The four of us can do anything we want. That's what families do—they help each other. And that's what makes them so strong. And that's why, in a few minutes, when they've loaded our cart, we'll push it back home together. Your father can't push it by himself. But when we work together, it will be easy."

Lek nodded. "Your mother's right. She's always right."

"Of course I am," Sarai replied, longing to see smiles alight on her children's faces. "Did your father marry me for my money? No, of course not. For my looks? No, he's not blind. So, he must have married me for my brain. And my brain tells me that everything will be fine, that if we always work together, we won't need the help of anyone else."

Though Suchin nodded, Niran appeared unconvinced. "But Patch was going to build me a stone pit. For my hermit crabs. We were going to do it together."

"You were?" Lek asked.

"Right over by the tree house."

Lek reached into his pocket and removed two pieces of hard candy. He gave one to each of his children. "I can build that pit. We can build it together."

"You won't have time."

"Look," Sarai said, pointing. "They've almost filled our cart. We need to pay them; then we'll push it home. While your father and I unload it, you two can swim. Then we'll make your pit, Niran. We'll make such a great hermit crab pit. It will be deep and wide, and if Suchin gets too feisty, you can stick her down there too."

Niran smiled, then picked at a scab on his elbow. "She's always feisty."

"You'd be feisty too if you had a little brother," Suchin replied.

"No, I wouldn't."

"Yes, you would."

A pair of men finished loading the cart. Sarai double-checked the inventory, then handed one man a roll of bills. A few months earlier, he had tried to raise the price of his delivery, but Sarai had refused him and started walking toward one of his competitors. Since then, their arrangement had been unchanged, though occasionally Sarai sent him back with a bag full of hot food.

Satisfied that the correct items were on the cart, Sarai once again turned to her children. "Are you ready to push?"

Niran thought about Patch, and felt sad that he would be leaving soon. Patch had always been eager to talk about fish, to play a game of soccer. The thought of Patch leaving seemed to create a dampness within Niran, as if a fog had settled inside him. But when his parents and sister placed their hands on the cart, he did the same. The cart began to roll down the pier, slowly at first, but soon gaining momentum. As Suchin started to tell their parents about a story she was writing at school, Niran put all his weight against the cart, wanting his muscles to grow, knowing that without Patch, he would have to help his father even more. Though Niran often pretended not to hear his parents' whispered concerns about money, he understood the obstacles they faced. So did Suchin.

Grunting, Niran pushed harder, thinking about how Patch had become the big brother he'd always wanted. "I'll miss you," Niran whispered, glad that he looked at the ground, that no one could see how his eyes glistened. When a tear fell, he wiped it away and continued to push, his legs and arms tired, but his determination stronger than ever.

"IF YOU HAVE TO WORK, of course I'm going to be your customer," Ryan said as he stepped into the massage parlor. "But you don't need to do anything to me. I'll just lie down and you can pretend to work."

She shut the door behind him and smiled. "But then I no get tip."

"Oh, I'll give you a tip. Tonight."

"You naughty, King Kong," she replied, slapping his shoulder. "Why you want to be so naughty?" She watched as he undressed and put on the thin shorts that she had handed him. "Your muscles look tired. You get too much exercise last night?"

"You wore me out."

"What you talking about? I only visit your room, say hi. Maybe you drinking beer before I come. Maybe you drunk and remember something that never happen."

He let her lead him to the massage table. "In that case, will you say hi again tonight? I'll get some more watermelon."

"Ah, watermelon is my favorite. Yes, please get more. So much more." She poured oil on her hands and started to rub his back.

"Wait," he said, stiffening. "You don't need to do that. I don't want you to work."

"I happy to work."

"I know. But I won't be happy if you work. At least not now. And if you work, you won't get that big tip."

Dao stopped pressing against the edges of his shoulder blades but held her hands against him, just in case someone stepped into the room. As she studied the width of his shoulders, she remembered how the watermelon juice had run down his spine, gathering near his tailbone. She'd tasted so many parts of him, the juice a constant presence during their lovemaking. The thought of repeating that experience was almost as arousing as the experience itself. Parts of her tingled. The room seemed to sway from side to side.

"Tell me your life's dream," she said, needing to talk. "That way, I see if my dream the same. And I can decide if I keep you."

He laughed, and then reached back and felt her leg. "I want to build something."

"What?"

"Two things, really."

"I waiting. Sure, sure I am."

"I want to build a company first. Then a family."

She started to rub his back, wanting to please him. "What kind of company? What kind of family?"

"I don't know about the company. The family . . . maybe a big one."

"If you want me, you better want big family," she replied, allowing herself to dream, just for the moment. "I not need big house, but I need big family."

"How big?"

"Three girls and three boys."

He turned over, reaching for her. "Seriously? You're so precise."

"Stop that. Customer cannot touch me." She slapped his hand away. "Never, never, never."

"You're sure sassy today."

Her laughter seemed to echo in the small room. "I be more sassy, King Kong, if you not stay still. Now tell me, what you want in wife? Big boobs? Tall and blond?"

"Dark haired and small. Someone . . . kind of like you."

"But you so big. I think you need big woman."

"Why would I need a big woman?"

Dao rubbed him harder, trying to maintain the fantasy that he would fall for her, trying and failing. "I think you need strong, smart American woman. She can help you with your company, your family. Yes, you should find woman like that. Then both your dreams come true."

Ryan saw that her smile had fled. He sat up, putting his hands on her hips and squeezing. "Let's stop talking about tomorrow."

"Why stop?"

"Because it's today. And everything about today is good."

"I not—"

"I'm lucky to have found you. Do you understand that? I was

ready to leave, but now I'm so glad I didn't. And that's because of you."

"But soon you must—"

"Dao, I'm here now. I want to be here. With you. Not with anyone else. You're just as strong and smart as anyone I know, and you won't ever hear me say differently. So let's just enjoy today."

She pushed him down, helped him turn over, and started to rub his back again. "I see you tonight, after work?"

"Yeah. Come back up. And tonight will be just like last night. Only this time . . . I'll have a surprise waiting for you. Something fun."

"What surprise?"

"It won't be a surprise, silly, if I tell you."

She slapped his hip, smiling once again, her fingers tracing the contours of his body. After glancing at the door, she bent lower, unable to resist giving his back a quick kiss. She then stood straight, her fingers still moving, her voice teasing and tantalizing him, hinting of what the early evening would surely bring.

THOUGH MIDMORNING HADN'T YET ARRIVED, the beach in front of Rainbow Resort was occupied by Thais and tourists. The sky was almost free of clouds, and since it was a Sunday, more locals were present than was usual. Sarai and Lek walked the beach, picking up plastic bags and other debris that the high tide had carried in. Yai sat in the shallows, Achara in her arms, both wearing sun hats. A soccer game unfolded near the water—Patch, Brooke, Suchin, and Niran matched against six other children. As Sarai and Lek worked, they often smiled at the laughter emanat-

ing from the game. Niran was doing better than usual. He'd
scored a goal and twice stopped the other team from doing the
same. Suchin soared around the opposing players, leaping nimbly
over outstretched legs, her mouth moving as fast as her feet. She
continuously told Patch, Brooke, and Niran where to go, giggling
when they were tripped up or missed an easy shot.

When the ball was sent careening toward the sea, a strange
thing started to happen. The water began to pull away from the
beach, as if frightened of the approaching children. The shoreline
was suddenly exposed, and yet the water continued to retreat,
revealing a massive expanse of wet sand. Niran had never seen
such a sight, and rushed forward, eager to find creatures that must
have been exposed. Suchin and Patch followed him. Yai held
Achara and was struggling to stand up. Sensing the older woman's
distress, Brooke hurried to help her. Somewhere a dog barked.

The wave that followed wasn't a wave really, but more of a
massive surge. The ocean seemed to rise up and rush at them,
engulfing the sand it had just revealed, roaring so loud that it
sounded as if a plane were taking off. Patch saw the water coming
and grabbed Niran and Suchin, shouting at Brooke as his feet
were swept out from under him. He tried to keep the children
above the surface, but everything went dark as he tumbled inland,
somehow still holding the two wrists, resisting the urge to let go
of them so that he might try to breathe. His feet struck something
solid, he saw light, and he desperately pushed up, dragging the
children with him. They broke the surface as one, drew a breath,
heard screams and crashing, and were yanked under again. The
water took them where it wanted—inland at first, toward Rainbow Resort. The bungalows that Patch and Lek had worked so
hard to repair were swept away like leaves blown by a storm. Peo-

ple shrieked, struggled, and disappeared. Longboats were thrust forward like spears, smashing through walls and trees.

Something hammered into Patch's side, the pain instant and overwhelming. As his mind threatened to go black, he concentrated on one thing—holding on to Niran and Suchin, keeping them alive when so many things around them were dying.

BROOKE HAD SEEN PATCH AND the children get swept away. She'd had time to grab Achara and run toward shore but hadn't gotten far enough, making it only to the bungalows when the water caught her. She screamed as what seemed to be an angry river, full of currents and white water, swept her up. Somehow Yai tumbled past them, disappearing and reappearing like a bobber pulled down by a fish. The strength of the wave was something that Brooke couldn't fathom. Compared to its fury, she was a grain of sand. A tremendous force hurled her forward, along with longboats, beach chairs, umbrellas, and people. She gasped, trying to hold Achara out of the water. Brooke's right leg became tangled in some debris, and she was dragged under. Shrieks went silent. Light was suffocated. A primeval instinct gave her an almost inhuman strength, and she kicked ferociously at whatever held her. A few seconds later her leg was freed and she shot to the surface. Achara was gagging but was alive and seemed uninjured. A coconut tree appeared, and as they continued to be swept ahead Brooke reached for it. The current threw her straight into the tree, however, and her outstretched hand was bent backward. She grunted in agony, slamming into the trunk, unable to hold on to it with her injured hand and spinning away. A mattress became trapped against the tree, creating a dam of sorts. Brooke heard someone scream Achara's name. Then the water rose over the mattress, tilting the tree, bringing it down. Brooke dived underwater as fronds flailed about her. Something struck her shoulder, separating her fingers from the baby. She shrieked, diving for Achara as the water tossed her about. The two went under together, and came up together.

Brooke tried to swim, but one arm was aching, and with the other she held Achara. In the distance she saw a building topple as if it were made of straw. A yacht floated past her, plowing into a half-submerged restaurant. A Thai man looked at her, their eyes met, a connection was made, and he disappeared beneath the dark water. Achara was screaming, muddy bits of debris speckling her face. Instinctively, Brooke kissed Achara's forehead, weeping now, her strength fading. She tried to kick, but her legs were bruised and bloody. She went under again, fought against the blackness, fought as she had never fought, and rose into the light.

Then a miracle happened. A hand reached for her.

Yai had managed to make it to the ladder leading to Patch's tree house and held on to the top rung, water swirling about her knees. Brooke tried to seize Yai's outstretched hand but missed, then screamed as Yai grabbed her hair and pulled her toward the ladder. The Thai's strength, for that instant, rivaled the fury of the tsunami, for despite the immense pressure of the swirling water, Yai dragged Brooke to the ladder. Yai snatched Achara, set her on the plywood platform, and then pulled Brooke to safety.

As Yai picked up Achara again, cradling her and weeping, Brooke fell to her hands and knees, retching. The swirling, raging water was only a few feet below them, and clearly rising. A man floated past, his eyes lifeless, his body stripped of its clothes.

Brooke moaned, then began to shout, calling out to Patch as Yai screamed for her loved ones.

Though it seemed impossible, the water came harder, thrusting against the tree, threatening to topple it, to burst their eardrums. Brooke turned to Yai, and the two women embraced, Achara pressed tight between them. They continued to hold each other as the island seemed to sink beneath the dirty, furious water. A bicycle struck the tree, became trapped, and was bent as if it were made of rubber. A face appeared, and Brooke dropped to her knees, her fingers finding those of a stranger. A tug-of-war ensued between Brooke's clasp and the water's push, and though a muscle pulled in her back, and the stranger's fingernails peeled away her flesh, Brooke lost the battle. The stranger disappeared. Screaming, Brooke looked for other faces but saw none.

In the distance, an overturned fishing boat tumbled in their direction, gaining speed, crushing everything in its path.

RYAN HEARD THE WATER BEFORE he saw it—a rumbling, grinding rage that sounded like an old building being brought down by explosives. He heard the screams next—shrieks of terror, pain, and confusion. Turning on his side, he had time only to realize that Dao was no longer rubbing his back. Instead, she had paused to look at him, her mouth open, but still. He leaped to his feet. "What the hell?"

A heartbeat later, the sea assaulted the massage parlor, spewing up through the wooden floor as if the room were being forced down into the froth by a giant's hand. Water shot up like miniature geysers between the gaps in the floorboards. It then raged inward through the windows, rising with each second from Ryan's ankles to his knees to his thighs.

Instinctively, he threw himself against the bungalow's door. The sea mirrored his action from the opposite side, though, crushing the door as if it were a battering ram—ripping off its hinges, hurling it inward against him. He tasted salt and blood. Dao screamed as she was lifted and then compressed against the roof. Suddenly they were underwater. As the sea stung his eyes Ryan tore at the thatched roof. He slammed his head against it. He bit it, ripped it, and kicked it. Though the hole he opened was no bigger than a toilet seat, it was big enough. The sea shoved them through it, and suddenly they were on the surface, being driven inland by a mass of water that seemed infinitely powerful and irresistible.

"Dao!" he screamed, kicking toward her, pulling her close. She clung to him, wiping blood from a gash above her eye, struggling to stay afloat. She tried to speak but no words came out.

The sea spewed forth, collapsing bungalows, toppling buildings, pulverizing everything in its path. A man clinging to a palm tree wailed as an overturned boat plowed into the tree, severing his hands from his arms. He shrieked again and disappeared. In his wake swirled bodies—those of cats and children. The bodies were torn and incomplete.

Something snagged on Ryan's shorts, and he was yanked underwater. In the blackness objects battered him, striking his head, ankles, and groin. He managed to get out of his shorts and, following bubbles upward, swam. Dao shouted when she saw him, and they were together again. Their fingers met and clutched.

Ryan was astounded by the speed with which they were pulled—at least as fast as a passenger train. Another boat tumbled past, punching a hole in an Internet café. Next a hotel disintegrated, its balcony falling atop a man clinging to a floating door. A woman wailed as she saw him die. She dived after him and was swallowed by the hotel. People on the upper level screamed as the building collapsed. They jumped from windows. They ran inside. Clinging together, they disappeared as the hotel and the sea consumed them.

A mound of steel and concrete remained slightly higher than the water. A Thai man swam frantically toward this island, only to be impaled upon the rubble. Ryan shouted at Dao to swim away from it, and she did, wincing as her feet struck debris. The brown water, laden with filth, choked her, and she spit and struggled.

A fishing net filled with thrashing creatures entangled the pair, and they went under for a few heartbeats. A dead shark hammered into Ryan's side as he desperately held his breath. Kicking upward, they emerged from the net, their bodies now bloodied in a dozen places.

Dao was weakening, angry welts all over her body. Her left arm hung useless, and Ryan feared it was broken. He shouted at her to fight, to clear her mind of anything except the need to survive. But to his dismay, she didn't seem to hear him, not even when he pressed his lips against her ear.

A life-size wooden Buddha floated by, and Ryan grabbed its torso with one arm and Dao with the other. They were moving slower now. For an instant the water ceased to flow. Then they were dragged backward, out toward the sea. Something ripped into Ryan's thigh, and he shrieked in pain.

As Ryan and Dao were pulled toward the deep, he struggled to keep her alive. He tried to do so many things—to hold her afloat, to kick toward a distant palm tree, to maintain his grip on the Buddha. The thought of losing Dao provoked a fear within him that made it difficult for him to breathe. His world seemed to spin, and he panicked, clutching her against him so hard that his fingernails made her bleed.

Again something struck his legs, raking them like an ancient weapon of steel. The pain was overwhelming. He screamed. He screamed again and again, and this newfound despair gave him the strength to lift Dao higher out of the water. She was barely conscious, and a large contusion dominated one side of her head. He begged her to stay awake, salt from the sea clouding his vision. Dao suddenly seemed to recognize his voice, and her lips formed into a fleeting smile.

Ryan prayed as he kicked toward a palm tree, kicked with his pulverized and aching feet. He prayed to God, to the Buddha he grasped, to anyone or anything listening. He cried as he prayed, four or five lifeless bodies swirling about him like flotsam in a river.

"Please . . . no leave me," Dao whispered through bleeding lips.

He pulled her closer and kicked harder, groaning when they became snagged on the outrigging of a half-sunken fishing boat. His body was caught within ropes and cables, as was Dao's. The sea continued to withdraw, and the pressure against them was enormous, unbearable, in fact. Debris jammed against them, striking their legs, slashing their faces. With a supreme effort, Ryan moved to his right, lifted Dao out of the water, and set her on top of the wheelhouse. The steel roof was secure, and the fishing boat was large, heavy, and seemingly immobile—wedged within a cluster of stout trees.

"You're safe," he said, feeling cold.

"Climb up here!"

He shook his head as the current pulled on him. "My brother. I have to find my brother."

"No!"

"I have to."

"Please stay," she said, and reached for him.

He kissed her hand. "Be happy. Always be happy."

"Please!"

His lips pressed against her skin again. "Thank you."

"Why? Why you thank me?" she asked, weeping.

"Because I know . . . I know you would have loved me." He turned then, leaving her, letting the current pull him toward the other side of the island, where he knew Patch would be. Though the water was red near him, red from his blood, he swam as hard and fast as possible, the bond he shared with his brother giving him a strength he had never known, a ferocity he hadn't dreamed possible.

The water tried to suck him down, to sever that bond, but he screamed and swam on, heedless of the dangers around him, of how the cold was spreading deeper into his limbs.

✎

SARAI HAD ALWAYS TRIED TO control her world, working hard to ensure that everything was as it should be. But now, as she struggled for her life, she felt so very small. She and Lek had been swept inland, like everything else, but had managed to grab onto a wooden sign that had once pointed tourists toward a pastry shop. The thick sign was five feet long and a foot wide, and was buoyant enough to keep them afloat. Resting their upper bodies on it, they kicked hard, trying to head back toward Rainbow Resort. Though they could have reached safe havens on several occasions, once they determined that none of their loved ones was amid groups of survivors, they continued to search.

Even as she bled and suffered, Sarai focused only on her children, constantly looking for them. No thought or action was for herself. She had seen Patch grab Suchin and Niran, and then the water had consumed them—just as it had swallowed up Yai, Achara, and the American woman. Her tears incessant, Sarai begged Buddha to give strength to her family and to those who were helping them. She had been tempted to leave the board, to try to swim toward their resort, but no one could fight against such currents. To swim meant death, and dying would not help her loved ones.

She beat her fist against the board, beat it until Lek stopped her. "You're going to hurt yourself!" he shouted, kicking so hard that he seemed to have the hip of a twenty-year-old. "Stop, Sarai! Stop doing that!"

"Where are they? Where . . . where have they gone?"

A woman's body floated past. To their right, a complex of new bungalows disintegrated, glass shattering, roofs collapsing. Screams came from inside one of the structures, which were simply lifted up and pulverized into shards by the sea. The screams were vanquished, though in the distance, other shouts and cries pierced the constant tumult created by the raging water.

Sarai's sarong caught on something, and she was dragged down. She kicked, her feet seeming to strike nails, and Lek pulled her up, his face contorted. The sarong ripped and disappeared. Suddenly she was free, though her feet hurt so badly that she could hardly kick. Thinking of her children enduring such pain, she began to beat the board again, wanting to take their suffering and make it her own.

Lek stilled her once more, assuring her that they were alive.

"How do you know?" she asked. "How, how, how?"

"I'm not—"

"Tell me!"

Her eyes seemed crazed, and he nodded. "Patch grabbed them. And Achara . . . the American woman—"

"The wave took them all! They disappeared!"

"Look," Lek said, pointing to a boy who had climbed a coconut tree. "People live."

"And people die!"

Lek, barely able to see, wiped tears and grit from his eyes. "We should have . . . sent Patch away weeks ago."

"So?"

"Why did we keep him with us?"

"To help! For selfish, disgusting reasons."

He shook his head. "No. He was meant to be here today. That's why . . . that's why, my love, I think they all live."

She put her head against his shoulder and started to sob, praying as she had never prayed, beseeching Buddha to let her husband be right.

As if her plea were answered, a longboat appeared ahead, vacant and seemingly undamaged. "There!" she shouted, kicking furiously as the water swirled around her, pulling her down. She wasn't afraid of death, but she wouldn't die now, with her children still out there. And so she called upon the last reserves of her strength and will, refusing to submit even as people around her were sucked under, even as the strongest and stoutest finally surrendered, disappearing beneath the sea that had always comforted them.

CLINGING TO A VOLLEYBALL-SIZE YELLOW buoy that might have been from a crab trap and that couldn't quite save them from sinking, Patch struggled to keep Niran and Suchin alive. Though both children were unhurt except for a variety of scratches and shallow cuts, they appeared to be in shock. Suchin's teeth chattered and her eyes were blank and unfocused. Niran tried to swim but seemed to have forgotten how. And while Patch's mind still sped and schemed, his body, which hung down into the debris-filled water, was bruised and bloody. The initial impact of the wave had twisted his right knee, and that leg now throbbed and was nearly useless. He could kick with his other leg, but his hands gripped the children and the buoy, and keeping everyone above the surface was becoming increasingly difficult.

The sea was now withdrawing from the island, sucking boats and trees and buildings back toward the bay. Here and there survivors gathered on the roofs of half-demolished buildings or concrete hotels. Though these people called out to him, Patch didn't expend his energy shouting for their aid, as there was nothing they could do. Instead he tried to comfort the children, humming to them, kissing their foreheads, and even joking on occasion.

Though he pretended otherwise, he was gripped by despair. Oil and gasoline coated patches of the surface, and his eyes stung from the chemicals. He'd swallowed so much filthy water that he felt nauseated. He tried not to panic, but his breathing was becoming ragged, and the world started to spin. The water seemed to be moving faster, pulling back, as if the island were a submarine breaching the surface. Objects too small or waterlogged to be of use swirled around them. Patch sought to shield the children with his own body, grunting as coconuts thudded into him. Suchin tried to climb out of the water onto Patch, and he was pushed under, debris striking his face and neck. With an almost superhuman strength, he kicked to the surface, shouting at her to be still and to pray.

With a free arm, he told himself, he could save one child. Letting one die would likely allow the other to live. A free arm would allow him to swim to a tree, to grab hold of something before they were swept into the bay. He wept as he wondered which child to release, which child to save and which to let die. Suchin was so happy, and that happiness shouldn't be extinguished. But Niran was bright and eager, and his love of science would surely lead to good things.

Patch swore at himself, cursing his weakness. He kissed each child again, deciding that all three of them would live or all three of them would die. A middle ground couldn't exist, as much as the practicality of that decision made sense on some level. No, Suchin and Niran would live or die together, and he would share their fate.

The last of the coconut trees was suddenly behind them, and Patch knew that they were being swept out to sea. Two hundred yards to his right, a large sailboat careened into several overturned longboats, sinking them. Life jackets surfaced but were too far away. People clinging to debris screamed for help that wasn't coming. Though plenty of boats were still afloat, they were vacant and headed toward deeper water.

"Your clothes . . . are too heavy," Patch whispered, struggling to stay afloat, weakening with every passing moment. "Take them off." As the children did as he asked, he looked skyward, wondering how he might comfort them if death finally came. "You have . . . you have to try . . . to kick," he added. "You have to . . . help me."

"Don't . . . please don't let us die," Suchin said, still shivering.

"That won't happen."

"Please, Patch. Please. We don't want to die!"

He started to reply, but something bumped into his injured leg, prompting him to groan. Dimly, he wondered what had happened. One moment they had been on the beach, the water had receded, and the wave had come. Where's Ryan? he asked himself, panicking once again, kicking harder. He looked around, calling out his brother's name, crushed by the thought of their fight, that it might prove to be their last moment together. If anyone could survive the calamity, Ryan could. Patch didn't fear for his brother's death, but for their looming separation, because with each passing moment, Patch grew more certain that he would soon die. His life would last ten or fifteen more minutes. And then it would be over, all his dreams and joys gone forever.

"I love you, Suchin," he said, tears cleaning his filthy face. "And I love you, Niran. You're my sister and my brother."

They answered and he kissed them, hugging them tight, protecting them from the unseen, from the weight of their own bodies. He couldn't imagine the world without them in it, and this thought was almost magical, for it gave him strength when it seemed he had none left. He kissed them again, making promises he could not keep, tricking them with smiles and with words.

But the sea could not be tricked or beaten, despite his resolve. It continued to pull them out, dragging them from the bay and into deep water. Patch looked for something to grasp, for a gift from the heavens, but no such lifeline existed.

Wanting to give the children a few minutes of solace and hope before his strength gave out, Patch began to tell them a story. Reaching inward, gathering what remained of his will, he whispered a tale about an American man, about how that man had come to a small island in Thailand where he met two children, a brother and sister who made him laugh so many times, who made him feel happy and loved. The three of them went for a swim one day, a swim way out into the ocean. They swam so hard, so far. Finally, when they could swim no farther, when they were so tired that they couldn't raise a finger, a whale surfaced beneath them. And the whale lifted them up into the air, into a world where they could once again run and play and be free.

AMID DISTANT SCREAMS AND CRASHES, Ryan thought he heard music, which seemed to drift down from above—a woman's voice, rising and falling, accompanied by violins. Ryan had listened to thousands of musicians create wonder with their voices, with the keys of a piano, but he had never heard such beauty as he did now. The woman sang in a language that was foreign to him, yet her words seemed directed at him. He saw her in a dark room, her lips red, her long hair pulled back. Surrounding her were musicians holding stringed instruments, everyone moving so gracefully, as if each arm and wrist were a snowflake, blown by a gentle wind, sent toward an unknown destination.

Supported by the life jacket he'd found, Ryan let the current pull him toward the bay. Though his blood, his warmth, continued to leak into the sea, the music comforted him. It seemed to come from the deeper water, and he followed it, believing he was being led toward Patch. His body, so cut and bruised and beaten, drew strength from the woman's voice, and from his own will. He pushed himself harder than he ever had, his arms and legs propelling him farther away from land, from safety. On several occasions he could have swum to a tree or a surviving building. But somehow he knew that Patch needed him. The woman seemed to sing of this need, her voice haunting and compelling. Ryan saw people clutching at debris, and bodies tumbling in the water, and he wondered whether they could hear the woman too.

He whispered his brother's name, shuddering, weeping as he kicked out into the maelstrom that had once been the tranquil bay. A handful of people called to him as they stood on the bottom of an overturned ferry. One of the men threw a rope in his direction, which Ryan ignored. The woman was still singing, her voice like a beacon from afar.

Something crushed against his injured leg and he groaned in pain. The world around him went black and then slowly re-emerged, colors and sights forming like the first dream of the night. He lifted up his leg and saw a deep, frightful slash in his thigh. Ripping a strap from the life jacket, he tied a tourniquet above the wound, pulling it as tight as possible.

The water was swirling ahead, and suddenly Ryan was sucked under. Blackness engulfed him once again. For a moment, he let himself be pulled deeper. The woman still sang beneath the waves, and under the surface he didn't seem to be as cold. But then he thought about Patch, about raking a massive pile of leaves together and jumping into those leaves. He kicked upward, memories flooding into him. He saw them playing in their parents' station wagon, saw them running through the rain. And as he broke the surface, gasping for breath, he called out for his brother, called out until his throat hurt almost as much as his leg.

More memories came to him then, as he swam as he never had, again following the voice, which carried him forward, through the footsteps of his life. He saw his mother as she painted Easter eggs, his father as he showed his sons how to build a campfire. His parents laughed; they smiled from distant places. They lived. Patch came next, and as Ryan swam and wept, he remembered how Patch had always wanted to play with him, regardless of what he'd been doing. They'd raced on their bicycles, hunted for crayfish at the creek, whispered about sports after the lights had gone out.

Another twisting eddy pulled Ryan under, and again he was tempted to let the water win. If the woman had stopped singing, he would have given up, but her voice didn't disappear, and so he fought the currents with all of his strength, his endless runs and workouts letting his muscles do what his mind commanded—wrench him free of the blackness.

The sun was out, shining powerfully upon him. He'd never seen such light.

"Where . . . where is he?" Ryan stammered. "Please . . . oh, please tell me where he is."

A plane passed above Ryan. And though the woman still sang and his mind swirled, he realized that if he'd left earlier, he might well be on that plane. He might be safe. But then Dao would have died. The wave would have extinguished the light of her life and she would have never experienced the happiness that he was certain she'd know someday. She would never have had the three daughters and three sons she wanted, nor rejoiced in all the laughter that was destined to spring from her lips. She would have died alone and afraid, and so he didn't regret staying on the island, didn't regret the numbness in his leg.

An arm waved from far out to sea. Shivering, Ryan called for Patch, called again and again and again. The arm disappeared, but the woman continued to sing. Sure that his brother still lived, Ryan followed the voice, not believing that it came solely from God or from some sort of divine intervention, but that now, as his life bled into the sea, the bond between him and Patch was stronger than ever, and that his little brother needed him, that Ryan had been summoned to Thailand not to save Patch from the police, but to save him as he had saved Dao.

Though the world was still angry—swirling and killing—to Ryan it made sense. He had been brought here to save his little brother. That was why he had always loved to run, to channel his will into movement and muscle. Though he had never known it, his whole life had been about preparing for this one moment— this one chance to save Patch. Because if only one of them could live, surely it had to be Patch, who had always been weaker but better, who had always given, not wanted.

Ryan knew that the voice marked the start of his own journey, that the voice would lead him to Patch, and then toward a world where he would always be able to run, where his feet would never grow tired and aching, where light would always be on his back. He knew why he had come to the island. He knew what he had to do.

~ຼ

Despite the withdrawal of the initial wave, the situation had worsened at the tree house. A stronger and higher wave had come from the other side of the island, reaching almost twenty feet tall and sweeping over Ko Phi Phi like a swollen river toppling a dam. The weight and fury of this water thrust buildings and trees and people back toward Rainbow Resort. Brooke and Yai watched in horror as the water climbed higher and higher, surpassing the top of the ladder, then swirling about their ankles, then their thighs. And still it climbed, creating a crest of white water around the platform and railings that Patch had nailed to the sturdy tree, boards that he'd fastened securely, but that weren't meant to resist an almost incomprehensible amount of power.

The torrent of water had forced Brooke and Yai to the edge of the plywood, where they leaned against a bent railing and clung to the tree's main trunk. Though they wanted to climb up, the trunk was slippery and to fall would mean death. And so they stood, fighting to not get swept to the sea, Achara held tight in Brooke's arms. Yai put her body between the American's and the current, trying to protect her granddaughter, knowing that she would be safer in Brooke's grasp than in her own. Yai didn't think about her other loved ones. In her mind, they had to be alive. She wouldn't have the strength to save Achara if she believed her loved ones were dead. And so they lived. Patch had saved Suchin and Niran. And Sarai and Lek were standing on top of a hotel, sending help their way.

The filthy water climbed higher, reaching Yai's waist, roaring in her ears. With each inch that it rose, there seemed to be another set of hands pushing against her. Yai screamed as Brooke slipped, unable to cling to the trunk with Achara in her arms. Dropping deeper into the water, Yai pulled up Brooke and didn't stop pulling even when something popped in her shoulder. "You climb!" she shouted, knowing that Brooke had to carry Achara higher or she would die. "You climb now!"

Brooke eyed the thick trunk, which glistened with water and was almost free of smaller limbs. She also realized that they couldn't remain on the plywood platform much longer. Soon they would be swept off, and when that happened, the end would come quickly. But climbing the trunk looked impossible. She'd have to shimmy upward, dragging herself higher until she reached a trio of wrist-thick limbs about six feet above her. Still, she had no choice. She could try to climb or she and Achara would die.

"Hold her," Brooke said, handing Achara over to Yai. Then she wrapped her legs around the trunk, clutched at irregularities in the wood, and pulled herself up. Twigs left gashes on her thighs, but she continued to climb.

"Hurry!" Yai shouted. "Hurry, hurry, hurry!"

Brooke tried to reach for a stout branch but felt herself sliding down. She wrapped her arms around the wood, and again sought to climb, and again slid down. She repeated this process three more times as Yai screamed from below. But no matter how deeply her nails bit into the trunk, no matter how hard she fought, it was impossible to go any farther. The trunk was simply too wet and too free of smaller limbs. Knowing that soon everything would be black, that the water would extinguish them as easily as it would a trio of candles, Brooke began to sob.

But then another miracle happened, for she felt one of Yai's hands against her bottom, pushing her up with an astounding strength. Brooke lunged away from the water, her fingers encircling a small branch and pulling on that branch with a ferocity she didn't know she possessed. Suddenly she was higher, and able to reach thicker branches. She grasped them, pulled herself to safety, and then reached down for Achara.

The water was up to Yai's chest. She squeezed Achara, kissing her lips and telling her to always be happy. Then, using both hands, she lifted her wailing granddaughter higher, shrieking with effort, rising to her tiptoes as the water knocked her off balance. She smiled as Brooke grabbed Achara's hand and pulled her to safety.

Yai blew her granddaughter another kiss. Then the water swept her away, dragging her into darkness. For a moment, she tried to fight this darkness, but it was too strong, too omnipotent.

And so she let the darkness carry her wherever it wanted. And while it carried her, she thought about her loved ones, how they were safe, how they would be happy and fulfilled. As a searing pain gathered within her lungs and chest, she pictured the treasures of her life, seeing their smiles, hearing their laughter. And these sights and sounds transported her through the blackness into a world free of doubt and fear, a world defined by beauty and hope.

Memories flooded into her, replacing her pain with warmth, filling her with light.

༄

A HALF MILE OUT TO sea, the water had ceased its tortured gyrations. Patch and the children were no longer sucked under. The current that had dragged them so far out was a shadow of its former self. The slicks of oil and gasoline were mostly dispersed.

Though such changes should have boosted Patch's spirits, he would have traded away all such tidings to find a large piece of floating debris. Such objects existed, but they were far away, too far to swim to with his swollen knee and in his weakened state. Much to his horror, it took all his will and strength just to tread water.

Suchin and Niran clung to the yellow buoy, which barely kept them afloat. They had offered to swim while Patch rested, but he'd refused. Help would come, he was sure, but that help would likely be hours away. And if the children exhausted themselves swimming, they wouldn't be strong enough to cling to the buoy. They'd drown before any rescuers arrived.

Patch had decided that the children must live. The buoy, the lifeline, was theirs. And though the decision gave him a sense of purpose, the thought of his own looming death seemed to steal the air from his lungs. Fighting to control his panic, he paddled with his hands. His right leg was worthless. Though normally, even without the use of one leg, he could have treaded water for hours, he'd used almost all his strength to survive the wave. Time and time again, he and the children had been sucked under, and he'd dragged them to the surface, gasping for breath, his body bloodied and aching.

Suchin started weeping once again, and Patch reached out, stroking her forehead. "Don't," he whispered. "You need . . . to be strong. Strong for yourself. Strong for Niran."

She bit her bottom lip, lost her grip on the buoy, and slipped underwater. Patch helped her up, kicking hard enough that the pain made his world spin. When she was secure, he stopped swimming for a moment, needing to rest, letting himself sink slowly beneath the waves. The children screamed his name and, using his hands, he propelled himself to the surface. Niran pulled him to the buoy, and his additional weight sent them all under. Realizing

that he was doing exactly what he feared most, Patch rallied once
again, swimming hard, helping the children back to the buoy.

As they floated, he looked again for debris, turning slowly. The
sea was getting choppier, however, and the waves made it difficult
to see far. Plastic bags and bits of wood topped the water, but
nothing significant enough to keep him afloat.

"You . . . you be good to each other," he said, his tears mixing
with the seawater as he thought about Ryan. "Love each other."

"Don't go under again," Suchin replied, shaking her head.
"Please, Patch. Don't go under."

He managed to smile at her. "I was looking for shells. For
Niran's tank."

"Don't go under!"

"I won't."

"You promise?"

A wave slapped him in the face, sweeping away his tears. "Stay
strong. Help will come. Your father . . . he's on his boat. He's looking for you."

Niran glanced toward Ko Phi Phi but hardly recognized the
center of the island. Most of the large structures and trees were
gone. "How . . . how did the ocean do this?"

"I . . . don't know," Patch said, spitting out water. "But someone . . . should learn why. You should learn why."

"I don't want to learn that."

"But if you did . . . you could help . . . in the future. You could
help the people of Ko Phi Phi."

Niran wished the ocean hadn't done such a thing. He wanted
to call out to his parents, to see their smiling faces. Thinking of
the bodies he'd seen twisting in the water, he started to cry. He
was terrified of his body going limp, of watching Patch die.

Patch tried to comfort Niran but was too weak. A wave rolled over him, and he rested for a moment, sinking. Then he swam up and breathed deeply, more aware than ever of how air felt within him. He held his breath, letting his expanded lungs keep him afloat. Seeing that Niran was about to break down, but lacking the strength to help, Patch asked Suchin if she would tell them a joke. She shook her head at first, but he winked and nodded at her, and she appeared to realize why he was asking.

"I'll tell an American joke," she said, holding on to her brother and the buoy.

"What joke?"

"What is gray, has gigantic wings, and gives money to elephants?"

"What?"

"A tusk fairy."

Patch smiled. "A tusk fairy. That's good." He tried to think of a joke to make her laugh, but his mind didn't seem able to put his thoughts together. "Can you . . . maybe you can tell us a story," he finally said, spitting out seawater, wondering how it would feel in his lungs.

"I'll finish your story," she said. "Your story about the whale."

He nodded to her as she spoke about how the whale had taken the three companions to a magical island where rainbows were born. While Suchin spoke, Patch imagined her island, and then the beauty of the reef near Ko Phi Phi. He knew that in a few minutes he'd go under for the last time. And he didn't want to think about suffocating in the dark, deep water. So he envisioned what he'd seen at the reef—angelfish, brilliant coral, the moray eel. Dying in such a place wouldn't be so bad, he told himself, trying not to cry in front of the children.

"I'm going . . . going to look for our whale," he said, interrupting Suchin. "I'm going to send her to you."

She shook her head. "No! You have to stay!"

"The whale . . . she's down there. I just need to find her."

Niran reached for him. "Stay, Patch!"

"I can't. But I'll—"

"Stay!"

The children tried to pull him up but sank in the process. He kissed their hands. He told them to be strong, to wait for the whale. Then he swam away, saying that he loved them, that he was proud of them, and that they would survive.

He looked around, saw the beauty of the sky, which was like a blue blanket draped over him. Reaching upward, he felt the sun's warmth, basking in it, hoping that he wouldn't be cold down below. He said good-bye to his loved ones, praying for them. And then he took a final breath and sank beneath the surface.

As a wave picked up Ryan, he saw a commotion not far ahead. A pair of figures had been flailing at the water, crying out, then disappearing. As the woman continued to sing, Ryan kicked hard and called to them. Another wave lifted him, and he saw two dark heads and thin arms belonging, perhaps, to children. He redoubled his efforts, shivering, fighting to keep his body moving.

The sea seemed to tilt down, to send him tumbling toward the struggling figures. He reached into the darkness and pulled them up. The voice grew louder, and he glimpsed a face, a version of his own face. He yanked up with all of his great strength; he saw himself open his eyes, and then the answer came to him.

Ƨ

PATCH COULDN'T BELIEVE THAT SUCHIN and Niran had reached so deep to pull him up with such force. But somehow they had. And he opened his eyes, stunned to see Ryan. Somehow his brother had found him.

At first, Patch wasn't able to speak. He clung to his brother, as did Suchin and Niran. He kissed the side of Ryan's head, holding him tight. The brothers wept together, shuddering as the waves lifted and dropped them.

"How?" Patch finally asked.

The word seemed to drift to Ryan. His ears didn't work properly. Though his mind still put thoughts together, parts of his body were shutting down. "The water."

"What?"

"It carried you. It carried me. The same direction."

"Are you all right? Your leg. What's wrong with your leg?"

"And a voice."

"A voice?"

"I followed . . . a voice."

Switching his grip on the life jacket that Ryan wore, Patch lifted his brother's leg out of the water, then closed his eyes at the sight of Ryan's wound. "Oh, no. No, no, no."

"It's all right."

"Oh, God. Please don't do this. Please."

"It's . . . done."

Patch put his arm around Ryan's neck, drawing him closer. He stroked his brother's forehead. "Help's coming. They're coming for us."

The cold seemed to be leaving Ryan. His leg no longer ached.

He felt so tired, felt himself slipping toward sleep. And though that pull was as irresistible as anything he had ever experienced, he fought it, biting his own lip, tasting his blood, awakening himself. "Do . . . you love her?"

"What?"

"Brooke."

Patch shouted for help and then felt the strength of Ryan's grip.

"Do you love her?"

"Maybe."

"Yes or no?"

"I'm . . . falling in love . . . with her."

Ryan nodded. "Good. She . . . she deserves that. And so do you."

"Why are you—"

"My passport. Take it. It's high up . . . in the Hillside Bungalows."

"But why—"

"You can leave together. Be me for a day. Leave Thailand . . . with her. And then . . . then you can be happy together."

"No. You'll need it. You'll need it, Ry."

"Promise me . . . you'll take it."

"I can't."

"You have to. For her. For you."

"It's yours."

"Run . . . for me. When you're me. On a beach."

"No."

Ryan smiled. "And Dao. Send her my money. Tell her . . . tell her it came from King Kong. For her . . . to go to college."

"You tell her."

"You . . . brought me here," Ryan said, squeezing Patch's hand. "But that was good. I saved Dao. And you. And the children. Four lives . . . for one."

"Five lives. We're five lives."

"I wouldn't . . . change anything."

"Please, Ry. Please."

"Four lives."

"Please don't go. You have to stay. You have to stay with me."

"Brothers . . . always stay. We always stay . . . together."

"Wait. Please wait."

Ryan squeezed his brother's hand again, no longer hearing Patch's words. He thought that the woman would stop singing, but her voice continued to fill him, comforting him. Now that he had found Patch, he no longer tried to resist the profound weariness that gripped him. He had resisted for so long, and now he wanted to sleep, to go to a new, quiet place, a place where he could rest.

"I love you," he whispered, unclipping his life jacket, slipping into the waves. He felt Patch pull him up, heard the love in Patch's voice and smiled at that love, knowing that it would endure, knowing that the sacrifice had been worth it, that four lives were more important than one.

The woman's voice grew louder, lifting him upward. He saw her then. Her brow was furrowed. Her hair was long and dark.

He reached for her and they touched and then he was within her.

FOR THE NEXT FIVE HOURS, Patch, Suchin, and Niran gripped Ryan's life jacket and the buoy. Patch had wanted to also hold on to his brother's body, but the weight had been too much, pulling them all under. And so Patch had kissed Ryan's forehead, prayed for him, and let him go. And he had wept until no salt or water seemed to remain within him.

Not long after his tears stopped, a longboat appeared. In it were Lek, Sarai, Brooke, Achara, and four strangers.

Patch watched as Niran and Suchin shrieked for joy. Their happiness reminded him of his brother's last words, of his sacrifice.

Sarai leaped into the water, swimming toward her children, shouting their names.

"Let him see this," Patch whispered, crying once again. "Please, God, please let him see."

MONDAY, DECEMBER 27

as one

Lek sat on the steps of their restaurant, one of the few remaining structures in sight. He cradled Achara, stroking her brow, gazing at the devastation around him. All of their bungalows were gone, as were some trees and portions of Patch's path. What remained was a gruesome mix of slabs of cement, ruined boats, piles of splintered lumber, rooftops, washing machines, a pool table, bicycles, and countless pieces of smaller debris. It was as if a nuclear bomb had gone off, destroying everything on the island.

At first light, Lek had left his family, crept down from the hills, and pulled the bodies from his property. He'd found eleven corpses—mostly children—and had wept as he carried them into the village, carefully laying them down next to hundreds of others that had already been arranged in long lines. After moving the last body, he'd fallen to his knees, thrown up, and then returned to his loved ones.

Now, as he sat in their restaurant and held Achara, he thought about his children's survival. Though he grieved over the loss of Yai, the fact that his children still lived was nothing short of a miracle. As he had many times already, Lek prayed, thanking Buddha for the safety of his family. He kissed the scratches on Achara's arm, left from where Brooke's fingernails had dug into her flesh. Looking up, Lek saw that Brooke and Patch were sitting on a coconut tree that had fallen over—one of the few places not covered in filth. She had her arm around him and his head rested on her shoulder. Though their backs were to him, Lek bowed deeply in thanks, tears gathering in the corners of his eyes. He shuddered, then wiped his cheeks with trembling fingers and stood up.

Moving carefully so as to avoid the broken glass, bent nails, and splintered wood, Lek walked into the hills, cradling Achara. He found the rest of his family where he'd left them, sitting on palm fronds a stone's throw above the waterline. Sarai was between her children, who were so close to her that they looked to be cold and seeking her body's warmth. Even though a wound on Suchin's shoulder had been bandaged and had stopped bleeding, Sarai's hand still pressed against the dressing. Two of her fingernails were missing.

"What did you see?" Sarai asked Lek, her eyes downcast.

He knelt in front of them, so that they formed a circle. "The restaurant . . . it's still there. Filthy, but there."

"And the rest?"

He shook his head.

Closing her eyes, Sarai held her children tight, her fingers throbbing. Her breathing sped up, and panic gripped her as she imagined trying to rebuild. She thought of her mother, about

Brooke's description of how she had died. And though she started to cry, she was filled with pride. Her mother had saved Achara and Brooke, had summoned an inner strength that only a few people had known existed within her. Sarai had always known, despite her teasing. And now others would share that knowledge.

Sarai used her pride to transform her own fears and doubts into something different, into resolution. She wanted to stay on the island, to rebuild. She wanted to start work right away. But she needed to ask her loved ones about their desires and would do whatever was best for them.

She squeezed Niran and Suchin, holding them tight, not wanting to ever let them go. "Can I ask you something?" she said, her voice strained from screaming. "Are you ready to talk?"

"Yes," Suchin replied, while Niran merely nodded.

"Do you know how much your father and I love you?"

Suchin nodded, tears dropping from her dark lashes. "We know."

"How much do we love them?" Sarai asked, looking at Lek.

He inched closer to his children. "Our hearts . . . they'll always beat together," he replied, and touched their faces, his fingers tracing the outlines of their scratches and bruises. "All our hearts, beating as one."

"That's right," Sarai said, wincing as she shifted her weight. "And whatever you want, we'll do. Whatever makes you happiest. Because you give anything to those you love. Anything in the world."

Suchin thought that her brother might speak, but his mouth merely opened and closed. "Why are you saying this?" she asked, wiping her eyes.

"Because we have two choices," Sarai replied. "We can stay

here. We can rebuild. Or we can go. We can have new lives in Bangkok, where you'll never have to worry about the sea rising up, where you'll sleep in a tall, strong building."

Lek studied his children's faces. He then thought about what he'd heard that morning in the village, about how there was talk of the government making money available to those who planned to rebuild. He wasn't sure what he wanted, other than the happiness of those he loved.

Niran saw his father watching him. He turned, looking at the bay, which was still filled with debris and was the color of cement. The previous night he'd had nightmares about the wave, about it dragging him underwater. He'd wanted to climb higher, to reach the summit of the island. For the first time in his life, he had no desire to be near the water.

As Niran imagined what it would be like to live in Bangkok, to explore an endless city, he noticed a hermit crab moving beside the palm frond beneath Suchin. Niran picked up the animal, and saw right away that it was much too big for its shell. "We'd better find you a bigger home," he whispered. "Or you'll get eaten."

The crab half emerged from its shell, and then tightened up again.

Niran took off his shirt, grimacing at the pain that movement brought, and made a pouch into which he set the crab. "Are there shells down there?" he asked his father.

"More than you can imagine. The wave . . . It brought in as much as it took out."

Nodding, Niran thought again about Bangkok.

"You want to stay, don't you?" Suchin asked. "You've found your little friend and you want to stay."

"I don't know."

She nudged him. "Yes, you do."

"Maybe. I think so."

Suchin looked out to the sea, believing that her grandmother was still out there, that she would always remain in these waters. "She'll want to hear us laugh. She'll want to see us play. And it will be harder for her . . . if we're in Bangkok."

Sarai squeezed her daughter's hand. "She's reborn by now. I know she is. So don't ever worry about her not being a part of your world."

Suchin started to cry again. "I won't."

"What should we do, Suchin?" Sarai asked, then bit her lip as tears obscured her vision. "Which path will be harder for you?"

"We should stay. Our family . . . has always stayed."

A ship materialized in the distance, an immense ship the likes of which Sarai had never seen. Help was coming, she knew. They weren't alone. They had survived their darkest hours and they were not alone.

"I think we should rebuild," Sarai said, committing herself. "I think Rainbow Resort was meant to be here. The restaurant, your tree house, those things are still here. They weren't meant to go. Just like we weren't. And if we weren't meant to go, I don't think we should leave."

Lek reached for his wife's hand. "If we're going to stay, we should help with the school. Let's rebuild the school. Let's start with that."

"Tomorrow," Sarai replied. "We'll start tomorrow."

"And today?"

"Today I just want to hold each of you," she answered, pulling her children closer, feeling her husband's head press against her own, tears running down her cheeks. "You're all miracles, you know," she said, shuddering. "Miracles that floated down to me, that I feel and love each and every moment, that fill me with the light of the sun."

TUESDAY, DECEMBER 28

footprints

At the end of the beach, far removed from the cleanup crews, the piles of wreckage, and the makeshift infirmary, Brooke and Patch stood at the edge of the water. Patch held Ryan's football and passport. He remembered throwing the football with his brother, remembered autumn days and jumping into piles of leaves. After bringing the football to his nose, he inhaled deeply, trying to detect Ryan's presence. The football smelled as it always did—like old leather. But something else might have lingered—the presence of his brother's hands, perhaps.

Patch had come to the water to throw the football as far out as possible, to play one last game of catch with Ryan. His brother had always taken the football with them on family trips, had always made sure that they had time to play catch. And so it had seemed to Patch that Ryan should have the football with him, should carry it wherever he went. But now, as Patch turned the football over and over in his hands, he was torn. He wanted to give Ryan a gift, and yet he feared separating himself from such a connection.

Tears glistened on his cheeks. He continued to spin the football. Then he kissed it, pulled back his arm, and threw with all his might. The football spiraled forward, arcing high, traveling straight and true. It landed with a small splash, skipped forward, and settled into the water. The tide was going out, and the football drifted toward the open sea. Patch wondered if his brother had seen his throw. He hoped so. Ryan would be pleased.

Patch watched the football until it was a distant blur. Opening the passport, he studied his brother's picture. They looked so alike. "It doesn't feel right to go," Patch said quietly. "Even if we help rebuild for eighty days until his visa expires."

Brooke shook her head. "Your visa. It's your visa."

"It doesn't feel right."

"Make it right."

"What do you mean?"

She took his free hand, her fingers cool against his. "Make your life count."

A longboat came into view, cutting through the water, heading toward the opposite end of the beach. The longboat was towing something wide and red.

Patch pondered Brooke's words, knowing that they would stay for eighty days, helping to rebuild Rainbow Resort. His parents would come, and they would help too. And somehow they would find the grace within themselves to absolve him. He knew that he wouldn't forgive himself for many years, at least until he had done as Brooke had said. His life would have to count. Not that every life didn't matter. Of course it did. But Patch would have to reach for something special, to aim so high. After his last eighty days in Thailand, he'd use Ryan's passport and travel to another place where his help was needed. And he'd stay for however long it took to cleanse what needed cleansing, to save what needed saving. He'd be called Ryan, and strangers would come to know that name. They would speak it. They would celebrate it. They would thank a god or simple luck for delivering this name to them.

"Will you help me?" he asked, holding the passport against his chest.

Brooke lifted up his hand and kissed it. "I want to go back to Dao, to see how she's doing. And then I'll come find you." She kissed him again, studying the redness of his eyes. "If you'd never come here, if you'd never gotten into trouble, Suchin, Niran, Achara, and Dao, they'd all be dead."

"But my brother would be alive."

"Would you give your life for those children?"

"Yes."

"That's what he did. That's what he chose."

His tears came again and he shuddered against her, his injured knee threatening to buckle. Pulling her closer, he squeezed her arms, needing her as much as he'd ever needed anything. "Don't leave me," he whispered. "Please don't leave me."

Brooke saw the pain in his eyes, a pain that threatened to overwhelm her as well. "Why would I leave you . . . when I'm falling in love with you?" she replied, and kissed his hand again.

"You are?"

"You know I am."

"How? How did that happen?"

"I don't know. But you . . . you see me. Not who you want to see. But who I am."

"I love who you are."

She smiled and wiped his cheek free of tears. "I won't leave you."

"But I have to . . . do things. To go places where I can help."

"So do I. We can do twice as much together."

"It'll be hard."

"I don't care."

"Really hard."

"The harder, the better."

He sniffed. "But what about business school? About your stud-ies? I know school is important to you and I don't want—"

"School can wait. I'd rather stay here. It's more important that we stay here."

He hugged her, holding her tight, stroking the back of her head. "That's how I'll honor him, how I'll repay him. He was never proud . . . of me. And he had no reason to be. But now . . . now I want to make him proud. I know he'll be watching . . . and I just want to make him proud."

"And you will. You'll make everyone proud."

"I have to."

"Let's go. Let's see Dao. And then we'll start working. We'll start making him proud."

They embraced for several minutes, saying no more but feeling each other, drawing strength from each other. Then they started to walk, hand in hand, down the beach. They walked near the waterline, leaving footprints that were filled, then washed away by diminutive waves.

Though their footprints were impermanent, in the days and weeks and many months to come, their touch would linger, on wood, on people, bringing beauty to ugliness, life to death, hope to misery.

Their footprints would be washed away, but their deeds would remain, tangible and resonant and cherished, like monuments built by past generations.

And then one day, years later, they would come to peace with their pasts. They would sit on a beach together and feel no more anguish, no more fear. They would smile in contentment, knowing that they had done their best, and that their best had been good enough, had been good enough to build a path to carry others forward.

The sea had come and taken, but some things couldn't be taken, because some things were stronger than even the sea.

afterword

I first traveled to Ko Phi Phi in 1992. Though I arrived with a horrible case of food poisoning, I was mesmerized by the island's beauty. I felt as if I had stumbled into some unknown slice of paradise. For three days, as I lay on the beach and recovered, I soaked up everything that the island had to offer. If one could fall in love with a place, well, I had fallen.

I returned to the island in 1994 and 1999. Each visit brought unwelcome changes—more tourists, fancier bungalows, higher prices, even a few cigarette boats. And yet the spirit of the island remained. The water was still turquoise and clear, the cliffs magnificent, the people friendly.

When the tsunami tore through Ko Phi Phi in 2004, I felt compelled to help, but my wife and I were in Colorado with our two young children, and international travel wasn't practical. And so I waited, returning in 2007 to research *Cross Currents*. I was astounded by how much of the infrastructure had been rebuilt.

And while I was disappointed by the nature of some of that re-building (too many shops, hotels, and bars), I was also inspired. The Thais had seen the worst that life could offer, and, though still haunted with memories, they had risen.

In late 2010, while I was putting the finishing touches on *Cross Currents*, my wife and children accompanied me to Ko Phi Phi. On the beach we watched our children play with other children from around the world, and that world felt small and good. It felt right. Though the tsunami had destroyed so much and so many, though wounds still existed, I felt hopeful. The sun was warm, the water still, and the laughter of others was carried on the wind.

acknowledgments

Cross Currents would not have been possible without the support of many people. First and foremost on that list are my wife, Allison, and our children, Sophie and Jack. I draw inspiration from each of you every single day.

I'd like to express my gratitude toward Laura Dail, my agent and friend, who has always had my back, and who believed in this novel from the start. Also, my sincere thanks to Ellen Edwards, my wonderful editor, who works as hard at her craft as anyone I know. Thanks also to my parents, John and Patsy Shors; my brothers, Tom, Matt, and Luke; as well as Mary and Doug Barakat, Bruce McPherson, Dustin O'Regan, Amy Tan, Chris Bohjalian, Karl Marlantes, Joan Silber, Kara Cesare, Pennie Ianniciello, Bevan Powrie, Sally Van Vert, Terry Naumann, Kamon Jungruk, Sahat Hod, Shawna Sharp, Bliss Darragh, Diane Saarinen, Kara Welsh, Kaitlyn Kennedy, and Davina Witts.

Giving recognition to the wonderful people of Ko Phi Phi

is also imperative. The people I interviewed who survived the tsunami taught me so much about what happened, about how they endured that day. My gratitude for their honesty and strength is profound. Also, my recent travels to Thailand were enhanced by the help of a variety of Thais and expats. I'd like to thank Robin, King, Aaron, and the friendly staff at www.railay.com for providing great accommodation.

For all that I have received, I am grateful.

PHOTO BY JIM BARBOUR

John Shors is the bestselling author of *Beneath a Marble Sky*, *Beside a Burning Sea*, *Dragon House*, *The Wishing Trees*, and *Cross Currents*. He has won numerous awards for his writing, and his novels have been translated into twenty-seven languages.

John lives in Boulder, Colorado, with his wife and two children. For more information, please visit www.johnshors.com.

JOHN SHORS

cross currents

A CONVERSATION WITH
JOHN SHORS

Q. It seems that you try to identify places and subjects that haven't yet been explored in novels, and then you do exactly that. Can you talk about how you choose the stories that you decide to tell?

A. It's hard to be completely original, since so many novels and poems and films are out there, but it has been my strategy to travel overseas looking for stories that haven't been told. For instance, a trip to India inspired my first novel, *Beneath a Marble Sky*, which is about the creation of the Taj Mahal. It's based on a story that is famous in South Asia, but not well-known in the West. I was surprised to learn that so little had been written about the Taj Mahal, and felt that the story would give me a wonderful opportunity to make a splash with my debut novel. Likewise, I felt that the Indian Ocean tsunami of 2004 was a global event that had faded quickly into the background. In my opinion, far too little had been written about this enormous calamity. Perhaps because of my many travels to the region, I continued to think about the people and places that were affected by the tsunami, and I wanted to honor those who survived and those who died by writing a novel inspired by them.

Q. *Many of the early pages of* Cross Currents *are devoted to exploring the relationships between locals and tourists. Why did you decide to devote so much of the novel to this topic?*

A. In my travels I've seen how locals and tourists interact. In some places, this interaction is characterized by resentment and bitterness, mistrust and suspicion. It's a complicated relationship, and often evolves from mutual need, rather than mutual respect. The good news is that in many other places around the world, locals and tourists mingle quite comfortably together. Thailand is such a place. While differences between Thais and foreigners do exist, and conflict is present, there is also genuine goodwill between these two sets of people. It's a joy to behold, and I savored exploring its nuances in my writing.

Q. *A pair of brothers, different from each other in many ways, are among the most important characters in the novel. Why did you decide to make Patch and Ryan brothers instead of best friends?*

A. I wanted these two characters to be involved with the same woman, and felt that by making them brothers, I was adding a layer of conflict and complexity to the relationships. Brothers know each other so well—their strengths and weaknesses, hopes and fears. And certainly sibling rivalry does exist. I wanted to explore such rivalry, as well as the bond between brothers.

Q. *Patch makes a colossal mistake early on in the book, and places himself in a difficult situation. Have you ever made such a blunder and found yourself in a predicament that seemed to have no way out?*

A. I've done plenty of foolish things, but have never been in trouble with the law. And yet, I can relate to Patch, because I think that life, despite all of its beauty, can be so unforgiving. One mistake can cost you so much. Experience has made me more careful and aware than I used to be. In my twenties I took lots of risks. I'm glad I took them, as they ultimately shaped who I am, but I won't make the same choices again.

Q. *The Thai family in the novel is faced with a dilemma—to try to make ends meet in Ko Phi Phi or move to Bangkok. Is that often a choice that Thai families must make?*

A. There was a time, not too long ago, when many of Thailand's outer islands were largely undiscovered. Locals fished and tended coconut plantations. Very few tourists knew about such places, despite the remarkably beautiful waters and beaches. Yet as the world became more accessible, such places were discovered, creating a boom in tourism. In some ways this boom benefited the locals, and in other ways it did not. One consequence is that many Thais from the mainland moved to the islands, seeking jobs. And these additional residents began to compete with the locals for work. In *Cross Currents*, Lek and Sarai face the challenge of operating their small resort in competition with much larger operations. From what I could see during my visits, theirs is a common dilemma.

Q. *Several characters, perhaps most notably Yai and Ryan, redeem themselves in the novel. Can you talk about their redemption?*

A. I wanted Yai to surprise readers. For so much of the book she makes fun of herself, lamenting her shortcomings. Yet at the end, she's remarkably strong-willed and brave. Her experience mirrors what I've personally witnessed. Sometimes people who seem weak on the surface have vast reserves of strength and resolve. When it came to Ryan, I gave him plenty of flaws, but wanted to show that he also has the capacity to be redeemed. He begins the book as self-centered and selfish, but ends up making the ultimate sacrifice for others.

Q. *After the tsunami strikes, Thais and tourists help each other, risking everything to save one another's lives. Was this the case in real life?*

A. I've spoken with dozens of people who survived the tsunami, and I've read many firsthand accounts of the disaster. People went to great lengths to rescue each other, regardless of their nationality. Countless lives were saved by such selfless acts. Moreover, in the weeks and months that followed, Thais and tourists continued to work together, rebuilding the infrastructure on Ko Phi Phi and cleaning out the bays. I've read that seven thousand tons of debris were removed, by hand, from the bays and the beaches.

Q. *What did it feel like to return to Ko Phi Phi after the tsunami? With whom did you talk? And how did those conversations influence* Cross Currents?

A. It was a bit surreal to return to the island. So many things had changed, and yet so much had remained the same. All of the physical beauty was still there, but almost everything man-made was either gone or newly rebuilt. Sitting on a beach where several thousand people had died a few years earlier was both haunting and a source of hope. I did a lot of thinking on that beach, about how our lives are just small ripples in a vast ocean, yet we each have significance, and we each can impact the lives of our loved ones, total strangers, and the world around us. As far as the conversations I had about the tsunami, I spoke with fishermen, hotel owners, masseuses, and children. These people helped me get a feel for how the tsunami struck the island, how waves came from either side, and the mayhem that resulted from their collision. I also learned how people survived—by clinging to trees, to pieces of lumber, to each other. Many of them had lost family members. Some still hadn't been able to go back into the ocean. Some had brought new babies into the world. These conversations were invaluable.

Q. Are you trying to impart certain messages to readers through Cross Currents?

A. No, not really. Some writers write with a specific message in mind, but for the most part, that's not how I go about the process. If there are messages in my novels, they're mostly unintentional offshoots of the stories I'm trying to tell. I will confess that one of the reasons I wrote *Cross Currents* is that I think it's important that we all think about global events. The world is becoming such a small place. We can help strangers and we can be helped by strangers. It's important to keep this notion in mind, because as the population around the globe continues to boom, and people live together in greater concentrations, we're going to see increasing numbers of human casualties from natural disasters.

Q. In your last novel, The Wishing Trees, *your characters went on a journey that spanned eight countries on two continents. Now, with*

Cross Currents, *you've taken readers to a little island in Thailand. Where will your next novel be set?*

A. I'm working on a historical novel set around Angkor Wat, the amazing temple located in present-day Cambodia. Angkor Wat was built over a forty-year period in the twelfth century, when a sophisticated society flourished in the region. But conflict with a rival group led to a series of wars that changed the course of civilization in Southeast Asia. I'm fascinated by the history surrounding Angkor Wat and am deep into imagining a story involving a cast of high- and lowborn characters. It's going to be an epic novel, in some ways similar to my first book, *Beneath a Marble Sky*.

QUESTIONS
FOR DISCUSSION

1. Where were you when the Indian Ocean tsunami struck on December 26, 2004?

2. What was your reaction to the catastrophe?

3. Some novelists avoid real-life subjects that are bound to evoke powerful negative emotions in readers. Do you think John Shors brings the story of the disaster to life in a way that honors those who suffered and died?

4. The author traveled multiple times to Ko Phi Phi before and after the tsunami struck. Do you think it's important for writers to have such personal connections with the places they write about?

5. *Cross Currents* explores the relationships between locals and tourists. In real life, do you think each set of people understands the other?

6. How do you think people from different cultures best learn from one another?

7. What do you think of Patch's initial decision to flee Thailand, rather than to turn himself in? If you were a member of his family, would you try to convince him to take another path?

8. Lek and Sarai assume a significant amount of risk when they let Patch stay with them for such an extended time. Do you think they make the right decision?

9. Why do you think Brooke decides to share her past with Patch? By doing so, does she knowingly or unknowingly bring them closer together? Why do you think John Shors chose to handle the issue this way?

10. What aspect of the changing romantic relationships in the novel do you find most interesting?

11. What do you think about the relationship between Ryan and Dao? What is each character looking for?

12. Lek and Sarai depend on their children to help draw business to their resort. Discuss their distaste at having to exploit their children in this way. Can you think of times when you might have exploited your children, in small or large ways, or incidents when you've seen other parents exploit their children?

13. Which character faces the greatest challenge and rises to the occasion most impressively?

14. If you had lived on Ko Phi Phi, and endured the tsunami, would you have left afterward?

15. Imagine that many years have passed since the tsunami. What do you think life is now like for Lek and his family? Do you think Patch kept his promise to make his life count?